Yinka,
Where Is
Your
Huzband?

Yinka, Where Is Your *Huzband?*

Lizzie Damilola Blackburn

———————

PAMELA DORMAN BOOKS / VIKING

VIKING
An imprint of Penguin Random House LLC
penguinrandomhouse.com

First published in hardcover in Great Britain by Viking, an imprint of Penguin Books,
a division of Penguin Random House Ltd., London, in 2022.

First published in the United States by Pamela Dorman Books/Viking.

A Pamela Dorman Book/Viking

LIBRARY OF CONGRESS CATALOGING-IN-PUBLICATION DATA
Names: Blackburn, Lizzie Damilola, author.
Title: Yinka, where is your huzband? / Lizzie Damilola Blackburn.
Description: New York : Pamela Dorman Books, [2022]
Identifiers: LCCN 2021022941 (print) | LCCN 2021022942 (ebook) |
ISBN 9780593299005 (hardcover) | ISBN 9780593299012 (ebook)
Subjects: LCSH: Nigerians—England—Fiction. | Self-actualization (Psychology)—Fiction. |
LCGFT: Romance fiction. | Novels. Classification: LCC PR6102.L3343 U56 2022 (print) |
LCC PR6102.L3343 (ebook) | DDC 823/.92—dc23
LC record available at https://lccn.loc.gov/2021022941
LC ebook record available at https://lccn.loc.gov/2021022942

Printed in the United States of America
1st Printing

BOOK DESIGN BY LUCIA BERNARD

To my very own *huzband,* Martin.

Thank you for encouraging me to pursue my dreams.

And to all the women who have questioned their worth.

Remember, you're always deserving of self-love . . .

Huzband

(pronounced auz • band)

NOUN

1. A male partner in a marriage
   e.g. Yinka's younger sister, Kemi, is married to
   Uche

2. A nonexistent man in a nonexistent marriage
   whose whereabouts is often asked, usually by
   Nigerian mums and aunties, of single British-
   Nigerian women
   e.g. "So, Yinka, where is your huzband? Ah, ah.
   You're thirty-one now!"

Yinka,
Where Is
Your
Huzband?

January

The prayer of the century

SATURDAY

It's two hours into my sister's baby shower and so far not one person has said, "So, Yinka, when is it going to be your turn?" Or the classic, "Yinka, where is your *huzband?*"

Thank you, God!

After going crazy with the party popper emoji and asking Nana what time she'll reach, I shove my phone into my back pocket. Let's just hope I haven't inadvertently jinxed myself by celebrating too soon.

Slouching back in my chair, I stare at Kemi and her friends dancing in the center of her living room: all bumping and grinding, serious expressions on their faces, as though they're competing in an Afrobeats dancing competition.

I look at those still seated: a red-haired woman and another with an eyebrow piercing who must be Kemi's workmates, and four of my aunties. Like me, my aunties are struggling to finish their plates of jollof rice. It's far too mild for our palates. I know everyone can't take spice, but whoever made this didn't represent us, Nigerians. Succumbing to defeat, I abandon the plate under my chair. When I look up, I spot Mum waddling through the throng of dancers, her wide hips swaying. When she gets to the front, she jabs her fingers against Kemi's phone, before giving up and swiveling around. Mum still owns a Nokia 3410 so operating an iPhone is beyond her capacity.

"Hello-o! Hello-o!" she cries in a thick Nigerian accent. The thick Nigerian accent, mind you, that she still has, despite having moved to the UK way back in the eighties. "Can I have everyone's attention, please?"

But the music drowns her out. Kemi and her friends carry on dancing to the song. Except my younger sister goes one step further. As though she has completely forgotten about the massive bump attached to her front, she dips her knees and bends her back and—oh, good Lord. She's twerking.

I chuckle. Ah, man. Such a shame that I don't see Kemi as much these days. Before she got married, we were in and out of each other's houses. It's not been the same the last year.

"Excuse me, everyone!" Big Mama's twenty-thousand-decibel voice punches through the music. "Can everyone stop what they're doing, please? Kemi's mum wants to say something."

This announcement from my aunt (Daddy's sister) does the trick. Within seconds, conversations end, phones are tossed away, and, like rolling snooker balls, the dancers disperse to the sides of the room. With one hand supporting her stomach, Kemi penguin-walks to the sound system and switches the music off.

"Thank you," says Mum, pressing her palms together. "And thank you to all of you for coming to celebrate my daughter's transition into motherhood." She swings her head around to Kemi and flashes her a proud smile. "As you know, motherhood is a verrry important chapter in a woman's life. So, I would like to dedicate this time to praying over Kemi, her *huzband* and the baby. Now, everyone, please rise to your feet and hold the hand of the person standing next to you."

A lot of shuffling follows as those who are sitting rise and form a circle with the already standing dancers.

"Don't look so nervous," I hear Mum say to Kemi's workmates, their faces now watermelon red. "If you don't believe in God, you can just bow your head as a sign of respect."

I catch the eye of the red-haired woman. I can smell her anxiety all the way from here.

Kemi's school friends are standing on either side of me, and I reach for their hands as I bow my head.

Mum clears her throat. "Dear Heavenly Father . . ."

What feels like ten minutes later . . .

"I thank you, Lord, for granting my heart's desire to become a grandma—an *ìyá-ìyá*. I pray that your love, peace and guidance will be with my daughter in the delivery room. She will be well, in Jesus' name. Her *huzband* will be well, in Jesus' name. The *baby* will be well, in Jesus' name."

"Amen," we all drone like gaunt zombies.

"I thank you, Lord, for bringing Kemi and my son-in-law, Uche, together while they were studying at the university. I pray that . . ." There's a stretch of silence; Mum's voice quivers. "I pray that like my late *huzband*, Kunle, Uche will be a wonderful dad. Give him long life and good health."

"Amen," I say in a low voice.

Mum continues to pray for protection, safety and security. *No weapon formed against Kemi shall prosper.* My legs are starting to ache and my knees begin to wobble. Then, at long last, Mum says what everyone has been waiting for:

"Lord, answer our prayers. In Jesus' sweet, holy, precious name we pray."

The last "Amen" is triumphant.

I open my eyes to see a wave of women collapsing on their seats, each breathing a loud sigh of relief—except for Big Mama. She's already slumped in her chair, shoes kicked off and legs outstretched. Her toenails look like pork scratchings dipped in red paint. I smile. Big Mama may not be the most decorous of my three hundred–odd aunties—because in Nigerian culture, every African woman who is older than you by at least ten years is by default your aunty, regardless of whether or not you're blood-related—but still, I can't help but love the woman.

"Hold on." She thrusts forward in her chair. "Tolu! You didn't pray for your eldest daughter."

Mum, who for the past two hours has been patting her bird's nest of a weave sporadically as if she has fleas, turns to me with wide eyes. "Oh, yes!" she exclaims, using one hand to hoist up her wrapper, while the other continues to pat her itchy scalp. "How could I forget about Yinka? The investment banker!"

Heads swoosh in my direction and despite my attempts to avoid eye contact with my aunties, I can tell they're grinning at me encouragingly. No matter how many times I've told Mum that I work as an operations manager *in* an investment bank, she still gets it wrong. Whether she does this due to pride or because it's easier to explain, I'm still unsure. And to be fair, it's the first thing that most people assume whenever I tell them I work for Godfrey & Jackson. No one ever thinks of the operations team, the unsung heroes who work in the back office, and work through all the processes to settle each banker's trade. (Okay, operations may not sound glamorous, but it's still a solid job, and I'm proud of it!) Anyway, whatever the reason, Mum sure does mention my profession as an "investment banker" a hell of a lot more than she mentions Kemi's job as a drama teacher—though not to the extent to which she gloats about Kemi being married or having a baby, of course.

"Yes! God has blessed me with two daughters. I should pray for them both." Mum claps. "*Oya!* Everybody, rise to your feet. We have to pray for Yinka."

The groans are somehow both quiet and yet loud enough to fill the room.

"Ah, ah! What is all this gr-gr-grumbling?" The remark comes from Big Mama, of course. And yet, while everyone is reluctantly rising to their feet, she's still sitting comfortably like she's on a throne. "If Yinka's mum said she would give twenty pounds to everyone who is standing, would you be moaning the way that you are now? *Abeg!* Get up, my friend. Don't you know it's good to pray?" She kisses her teeth. "Nonsense."

The woman with the eyebrow ring snatches her jacket from behind her chair and stomps out. "This is too weird," I hear her mutter as she marches past me toward the door.

The red-haired woman looks desperate to leave too, just not as brave. I give her a rueful smile.

"How about I pray?"

A familiar voice makes my brows shoot up. I turn around. My heart plummets. Standing at the doorway is none other than Aunty Debbie.

"Funke, what time do you call this?"

Mum is the only person to still address her younger sister by her native name.

"Did it not say two o'clock on the invitation that I gave you, ehn? Seriously, you take 'African time' to the next level."

Aunty Debbie tuts and pulls off the huge Chanel glasses that have been sitting on her heavily contoured nose.

"Tolu. I live all the way in Hampstead, you know."

A ripple of suppressed chuckles fills the room and I resist the urge to roll my eyes. Yes, Aunty, we all know that you and your husband make a tidy sum thanks to your flourishing property investment business. You don't have to constantly remind us.

"The drive took over an hour," she drawls in her best attempt at a

"British" accent which she tends to put on and take off like a coat. "That reminds me"—she folds her glasses, hanging them over the V-neck of her white silk blouse—"will my Porsche be safe outside?"

Mum's mouth hangs open. Big Mama kisses her teeth.

"Debbie, Peckham isn't how it used to be, you know," pipes up Aunty Blessing, the oldest of the three sisters. Unlike Mum and Aunty Debbie, Aunty Blessing has what I call a BBC newsreader accent, one she developed over her thirty-plus years of being a barrister. "In fact, the place is pretty much gentrified."

"*Gentri-what?*" Mum looks confused.

Kemi butts in before they start arguing. "Mum, I thought you wanted to pray for Yinka?" She folds her arms over her protruding stomach, then cocks her head at Aunty Debbie. "And Aunty," she says with a small laugh, "Don't worry. Your car *is* safe outside. Uche and I have lived here for close to a year, and no one has nicked our Ford Fiesta."

"Well, who would want to steal— Never mind. Anyway, Tolu, let me pray," says Aunty Debbie, and immediately my stomach tightens with dread. "We could all do with a change of voice, yes? And besides, I'm late." She fluffs her wig. "The very least I can do is pray for my niece." She flashes me a wide smile. I return to her a tiny, begrudging one.

I haven't forgotten what you did at Kemi's wedding, I think, scowling at her as she closes her eyes.

"Dear God . . . we thank you for the life of Tolu's eldest daughter, Yinka Beatrice Oladeji."

I feel a tug at my right hand as the lady beside me pulls hers away.

"Sorry," I whisper. I must have been clenching her fingers.

"We thank you for the excellent job you have blessed Yinka with, and the house she bought a few years back. She is quite an exemplary woman and has achieved some remarkable things."

My hunched shoulders relax. *Okay. This isn't too bad.*

"Lord," she continues. "We've not long entered the new year—"

"New year," Mum echoes.

"And the Bible says that through you, all things are possible—"

Mum claps. "Yes, Lord!"

"So, with this in mind, Lord, I pray that this year will be the year . . . the year that Yinka finds her *huzband*."

What the—

I glare at Aunty Debbie, who has paused for a hot second to allow everyone to say their Amens. Obviously, Mum and Big Mama's are the loudest, and they raise their arms to the ceiling as though any second now my miracle husband will descend.

I grit my teeth.

"Lord," Aunty Debbie rattles on. "Yinka is thirty-two—"

"Thirty-one," I mutter under my breath.

"There is no reason why, at the age of thirty-two, a woman of her caliber should still be single."

"God forbid!" Mum inserts.

"In the same way you brought Kemi a *huzband*, Lord, bring Yinka a *huzband* of her own. Don't delay your blessing. Bring him this year."

The loudest Amens come from two other "aunties" standing in front of the sofa—one, vigorously shaking her head, the other mouthing her own prayer. Some of Kemi's friends are sucking in their lips to hold back a laugh, but one isn't as tactful and snorts.

I inhale to stay calm.

"Sorry," Kemi mouths with a pitying expression on her face—which I've grown accustomed to *a lot* lately.

This isn't your fault, I want to tell her. I mean, all you did was fall in love with a guy you met at uni who you got married to at twenty-five. And yes, I would have had a lot less pressure to settle down if you hadn't got knocked up during your honeymoon in Costa Rica and waited, I dunno, maybe another year or two? But everyone finds love in their own time, and yours just happened to be before mine. My time will come. I know it will.

While I try to telepathically say all this to Kemi, Aunty Debbie starts up again.

"Lord, bring Yinka a good, good *huzband*. A man who is God-fearing, tall and educated—"

"Okay, in Jesus' name we pray, Amen." The interjection comes from Aunty Blessing, and I resist the urge to hail her.

But never one to take hints, Aunty Debbie doesn't wrap it up. Instead, she remains silent, tilting her chin toward the ceiling, eyelids firmly closed. The silence is so uncomfortable, a few of Kemi's friends begin to twitch.

"Lord," she declares finally, waving a hand in the air as she does at All Welcome Church when she catches a whiff of the Holy Spirit. "Do what only YOU can do. Intervene, Heavenly Father. Intervene! In Jesus' name we pray, Amen."

Everyone utters, "Amen," all eyes wide open. And who are they staring at? Me, of course. The lady with red hair now looks as though she's about to cry, and one of Kemi's friends says loudly, "Gosh, man." Two aunties in front of the sofa are busy chanting, *"Àmín ní orúko Jésù!"* which, despite my basic knowledge of Yoruba, I know translates to, "Amen in the name of Jesus!" Mum is still striking a Rafiki. And Aunty Debbie . . . well, she looks delighted.

I want to punch a wall. I am desperate to leave but I can't. Not when everyone is watching me. To my relief, the music resumes and Aunty Blessing gyrates to the center of the room.

"Isn't this supposed to be a party?" She's swinging her head from side to side. "Come on, now!" she yells at our awkward faces. "You're not about to leave me dancing solo." She pulls Kemi, twirling her around, then begins to do God knows what with her hips.

"Heeeey! Heeeey!" She's mimicking Kemi's dance moves from earlier; when the chorus comes in, it doesn't take long for Kemi's friends to gravitate toward the center. They wail the wrong words over the pidgin English lyrics, their bums never failing to miss a beat. I exhale for what feels like the first time in the last hour.

With everyone now distracted, I scurry out of the living room and race down the corridor. I just have to grab my jacket from Kemi's bedroom, then I can leave.

"Oh." I halt at the doorway, my rapid heartbeat kicking the breath out of me. "You're here."

My cousin Ola is on her knees by Daniel, her youngest.

"Hey," she says, focusing back on the nappy in her hand. "Yeah, I arrived with my mum, but Daniel needed changing."

Daniel squeals and kicks his pudgy legs.

For a moment I'm distracted by his cuteness, then I make my way to the bed where there is a mountain of coats and jackets. I waste no time in disassembling it.

"Is Rachel here? Nana?" Ola asks, and when I glance down at her, I notice that she has changed her hair. Again. When we went shopping on Boxing Day with Rachel and Nana her hairstyle was a long, black weave. That was what—two weeks ago? It was Brazilian hair, I think. Or maybe it was Peruvian? As a lifelong natural hair wearer, I wouldn't know. Now her hair tousles in waves down her back, the color of golden syrup. Her makeup is the same as usual—lots of foundation, blush, false lashes. There is never a day when Ola isn't glammed up.

"Not yet," I reply, still rummaging for my jacket. "Nana has gone AWOL. I'm hoping Rachel will be here soon. Her mum's just arrived—finally!" I wrench my jacket out of the pile. But it's too late.

"Ah! You're not going yet, are you?" says Mum, pulling up her wrapper and marching into the room followed by Aunty Debbie. "Your Aunty and I need to speak to you." She grabs me by the wrist, and before I know it, I'm sandwiched between the two sisters on the bed.

"Yinka, how are you, hm?" Aunty Debbie flutters her fake lashes, as if the Bambi act will make her look innocent. "How's life? In fact, how's work?" Her lips curl into a smile. It's as though the prayer of the century never happened.

"Uh, work's fine." Suddenly, I get a flash of inspiration. "Actually, this coming Tuesday I'm getting promoted."

Okay, pause. What I meant to say was, "On Tuesday, I find out *whether* I've been promoted." But before I can correct myself, Aunty Debbie throws herself at me.

"A promotion!" She gasps. "Yinka! That's wonderful."

"This is news to me," I hear Mum say.

"So what's the new role, hm?" Aunty Debbie's eyes are sparkly with interest.

"Well . . ." I begin, fluffing my fro. No point backtracking now. "I'm being promoted from a managerial position to a vice president. In the operations team."

Mum's hands have flown to her head. "Vice president!" she cries. "Yinka, for the love of God, why do you want to run the bank, ehn? This job they want to give you is a man's job, you know that? Not for a woman who wants a *huzband* and kids."

"Mum!" I can't help but laugh—what she's just said is wrong on so many levels. "Not *that* kind of vice president." God, bless her. "This new role is just a step up from what I'm currently doing. And besides, there are loads of vice presidents at Godfrey. None of them are close to running the bank."

"Well, I think it's brilliant," says Aunty Debbie, giving me a wide smile. She swings her head to her daughter. Sniffs. "Ola. Aren't you going to congratulate your cousin?"

A pang of guilt hits me while I watch Ola slowly dispose of a wet wipe into a plastic bag.

"Congratulations," she says, as though I've beaten her to become prom queen.

"You see, that's why having a degree is so important." Aunty Debbie has moved on. "It's like having a passport. It can take you almost anywhere."

I want to kick myself and hit the rewind button. Yinka, why, why, why would you bring up the promotion? You know Aunty Debbie hasn't forgiven Ola for dropping out of uni when she fell pregnant the first time.

"Well, Nana doesn't have a degree," Ola mutters as she wrestles Daniel's legs into his trousers.

Aunty Debbie belts out a theatrical laugh. "Nana!" She scoffs. "The same Nana that is *still* working as a bartender and doing shifts at H&M? Ola, please."

"And she's a fashion designer!" I race to my best friend's defense.

Aunty Debbie rolls her eyes. "*Aspiring* fashion designer." She bats a hand. "Anyway, how do you fancy attending your mum's church tomorrow?"

"Uhm, what about my church?" I say, and Mum scoffs. Mum has never been a fan of St. Mary's. It's not that she holds anything against the Church of England denomination; though she does question whether one can learn anything in a one-hour service as opposed to All Welcome Church's three-hour Pentecostal marathon. No, the thing about my church which gives Mum great concern is . . . let's just say the "makeup" of the congregation.

"Yinka, how do you expect to meet a *huzband*, ehn?" she would say, punctuating each word with a clap. "This church of yours, it's full of old, *oyibo* people!"

"Well, tomorrow," Aunty Debbie continues, "you'll go to your mum's church. There's a young man I want to introduce you to. His name is Alex. He's one of my tenants. He's new to London but originally from Bristol. Tall. Handsome. You'll like him."

While Aunty Debbie rattles on about Alex's profession—a website designer, makes good money—Mum literally rubs her hands in delight.

"Thank you for thinking of me, Aunty," I say. "You really didn't have to. I'm not in a rush to meet someone." Then quickly, I add, "I think it's best to wait on God's timing, you know?"

Aunty Debbie's jaw drops. Then—

"Yinka! For the love of God. Do you just expect a man to fall from the sky, ehn?" Mum glares at me. Her question isn't rhetorical. She wags a finger. "Don't tell me you're still crying over Femi."

"No, I—"

"Look at your cousin." She points at Ola, who finishes packing up her nappy changing bag. "Married with three kids."

I raise my brows. Clearly Ola and Jon's shotgun wedding doesn't matter so much to her.

"And look at your junior sister. Married and pregnant."

I knew it was only a matter of time before she brought that up again.

"And look at your cousin, Rachel—"

"She's not married!" I point out.

"Ehn, not yet but she will be soon. Yinka, what is wrong with you? Why are you being so stubborn when you're no longer a young woman—"

"Do you want to end up like Aunty Blessing?" Aunty Debbie says.

"Kai! God forbid." Mum swings a hand over her head, clicking her fingers, yelling, "God, don't let my daughter end up like Blessing o. No *huzband*. No children. No grandchildren."

How rude! I want to shout. I would do anything to be as accomplished as Aunty Blessing. Who knows, maybe she struggled to settle down because men were intimidated by her? Back then, being a career-driven woman wasn't as widely accepted as it is today.

"God, if only I had a photo of Alex." Aunty Debbie slaps a hand to her head. "I will add him on Facebook. Your mother's right. This stubbornness will get you nowhere."

"Aunty, I appreciate the offer. It's just—"

"Oh, for goodness' sake, Yinka! Stop being so goddamn closed-minded." The outburst comes from Ola, who is now on her feet, hoisting Daniel on her hip. "No wonder you're still single." She hisses like one of those angry commuters after they fail to squeeze themselves into a packed train.

A lump the size of a melon fills my throat. Ola can be harsh sometimes, but she rarely raises her voice.

What did I do to deserve that?

Just as I swallow back tears, shrieks erupt from the living room. Fela Kuti's "Water No Get Enemy" is playing in the background. But the screams sound like more than just the guests cheering at someone busting a sick dance move.

I clamber to my feet, avoiding Ola's eyes as I rush out the door.

Back in the living room, there's a huddle. Rachel's here and she's standing with her mum, Big Mama. The pair look excited.

"Yinka! You won't believe what happened yesterday!" Rachel thrusts a hand forward and a diamond rock shines from her third finger. "I'm engaged!"

The plan

Thrusting my duvet to one side, I stare up at the ceiling, spread-eagled. Outside, the wind is whistling and rain is pattering against my window.

I can't sleep. I've been tossing and turning, today's events taunting me. After Rachel dropped her bombshell of an announcement, I didn't stick around for long. I told her that I'd catch up with her over the phone, or next Friday when she and Gavesh are having their engagement party. Although whether she heard me is another question. She was too busy chatting with her BFF, Ola. Kemi was sad to see me go, but she understood. As always, she apologized for Aunty Debbie's behavior.

"Yinka, I feel so bad," she said as she walked me to the front door. "If I had known, I would have offered to pray."

"Let's face it, Kemi. No one can stop Aunty Debbie when she is on a roll." I forced a small laugh. "Don't feel bad. It's not your fault."

As for Nana, my so-called BFF who was meant to be there for support, I texted her saying that I was leaving early and that she no longer needed to come. She messaged saying she was sorry and she'd see me tomorrow after church. Which will soon be today.

I toss again and stretch over to switch on my bedside lamp. I squint, catching sight of my dark reflection in the mirror.

I can't believe what happened. I can't believe Ola called me out like that. And how dare Mum bring up Femi—

Femi. I grip my duvet.

If you hadn't got that stupid job in New York, we would be married by now. I was ready to give up everything for you. My home. My career. My family and friends. But no. You had a change of heart. You said moving to the Big Apple had made you realize that you weren't ready to settle down. What happened, Femi? We had discussed marriage, even thought of baby names for the two kids we both wanted. I couldn't have dreamed of a better partner. You were kind. Attentive. You made me feel beautiful. How could you throw away everything just like that?

Curling my hands into fists, I push them against my eyes. *Come on, Yinka. It's been almost three years now.* I'm praying to God for comfort, reciting Bible verses in my head until I calm down a bit. Suddenly, I remember something.

I clamber out of bed, grab my laptop and climb back in again. After I returned home from Kemi's baby shower, I had needed a bit of reassurance, so I typed into Quora, *What are the chances of meeting a guy and getting married when you're a thirty-something woman?*

And hey, what do you know? I've already got an answer. I hope this will make me feel better . . .

 Julia N. King, feminist and proud

If you think that your chances to find a man and get married increase just because some thirty-something woman on here tells you about her experience, then you must be naive. That's like me coming on here and asking, "What are my chances of living till I'm eighty?!!!" And why set a deadline for yourself? The last time I checked, one can get married at any age. The fact that you're asking this question in the first place tells me your values are misplaced and that you're one of those desperate types that needs a ring to find happiness. Well, newsflash, woman. We're not in the 1950s! Start by loving yourself!

 Upvote 22   Share

I blink. "Wow." *And* she got twenty-two likes.

Obviously, women don't *have* to get married to be happy or find value in themselves. Well, at least, that's not why I want to get married. I always just loved the idea of spending the rest of my life with someone I made a vow to and building a home and family with them. So does this make me a bad feminist? Well, according to Julia N. King and twenty-two other Quorarians, yes. Yes, it does.

I type the same question into Google. An ad appears at the very top of the search list: *What are your chances of finding love? Take our free quiz today.*

Curious, I click on the link. A message pops up.

> Waiting for a new guy to show up in your life? Well, fear no more! By taking this quiz, we'll determine when you'll meet your next boyfriend based on your personality. So, what are you waiting for? Take our free quiz today!

Under normal circumstances, I would run a mile from something like this, but after being publicly prayed for, I think it's fair to say that things are far from normal right now. I click on the button and begin the quiz. It's multiple choice.

Question 1

To date, how many relationships have you been in?

A. ◯ So many I can't remember

B. ◯ Two or more

C. ◯ One

D. ◯ None

Next

I click "C." Femi is my one and only boyfriend. Well, he *was* my boy-friend.

Question 2

How are you around guys?

A. ◯ Confident and carefree

B. ◯ A bit hesitant

C. ◯ Super-duper shy

D. ◯ I rarely talk to guys

`Next`

I drum my fingers on my laptop. Now that I think about it, I don't really have a lot of male friends. I went to an all-girls secondary school and sixth form, so I didn't have much interaction with men in my age group until I started uni. Even then, I still didn't make a lot of male friends. Well, there was Jon, the guy in my lectures who later became Ola's boyfriend, and shortly after, her daughter's father. But he was more Ola's boyfriend than my friend. So I guess the only reference point I have is how I was when I first met Femi.

I remember the day I met him like it was yesterday. It was at a small gathering that Rachel threw for Gavesh's twenty-fifth birthday. It was Gavesh's older brother, Sanjeev, who had invited Femi—they're best friends. During the evening, Femi and I got chatting. I don't think he approached me with the intention of making a move—in fact, I think he said some-thing along the lines of, "Can you pass me a napkin, please." But two hours of solid conversation later, we were talking like old friends. It was so effort-less, I didn't even notice it happening.

"Do you mind if I get your number?" he asked as I shrugged on my coat to leave.

"Who, me?" I pressed a hand to my chest. It was only then that I noticed how attractive he was: taper fade haircut, light stubble, cinnamon-brown skin.

Suddenly, I felt jittery and nervous.

Femi laughed and handed me his phone. I could barely type the numbers in—I couldn't believe someone as gorgeous as him would take an interest in someone like me.

That same nervous-excited feeling stayed with me for our first few dates, constantly thinking, *What's the catch?* Pinching myself in disbelief.

"So, in that case, B," I say aloud, clicking on the button on the mouse. I think that around guys, I'm somewhat confident but a bit hesitant.

I carry on with the quiz, answering a few questions about myself—but why do they need to know my ethnicity and age, though?—and I hit the "Submit Answers" button with a loud exhale. *Come on, Yinka. You're not applying for a job.* I cross my fingers anyway.

It doesn't work.

"Five point five years!" I gape at my results. That means I'll be, what, thirty-six, thirty-seven, by the time I get into another relationship? I know I've always said I'm happy to find love at the right time, but come on, five years is way too long.

Pushing my face toward the screen, I read the report explaining how this number was reached.

You got: Who needs a man?

According to your answers, you're the type of person who takes a laid-back approach to dating and values long-term relationships. Since you're not signed up onto any dating sites and tentative about joining, we can only assume that you've got other priorities in your life right now, and if you have to wait 5.5 years to meet that special someone, then "so be it," is your mantra. We admire how independent you are. You don't need a man to be happy.

I slam my laptop shut. The Internet isn't helping. I drag my fingers through my kinky hair, raking it up and down.

What if Ola's right? What if I am the problem?

Okay, maybe not the problem. But there might be some truth in the idea that I am stopping myself from finding love. And if I don't want to suffer more public humiliation, then I need to find a man in time for Rachel's wedding. I need a plan. A plan with clear aims and objectives, like the ones we produce at work.

I fetch my notebook and eventually find a pen at the bottom of my bag, before returning to bed. With a fresh page open, I jot down the title, "Operation Wedding Date: My plan to have a date for Rachel's wedding." I inhale. I already feel better.

The next thing I do is draw a table. At Godfrey, every time we begin a new project, we draw up a plan with columns for "objectives," "tasks," "deadline" and "key performance indicators." Within a matter of minutes, I've finished.

OPERATION WEDDING DATE: MY PLAN TO HAVE A DATE FOR RACHEL'S WEDDING

OBJECTIVES	TASKS	DEADLINE	KPIs
1. Meet a guy in person	• Make an effort to speak to any single men at Rachel's engagement party	• Next Friday	• I exchange numbers with a guy
2. Meet a guy virtually	• Sign up to online dating if I don't meet anyone at Rachel's engagement party	• End of Jan	• I connect with a guy I've met online • We exchange numbers, speak on the phone and go on a date

I scan my plan, wondering whether I should add as another objective, "Take up Aunty Debbie's offer to meet Alex"—and quickly decide against it. No. If I don't like Alex, Aunty Debbie will forever remind me of how my singleness is my fault until the day I get engaged. Best to leave that option out. Besides, I'm sure there's bound to be at least *one* decent-looking single guy at Rachel and Gavesh's engagement party. If I could meet Femi at an event all those years ago, surely it isn't too far-fetched to think that I can meet a guy next Friday?

I take one last look at my plan before closing my notebook. Operation Wedding Date. Bring it on.

Like a sister

YINKA

Mum's right. I'll never find a huzband at St. Mary's Church lol

NANA

Uh, tell me something I don't know. You coming over? x

YINKA

Yep. See you soon. You better prepare your apology! x

"So . . . you didn't quite make it to Kemi's baby shower then?"

It's an hour later, and I'm stepping through the trillions of sequins and loose bits of thread all over Nana's carpet at her place in New Cross Gate.

"Actually, I was en route to Kemi's when you texted me," she says, tying her long locs into a high bun, which immediately sags to one side because of the weight. Her skinny legs are outstretched on the bed under a baggy dashiki. "But you know how I am with big crowds. I don't do well with mixed energies. It just . . . I dunno. Disturbs my inner peace."

I roll my eyes. "You thought you'd come when everyone had left then?" I plonk myself on her bed.

She laughs and shrugs. Nana has not changed one bit in the fifteen years that we've been best friends. We met during sixth form after she handed me a clipboard.

"It's a petition to end hair discrimination against Black people," she had said.

From that moment, I knew we would get on. And we got on so well that I immediately welcomed her into the fold. Or rather, "Destiny's Child," which is what my cousins Rachel, Ola and I called ourselves in secondary school, even though we couldn't sing to save our lives. Of course, Ola claimed Beyoncé and Rachel claimed Kelly. In my thirteen-year-old mind I was convinced I should have been Kelly since I'm darker, even though none of us looked anything like the band. And though they were always saying, "We're all best friends," deep down in my heart I knew I wasn't as close to them as they were to each other. And I also knew that Ola probably wouldn't have been my friend at all if it wasn't for Rachel.

"What do you mean?" Rachel cried when I confided in her about how I felt one day when Ola was off sick from school. "Yinka, don't be stupid, you're family. She loves you. If she has a problem with anyone, it's her mum, not you."

I couldn't contest this. Aunty Debbie was hard on Ola growing up, constantly comparing us like two kitchen appliances she was deciding between. If it wasn't our grades, then it was the length of our hair, and if it wasn't our behavior in class, then it was who had the clearest skin. That wasn't my fault, though. And I had my own problems with Mum always pushing me.

When I met Nana and we clicked, I thought, *Finally, I have my own best friend.* I clung to her like a sister. There's something about Nana's chilled energy and her bohemian swag, which is both refreshing and admirable. Despite our very distinct personalities, we looked like sisters, according to some. Same dark skin, slim frame and what I've coined the J-shaped bum.

I don't know why my obsession with women's bottoms started—I think maybe it's because God didn't endow me with a big one—but I've grown the habit of labeling women's bum outlines with letters of the alphabet, a bit like how women's body shapes are named after different fruits. I've concluded that both Nana and I have a J-shaped bum. There is no demarcation between where our back ends and bum starts, just a slope with the tiniest bit of fat residing at the base. Still, Nana wears anything she feels like—she has this African meets grunge style (Afropunk, I think it's called?)—as for me, I hate any clothing that shows off my flat behind. I practically live in long cardigans.

"So . . . Rachel's engaged," says Nana now, rubbing the side of her shoulder, two black ankh tattoos on display.

"And we're bridesmaids."

Nana grins. "Guess who's making the bridesmaids' dresses?"

I give Nana's foot a light squeeze. "Well, in that case, I know we'll look amazing." I gaze at the opposite wall covered with dozens of sketches and photos of her designs made out of bold wax fabric, inspired by her Ghanaian heritage. "I swear, Nana, you need to leave your job and do this full time. Honestly, you're so talented. I mean, look at that jacket!" I swing my arm toward a mannequin where a blue blazer with giant shoulder pads and a lapel made out of Kente cloth is draped. "It's like something out of *Black Panther*."

Nana laughs and twiddles her nose ring. "I know, I know. But bills have to be paid." She slaps her thighs. "Anyways, how was the baby shower? Why did you suddenly decide to bounce?"

"Ah! Where should I even start?" I shuffle until my back hits the wall, and then tell her *everything*, barely stopping to take a breath. Well, everything except the part when Aunty Debbie said those not-so-nice things about her, and when Ola called me closed-minded.

"Damn," Nana breathes after I've spilled the tea. I'm parched from all the ranting. "Aunty Debbie *definitely* took the piss. I mean, praying publicly over your singleness. *That's* a new low."

"Thank you!"

"And this guy she wants to introduce you to—"

"Alex," I say, ready to launch into another rant.

"Remind me why don't you want to meet him again?"

I stare at Nana, speechless.

She stares back. "You're single, sooo, what's the problem?"

"Nana, weren't you listening? Aunty Debbie *em-bar-razed* me," I say, putting on a Nigerian accent. "No, scratch that, she humiliated me *and* she got my mum in on the act," I add before she can jump in. "And what would happen if I met Alex and didn't like him? You think Aunty Debbie wouldn't kick up a fuss? Puh-lease. Let's not forget what she did at Kemi's wedding."

At this, Nana purses her lips.

"Exactly."

What happened was that when I had failed to catch the bouquet, Aunty Debbie had made a mad dash to the dance floor, grabbed the mic from the MC's hands and called back the winner, demanding to know how old the woman was before insisting that her niece needed the bouquet more than she did. When she discovered we were the same age, she snatched the bouquet from the woman's hands, split it in two and then announced, "Now both of you will get married," and my three hundred uncles and aunties chorused, "Amen!"

Nana shakes her head. "I see your point. It's just . . ." She trails off. Bites her lip.

I sigh. "Go on, you might as well just say it."

"Well, I know you believe in love, yeah. And it's great that you believe that one day you'll find it. But don't you think you actually need to, you know, step out to find it?"

I laugh. "Oh, that's rich coming from you." My girl hasn't had a boyfriend in a million years. Lucky for her, she can get away with it because her parents are those liberal, laid-back types. My mum would have killed me if I'd told her that I had no plans to go to uni.

"Hey, this is not about me," she says. "There's a big difference between you and me. I'm okay if I never find love and grow old on my own. I prefer my own company, to be honest." She points a finger at me. "*You* are a hopeless romantic. You believe in love and all that *ish*."

"And I'll find it, but *not* with the help of Aunty Debbie."

"Then how?" Nana grips her hair, the messy bun sagging even lower. "How will you find a man when all you do is work these days?"

"I have to bloody work," I protest. "Besides, these last three years I wasn't focused on getting a man, you know that. But nowww . . ." *Do I tell her about Operation Wedding Date? No, too embarrassing.* A coy smile slips across my face. "Now I think it's time for Yinka to get her groove back."

Nana quirks a brow then leans forward and places a hand on my forehead, as though to check whether I've got a temperature. I shrug her off and she laughs.

"Nana, I'm serious! In fact, I've got a plan. This coming Friday at Rachel's engagement party . . . I'm going to speak to a few guys."

Nana snorts. "I wouldn't ride all your hopes on this Friday."

I frown.

"Isn't it more of a small gathering? I'm sure Rachel told me it's *not* a party. Anyway, isn't online dating easier?"

"That's my next option. I've heard way too many harrowing stories to try that unless I have to. Plus, you know I'm old skool."

"True." Nana laughs. "Well, I'm just happy that you're actually putting yourself out there. I was getting worried that you were still hung up on Femi."

I fold my arms. "Err, excuse me. I don't even stalk the guy on Facebook."

Nana scoffs. "You're the only person I know who still uses Facebook."

We laugh, then I start thinking back to my plan. I really do hope there are a few single guys at Rachel and Gavesh's engagement party—gathering, whatever. But maybe, like Nana said, I should look at other options too.

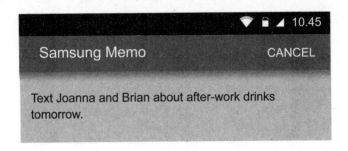

"Hey, Yinka?"

"Huh?" I look up to see Nana fiddling with her many ear piercings. "Don't tell me you need me to be a mannequin again."

"No, not that." She rubs her finger over her Cleopatra tattoo on the back of her left wrist. "The landlady wants to put the rent up."

"Seriously? That's insane. I swear you only just moved in about six months ago."

Nana sighs. "I know, right. Who would have thought that New Cross would be an expensive place to live?"

"Damn. That sucks."

"Yup," she says glumly. "So I was thinking . . ." She pushes out her lips. "You know you have two bedrooms . . ."

"Oh, no, please . . ."

"It won't be forever," Nana cries. "Please, Yinka. Otherwise, I have to move in with my sister and her three kids. Where would I put my stuff?"

"But it will ruin our friendship," I whine. "Also, wouldn't living with me affect your energy?"

"So *now* you want to be all spiritual." She hits my knee with a pillow. "Yinka, come on. What's the real reason you don't want me to move in?"

I glance down, fake-cough. "You're messy."

"*Messy?*" Nana gasps like I've just dissed Beyoncé. Seriously, can she not see the evidence? In addition to her carpet, which could do with a deep Dyson clean, tons of yarn, fabric and plastic bags spew out of every corner. Nana's sewing table is a mess—you can hardly see her sewing machine—and oh, no, is that old tangerine peel I see?

"It's called Art," she says proudly, but even she can't keep a straight face. "Come on, Yinka." She laughs. "You're my last hope. How can I bribe you? I know. You love my cooking, right? Now imagine this. Jerk chicken. Jollof rice. Every night."

For a moment, I'm slightly swayed. Nana is an amazing cook.

I throw her pillow back at her. "I'll think about it."

Can I have tap water, please?

History	Ctrl+H

Recently Closed

How to approach a guy at the bar without looking like a complete weirdo—*Elle*

"I can't believe they actually prayed for you," says Joanna, hand over her mouth, spluttering laughter. "Like *kumbaya* prayed for you."

It's seven in the evening and I'm standing near the bar with my favorite colleagues, Joanna and Brian, at our usual after-work spot—All Bar One. As always, the place is buzzing. With Operation Wedding Date now in action, I've worn my best white blouse and tucked it into my black A-line skirt from H&M. I did consider the bare legs look, but it's too cold. Joanna, on the other hand, is wearing a figure-hugging pencil skirt, and what, for her sake, I hope are nude tights.

I met Joanna about five years ago after she ever so kindly passed a wad of tissues under my toilet cubicle, when silly me forgot to check the tissue dispenser beforehand. We quickly grew from stall mates to good friends, and thanks to her working in PR, I've seen Jorja Smith live. Brian joined my team last year as a graduate analyst and during his first week, my manager

Louise gave him an earful—"You're here to work, Brian, not to chit-chat." Feeling sorry for him, I invited him out for coffee with me and Joanna, and since making the introduction, they've become inseparable. I call them Jo-Brian whenever I'm feeling lazy (which is often).

"Man. Sorry, babe," says Brian, visibly distressed. He slings his gray blazer over one shoulder. "You have it worse than me. When I came out to my mum, she only said, 'Well, I better put the kettle on.' And she's a Roman Catholic."

We laugh.

"Welcome to my life," I say, projecting my voice over the buzz of chatter as more and more people in smart shirts and loose ties pile into the venue. There are loads of men here, but no one has caught my eye, which is a bit rubbish given that the article I read earlier suggested making "smoldering" eye contact (whatever that means). To make matters difficult, most of the men are drinking in huddles and some are being annoyingly shouty. And what if they work for Godfrey? Dammit, I didn't think about that. Would that make things awkward?

"That's the thing with coming from a Nigerian family." I drag my eyes back to Brian. "They forget that love is a process. That you need to fall in love *first*, not just meet a random guy and decide he's the one to marry."

"Are you going to meet this Alex guy then?" Brian clearly hasn't been listening.

"Of course not." A man brushes by and nearly yanks my arm off.

"Why not?" Brian pushes up his glasses. "He sounds like a catch, sooo—"

"Don't encourage her!" Joanna flicks her fringe away from her eyes. "If she gets with Alex, then what about Derek?"

I put down my drink so that I can properly scowl at her.

Ever since I told JoBrian about Derek, I've had to put up with them constantly saying, "*He's the one.*" It doesn't help that they both know what he looks like—my fault, showing them Derek's Facebook photos. *Why did I do that again?*

Derek and I go way back. We attended the same Sunday school at All Welcome Church, but we became proper friends when we were eighteen and both studying hard to get into our first-choice university. We provided each other with moral support, hung out in the library together. I thought our relationship was platonic, but then one day, Derek showed up at the bar while I was having a pity party with Kemi over my breakup with Femi. I spent God knows how long talking to him. He was a shoulder to lean on. Literally. Then, when Kemi was in the toilets, he said in a low voice, "Yinka. Femi may not want you, but . . . but I do."

I jerked up as if he was a spider. Then, as now, I saw Derek as a nice guy but still *Derek*. Zero chemistry. I've just never seen him in a romantic way.

"I like you, Yinka," he said, just about managing to hold eye contact.

My stomach twisted in knots. I knew how painful unrequited love is and how it feels to have your heart broken. So rather than telling him how I really felt, I said, "Derek . . . I just got out of a relationship." And thankfully, he didn't say anything else.

I haven't seen him in a while now. Hmm. Another reason why I shouldn't attend All Welcome any time soon.

"Yes!" Brian turns to Joanna, mouth wide. "How could I forget our beloved Derek? Yinka, I kid you not, you would make a beautiful couple."

Clearly, I must have forgotten that I'm with my white friends because in true Nigerian style, I swing a hand over my head, clicking my fingers, repeating, "God forbid. God forbid," like Mum does.

Brian and Joanna stare at me.

I clear my throat and reach for my drink. "Besides, I've already got a plan for how I'm going to get a man." I watch Joanna's brows flicker with interest.

"A plan?" she says, bobbing her straw in her glass.

"Ooh. Tell us more," Brian adds.

"It's no big deal," I say. "I just plan to, you know, put myself out there a bit more. Maybe talk to a couple of guys at my cousin's engagement this

Friday. If that doesn't work then, I dunno, maybe try online dating or something—"

Brian's mouth falls open. "You're not even on Tinder?! God, Yinka. No wonder you're bloody single."

I take a slow sip of my G&T. "Apparently, the guys on there are only after sex."

"Is that a bad thing?" Brian smirks. "Just kidding. Though I'm not going to lie to you, you have to do a bit of weeding. But don't forget! I found the love of my life on Tinder. Ricky and I are going two years strong."

"Hey, I'm not the only one that's single," I point out, nodding to Jo.

Brian shoots Joanna a playful glare. "Oh, I'm on to her too."

"I'll stick to my paid online dating sites, thank you very much." Joanna knocks back the rest of her wine. "My theory is this—if a man is happy to pay to search for love, then surely he must be after a serious relationship, right?"

"Maybe." I shrug. "But that doesn't stop them from being bad dates."

Brian gasps. "Ohmigod, yes! Remember that time when Jo got catfished?"

While Brian recounts the date that Joanna had a few months back with an FBI-looking IT technician who refused to take off his sunglasses, I spot a chiseled Black man making his way from the men's toilets. My brows rise. He is definitely not a Godfrey employee, because as a Black minority, I'm convinced that I know all the Black people in the office—and trust me, I *definitely* would have remembered his face.

Brian is still talking as I sneakily watch the man weave through the crowd. "Hey!" I'm suddenly thrown forward after someone knocks into me from behind.

"What a moron." Brian raises his voice. "Aww, look. Your drink's all over the floor."

"Let me get you another." Joanna rummages in her bag.

"No, it's okay. There was only a little left." I look around frantically.

Chiseled Black Man walks straight out of the bar. Well, that ended before it even started.

Joanna flaps a hand. "It's cool. I got it."

"It's fine, thanks. I don't drink that much anyway."

Joanna lets out a belly laugh. "Yinka, what you do doesn't class as drinking. How about you, Brian? Fancy another?"

"Well, if you're paying," he sings.

Joanna flags down a bartender. I place my empty glass on the counter and glance away.

Great. Once again, Yinka is the boring one. I just don't want to have to explain my limited alcohol consumption for the hundredth time.

Yes, Christians are not technically forbidden to drink alcohol—hey, even Jesus turned water into wine—but the Bible does encourage Christians not to get drunk. "*Sooo, if you can't get drunk, then what's the point of drinking?*" I imagine they would say while exchanging fleeting glances. Then I would have to explain the whole virtue of being sober-minded and in control of yourself thing. Or I could chicken out and say, "God just wants to save humanity from a few hangovers." Either way, this is something I refuse to get into.

Just as Joanna is about to order their drinks, I tap her shoulder.

"Actually, can I have a tap water, please?"

Our drinks arrive, and Joanna hands them out. "Ooh, we should make a toast," she says.

"What to?" Brian takes a sip of his cocktail. "And *please* don't say to the New Year. It's so over."

"How about my promotion?" I suggest.

"Oooh. Someone's confident." Brian nudges me.

"Yes, because I damn well deserve it." I raise my glass of tap water in the air. "Seriously. Eight years I've been at Godfrey. With all the long hours I've put in, I should already be VP by now."

"Yeah, you're right. You do deserve it," Brian admits. "Especially with all the sucking up to the MDs you did."

I snort. "Oh, yeah. I forgot about that."

"Well, in that case. To Yinka!" Joanna raises her glass. "To getting the promotion that you truly deserve tomorrow."

We all clink our glasses. "Cheers!"

This actually cannot be happening

Oh, God, no.

No, no, no, no, no.

This can't be happening.

This actually cannot be happening.

I read the subject line on the printed letter over and over again:

RE: TERMINATION OF EMPLOYMENT BY REDUNDANCY

I'm being made redundant! My heart is pounding in my chest, the letter that my manager Louise slid across the table trembling in my hands.

"I'm sorry," says my manager in that patronizing voice of hers. "But, as you know, Godfrey & Jackson is going through a very difficult period. Budgets have been slashed and cuts have to be made."

"But this doesn't make sense." I'm struggling to breathe. "What about the promotion? I worked hard. You even said so yourself—"

"Well." She shrugs. "What can I say? That's life. Do get in touch if you need a reference, though."

Seven hours later...

I'm sitting in front of what is now my former desk, the sound of a hoover blasting in the background. After sobbing my eyes out in the disabled toilets, I decided to go home and come back in the evening to clear my desk (I had to sweet-talk security to let me through the barriers, though). Better this way with just the cleaners around, than in front of my entire team.

"How are you feeling?" asks Joanna as I throw a handful of Biros in an orange Sainsbury's bag with all my other desk belongings.

"How do you think she feels?" Brian whispers. "Why would you ask her such a stupid question?"

"I feel like shit." I slump back in my chair. "I feel like someone is playing a nasty prank on me. I mean, eight years, Jo, and this is how they repay me?"

Like a film reel, my time at Godfrey flashes through my mind. All the late nights. The early starts. The arse-kissing. The sacrifices, the compromises. The exhaustion, the unfair reprimands.

And yes, granted, I never *loved* my job, or my manager, or the high-pressured work culture, but I felt comfortable in this role, *and* I was good at it. I never once complained about the repetitiveness of analyzing each trade to make sure they were settled properly. Never said, "Figure it out" when junior members in my team needed help. I was the first one in, last one out. I took up the slack.

In the end, it has all been for nothing.

"Well, at least you didn't get the chop," I say to Brian, trying to find the silver lining in this nightmare of a situation. He drapes his long arms over my shoulders and nuzzles his chin into my hair.

"Why did they have to let you gooo?" he says overdramatically. "I don't know how I'm going to survive without you, Yinka. You know they only kept me on because I'm a graduate. Cheap labor. And I can't believe Mary's gone too. I almost fainted when I saw the e-mail."

Yes, in addition to me getting the boot, a load of other people have been let go, including Mary, which took me by surprise. She just got promoted last year. Then there's Sanjay and Bobbie. Gayle and Tony too. Tony hasn't even completed his probation.

"So what's the deal with PR and Media?" asks Brian, lifting his arms away. I still smell his Paco Rabanne on my cardigan.

"Who knows?" Joanna tosses a crumpled-up Post-it into a nearby recycling bin. "But believe me when I say I'm not waiting around to find out. Starting this weekend, I'm looking for another job."

I feel a swoosh of nerves. I haven't applied for a job since my early twenties. Even then, I was applying for graduate schemes as opposed to a position at a company. I'll have to update my CV, trawl the Internet, finesse my LinkedIn page, brush up on my interview skills, and who knows what else.

I swallow. I'm getting sick just thinking about it.

"Are you okay?" Joanna places a hand on my back.

I shake my head to dislodge the thought. "It's just . . ." I sigh. "I've only just realized that I'm effectively . . . unemployed."

A lengthy silence follows as the reality of my situation kicks in.

"Aww, you'll get a job in no time," says Joanna, trying to lighten the mood. A cleaner with a mop and bucket in hand strolls by and nods. "And with Godfrey on your CV, I can't imagine you'll be out of a job for too long."

"Yeah, and at least you no longer have to deal with Louise, eh?" Brian spreads his hands. "It's humanly impossible to have a worse manager than her."

"True," I say flatly. "I still wish I hadn't lost my job, though."

Brian pushes out his lips. "Sooo," he says after an awkward pause. "Do you want me to pop these back in the stationery cupboard then?" He gestures at the array of neon colored Post-it notes that I've been hoarding in my drawer.

"No," I say more forcefully than I intended to. "Pop them in the Sainsbury's bag. Please."

We tackle my pedestal next, sorting through piles of paper, and all the while I try to ignore the hotness creeping into my eyes. Today will be the last time that I see this desk, sit in this chair and look at these two screens. I feel as though I'm going through a breakup and I'm getting kicked out, right after being served with divorce papers. *God, this is so unfair.*

In silence, we finish clearing my desk, dumping unwanted papers in the recycling bin. I stand and tuck in my chair. Joanna and Brian bow their heads.

"Good-bye, Godfrey & Jackson," I whisper, my voice cracking on the final note. I'm just about to launch into a good-bye speech when I realize my chest is buzzing. I grab my phone from my pocket and when I look at the screen, I taste bile in my throat.

Shit. It's Mum.

Now I've got another problem to deal with. My big mouth just had to tell Mum that I'd got a promotion, didn't it?

What would I do without my favorite aunt, eh?

THURSDAY

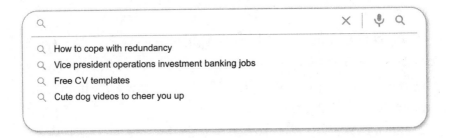

I'm upstairs in Aunty Blessing's study at her terraced house in Poplar, sitting in my usual chair. It's where I share my life problems with my favorite aunt, in the hope that she'll offer me advice and help me to see things objectively. Aunty Blessing is like a second mum to me. She was there for us when Daddy passed away—braiding my hair and Kemi's, helping with our homework or with food shopping. Over the years, we've become really close. In fact, I open up to her more than Mum. Where Mum is set in her ways, Aunty Blessing can see things from a different perspective—for example, she helped me to navigate some of the politics at work, when Mum just said, "Well . . . may God give you wisdom." Most days, I love Aunty Blessing for this, but today . . . hmm, not so much.

"*Aunty!*" I stare at her dumbfounded. "How is losing my job a blessing in disguise? We worked hard putting my promotion case together, re-member?"

As I had recounted what happened, Aunty Blessing had inhaled her be-loved e-cigarette, blowing billows of citrusy smoke in my face, but now she puts it down. "I do remember," she replies, and yet there isn't an ounce of outrage in her voice. "Come on, Yinka, it's not like you even like your job. In fact, how many times have you sat in that very chair and complained about your manager, the culture, how stressful work is?"

I wince.

"I love *my* job." Aunty Blessing places a hand on her chest, and I pull a face.

"Why wouldn't you? You get to be Annalise Keating."

She frowns.

"You know, Viola Davis from *How to Get Away with Murder.*"

She rolls her eyes. "I'm just saying, maybe it's time for you to work else-where. Eight years is a long time. They passed you over for a promotion. Twice! Honestly, Yinka, I'm surprised that you stayed as long as you did."

I dig my foot into the rug. We've had previous conversations like this. But why on earth would I want to leave one of the most prestigious banks in the world? Godfrey & Jackson is like the Google of the financial sector.

"Anyway, you have to move forward. What other banks are you look-ing at?" she asks. "Oscar Larsson? Citi? Deutsche Bank?"

I blank-stare guiltily at her.

"You haven't started looking, have you?"

"I just lost my job. I need a few days to recover." I also need a few days to binge-watch TV, but I don't tell her that.

Aunty Blessing gives me a warning look. "Well, don't wallow in self-pity for too long. How will you cope financially? I know they've given you a package, but it can take a few months to get a new job."

"I've got savings," I say. "Also, next weekend Nana is moving into my second bedroom. She'll pay me rent."

That's one thing I've done at least. After I had returned home from clearing my desk, I got straight on the phone to Nana. She was ecstatic for a moment, before remembering she had to be sad that I'd lost my job.

"Well, if you ever need any assistance—whether that's looking over your applications or you're low on cash." Aunty Blessing raises her brow. "I mean it, Yinka. Come to me. Any time."

"Thanks." I smile at her. "What would I do without my favorite aunt, eh?"

She reaches forward, opens her bottom drawer and stashes her e-cig away. "So how did your mum take the news?"

I give her another one of my blank-guilty looks.

"You haven't told her! Why not? She's your mother."

"I haven't got round to it," I lie. I will never get round to it.

"*Yinka, how will you find a* huzband *now?*" she would say, clapping after each word. "*How will you find a* huzband *when you're jobless, ehn?*"

"Make sure you tell her," says Aunty Blessing, pulling me out of my thoughts. "It's not right that I know and she doesn't."

"Okay," I say. Still, I'm thinking, *hell no.* I'm not even going to tell Kemi in case she tells her. Besides, I'm sure it won't take me *that* long to find a new job. I mean, I've got eight years' experience.

"Do you know what?" she says, as she leans back in her swivel chair and digs her finger in her thick, natural hair, which she tends to tie back in a bun. "While you were talking, something came to mind. Do you remember after you graduated you went to Peru?"

"Yes," I say, wondering where she's going with all of this.

"Well, didn't you come back saying you wanted to work for a charity? Maybe now is your chance."

A snort comes out of me as I laugh. Aunty Blessing gives me a look.

"What's so funny?"

"Aunty. I haven't wanted to work in the charity sector for donkey's years."

"But you were so adamant at the time," she insists. "I just thought it was a passion that you might want to revisit. I haven't seen you so passionate about something in a long time."

My gaze shifts to a glass award on the wall shelf, ten-year-old memories flooding in. Aunty Blessing must have noticed as she doesn't try to fill in the silence.

After I graduated, I wasn't keen to rush straight into work—I'd spent sixth form busting my arse to get straight A's so I could study Economics and Management at Oxford, then when I got in, I spent most of my days in the library busting my arse to get a 2.1. So I went on a gap year abroad, despite Mum's disapproval. It was me and four other Brits: Kathy, Jojo, Donovan and Hailey. We went with an international charity called Action 28. It was such a brilliant time. Every day we would set up a homeless shelter, handing out food and essential toiletries, and we would provide companionship using our basic Spanish. I loved talking to the people who came through the shelter, hearing about their lives, and being able to do small things for them that would make a difference.

When I returned to the UK, I was *this* close to terminating my allocated graduate position at Godfrey.

But Mum was having none of it.

"Are you crazy?" is what she actually said. "Is this what you went to Oxford for, ehn? To be asking money from people. People on the street." (Mum had a very limited view of the charity sector, unfortunately.)

"How will you save for a mortgage?" she rebutted after I tried to show her a job ad for an entry-level position at a national homeless charity called Sanctuary. "A position that is paying less than minimum wage. Why would you give up Godfrey for that, ehn? You want to live at home with me forever?"

I kept my secured place at Godfrey. I told myself that I would work there for five years, save hard, get a mortgage and bounce. With all the transferable skills I had gained, I would find an operational role in the charity sector, or even better, a role where I would get to work directly with the people. And for many years, I was on track. I even volunteered at one of Sanctuary's local homeless outreaches. Every Saturday for nearly three years, come rain or sun. I got a mortgage—thank God—and moved out of Mum's at the age of twenty-seven. Then over time, I don't know how it happened, but I became reluctant to leave. I had risen in the ranks. I didn't want to throw all I had achieved away. And honestly, I felt comfortable in the private sector. Since then, I haven't volunteered at all.

"What about the others you went to Peru with?" Aunty Blessing interrupts my thoughts. "What are they doing now? Wasn't the other Black person from around here? You could speak to him about jobs."

"Who, Donovan?" I shrug. "Beats me. After I returned, I lost contact with all of them." It's strange that I haven't bumped into Donovan or Hailey during the last ten years, as they both lived in south London. Not that it's a shame on the Donovan front—he was the one I liked the least.

"Anyway, that's in the past," I say finally, raising my eyes to meet my Aunty's. "I'd rather stick to the banking sector. It's what I'm good at."

"Well, if that's what you want." Aunty Blessing gives a light shrug then rubs her hooded eyes. "Right," she says, standing up. She pats the back of the chair. "Come on. Get. Don't you have some job hunting to do? Oi, don't give me that face. Here, you can use my laptop." She scribbles on a piece of paper and hands it to me. "That's my password. And that's a number five, not an S."

I drag my feet to her desk.

"I'll be in the living room if you need me, okay?"

"Yes, Aunty."

———

An hour later, I've updated my LinkedIn page and sent a couple of recruitment agencies my CV. Mentally unable to do more (or rather stubbornly refusing to) I log into Facebook and stalk the two of my gap year buddies I can find—Hailey and Jojo—until I'm bored stiff of looking at weddings and babies.

Then, as though I'm looking for something illegal, I quickly type "Femi Ajaye" into the search bar.

"*Nostalgic,*" his latest post reads. I screw up my nose.

It's attached to a photo of his palm holding out a Yorkie chocolate bar. Femi hardly posts on Facebook. I know this not because I stalk him (honest), but thanks to his lack of presence on my notifications.

I rub my chin. Maybe he's missing the UK, because from what I know, they do not sell Yorkie bars in the U.S.

Unable to stop myself, I trawl through his timeline and all his tagged photos. Annoyingly, most of his albums and status updates go back to two years ago. Nana is right. No one really uses Facebook any more. Though I still find it strange that out of all the things he could have posted, he decided to post a picture of my favorite chocolate.

I wonder if he's missing home . . . his former life . . . me.

"Well, kiss my arse, Femi," I say aloud with a stagy cackle. "You made your bed, so go and lie in it."

Just one last look at his photos—God, he does look good with a beard—then I hear a pinging sound. It sounds like one of those notifications you get when you're sent an instant message, though not on Facebook.

My eyes pan across the top of the screen. Ugh, why does Aunty Blessing leave so many tabs open? No wonder the Internet is slow.

The pinging sound continues. Hmm. It could be one of those spam sites—like the ones that pop up suddenly when you're trying to stream a movie.

Clicking through each tab—Amazon, Twitter, chin hair removal?—I'm about to give up and hit the mute button when I stop.

Infiltrating the entire screen are lots of thumbnails of . . . men.

"Elite professional dating?" I gape.

The men on the screen look old enough to be my dad. There's Black, White, Asian and Mixed. On the left-hand side is a thumbnail of Aunty Blessing and alongside it, her username.

O-kaay. Aunty Blessing is online dating. For some reason, I'm shocked. She always comes across so . . . so . . . sure of herself. A happy, single, independent woman.

My chest tugs a little. I didn't know that Aunty Blessing still longs to find love. I thought she had accepted her life as a single woman. Preferred it, even. Then again, I've never asked her.

The pinging sound goes off again, and this time, I know exactly where it's coming from. It's from a man called Jazz, who, as I hover the mouse over the screen, is direct messaging Aunty Blessing.

"Let me just get a pen." I hear Aunty Blessing's voice as she approaches the room.

Shoot. I scramble to find the LinkedIn page, clicking blindly through each tab.

I hear the door swoosh open, then, "Sorry to disturb. Just need to grab something." By this point, I've swiveled my chair around, my back facing her laptop.

Her phone pressed to her chest, she leans over her desk. There's a clattering sound of pens clinking in her mug. I wait for her to stand, but she doesn't.

"Yinka!" she cries.

"Aunty, I can explain . . ." I start, and swivel around. I'm about to waffle my way through breaching her privacy, then I realize what's on the screen.

"Why are you on Facebook?" she demands. "On Femi's profile!"

I laugh in relief.

Aunty Blessing blinks. "Yinka!" Then to the person on the other end of the phone, she says, "Sorry, I'm just reprimanding my niece."

"I was on a break," I explain. I log out of Facebook and reopen the Linked-In page. "There's nothing to it. I was bored."

Aunty Blessing looks me up and down, then with a pen in hand, she leaves the room and I hear her say into the phone, "Sorry about that."

I listen for the pattering of footsteps. I think she's downstairs now.

Not long after she has gone, the pinging sound returns, and this time, I immediately hit the mute button.

"That was close," I sigh, slumping back in my chair.

A real honest-to-God pumping party

History	Ctrl+H

Recently closed

How to approach a guy like a don—YourTango

Relationship expert gives tips on how to meet a guy in REAL life—*Daily Mail*

WE'RE ON THE ROOF! COME ON UP:)

I stare at the note scribbled in thick black marker, stuck to the front door of Rachel and Gavesh's apartment.

Here I was looking forward to a nice, cozy gathering *inside,* and now I have to go all the way upstairs and hang out in the freezing cold. The bag of "buy one get one free" beverages that I bought from Tesco's earlier is already beginning to hurt my arm as I toddle down the hallway, jab the button to the lift and enter.

In the wide mirror inside, I peer at my outfit. As today's engagement do is a small gathering and *not* a party, I decided to go for a cool, effortless look. Inspired by a photo I once saw of Rihanna, I've thrown on my *Game of Thrones* T-shirt under a woolly cardigan paired with skinny jeans and flat boots (because I don't own a pair with heels). I sigh. Rihanna definitely pulls off the outfit better.

As the door rattles shut, I think back to Operation Wedding Date, which I've had to abandon for a few days while I recover from the shock of losing my job. According to the *Daily Mail* article that I read before leaving home, there are four steps to approaching a guy.

Step one: make good eye contact. Step two: smile. Step three: break the ice by commenting on the surroundings, or if you're feeling really brave, compliment him on what he's wearing. Step four is what Dr. Nicole refers to as "the turning point," because this is when you'll ask open questions and decide on what to do next. If the guy holds his cards close to his chest, gives short answers or if the vibe seems off, then you need to leave him the F alone—he's not interested—but if the guy is receptive and begins to ask questions, *then gurl,* you may be on to something.

The lift pings open, and I'm greeted by the bass of Afrobeats soundtracked with buzzing chatter and laughter.

Okaaay. I walk down a narrow corridor toward the door at the end where the noise is coming from.

Great. It's a real honest-to-God pumping party. I gaze at the DJ and outside heaters and fairy lights. "Congratulations" bunting is draped along the walls, and two trestle tables have been pushed together to form a bar.

There are so many people.

Lots of *well-dressed* people, I notice as I peer at the sophisticated crowd, which mostly consists of women wearing brightly colored heels and guys in smart shirts.

I look down at my outfit, my *Game of Thrones* T-shirt. I swear, I'm going to kill Nana when she gets here. Why did I wear this stupid outfit? I don't know what made me think that I looked cool.

I turn around, not quite sure where I'm running to, when I hear a familiar voice call my name.

"Yinka! Come here, give me some sugar!"

I turn around. My cousin Rachel is sauntering toward me like a goddess. Green sequin dress. Thick natural hair. Makeup on fleek.

"Rachel! You look amazing!" I fold her into a hug.

Rachel leans back and rubs her full hips. "Are you sure? You don't think this dress is too tight on me, do you?"

I frown. "Trust me, girl, you look banging. And look at your hair! Hashtag: hair goals." We laugh. "Oh, Kemi sends her apologies. It's her mother-in-law's birthday. And I brought you these." I hand her the plastic Tesco's bag.

"Yasss, girl! More alcohol!" Rachel looks inside. "Oh, my bad. Soft drinks. Honestly, Yinka, you shouldn't have."

I slap her arm and she lets out a loud laugh.

"Um"—I take another fleeting glance at the crowd and draw my face closer to hers—"did you tell Nana that tonight was going to be a small gathering?"

Rachel giggles. "I only told her that so that she wouldn't rock up late. You know how that girl is funny about crowds."

I manage a fake chuckle. I feel so underdressed. What guy is going to look at me now? Dammit. If only Rachel and I were the same size, I could borrow one of her dresses.

"So, let's see your ring again." I try to force a bright smile, and just as she's about to show me her rock, her fiancé shows up.

Gavesh and Rachel are *the* ultimate couple. They met at uni—Gavesh was studying Medicine, Rachel, Media Studies—and have been together for more than ten years. With Gavesh being a doctor and Rachel a journalist, they've been able to rent a lovely apartment in Bermondsey. And they have a pug. And they coordinate their outfits. Tonight, Gavesh's suit is also a dark green.

"Gavesh! Congratulations!" I throw my arms around his neck, thankfully missing his perfect quiff. "Finally, you put a ring on it," I tease, and at this, Rachel rotates her hand like Beyoncé.

"Better late than never," comes a male voice from behind.

In unison, we turn our heads to see Ola's husband striding toward us, Ola by his side, carrying a massive bouquet. Over a black turtleneck, Jon is wearing a wool coat in a similar shade to his sandy-brown skin, while Ola is glammed up as usual: big hair, fur coat, high heels. The smile that I had earlier slips away.

"Jonathan! My guy!" Gavesh embraces Jon with one of those macho hugs where men slap each other on the back as though the other is choking on a hot dog.

Meanwhile, Rachel greets Ola like she has not seen her in years. She lets out a seal-like squeal and nearly topples the girl over as they hug.

"Aww, you shouldn't have." She cradles the bouquet of flowers like it's a newborn baby.

The 99p engagement card that I bought from Card Factory earlier is still sitting in my handbag with my half-eaten sausage roll from Greggs. *I'll give it to Rachel later,* I conclude, scratching the back of my ear. *Or maybe, you know, I'll just buy her a new card.*

As the BFFs compliment each other's dresses and shoes (clearly, someone got the memo), I glance at Ola.

"Sorry, Yinka. Didn't see you there." She hugs me. I taste her perfume and strands of her weave in my mouth.

So you called me out last Saturday, and now we're hugging as though everything is okay?

But sadly, this is the routine that Ola and I have fallen into ever since we were teens—brushing things under the carpet, and Rachel pretending we're all getting on great. I should just let things go, though. Maybe she was having a difficult time at Kemi's. Her mum was pretty mean to her.

"And Gavesh! Congratulations!" Ola gives Rachel's fiancé a proper hug. I go to greet her husband.

"Hey! You cut your hair," Jon says. It's been ages since I've seen him.

Intuitively, I touch my kinky, "4c" hair. "Yeah, I did the big chop a few months back. It was breaking. My mum wasn't happy, though." I laugh.

"Damn, I can imagine." Jon chuckles. Though his dad is Dutch, Jon's mum is also Nigerian. "I remember how long it was back at uni. But this short hairstyle suits you."

"So have you lovebirds got a date yet?" says Ola after I thank Jon for his compliment.

Rachel and Gavesh look at each other as though they have another big announcement to make.

"We're getting married in July," Rachel says after Gavesh has taken the bag of soft drinks from her.

"This year," she clarifies.

"*July?*" Jon looks incredulous, as though he's the one getting married in only six months' time.

Gavesh laughs. I take a quick look at the crowd. Can I actually get a boyfriend within six months?

"But come on!" I hear Gavesh say, and I drag my eyes back to him. "It did take me nine years to propose."

"Er, *ten* years," Rachel corrects him, and Gavesh laughs again.

"See. A long engagement wouldn't have gone down well." He nods to Jon. "Didn't you and Ola get married in three months?"

"Yeah." Jon laughs. "But our situation was different, as you know." He emphasizes his point by rubbing his invisible pregnant stomach. "And we all know how parents can be about these things."

Jon is the only one laughing at his joke.

"I need to use the bathroom," says Ola, throwing daggers at her husband. "Rach, is your front door open?"

Rachel shakes her head. "The key's under the mat. Actually, I'll come with." The two of them link arms, and I wait for Rachel to invite me, but instead they strut away.

"Wait, did I say something wrong?" says Jon after they've departed.

Gavesh pats him on the shoulder. "Remind me to never take marriage tips from you, yeah. Anyway, let me fix you a drink. Yinka, what do you fancy?"

I shake my head. "Don't worry, I'll grab one later." And with that, I scamper to the back to hide.

So, how do you know the engaged couple?

After two failed attempts to get hold of Nana—*she's probably on the Tube*—I lean against the wall and exhale. I don't know how I'm going to meet a guy tonight. I feel so unattractive. Maybe I should start my plan another day.

"For goodness' sake, Yinka, stop being so closed-minded." I'm hearing Ola's voice in my head. Then I imagine the worst—Aunty Debbie praying over my singleness at Rachel's wedding.

I inhale through my nose. No. I'm not going to back out.

I lift my chin high and do a full sweep of the rooftop. Similar to the crowd at All Bar One, most of the guys are standing in huddles, though there are a handful that are dancing. Hmm. How awkward would it be for me to slide right in and join them? Maybe not. I don't want any of the women on the dance floor to rip my hair out.

With a sigh, I turn to the left and almost jump out of my skin. A man has suddenly appeared, standing against the wall a couple of feet away from me. Ooh, he's quite cute. He's wearing a Budweiser T-shirt which makes me feel ten times better, and he looks like someone I'd happily introduce Mum to. And he's not wearing a ring. *Thank you, Jesus.*

As I glance away, I remember the *Daily Mail* article. Oh, yeah. I'm supposed to hold eye contact and smile.

I turn my head slowly, hoping I don't look like a creepy Chucky doll. But the man is scrolling through his phone now, taking sips of his 7up while he bops along to the music.

Fab.

After five excruciating seconds of staring, I decide to abandon steps one and two. On to step three—comment on the surroundings.

"So, you're a fan too?" I raise my voice, and thankfully, the man looks up. I bop my head, hopefully on beat.

He frowns.

"J. Cole." I take a step forward. "I saw you bopping along."

The man's face lights up and he smiles. "Ohhh, right," he says, and I grin, pleased that I've broken the ice. "Yeah. Cole's music is dope, right? So what's your favorite album, then? I'm torn between *Forest Hills Drive* and *The Blow Up*. Although, *The Warm Up* is pretty sick too. How about you?"

The smug smile I had on my face now feels frozen in place. Okay. That was a bad move. Yeah, I know a couple of J. Cole hits, but I'm not going to pretend that I'm a hip hop head.

"Err . . . the last one," I say, nodding. "That album was the bomb, right?" *Seriously, Yinka. The bomb?* "Anyways, I'm Yinka." I stick out my hand and the man shakes it.

"Karl," he says with a bright smile.

"So, how do you know the engaged couple?"

"Through my girlfriend."

My heart plummets to my knees.

"She works with Rachel," Karl is now saying. "Speaking of which, here she comes now."

Just when I think my heart can't sink any lower, a stylishly dressed woman joins us. She's wearing an expensive-looking leather jacket and one of those bold patterned topknot head wraps that I tried to pull off once but couldn't because I was rubbish at tying it. Honestly, it looked like a deformed pineapple.

Karl does the introductions. Her name is Taleesha.

"Sorry to interrupt." She places a hand on my elbow and turns to Karl. "Can you take a photo of me and the couple, real quick? Actually, you should join us." She turns to me and proffers her phone. "Sorry, Yinka. Do you mind?"

After being photographer for five whole minutes and then reluctantly joining one of the group photos, I retreat to my spot by the wall, no longer in the mood to go man scouting. I rest my elbows on the concrete brick. Despite the dark sky and the distance, I can just about make out Godfrey & Jackson's shiny high-rise building in London's skyline, Canary Wharf, next to the tower with the flashing beacon.

My lips wobble.

No, I won't be upset. I roll my shoulders. I won't be upset at my cousin's engagement party. Besides, I've applied for a couple of jobs already; I'm sure I'll get one soon. I just have to pray, have faith and be optimistic.

"Yinka! What are you doing here?"

I wrench away my view of the skyline and glance to the right.

"Derek?"

Derek throws himself at me and gives my shoulders a squeeze. I give his back two ineffectual pats.

"Hey! We're both *Game of Thrones* fans!" He points at his own T-shirt. It's exactly the same design as mine.

"I guess we are," I reply, wanting to rip the damn thing off. I fold my arms. "So, how do you know Rachel and Gavesh?"

"Gavesh and I work at the same hospital." Derek flashes me a smile.

"Wow! Small world." I clear my throat. "You work as a nurse, right?"

Derek smiles. "You remember."

Bugger. People are always confusing my weirdly good memory with being a stalker. Or fancying them. My brain is like superglue. Things stick.

"How 'bout you? How do you know the couple?" He touches a bald spot on his head. "Let me guess. You work with Rachel, right?"

"Actually, Rachel's my cousin," I correct him.

Derek leans back. "No way! Your mum's side?"

"No, my dad's, actually."

He nods a few times. "So . . ." He leans against the wall. "When are you next planning to visit All Welcome?"

It's a simple question, and yet I'm floundering.

"Not for the foreseeable future," I say, wincing at my own formality. "I attend a new church now. It's just down the road from where I live in Denmark Hill. Actually, Derek, are you thirsty? Because I am. Can I get you a drink?"

"Let me get it. Anything in particular?"

"Er, G&T, please."

"Coming right up."

Derek shoots me the finger gun and stupid me does one back. At last, he wanders away.

It's going to be a long night. I exhale and look up at the sky. *God, I wanted to meet a new guy, not spend my evening talking to Derek!*

Frustrated, I whip out my phone and I'm about to text Nana when I spot a very attractive woman hanging by the entrance in the way that people do when they show up to a party alone. She's curvy, wearing a mustard-colored dress, and her complexion is so, so light. She's stroking her hair, looking all Nicole Scherzinger–esque in that shampoo ad.

Suddenly, she heads in my direction, and in the same way that Moses split the Red Sea, the crowd parts.

"Oh, shit," I hear a guy say as he eyes her from behind.

For some reason, I glance at Ola. It appears she has spotted the woman too because she's glaring over at Jon as though to say, *if you dare.*

Clearly unaware of her magical powers to completely stop a party without doing anything, the very attractive woman stops a few feet from me. While she is resting her elbows over the ledge, my eyes shoot down to her bum.

Yes, because if my bum's profile resembles the letter J and Kemi's bum profile resembles the letter D, then this woman right here has what I can only assign to be the letter P. Pert. Plump. Perky. Huh, how ironic. I can't stop staring at it. I wonder if it's real.

"Hey, I'm Latoya."

My eyes shoot up. The woman has extended an arm. *Oh, God. How embarrassing!*

"Hi, I'm Yinka!" I pump her hand enthusiastically. She has hazel eyes too.

"You been here long?" She strokes her hair. Definitely not wearing a weave.

"Err, just under an hour," I reply, trying not to give weirdo vibes, but she does look like a real-life Instagram model. Then something hits me. "Your accent. You're not from the UK, are you?"

Latoya smiles. *God, her teeth are pretty.* "New York."

"Nice."

"You been?"

"Who, me? Oh, no, no, no. I just know someone who lives there. So . . ." I look around. "How do you know the engaged couple?" I notice that a few guys are now looking at me. Or rather, her.

"I don't," she says matter-of-factly. "It's my fiancé who knows them actually. He should be here soon. He's just looking for parking."

She shows me her ring. The diamond is obscenely large.

"Oh, wow! Congratulations! Do you guys live here?" I ask after I have given the ring enough attention and found out how he proposed—Central Park. Sooo romantic.

"We're just visiting," she says airily. "We actually fly back in two days."

"Nice. What have you guys been up to?"

Latoya cranes her neck. I'm not sure if she heard me.

"We did a bit of touristy stuff," she says eventually. "Saw a few landmarks. But I actually came to meet his family. My fiancé used to live here, you see."

"Ahh, so he's a native."

She glances away again. "Yeah. He knows London like the back of his hand, which was super helpful. Sorry, you must think I'm being incredibly rude. I'm just checking to see whether he has arrived yet."

"No, not at all." I bat my hand. "Do your thing."

As she swivels her head this way and that, I admire her blushed cheekbones.

"Babe!" she cries. "Over here!"

I follow her voice in the direction she's hailing, and I nearly faint on the spot. Standing by the entrance is none other than my ex-boyfriend, Femi.

My fragile ego

I wheel around as if I'm a wanted fugitive, my heart beating like a galloping horse. Instinctively, I grab the ledge for support.

Oblivious to my mini panic attack, Latoya calls Femi's name.

She grabs my wrist. "Let me introduce you to my fiancé," she says, tugging me along.

Before I can object, we come to a standstill. I keep my head down.

"*Yinka?*" Femi says almost questioningly.

I slowly look up.

You know, Femi has always been a good-looking guy. Nice teeth, nice eyes, all that jazz. And although he's never been particularly fashionable, his shirt always matched his jeans. But today, Femi is something else. Femi looks like an upgrade. If he was a BlackBerry back then, he's definitely an iPhone now.

"Hey," I croak wearily, admiring his crisp white shirt which shows off every line of muscle he didn't have when we were dating.

Latoya stares between us. "Wait, you guys know each other?"

"Yinka's my ex-girlfriend," Femi says quickly. He coughs and gives her a look as though to say, "*You know, the one I gave you the heads-up about.*"

Latoya blanches. "Ohhh." She looks at me. Covers her mouth. "Well, this is awkward. Yinka and I have just been chatting for the last five minutes."

She's beautiful, I can't help but think. *And she looks nothing like me.*

"You look well." Femi cuts through my thoughts and instinctively, I say, "Thanks."

"Well" isn't a compliment, Yinka. "Well" is something you say to your granny.

"And you cut your hair!" Femi spreads his arms, and I touch my hair, waiting for him to comment further. He doesn't say anything else, and I hate myself for immediately feeling a twinge of hurt.

"So, you're engaged," I splutter.

Femi opens his mouth and closes it again. He nods. Then, like an afterthought, he adds, "For three weeks now."

So they're newly engaged. Christmas wasn't that long ago, so he probably came here to tell his family. And then I remember his Facebook post. *Nostalgic.* Now it all makes sense.

"Congratulations," I say suddenly. My voice comes out high-pitched like a dolphin's.

Femi scratches the back of his head. "Well, it was good seeing you." We give each other that *"Would it be weird to hug?"* look. Thankfully, our decision is made for us by Derek, who shows up holding two glasses.

"Sorry to keep you waiting," he says, slightly out of breath. My eyes pan down and I notice his combats are drenched on one side.

"Had an accident," he explains. "Err, not that kind of accident." He hands me my drink and I make a face at how sticky the glass is.

"Thanks," I mutter.

Derek says, "No worries," then to Femi and Latoya, "Please forgive me. Where are my manners?" He wipes his hand down his side before extending it. "I'm Derek. And you are . . . ?"

"Femi." They shake hands, and I search Derek's face to see if he remembers which Femi this is. But if he remembers, he sure is hiding it well.

"And this is my fiancée, Latoya." Femi slides his hand and rests it just above Latoya's bum. My heart stings.

"Nice to meet you," says Latoya. She gives Derek a polite wave. Strangely, she doesn't look as desperate to leave as Femi does.

Derek brushes his hand along his side again, then in a moment of inspiration, he says, "You guys don't have a drink. What can I get you? Soft drink? Champagne?"

"We'll sort ourselves out," Femi replies quickly, at the same time that Latoya says, "Ooh, champagne!"

Femi shoots her a look.

"*What?*" She shrugs. "He was offering."

Derek smiles. "Champagne for the lady, coming right up."

I watch Derek leave again, his combats swishing to the music.

"Well, he's a gentleman," Latoya says, winking, and I'm not prepared for this so I say, "Um, I suppose so."

"You're even wearing matching T-shirts," Latoya gushes after I take a sip of my drink, and it nearly snorts out of my nose. "Spill the beans, what's your story? How long have you guys been together?"

"We're not together!" I cough.

"No?" She looks embarrassed. "Sorry, I saw your matching T-shirts and assumed—"

"It's fine." I wave my hands and shake my head. I'm aware that Femi is looking at me weirdly.

"Sooo," he says, as though he's walking on eggshells. "*Are you seeing someone?*"

I blink. Sorry, why the heck is he asking me this? Actually, I've known Femi for enough time to know the answer to this question. Femi is the nice guy. He's simply asking because he wants to know whether I'm doing all right after he broke my heart three years ago. But if I tell him the truth, then what? To be honest, I'm not too bothered about how news of my terminal singleness will affect him. It's my fragile ego that I'm concerned about.

"Yes, I am seeing someone," I say, forcing a bright smile.

Femi looks relieved.

"Yinka, that's fantastic. So where's the lucky fella, eh?" He grins as he swivels around.

I purse my lips. Shit.

"Err, he's at home," I say finally. Best not to pick a random guy in the crowd. "He's sick," I say as an afterthought. "Very, very sick. Oh, not that sick," I backtrack, reading their concerned brows. "Just, you know, man flu."

"Aww, poor thing." Latoya actually looks concerned. "Well, you'll give him our love, won't you?"

I smile and manage a shaky nod. *I need to leave. Like right now.*

"Anyway, it was nice seeing you," I say at the exact moment Femi says, "So what's his name?"

I blink. "His name . . . err, Alex. We've been together for, what, seven, eight, nine months. Yes, nine months sounds about right." I swallow.

"Oh, nice." Femi looks delighted. He must have forgotten that thing I do with my face when I lie.

"Actually, I should probably call him." I pull out my phone and point at it. "You know, check he hasn't died or anything."

Femi says, "Yes, of course," and as Latoya waves me a good-bye, he adds, "Good seeing you."

I wish I could say the same, but I can't, so I let out a strangled, "Hmm," then walk away as fast as my wobbling ankles can carry me. I spot Rachel and pull her to one side.

"Femi's here," I hiss.

"Who?" Rachel clearly doesn't register what I'm talking about. She's rocking slightly and I can tell she's a bit tipsy, as her glass is empty but she tips it back anyway.

"Femi. My ex-boyfriend, Femi." I slap my hands to the sides of her head and rotate it.

Rachel gasps. "Shit! What the hell is he doing here?"

I fold my arms. "You tell me." I'm aware that I sound very accusatory, but Rachel's the host, so surely she knows who she invited. "Did you know that he was coming?" I hiss. "Did you, Rach? Did you?"

"No!" Rachel looks shocked. "Gavesh didn't know either. He would have told me if he did."

"Bruv! What you doing here?"

We turn our attention to see Gavesh with his hands on his head and looking just as shocked to see Femi, while Gavesh's brother, Sanjeev, who is trailing behind, says, "You came!"

"See." Rachel turns to me and cocks her head.

"Fine." I glance away. "Rach, Femi's engaged," I croak miserably. "Like, actually engaged."

"Shit, *already?*" Rachel screws her face, then mutters, "He didn't waste no time."

I frown. "What do you mean by that?"

Rachel blanches and covers her mouth.

"Wait. Hold up, hold up, hold up. Are you telling me that you *knew* that Femi had a girlfriend? You *knew* and you didn't tell me? How long have you known?"

She tilts to the side, clearly drunk as she tries to count back the months. I stop her.

"How did you find out?"

At this, her answer comes quickly.

"Oh, through Instagram."

Of course. God, I really should get an account.

"In my defense, it was Sanjeev's Instagram." She tips back her empty glass again and then frowns, disappointed. "But that was like, what, three months ago. Sanjeev said they had only just met."

"What?" I raise a hand. "Why didn't you tell me? So they've only been together for three months?"

For a moment, I have an out-of-body experience. Everything around me fades. *"Two years,"* I'm telling Femi. *"Two years and yet you never felt as though I was the one."*

"You okay?" says Rachel, putting a hand on my shoulder.

Suddenly, we're interrupted. "Who died?"

Nana. She gives Rachel a hug first, says, "Congrats, hun," then hands her a bottle of Prosecco.

"Now *that's* what I'm talking about!" says Rachel, sticking out her tongue.

Nana turns to me and frowns. She's wearing a brightly patterned jumpsuit, big hoops, and all ten of her piercings on each ear.

"What happened to you?" she says. "You missed me?"

Rachel clears her throat. "Femi's here."

Unlike Rachel, Nana doesn't need any further clarification. She swivels her head, then stops.

"*Shabba,*" she says, almost breathless, but then adds, "But that's okay, hun, because you're over him, right?"

"Nana, he's engaged," I say weakly. Nana's mouth shrinks into a small "o." She pulls me to her and squeezes my shoulder.

Rachel shoves the Prosecco under her armpit. "You should take a rain check."

"Rain check?" I frown, and she nods. "But Rachel, it's your engagement party."

"So? By the time I wake up tomorrow, I won't remember who came anyway"—she pulls the Prosecco from under her arm and waves it around—"because I'm getting *turnt* tonight!"

I don't know how, but I smile. "Thank you, cuz."

I give her a hug and Nana says, "I can come with you."

I shake my head. "Thanks, but it's okay."

"I'm coming with you," she insists.

"Please, Nana. I want to be on my own."

I glance at Femi again and immediately wish that I hadn't. With his arm resting on the curve of Latoya's back, he pulls her into him. They kiss. It's only a short kiss, but enough to make me turn on my heels. I elbow my way through the crowd and back into the building, not stopping until I'm in the lift again. Then I allow myself to cry. One fat tear rolling after the other, my heart breaking all over again.

The updated plan

It's the middle of the night and I wake up to a pitch-black room, feeling numb. I reach under my pillow for my phone, squinting at the bright light as I unlock it and read the WhatsApp message from Nana.

NANA

Hey hun, hope you're okay. If you want to talk, I'm here. And if you would prefer that I never mention Femi's name ever again, then that's fine. I'm here for you either way xx

Then my heart thuds. There's a voice note from an unknown number.

Hey, Yinka, it's Femi. Er, just wanted to say it was good seeing you earlier . . . Not gonna lie, I was kinda nervous about showing up tonight. I met up with Sanjeev the other day, and he told me about the engagement and the party, but I told him it was unlikely that I'd be able to come . . . but yeah, guess I changed my mind. Anyway, it's a shame that we didn't get to catch up properly. I was actually looking for you at one point, you know, but Rachel said you had to go. I'm guessing you had to check on your mister and his "man flu." (Chuckles, then clears throat.) But yeah, I'm glad you've found someone. We both deserve to be happy . . . Well . . . I fly back to New York in two days, so I guess I'll see you in July. Maybe you could introduce me to Alex at the wedding . . . Anyway, take care, Yinka— oh, and my bad, how's your family doing? I know your mum hates me, but I hope she's doing well. And work? Do you still work at Godfrey? Okay, this voice note is getting long. Bye now. Bye.

After the voice note comes to an end, I stare at my phone, dazed. Femi's WhatsApp display picture is of him and Latoya and I fight the urge to view it in full-size. Instead, I clamber out of my bed, flick on the lights and fetch my notebook and pen. Drastic action is needed. ASAP.

OPERATION WEDDING DATE: MY PLAN TO HAVE A
DATE FOR RACHEL'S WEDDING IN JULY!!!

OBJECTIVES	TASKS	DEADLINE	KPIs
~~1. Meet a guy in person~~	• ~~Make an effort to speak to any single men at Rachel's engagement party~~	• ~~Next Friday~~	• ~~I exchange numbers with a guy~~
~~2. Meet a guy virtually~~	• ~~Sign up to online dating if I don't meet anyone at Rachel's engagement party~~	• ~~End of Jan~~	• ~~I connect with a guy I've met online~~ • ~~We exchange numbers, speak on the phone and go on a date~~
3. Take up Aunty Debbie's offer and meet Alex!!!	• Go to Mum's house tomorrow and let her know I've changed my mind • Attend All Welcome Church on Sunday	• This weekend	• God knows

You're so British

History	Ctrl+H

Recently closed
How to approach a guy like a don – YourTango
Relationship expert gives tips on how to meet a guy in REAL life – *Daily Mail*

I'm in a rush to get to Mum's by one o'clock. I struggled back to sleep last night and didn't wake up till about eleven this morning. Shortly after I'd texted Mum to ask if I could come over, I received a call from a slightly hungover Rachel.

"Don't send him a voice note back," she said after I told her that Femi had left me one. "Send him a message. A short, cordial message."

I got off the call and sent Femi a reply. Well, I did after three attempts.

> Hey Femi. Hope you slept well. Congrats again on the engagement! I'm so happy for you! Latoya seems really nice. And yes, you'll meet my boyfriend at the wedding. Hopefully, he won't be sick again. Lol. Have a safe flight back.

Showered, dressed and ready, I throw myself into my car, then I remember: my annual inspection is overdue. So I hop on a very busy train from Denmark Hill to Peckham Rye station, which thankfully is a short commute.

Leaving the station, I dodge my way down a busy tunnel with cafés and market stalls on either side, then I reach the high street where there are several Afro-Caribbean hair shops. Just as I'm passing one, I'm ambushed by a woman lurking outside.

"Darlin', darlin.' Do you want your hair done?" The woman has super-thin braids and what sounds like a Ghanaian accent.

I sigh and shake my head. This is a common occurrence whenever I visit Peckham. Just because I wear my hair natural doesn't mean I want it done.

Quickening my steps, I pass a market stall that's been there for ages, still selling those Ghana-must-go bags—but damn, were there always this many pound stores? I pass the McDonald's, remembering a fight that broke out inside once, before bustling through the human traffic—the preachers, the pushchairs, the shoppers with bulging plastic bags who always seem to congregate outside the massive Primark—and I'm approaching Costa, turning to peer inside.

It is all lace wigs, hijabs, Rasta hats and hoodies out here, but inside the coffee shop is a different picture. I see beanie hats, denim jackets and white socks poking out of Converse. Peckham has changed. *A lot.*

As I near the pedestrian crossing, I catch a glimpse of Peckham Arch— an outdoor platform, its roof shaped like a dome. I'm pleased to see the library, my favorite place, still up and running, scaffolding-free. It is the heart and soul of the community.

As a kid, Daddy would rescue me from the pressures at home by taking me there—he was always, "*Just do your best,*" while Mum was more, "*You must get A's."* Upstairs in the children's section, we would huddle on a bean-bag as I would read aloud a Jacqueline Wilson book.

I'm about to cross the road when I remember Mum's text message, and I make a quick stop at the African supermarket. After purchasing a bag of pounded yam, I power-walk all the way to Mum's, thinking about how I'm going to bring up Alex with her.

A s soon as I enter Mum's—a third-floor apartment which is still decent enough in its appearance that the council hasn't knocked it down yet—the aroma of dried crayfish hits me. Then I hear Mum's singing, loud and hoarse. I shut the door quickly before the neighbors complain; the metal letter plate makes a loud clattering sound.

"Ah, ah! Why are you slamming my door like that?" Mum's voice reverberates from the kitchen. "Are you now an immigration officer?"

I roll my eyes. After wrestling out of my coat, I fling it on the stand nearby that is in front of a portrait of a blue-eyed Jesus. Mum emerges.

"Hello, Mum." I genuflect to greet her in the traditional Yoruba way, and then I hand her the shopping bag. She pokes her nose into it and frowns.

"Ah, you bought the expensive brand," she says.

"Sorry." I rub the back of my neck. "Mum, are you busy right now?"

At the same time, she says, "Your sister is in the living room."

"Kemi's here?" My eyes widen. I love Kemi but I really don't want to talk about my love life in front of her. I mean, it's embarrassing enough that she's half a decade younger than me and already married.

"What is it?" Mum asks.

"Oh, nothing. It can wait."

She takes the turn to the kitchen, leaving me to squeeze past a broken drawer that she refuses to throw away.

"Fine girl, Yinka!" Kemi says when she sees me.

I spread my arms and we hug. She smells like cocoa butter. "I swear, this bump of yours is growing every single day."

"It's the puff-puff." She beams, then pats her stomach and we both laugh.

"What you up to?" I pluck a fluff from her short, relaxed hair.

"Just looking at old baby photos," she says. "You know, to get an idea of what the baby might look like." She nods to the cabinet where there are dozens of family photos crammed on each shelf and fighting for space. My throat catches as I spot one of Daddy, leaning against a vinyl record player. Like me, he is skinny in stature and has skin the color of coffee beans. Kemi is more like Mum. Fleshy and mocha.

I was ten when Daddy passed away. Kemi was only five. It was cancer that took him. Prostate cancer.

When Daddy was alive, he was my everything. My comforter. My best friend. He made me feel . . . seen. In primary school, I got bullied for having such dark skin. "Dog poo" I was called. I kept it to myself and would cry in bed, and yet somehow, Daddy always knew what to say. "You're a beautiful girl," he would often say to me. "Yinka, don't let anyone tell you otherwise, okay? Remember what I told you? What did I tell you, ehn?" And between sobs, I would say, "The midnight sky is just as beautiful as the sunrise."

There have been many times when I've wondered how my life would be if Daddy was still around today. Though I'm not sure I could've asked him for advice on my love life.

"So, how's things?" Kemi asks, stealing my attention. "Ooh, Mum said you got a promotion."

My mouth falls open.

"Yes, she's now a vice president," says Mum, strolling into the living room. My heart pounds frantically in my chest.

"Wow! Congratulations, sis!" Kemi bundles me into a hug. "I swear, you're bossing it. So, when do you start your new role? And what exactly will you be doing?" She is too busy firing questions at me to sense my discomfort.

"Th-th-thanks," I say, my thudding heart now in my throat. I shoot a quick glance at Mum, who's connecting her charger to her phone. "I don't start for a few weeks," I finally say. "It's really just a change in job title. Anyway, we missed you yesterday. How was Uche's mum's birthday dinner?"

By the time Kemi is mid-sentence, Mum is thankfully out of the living room, and hopefully, out of earshot. I'm about to interrupt Kemi to tell her the truth, when I think, *Do I really want to?* She would only give me that pity-guilty expression of hers. It's as though ever since she got engaged, anything bad or humiliating that happens to me is somehow her fault. I can't bear her tiptoeing around me, and I know it's why she doesn't ask me about my love life—not like there's much to tell anyway. Besides, she's starting to hang out with Mum so much that she makes it easy for me to stay away.

"How was the engagement party?" Kemi asks, rubbing her stomach.

Femi and Latoya flash to mind. "It was fun, I guess . . . Oh my gosh! Do you remember this photo?" I swing the glass door open and pull out the first photo that I see worthy of that exclamation. The photo I've picked is one of Kemi when she was about eleven, wearing a black leotard. Her complexion was even lighter at the time, and her hair is standing on end in giant *dudu* plaits.

"Argh!" Kemi snatches the photo. "Mum did not rate me. Look at my hair!"

I laugh as I peer over her shoulder. "But look at your posture. You know you were made to perform, right? Best in your class, I remember."

"Well, Mum didn't rate my acting." Kemi pulls a mocking face.

"What are you talking about?" I laugh. "Mum thinks you can act. We used to say you'd win an Oscar."

"Come on, Yinka. Mum did not give two hoots about my acting. It wasn't academic enough," she says in a sardonic tone. "Do you know what

Mum said when I got an A in drama? '*But what use is that?*'" she finishes in a Nigerian accent.

I wince. Mum has always been more of a fan of STEM subjects. Whether her preference had anything to do with her being a nurse and Daddy being an engineer, I don't know. I do know that when Kemi told Mum that she wanted to be a drama teacher, she wasn't impressed.

"I thought this was just a hobby," she said to Kemi with that baffled expression of hers which read, *My daughter has clearly lost the plot.*

Growing up I knew it was hard for Kemi to watch Mum praise my academic achievements, and that's why I made it my priority to be her biggest cheerleader. I helped her practice her lines, and I made an effort to attend all of her drama productions, especially when Mum said she couldn't because she had to work.

"Well . . . you're in Mum's good books now," I say, substituting the photo for another one. This time, it's a photo of Uche and Kemi on the day of their traditional wedding. Kemi looks like she could grace the wedding section of BellaNaija with her gold gèlè and her lace-sequin *aṣọ ẹbí* and her regal-looking feathered fan. As for Uche, he's all swaggered up in his matching *agbádá* and faux elephant-tusk beads.

"Aww," says Kemi. She tilts her head to my shoulder. And for a moment, we just stare at the photo.

"Daddy would have been so proud," I whisper. Kemi squeezes my hand.

"Okay. Now your turn." She snaps back to the present and returns the photo, grabbing one of me on my graduation day. "My God, Yinka. Look at how long your hair was!"

"And she went and cut it all off!"

Kemi and I jolt apart. Mum is back, and she gives her wrapper a hoist before shuffling toward us.

"Let me see." She beckons for the photo and stares solemnly at it.

"So long," she says with great remorse. She shakes her head, glances up at me and screws her brows. "Yinka. Why did you have to cut your hair? This one suits you now." She dabs a finger at the photo to emphasize her point. "You know this hairstyle you have on your head is for boys, ehn?"

"Mum!" Kemi covers her face.

"What, now?" Mum pushes out her lips. "You have your own preference and I have mine. My preference is long hair. Long hair! And Yinka's not yet married," she adds. Oh, great. I was hoping she wouldn't mention the m-word for once. "If she was married like you, *eh-hehhh*, then she could do whatever hairstyle she likes."

"Mum!" Kemi says again, emphasizing the indignity of the conversation.

I shake my head. "Okay, Mum. I know you don't like my hair." I return the photo into the cabinet, ignoring Kemi's guilty expression. Then I spot something. "Well, well, well. Look at what we have here." With a delicious smile, I pull out an old photograph of my parents. Daddy has a massive afro while Mum has a mop of Jerri-curls.

"Is this short hair I see?" I tease, brandishing the photo under her nose.

"*Abeg.*" Mum flails her arm. "That was the fashion at the time."

"And you weren't even married yet," I wail, and Kemi laughs. "Aunty Debbie told me that this photo was taken on your first date. Tell us, where did he take you? Was he a nervous wreck? Did he even talk?"

Mum snatches the photo. "Yinka, you ask too many questions. Every time you come, you *dey* ask question as if you're a news reporter." She returns the photo to its place and stands in front of the cabinet.

Mum's always like this. Never wanting to talk about Daddy or anything in the past, always shutting me down. I know she can be superstitious—she doesn't like to talk about the dead. But come on, we're talking about Daddy.

"Anyway, food is nearly ready. I just need to prepare the pounded yam."

Mum wipes her brow, and I make a mental note to talk to her after we've eaten.

"I'll lay the table," I offer.

"No, Yinka. You'll help me in the kitchen."

I turn to Kemi. She normally helps Mum.

"Or I can help," Kemi says.

Mum shakes her head. "Kemi, tell me. Who is it that is pregnant? You or Yinka?"

O n the stove, there's a pot of red stew and what looks like spinach inside, simmering.

Mum grabs the kettle and pours boiling water into another pot filled with fine yam powder, then hands me a wooden spatula. "Prepare the pounded yam," she says.

I swallow. I hardly *ever* make Nigerian food.

"Go on, then," she cries, and I edge tentatively toward the stove, clutching the spatula like a toilet plunger. Looking down at the pot, I dip the spatula inside. I tell myself, *It's just like making mashed potatoes.*

"Ah, ah! Start now!" Mum cries, jolting me. "Don't just stand there. Use your arms."

I get to work, turning the spatula this way and that. The pot is rocking so badly, I worry it might fall off the side.

"Put some umph into it," Mum keeps saying. She's peering over my shoulder. "Come on, Yinka. Pound the yam well, well."

I increase my pace. I exert more force. I'm working the spatula, although I might as well be doing battle ropes. I break into a hot sweat.

Sadly, it's not enough.

"You this girl, you're so British." Mum nudges me to the side and takes over. "What will you feed your *huzband*, ehn? What will you cook him when you get married?"

"Well . . . I won't be the only one doing the cooking."

Mum kisses her teeth. "Don't be feeding your *huzband* chicken and chips *o*."

I laugh. Growing up, I *loved* chicken and chips. I still treat myself to Chicken Cottage every now and again. Okay, maybe a bit more than that.

"Bring me three plates." Mum is done in nanoseconds. Only she could transform what looked like white mushy baby food into the smoothest, oval-shaped dough.

I do as I'm told and fetch three mismatched plates from the dish rack. After laying them on the freezer top, Mum plonks a slab of hot pounded yam onto the first.

"Small, please," I blurt as she's about to dish the final one.

"*Small?*" Mum parrots. She slaps me a portion as big as an ostrich egg. "Yinka, you're too skinny. You need to put on some weight. Look at your sister, Kemi." She moves on to scooping the stew. "Her bum-bum is bigger than your own."

I pull down my cardigan, my cheeks burning.

Once Mum has finished dishing the plates, I pile them onto a tray with a bowl of soapy water and a spoon. Mum shouts at me to put the spoon back.

"Eat with your hands!" she yells. "*Nawa o!* You're so British."

Yeah . . . well . . . I was born here.

I'm just about to carry the tray to the living room when Mum places a hand on my shoulder.

"Yinka," she says in a hushed tone. "Please. I don't want to pressure you, but for the love of God, give Aunty Funke's offer some thought. Don't be stubborn now. *Abeg*, come to my church tomorrow." She looks so desperate, I almost want to laugh.

"Okay," I say breezily. Well, that saves me from having to initiate the conversation. "But on one condition, Mum. We keep this between us. Seriously." I look over my shoulder. "I don't want Kemi knowing either."

Mum pretends to zip her lips, which have now stretched into a wide smile.

"Thank you," I say, and I pull aside the beaded door curtain to leave.

"Jesus is Lord!" I hear her yell.

Preach!

SUNDAY

RACHEL CREATED GROUP "I'M GETTING MARRIED, BIATCH!"

RACHEL

Hey chicas, good seeing y'all on Friday.

I'm sooo excited to share my special day with you

Now as you know, we only got only SIX MONTHS! 😨

There's A LOT to do

Will arrange a bridal meeting ASAP

Keep you posted

OLA

Can't wait! Your wedding is going to be sick! 🔥🔥🔥

And babes, call me if you need anything, okay

NANA

Jheeze, unleash the bridezilla

Now I know to put this group on mute

Autocorrection: **You** only got six months

Lol

YINKA

Nana you crack me up

Don't worry, Rach. We got you x

"We are singing thank you, Jesus. Thank you, my Lord. We are singing thank you, Jesus. Thank you, my Lord."

After what feels like hours of the congregation singing the same line over and over again, the worship team lower their tambourines, and the song comes to an end.

"Let's give them a hand." Pastor Adekeye steps toward the pulpit.

The congregation applaud the worship team as they leave the stage.

I can't believe I'm here. Back at All Welcome Church after God knows how many years. But I guess it makes sense for me to meet the man that I've appointed as my boyfriend. After showering this morning, I rummaged through my drab wardrobe, tried on a few outfits, and took a few selfies to help me decide. In the end, I decided to go for a bit of color, and paired my fuchsia turtleneck with my stonewashed skinny jeans.

I just hope he doesn't notice my flat bum, I'd thought, as I swiped through my photos again.

"Repeat after me!" Pastor Adekeye's voice makes me jump. I look up at the projection screen. Pastor is a charismatic character who likes to wear crocodile skin shoes.

As though he is preparing for a big dinner, he tugs his blazer behind him, then booms, "This is my year!"

"This is my year!" the congregation echo.

Pastor Adekeye grimaces and stops in his tracks. "What was that?" he spits. "Are you still asleep? I said, THIS IS MY YEARRRR!" he repeats with ten times more vigor, and the congregation does the same, fists pumping the air.

I crane my neck, trying to spot Aunty Debbie, but there are too many people. Too many gèlès.

"Let me tell you sometin." Pastor Adekeye is pacing to the other side of the stage. "God wants to bless you this year, do you know that? He wants to bless you abundantly. *Financially.*"

This arouses the crowd, who, with arms outstretched wide, declare, "Amen!"

"Amen," I say a second after everyone else. Now that I'm unemployed, I could do with some money—Oh, no. What would Alex make of me being unemployed? Well, I was made redundant. I'm sure he'll understand.

While Pastor Adekeye strides to the other side, I can't help but picture what Alex might look like. I wonder if he has a goatee? Stubble? He could be clean-shaven? Who knows, he might even have a full-on Babylonian beard? My thoughts are interrupted again.

"He wants to bless you with good health!"

"Yes, Pastor," a few heckle. "Preach!"

"And for some of you, He wants to bless you with children."

"Amen!"

"And for some of you—" Pastor Adekeye pauses for dramatic effect. "He wants to bless you with *grandchildren.*"

Ah, yes. This really fires Mum up. As though she's in a pool and can't swim, she thrusts her arms up and waves them side to side.

"Hallelujah o!" she yells, and I swear there's a ringing sound in my right ear. "Give me grandchildren. Lots and lots of grandchildren."

"That request is for you," I whisper to Kemi, leaning closer. She sniggers and pinches my waist. Honestly, she should have sat next to Mum. She's the one who still attends All Welcome Church—she's probably used to Mum's antics by now.

Back on the stage, Pastor Adekeye is sweating. He pulls out a crumpled handkerchief and dabs his forehead.

"Ho, ho, ho. You're all awake now," he laughs. "And for some of you"—he stops—"oh, I don't think you're ready for the next one."

"Tell us, Pastor." More heckles. "Tell us."

He smiles. "Okay, since you asked for it . . . God wants to bless some of you . . . with . . . aaa . . . huzbaaand!"

The congregation goes crazy. And I mean bonkers. Everyone stomps their feet and flails their arms. Mum begins to shake. She gets what I call "James Brown fever" and begins to speak in tongues.

I suppress a rising laugh. Clearly not every woman here is single. So I can only assume that a good number of them are screaming and howling on behalf of their single daughters.

I feel like we're on that episode of *The Oprah Winfrey Show*. You know, the one where she said, "*You get a car. You get a car. You get a car.*"

I'm looking around, bemused, then spot Derek in his all-black usher uniform strolling down the center aisle.

Our eyes meet.

Argh! I turn away quickly. Dammit. I told Derek that I wasn't going to be visiting All Welcome for a while.

I feel a knot in my neck as I watch Pastor Adekeye return to the pulpit.

"You may all take your seats."

There's the shuffling sound of a mass of bodies moving. It's only when I'm in my chair that I realize something.

Hold on. What about the men in the congregation? I know that there aren't as many men here as there are women, but surely Pastor Adekeye has to be consistent? How about *their* marriage prospects?

But Pastor is already flicking through his Bible. "Okay. Let's open up the Word..."

Twenty million hours later...

I'm mentally exhausted. And somehow, I have to get up enough energy to impress Alex. Perhaps this wasn't such a good idea.

Around me, people rise and bustle their way to the exit. I look over to Mum. She's busy talking to the passing aunties making their way down the aisle. That woman is so popular.

"You didn't mention yesterday that you were coming today?" says Kemi.

I turn to her. She's resting her head on Uche while he runs his thumb over her shoulder.

"Oh, you know...I just fancied a change. Uche! Good to see you. Not long now until you become a dad."

As Uche tells me about his excitement to become a father and the various YouTube channels he's been following to prepare, I feel moved. He's such a good guy. I could not have picked a better brother-in-law.

"Sorry, remind me. When are you due again?" I ask, after Uche has finished speaking.

"Come on, Yinka. April twelfth!" says Kemi. "I swear I've told you like ten times already."

"I know, I'm sorry." I pull out my phone. "Okay. I'll put it in my diary so that I won't forget."

After I tap open my calendar, I think back to my plan. Once Kemi has a baby, I'm sure I'll be seeing Mum and my aunties more often. I really hope this meeting with Alex amounts to something.

Kemi sits up. "We need to head off. I have to return something to Argos. Then we're going to meet up with Mum and head to B&Q."

"We're buying paint for the nursery," Uche explains, and he stands first before helping Kemi to her feet.

"You should come," Kemi says, shoving each arm into the coat that Uche is kindly helping her into.

I look over at Mum, who is proudly telling a passing aunty about her "expecting daughter." Where's Aunty Debbie? I can't meet Alex without her. "Hmm. Maybe next time."

Thankfully, Kemi doesn't pursue the matter further, and I hug her and Uche good-bye.

Suddenly, I feel a tap on my shoulder.

"Ah, Yinka. I thought it was you."

I clamber to my feet and genuflect to greet Aunty Chioma, who owns a hair salon and knows everyone's business. She has a distinctive mole on her nose, and her face foundation never quite matches her neck. The flamboyant gèlè she's wearing today is so large that I feel sorry for the person who sat behind her.

"So how far, Yinka? How's it going? I haven't seen you in a while now." Aunty Chioma's red lips pinch into a smile.

"Fine, thanks, Aunty." Keep it short and sweet.

Aunty Chioma is swaying ever so slightly. Then she moves her head about as if she's looking for something. I frown and look around me too.

"Tell me. Where is your *huzband*, ehn?"

I fake smile. Why didn't I see this coming? Mum told me that Aunty Chioma has been trying to marry off her son for a while now. The same son I used to attend Sunday school with, and from what I've heard from my old friends here, is now a bit of a player. Thankfully, before she can introduce him, our conversation is cut short by Mum, who greets Aunty Chioma hastily and tells her that we have to get going.

"Tolu! Don't forget to speak to Yinka about my son Emmanuel, okay?"

"Yes, yes." Mum waves a vague hand and prods me along.

"Mum!" I huff.

I follow Mum through the body traffic occupying the center aisle. I'm nervous now. What if Alex is not at all what Aunty Debbie hyped him up to be? But it's too late to change my mind, because we are nearing the stage where the traffic clears a little, and lo and behold, Aunty Debbie is waiting there, dressed as though she's going to Ascot.

"Yinka! You came." She smothers me into her bosom, and I get a mouthful of her pearls. "I haven't told Alex about you," she says. "So this introductory meeting should be pretty spontaneous." I watch as she eyes my hair then fluffs the ends without permission. "Come with me." She grins and pulls my hand.

We walk down a row of chairs and sidestep over legs and handbags, Aunty Debbie leading the way, Mum at my back. Eventually, we stop behind a man in a blue shirt who's sitting in the front row.

My heart thumps. Well, at least the back of his head is nice.

"Alex." Aunty Debbie taps the man on the shoulder. "I want to introduce you to someone."

He turns around, and I swear, I lose my breath.

Shit, my brain immediately thinks. *Sorry, God.* I mean, holy macaroni. Alex is *foine.* And I mean, dead fine.

Alex rises to his feet and stands over six foot tall. He has chocolate skin so smooth, it makes me think of cocoa butter, and he has this Tyson Beckford air about him. I think it's his eyes and his cheekbones. And his lips. Oh my gosh, his lips. He has that pink bottom lip that I like.

I swallow. "Hi," my mouth says for me, clearly not waiting for Aunty Debbie to do the introduction. "I'm Yinka." *And you're friggin' hot.*

"Yinka's my niece," Aunty Debbie chips in while I'm still staring. "Yinka. This is Alex. One of my tenants."

"Nice to meet you," Alex says, and my thighs wobble. He has one of those deep, sexy voices that I can picture myself happily staying up all night listening to.

Alex sticks out his hand, and I shake it slowly. *Ooh, someone has quite a grip.*

"And this is my sister. Yinka's mum."

Alex proceeds to greet Mum in the traditional way of Yoruba men. Or tries to. He bends forward to prostrate but because the space is limited, his hand doesn't quite graze the floor.

"Ah!" Mum shrieks, clearly impressed by his efforts. "I like this man *o*. I really like him."

Cringe!

She stares at his face for a while, then says something to Aunty Debbie in Yoruba. Alex clearly understands, as he says, "Ẹ̀ ṣe, Ma," which I know in English means "Thank you, Ma."

"So you understand Yoruba!" Mum exclaims, officially hijacking this meeting.

"Of course." Alex says this as though to say, *Why wouldn't I?* Then in an impressive Nigerian accent, he says, "I may be born here, but I'm a Nigerian first."

Mum claps, then pats him on the shoulder. "*Eh-hehhh.* Very good. So, how did you learn Yoruba? Because my daughter here can't speak it at all."

"A little bit!" I squeak, and Mum makes a scoffing sound.

"*Ehhhn*, Alex." She bats her lids. "Maybe one of these days you can, you know, teach my daughter?"

I press a finger to my temple. Someone shoot me now.

"Yinka." Aunty Debbie steps in. I never thought I'd say this, but *thank God for Aunty Debbie.* "Alex just moved here from Bristol."

"Bristol. Nice." I'm pretending all this is new information, which means I seem to be nodding my head quite a lot.

"Yeah, I moved here for work." He smiles. "I'm a website designer. How about you? What do you do?"

I stall, and Mum jumps right in and says, "She's an investment banker. A top one, as a matter of fact. At Godfrey & Jackson. *Shebi*, you've heard of it? Now the other day, my daughter got a promotion, didn't you, Yinka?"

Alex congratulates me. *How do I stop this?*

"I'm actually not an investment banker," I croak, pulling down my sleeve. "Remember Mum, I work in operations—"

"Same thing." Mum pushes out her lips. "Isn't your employer an investment bank?"

"Y-y-es," I stammer.

"So how's the new job going?" This question comes from Aunty Debbie.

"And what's the new role?" asks Alex.

I flicker between them, fake grinning. *God, forgive me for what I'm about to do.*

"Oh, I'm a . . . vice president in the operations team," I say, suppressing a wince.

"Fancy." Alex looks impressed. "Well done."

"Thanks. So how did you find the service?" I quickly deflect.

"Loved it," Alex replies without missing a beat. "In fact, this church kind of reminds me of my home church back in Bristol."

"So you'll come back next week?" Aunty Debbie flutters her lashes.

"Of course!" Alex turns to me. "Yinka, you're a regular member, right?"

"She is!" Mum cries before shooting me a glare. "Now Alex"—she gives him a sweet smile—"you will stay for lunch, won't you? We usually go for Chinese buffet, just down the road by Aldi. It's the church favorite."

Alex places a hand to his chest. "I would love to, Aunty, but sadly, I promised my brother that I'd help him with his uni project. Maybe next Sunday?" Alex turns to me when he says this and my belly flutters.

"Brilliant," Aunty Debbie shrills while I'm trying to think of something to say. "Now we better get going. Tolu and I need to speak to Pastor about something."

"Which something?" Mum looks confused, but thankfully, Aunty Debbie is already prodding her to move along.

As Alex and I watch Mum and Aunty Debbie navigate their way toward the center aisle, my first thought is, *Thank God*, then, *What should I say to him?*

"Sooo." Alex speaks first.

I blink. *God, he's so damn sexy.*

"You really don't know *any* Yoruba?"

"A few words here and there." I wave a vague hand. "And although my mum may say otherwise, she never really made an effort to teach me."

Alex laughs, and I admire his symmetrical teeth. "Yinka. Your mum. She's a character, she is."

"Quite." I blow out my cheeks. "Oh, and earlier, she said something to you in Yoruba and you said, 'Thanks'?"

"Oh, she said I was handsome." Alex swivels his head this way and that. "Don't you agree?"

In my head, I cry, *Hell yeah!* but in real life I just roll my eyes.

He laughs. "Just kidding. Just kidding."

Handsome and modest.

"So how come you speak Yoruba?" I ask, trying to not stare too much.

"I actually worked in Nigeria for a bit," he replies. "A few years after I finished uni."

I wait for him to start moving—we can walk and talk—but he stays put and carries on. *He wants to talk to me!* Alex tells me how he studied Computer Programming at Cardiff University before going to Lagos to work for his dad's catering business, where he helped to set up the website, handled all the client affairs and gave a hand in the kitchen. When he arrived, his Yoruba was okay, but some of his dad's clients didn't take him seriously. So Alex practiced Yoruba, until one day, he surprised them by suddenly replying in his dad's mother tongue. In a blink of an eye, they wanted to do business with him.

"What made you come back to the UK then?" I ask, trying not to get distracted by his kissable lips. "Let me guess, you missed the rain, huh?"

Alex's expression changes but not in a good way.

"My sister passed away," he says after clearing his throat. "My twin sister."

I slap a hand over my mouth.

"Car accident. I wanted to be close to my mum."

"Alex, I'm so, so sorry." I have a sudden urge to hug him. Instead, I say, "I know what it's like to lose a loved one. My dad," I clarify after he raises his brows. "Cancer. I was ten."

"Damn. Sorry to hear that." He blows out his cheeks. "Grief sucks. May I ask . . . does it get easier, you know, as the years go by?"

I give him a warm smile. "You learn to cope."

For a hushed moment, Alex and I just stare at each other in the silence of unsaid words, and it's . . . magical. It's not forced or one-sided or awkward or stifling. It feels . . . it feels . . . genuine.

"We should probably get going." My nerves get the better of me and I break the spell.

As we walk down our respective rows and reconvene in the center aisle, I suddenly realize how empty the hall is. We must've been talking for ages.

"So, what do you do for fun then?" Alex says in a cheerier tone.

"Oh, I like to eat out. Binge on Netflix . . . while I'm eating." I chuckle.

"Yeah, I'm a foodie too," he says, and I glance up at him. He turns to me. "I like to cook."

"Oooh. What's your specialty? Italian? Indian?"

"Come on, man. Nigerian. Always."

Ah, yes. Of course.

"And how about you?" he asks as we reach the back of the hall. We take the turn toward the exit. "Do you like to cook? Can you make Nigerian food?"

"Well, um, to be honest with you . . ." *Please, God, don't let this be a deal-breaker.* "I don't really make Nigerian food. Because I often work late," I add quickly. "By the time I get home, I'm shattered."

"So what do you usually have for dinner?"

"Oh, something quick like pizza."

"*Pizza?*"

"Or pasta. Or, if I really want to treat myself, I have a chicken dinner."

"Nothing beats a chicken dinner," Alex says, and I chuckle quietly to myself. He doesn't need to know that I meant chicken and chips.

"Ooh, Yinka." He comes to a stop, digs his hand into his pocket and pulls out his phone. "I was thinking, since I'm new to London, maybe we can exchange numbers?" Then quickly, he adds, "Only if you want to, of course."

"Of course! I mean, sure. Why not?" I try to shrug nonchalantly.

I rummage through my bag. "Here you go," I say, quickly unlocking and handing him my phone while suppressing the biggest of smiles.

Alex looks down, then chuckles. "Nice photo." He holds my phone up and lo and behold, there's one of the selfies I took this morning.

"Oh my gosh. I'm so sorry." I snatch it back and jab the delete button. Argh. And it was a photo that I took of my bum!

Trying not to die of shame, I open my contacts and pass it back as Alex proffers his phone.

"Damn, that was quick," I say as he returns mine.

I just need to double-check . . . Eleven digits. No typos. Yup, all correct.

Numbers exchanged, I glance down at my screen. Yesss. He included his last name. Alex Balogun.

"Call me any time," I say. "You know, if you have any questions about London."

Questions about London? What are you now, Yinka? A tour guide?

"Thanks." Alex grins. "I'll bear that in mind on my first night out."

I can come with you, I'm thinking, but instead I say, "No problem."

He smiles again and licks his lips, and I go all shy as I smile back. Note to self: Google "What does it mean when a guy licks his lips?"

I shove my phone into my bag, feeling excited and really good about myself. *God, I can't believe my plan is working.* And who knew Alex would be so fit! I can't wait to tell JoBrian when I see them tomorrow.

"So," Alex says as we resume a comfortable stride, "what does Yinka like to watch on Netflix then?"

The updated, updated plan

OPERATION WEDDING DATE: MY PLAN TO HAVE A

DATE FOR RACHEL'S WEDDING IN JULY!!!

OBJECTIVES	TASKS	DEADLINE	KPIs
1. Find out more about Alex	• Find him on Facebook and do a bit of snooping • Set up an Instagram account and find him • Spend time with Alex	• By next Sunday • At lunch after church next Sunday	• I like what I find • Alex is not a douche

Giant pandas

MONDAY

RACHEL
Hey chicas
So, bridal meeting's this Friday
Nando's. Holborn. 6 p.m.
And pls . . .
NO AFRICAN TIME!!!

Love ya Xxx

"And *theeen . . .*" I deliberately pause for effect, glancing between Joanna and Brian as I relish their anticipation. Brian drums the table. "He asked me for my number."

"Get out of here!" Joanna is genuinely surprised.

"Are you being serious?" Brian's eyes widen.

"Yup." I beam and reach for my G&T. "*My* number."

It's eight in the evening and we're catching up at All Bar One, though not the one that we usually go to (God forbid I bump into my former

co-workers). Instead, we're at the one not too far from London Bridge station. I can't wait to tell them about the phone call I just had too.

"Do you have a photo?" asks Joanna over her glass of red wine.

"Sadly not," I admit, shifting on my stool. "His WhatsApp picture is
currently one of a beach, and despite playing with the search filters, I
couldn't find him on Facebook. Or Instagram. Though I'm not sure if I'm
using it right. I only just joined."

"Perhaps his profile is private," says Joanna, crossing her legs. "I think
there's a setting on Facebook where you can choose to only be looked up
by your friends."

"And not everyone uses their real name on Instagram," Brian chips in.

"Oh, right." I nod. "Oh, that reminds me." I whip out my phone. "What's
your Insta Name? I mean, handle. Whatever it's called."

"We'll tell you later," Joanna says, flapping her hand. "We want to hear
more about Alex—who, by the way, sounds gorgeous."

"He is," I breathe. I wonder what Nana and Rachel will think of him. I
can't wait to tell them this Friday. And Ola. Let's see if she'll still have the
balls to call me closed-minded.

"So what made you change your mind?"

This question comes from Brian, who is stirring his drink, a mischievous grin on his face. "How come you suddenly decided to meet Alex? The
last time we spoke, you were against the idea."

"I dunno." I shrug. "Guess I just had a change of heart."

Joanna and Brian narrow their eyes. They can sense BS.

"Fine, okay." I put down my drink. I tell them about my ex-boyfriend's
impromptu visit and our awkward interaction and how he's now engaged
to a might-as-well-be Instagram model.

"No, my decision has nothing to do with him being engaged," I have
to stress far too many times. "I simply need a plus one for my cousin's

wedding so I don't have to admit I lied. A plus one who happens to be called Alex or is happy to be called that for the day."

"Well, I could have pretended," Brian says. He doesn't even manage to keep a straight face, and we all cackle.

Then Joanna gasps. "Oh, no. Does this mean that Derek is out of the picture?"

"Jo, if you like him that much, then you date him! Anyway, enough about me." I take the tiniest sip of my drink. This has to last me a few rounds. "What's going on at Godfrey? Any word on redundancies?"

"Well, Louise is still around," says Brian, scrunching up his nose as though he's got a waft of something foul. "And everyone in the team is pretty anxious. So, yeah, it's a shit time."

Joanna sighs. "No whispers of more redundancies yet, but that hasn't stopped me from looking for a new job. Oh, sorry, Yinka—how's the job hunt going?"

"Yeah, I forgot to mention. I've got an interview next Thursday."

"Oh, wow. Congratulations!"

"Already?"

"What company?"

"Why didn't you say anything?"

Joanna and Brian speak over each other.

"I only got the call this morning." I ignore Brian, who says, "Too busy thinking of Alex, eh."

"It was from a recruitment agency," I carry on. "They think I'd be perfect for a VP Operations role at Oscar Larsson."

"Oscar Larsson," echoes Joanna.

"Oooooh, the enemy," says Brian.

"Yup." I nod. "Anyway, the interview next Thursday is only the first round. It will be with HR, obviously."

Joanna snaps her fingers. "This means we could do lunch. Larsson's office is literally next door."

I laugh. "Jo, when was the last time we had lunch together? We always ate at our desks and I imagine I'd be doing the same thing at Larsson. And yeah, let me get the job first."

"Well, we can do after-work drinks," says Brian, raising his glass.

And Joanna says, "Yeah, and we'll be keeping our fingers crossed for you."

Brian holds up his crossed fingers.

"Thanks. I appreciate it."

As I take another sip, I feel a fizzle of excitement. How did I go from being booted out of my job to getting an interview and bagging a hot guy's number in a matter of days? That magical moment Alex and I shared—the bit when we looked into each other's eyes—I've replayed it in my head like ten times already . . . I'm replaying it right now . . . and when he licked his lips. Damn, so sexy.

"Guess who recently signed up to Tinder?" Joanna says, flashing her phone at us.

"About time too," Brian says as I quirk a brow. He reaches for Joanna's phone and taps away. "I mean, look at this beauty of a man."

Ooh, the guy on the screen is cute. His display name says Marcus, and he has the bluest eyes and a kind smile to match.

"Twenty-eight. Lives in south London." Brian flickers his brows at Joanna. "I'm telling you, Jo. You've been depriving yourself for months. Want me to swipe right, yes?"

"Brian. I like older guys." Joanna snatches her phone. "I know I don't look it, but I'm kicking forty, you know."

Oh, yeah, I always forget Joanna's a few years older than me.

"What about all those paid dating sites? What made you suddenly change your mind?"

"Sex," says Joanna matter-of-factly. She's so blasé about it, I nearly spill my drink.

"But I thought you were after something serious?" I ask.

"I am," Joanna cries. "I mean . . . but . . ."

"She hasn't had sex in a long time," Brian finishes.

"Two years," Joanna clarifies. "*Two* whole years. Not saying that I want to jump in bed with the next Tom, Dick or Harry—"

"But what she is saying *isss*," Brian cuts in, "she can't afford to make it three years."

"Yeah, three years is definitely pushing it," says Joanna, shaking her head as though to even fathom the thought was too much to bear. She puts down her wine. "Yinka, be honest with me. Two years is a long time to deprive your vagina, right? Hasn't it been that long since you and Femi . . ."

"Hmm?" I reach for my glass. I need to hold on to something.

Brian and Joanna stare at me.

I take a sip. "Well . . . it could be longer."

"Yinka!" Joanna exclaims.

Well, two years is nothing compared to thirty-one, I'm thinking as Brian is practically tittering. Not that I'm complaining about being a virgin. I made the decision a long time ago that I would save my virginity until I got married, and since Femi was a born-again Christian practicing celibacy, not having sex was easy. We just didn't have sex. But I can't tell Joanna and Brian this. They will look at me like I'm crazy. How can I explain that sex is sacred to me, when, let's be honest, the very act looks far from sacred. And these days, virgins are like . . . I dunno . . . giant pandas. They're rare. You say the word "virgin" and people think of Mary and nuns. No, I can't tell JoBrian. I won't tell them. They'll think I'm a freak. Besides, they're my work friends. They don't need to know everything about me.

"Anyone fancy another round?" I dash to my feet and nearly knock down my stool.

Their eyes flicker down to my glass.

It's still full.

"Well, if you're offering," says Joanna, to my relief. She knocks back the rest of her wine. "Another red, please."

"Martini, please," sings Brian, giving me a sunny smile.

"Fab. One red. One Martini. Coming right up!"

How can someone *that* handsome be single?

FRIDAY

ALEX

Hey

YINKA

Hey! How's it going?

ALEX

Good thanks

What u got planned for this evening?

YINKA

En route to see my friends

My cuz is getting married! It's her bridal meeting

Why?

ALEX

Wehey! Congrats

Ah, ok cool

It's a Friday and my co-workers went straight home
Wish I had friends in London

YINKA

Ah, thanks

ALEX

What?

YINKA

So you have **no** friends in London, yeah?

ALEX

Loool

Cmon now. U know you're my dawg

YINKA

😃

ALEX

Anyways, just got in

Have fun. Enjoy your night

I skim over Alex's WhatsApp messages. I think I've read them more than ten times now. After five days without hearing from him after *he* asked *me* for my number, I was beginning to think that I'd read too much into our first meeting. But then, today at 6:25 p.m., the Lord answered my prayers.

Alex got in touch. He asked me what I was up to. On a Friday night! That could only mean one thing: he was going to suggest we meet up. But then I had to tell him I had Rachel's bridal meeting. Bugger bugger bugger.

"Ooh, what about this one?" Above the samba music, Rachel's loud voice interrupts my thoughts. Along with Ola and Nana, we're sitting in a booth at Nando's. She thrusts a bridal magazine on the table beside the many bottles of mayo and ketchup. "Do you think this mermaid dress would suit me?" she says as I put my phone on the table. She lifts up the magazine and holds it beside her now sucked-in cheeks.

"I'm sure you'll look beautiful," I say as I resume eating my lemon and herb chicken. "What matters most is that you feel comfortable."

"*Comfortable?*" Rachel looks insulted. "Yinka, I want to look sexy on my wedding day. Do you think Kim K is comfortable when she wears those waist trainers?"

We all laugh, except for Ola, who is opposite Nana and has been awfully quiet since we sat down. She's still bundled up in her fur coat and rubbing what looks like a hormonal spot on her chin. Her hug earlier was a bit off, and when I complimented her on her new short hairstyle—a razor-sharp bob with a fringe—her "thanks" was a bit flat. I hope that she's still not in her feelings about what happened at the baby shower. Her mum has been comparing us for years. You don't see me carrying a chip on my shoulder when my mum compares our relationship statuses. And hold up, she was the one who called me out, so surely if anyone should be angry it's me.

"Ah! Weddings, weddings, weddings," says Rachel, putting on a Nigerian accent. She switches to a cockney one, and says, "I tell ya, darlings. There's just so much to do." She sighs. "There's the venue, the dress, the decorating, and the food. Seriously, how am I supposed to find a caterer that can do both Nigerian *and* Sri Lankan food, huh? Well, at least the cake is sorted."

"Already?" says Nana.

"Err, ya!" Rachel says exaggeratedly, shoving a forkful of rocket lettuce into her mouth. *Who goes to Nando's and orders a salad?* "In fact, do you re-member Carla from college?"

"Yeah, what about her?" I say, stopping between mouthfuls to drink.

"Well, you know her younger sister, Vanessa, yeah? She's gonna make the cake—"

"I used to babysit Vanessa," I interrupt.

"Oh, yeah, you did. You know that she runs her own cake business now? I'll show you her Instagram page. She's friggin' amazing—"

"I can't do this any more." Ola's fork clatters against her plate and we all blink.

"Ola, what's wrong?" Nana says.

Ola breathes out through her nose. "There's an elephant in the room."

"*An elephant in the room?*" Nana echoes.

"Yes," Ola says. "And we all need to discuss it."

Nana and I turn to each other. Then we glance over to Rachel, who looks just as confused.

Ola purses her lips as though she no longer wants to speak, then she word-vomits, "I'm talking about Femi. Are we *really* not going to discuss what happened? Yinka, how do you feel? I can't imagine it was easy, seeing him out of the blue like that, then finding out he's engaged. I did try to look for you but Rachel said you'd gone home. And I was going to call, but, you know . . . the kids."

I sit back in my seat. Wow. I wasn't expecting that. Ola's clearly digging to see if I'll get upset.

"I'm actually doing great."

Ola gives me a look that says, *Oh, really?*

"To be honest, I haven't given Femi much thought. In fact . . ." This is the perfect segue. I've been waiting all week to share my news with them. "I met a guy recently."

Rachel drops her fork, stretches her arms in the air. "Thank you, Jesus."

"So does this guy happen to be Alex?" says Nana, and I grin so hard as I nod.

Ola frowns. "Wait, is this the same guy my mum wanted to introduce you to?"

"Um, how come this is news to me?" Rachel folds her arms.

"It happened at Kemi's baby shower," says Ola just as I'm about to answer. "Just before you came, my mum was trying to set Yinka up with one of her tenants, but she was being all stubborn." She laughs. "So you took my advice, yeah?"

The corner of my lip twitches. *Let it go,* I tell myself. *Let it go.*

"Anyhoo," I say brightly. "He asked me for my number."

"And you didn't call me?" Nana nudges my shoulder and I nearly fall out of the booth.

"Wedding planning can wait." Rachel closes her magazine. "Don't leave us hanging, girl. Tell us what happened."

After one smug look at Ola, I do. I recite every moment of my magical meeting with Alex.

Rachel wastes no time in celebrating. She pretends the bottle of ketchup is a microphone and sings an off-key version of Ella Mai's "Boo'd Up."

"Do you have a photo?" Nana says.

I sigh. "Sadly, not. I tried searching for him on social media—"

"Found him!"

I glance over at Ola. I actually thought she had stopped listening.

"I have access to my mum's Facebook account," she explains. "She adds her tenants on Facebook for, you know, background checks. Anyway, is this him?" She props her phone on Rachel's magazine, and I gasp.

"That's him! That's him! That's him!"

Rachel snatches the phone. "Damn, Yinka. He's buuuff."

"Rachel!" Nana cries. "Can we all see the photo, please?"

Rachel reluctantly puts the phone on the table, and we're all hunched over, trying to get a glimpse. In his profile pic, Alex is dressed head to toe in Nigerian native attire (of course) and he's throwing up the deuces sign while standing in front of a palm tree.

"He's hot," Rachel says breathlessly.

Nana blows out her cheeks. "I have to agree."

"Sorry, but how can someone *that* handsome be single?" Ola's question sounds almost accusatory. "There has to be a catch. Let's check out his other Facebook photos." She raises a brow and adds, "Let's see what he's *really* like."

"What he's *really* like?" I scoff, but Ola is already tapping her shellac nails against the screen.

"Most of his pictures are private," she murmurs. "Wait, hang on." She rests her phone on the table.

I gaze at the photo on the screen. This man right here with his adorable smile and piercing eyes asked me for *my* number. *Kai!* God is good *o*. I'm about to comment on how chiseled Alex's jawline is when another photo pops up—Alex with a woman who might as well be a *Baywatch* model. He has his arms around the woman's waist. In the next photo too. And the one after that.

"Seems like he's a fan of the ladies," Ola says with a sniff, and the excitement I was feeling only seconds ago plummets. "I bet you, he's a player."

The woman he's holding is ridiculously curvy and . . . fair. In fact, she looks the total opposite of me. Maybe I read it all wrong, jumped to conclusions too quickly. But he was the one who asked me for my number. We've been WhatsApping! And he licked his lips at me—which according to *Cosmopolitan* is one of the top signs that a guy is into you.

Ola has stopped swiping, leaving me to stare at the mystery woman's ample cleavage. "I'm telling you, cuz," she says. "These men. You can't trust them."

"Wait. Aren't you married to one?" Nana lets out a laugh.

"These photos are old!" wails Rachel, pointing at the album date. Five years old to be exact. "And for Pete's sake, he's in Ayia Napa!" She points at the location below the photo. "Of course he's going to be living it up."

"Ola, I think you're being too judgmental." Nana wipes her fingers with a napkin.

"I'm just sharing my opinion." Ola huffs.

I inhale slowly.

"Let's look at the rest of the photos." I swipe manically across the screen, pretending not to see the club night photos where Alex is surrounded by even more women.

Then suddenly, I whiz past one photo that intrigues me, and I take a few swipes back. Again, it's an old photo of Alex but this time he's with a dark-skinned girl. She has long braids and she looks about a size eight. I have no idea what their relation is, and quite frankly, I don't care—seeing Alex with a girl who looks like me instantly raises my spirits.

I reach for my phone and unlock it in a hurry, desperate to show the girls Alex's WhatsApp messages. To show them that I'm not delusional and that Alex is clearly feeling me.

I'm just about to speak when Ola says, "Yinka, I wouldn't get my hopes up if I were you. And can we go back to talking about the wedding, please?"

"Okay, calm down." Nana laughs.

I look over at Rachel, hoping that she too will call out Ola for being a jerk. Instead, she says, "Actually, this is perfect timing," and I bury the feeling that I get with Ola, always getting snubbed. *Why is she such a hater?* I stab my chips with my fork.

"So I was reading this blog the other day, yeah," Rachel is saying. "And it talked about setting bridesmaids' goals—"

"Count me out," says Nana, and I laugh and feel instantly better.

"Hang on," Rachel cries. "Give me a chance to explain what it is first. Now, bridesmaids' goals"—she leans forward—"are all about supporting the bride-to-be. Motivating her. Anyway, given wedding diets can be stressful—"

"Wait. Is that why you got the salad?" I connect the dots.

Rachel looks down at her bowl, mighty pleased with herself. She shoots a finger gun at me. "Exactly. Anyway, the whole point is that each bridesmaid makes a goal of their own to support the bride. It's just a bit of fun," she adds, looking over at Nana, who appears incredibly dubious right now. "I mean, you don't *have* to do it if you don't want to."

"No, I think it's a pretty cool idea," says Nana, and my brows shoot up in surprise. "And I have a goal. One that I've been thinking about for a long time." She takes a breath. "This year, I want to officially launch my fashion business."

"Oh, Nana, that's amazing!" I lean sideways and hug her.

"I'm planning to host a fashion show," she carries on animatedly. "Sometime this summer. Obviously way before your wedding," she adds quickly, nodding to Rachel.

Rachel blinks in shock. "Err . . . that's not what I had in mind. *But* you're already making the bridesmaids' dresses, so I guess I can't object. On one condition"—she fluffs her hair—"I get to be one of your models."

Nana rolls her eyes. "Fine. Okay, that's my bridesmaid's goal sorted. Yinka, how about you? I was going to suggest that you join Instagram, but it looks as though you've done that already." She laughs.

"And remember, it's got to be relevant to the wedding," Ola interrupts, just as I'm about to answer. "We all know that you're doing well, what with your recent promotion."

"You got a promotion!" Rachel's voice makes the nearby party of four turn toward us. "Congratulations, hun! Why didn't you say anything?"

I glance over at Nana: the only one who knows the truth.

"Thanks," I mutter, glancing down. "But really, it's no big deal. It was only a small promotion—"

"Well, my mum didn't think so."

I stare at Ola.

"Anyway," I say quickly, feeling my irritation rising. "I already know what my goal is. My goal is to have a date for the wedding." *And get a job,* I think. *God, I need to smash this Oscar Larrson interview.*

Rachel claps in excitement. "Your date could be fine boy Alex."

Nana nods. "I'm proud of you, sis. You're actually putting herself out there."

"Yeah, I'm tired of my mum and aunties praying over my love life as though I'm terminally ill."

"You know they're only going to call Alex your *huzband*, right?" Rachel lets out a booming laugh.

"Well, beats being prayed for at every family function," I say, wiping my hands with a napkin. "I'm looking forward to the days when that becomes a thing of the past. Anyway, how about you?" I glance over at Ola, who is quietly sipping her drink with a straw.

Ola lets out a small laugh. "Well, if anyone can tell me how to get my kids to tidy their room, then that's my goal."

"How about doing an online course?" I suggest. "It's really flexible so you can study at home." Ola's laugh halts like a driver slamming on the brakes. "Loads of people enroll to open universities these days. You could even resume your degree."

My intention was honestly to be helpful—after all, Nana's goal was personal—but from the glare in Ola's eyes, which have now become two slits, she clearly doesn't see it this way.

"Are you having a laugh?" she says, her voice like ice. "Sorry, how do you expect me to study for a degree when I have three kids at home, huh? And what's wrong with being a stay-at-home mum?" She throws her napkin on the table and Nana jerks. "Jeez, Yinka. It's bad enough that my mum's constantly at my throat, but now I have to explain myself to *you.*"

"Sorry, it was just a suggestion," I manage over the salsa music. Ola scoffs and rolls her eyes.

"Yinka, you have no idea what it's like being a full-time mum. No idea!"

"Okay, let's forget about the bridesmaids' goals for now," Rachel says, glancing at the nearby tables.

Nana tries to lighten the mood. "Girls," she's saying, pressing her palms together as though she's a monk. "Remember your energies. Now on the count of three, everyone take a deep breath in."

By two, Ola is already on her feet.

"I'm off!" she spits angrily.

"Seriously?" Rachel exclaims, and Ola demonstrates how serious she is by wrestling her scarf around her neck.

"Ola, you don't have to go. I said I'm sorry."

But Ola ignores me, scooting out of the booth.

"I'd better go after her," says Rachel, bundling her coat and stacks of magazines to her chest. "I'll catch up with you later, yeah." In a blink, she's gone.

"What just happened here?" I wheel around to Nana, who looks remarkably calm, still chewing her food. "How did we get from ten to one hundred?"

"You know Ola has a temper," says Nana, reaching over to grab Ola's plate. She slides her remaining chips onto her own. "The fresh air will calm her down."

I glance over at Rachel's and Ola's empty seats, my heart heavy in my chest. "It's not fair. She was being rude to *me.*"

No longer hungry, I push my plate to one side. I need to learn to stick up for myself. I'm no longer that bullied little girl. But sometimes, sadly, I still feel like her.

Abeg. Give her a discount, ehn?

After I helped Nana move her belongings into my spare room, we drove to Deptford—the Mecca for ankara fabrics—as Nana wanted to buy some material for a particular dress she plans to make for her fashion show. With the exception of her stinking out my second bedroom with her sage and palo santo incense, the move has gone pretty well. We're in a small fabric shop now, strolling in between the aisles while I make another attempt to get ahold of Ola. There are tons of patterned fabrics, all folded on top of each other on giant wide shelves. I finger one sparkly lace material with silver swirly patterns while I listen to the ringing down the line.

"Any luck?" Nana asks.

I hold up a finger, phone to my ear. I hear a click.

"*Hi, this is Ola. I'm unable to reach the phone right now—*"

Disheartened, I end the call.

"Look, there's not much you can do," says Nana. "You've called her like three times already."

"Actually, five," I mutter.

"Just give her some space." She sighs. "You know what Ola's like when she's in her feelings. She'll come around . . . eventually."

Nodding, I put my phone away. I was really hoping to patch things up with Ola. But Nana's right—whenever we've fallen out in the past it's always me rushing to make up and her holding out. The girl needs to be angry for a while.

I step to one side so that an aunty can pass, bending my knees to greet her. Meanwhile, Nana pulls out a sparkly orangey-gold fabric with splashes of gems and flower-shaped appliqué on it.

"I can't believe you have a design in mind already."

"Trust me, girl," she says. "I've racked up tons of ideas for my fashion business over the years. I was just too chicken to do anything about them. But now . . ." She winks at me. "I'm putting myself out there too."

Nana continues to browse the shelves, like she's looking for a book in the library. She bends, pulls out different fabrics and ponders for a moment before returning them.

"Right. What are we looking for?" I ask. Might as well be useful instead of just standing here, mesmerized by all the colors.

"A gold nude," she replies after returning another fabric into its pile. "Oh, Aunty!" She turns around. Behind the glass counter, a round-faced Black woman appears, wearing a red chiffon blouse and a crucifix.

"Nana." She smiles. "My favorite customer. How may I help you today?"

Nana greets the woman and then introduces me. She pulls out her phone, taps on it and hands it over to the aunty.

"Wow-wee!" the aunty exclaims. "This is niiiiiice. I really like it."

"Nice" doesn't do justice to the dress that Nana has sketched. The dress is, in one word, *fire*. It has a Grecian-style bodice with a see-through mesh underneath which goes over the shoulder and falls like a cape. The bottom half—I learned this from Nana—is called a godet, with triangular fabric inserted at even intervals around the hem. A dress like this would make any woman feel like a supermodel.

"I'm looking for a bronzey gold color," Nana says. "Oh, in Swiss voile lace, please."

The aunty grins. "Don't worry. I have." She hands Nana her phone back. The aunty ambles around the counter, grabbing a stepladder en route. She props it against the shelves and pulls out three gold lace fabrics from the top.

"See, Aunty, this is why I love you," says Nana, reaching for the fabric in the middle. I look between the three laid out on the counter. They all look the same to me. Nana thoroughly inspects the material. "For five yards, how much?"

"One hundred," says the aunty.

I cough. "One hundred!" Mum buys material all the time and she doesn't pay half that price.

"Aunty," I say, stepping in, placing a hand on Nana's arm. The girl is already rummaging for her purse. Is she crazy? "Nana is a loyal customer of yours. *Abeg.* Give her a discount, ehn?" I clap the back of my hand in the same way that Mum does when she haggles.

"Okay," the aunty says. "For you, ninety-five."

Before I can counter her price again, Nana pulls me away.

"What are you doing?" she hisses, and I'm stunned by the agitation in her voice.

"What am *I* doing?" My eyes widen, and I hiss back. "Nana, you're getting bumped. And I know what you're going to say: the material is high-quality, yada, yada. But even I know she's charging way too much—"

Nana holds up her hand. "Would you ask for a discount at Prada?"

"Me? Walk into Prada?" I laugh.

"Seriously, Yinka, would you? At Gucci? Louis Vuitton? Dior? No, you wouldn't, would you? So let's keep the same energy with small businesses. Small *Black-owned* businesses, mind you."

I bite my lip. "I see your point."

That's one thing about Nana—she's not afraid to call me out. But whenever she does, she does it out of love.

Nana rubs my shoulder. "We have to support each other and part of that means paying full-price for things. If we don't, then God knows what our communities will look like three, four years from now. And don't forget. I'm going to be a small business owner too."

I think of my beloved Peckham and how it's gradually changing. Barber's shops are being replaced with coffee shops, and pubs and bars are the "hidden gems" it's now known for. I think of all the hair shops and the market stalls selling those Ghana-must-go bags. I would hate to see them pushed out.

We head back to the counter arm in arm, and Nana pays the aunty full-price.

"I've put some beads in the bag for you," the aunty says, handing Nana a sturdy carrier bag. "On the house." She winks.

In the spirit of supporting Black-owned businesses, Nana and I head next to a Caribbean takeaway nearby. We sit by the window, and tear into our yellow, crusted patties—I went for the beef, Nana went for the lamb—while downing KA grape punch.

Nana fans her mouth. "Damn, this is spicy."

I laugh then kiss my teeth. "Come on, girl. You're African. You can take the heat. Ooh, I forgot to take a photo." I return my half-eaten patty to my plate, positioning it next to my soda, shrill, "One for the gram!" and take a shot.

Nana laughs. "Oh, no, don't tell me you've become one of *those* people."

"My page is just looking a little sparse, that's all. Ooh, let's take a selfie."

"I'm good," Nana says quickly, then when she sees my face, "But I can take a photo of you."

When she's taken a few, I swipe through them and my excitement dwindles. I can hardly see my features because the restaurant's lighting is so dim. Half-heartedly, I go for the one where I look the most natural, then upload it to Instagram, selecting the Clarendon filter to brighten it up.

I put down my phone, mulling over the thing that I've been feeling bad about all morning. "Thanks for not bringing up my redundancy last night."

"How come you didn't tell the girls? No offense, hun, but that's pretty messed up."

I slump in my chair. "I know. But if I had told the truth, Ola would've told her mum, then her mum would tell my mum, and then I would have to deal with all the drama."

"But you can't just never tell your mum."

"Oh, don't worry, I'm going to get that job at Larrson." I press my hands in prayer.

"On the topic of Ola," Nana says slowly. She reaches for her napkin and dabs the corner of her mouth. "I know you guys have never been the chummiest of cousins, but yesterday she was really hard on you. What's that all about?"

"I don't know exactly . . . but I'm starting to think that there's more to what happened at Kemi's baby shower."

"Say what now?" Nana lowers her patty from her mouth. "What else happened at Kemi's baby shower?"

I nibble my lips. I might as well just say it. "I didn't want to make a big deal out of it, but basically, when I said I was against the idea of Aunty Debbie setting me up, Ola yelled at me. Called me closed-minded in front of Aunty Debbie. And my mum."

"Are you serious?" Nana's eyes widen.

I nod. "It actually really hurt. She seemed so angry with me. But as per usual, I let it go."

"Damn."

"Yeah, but before that . . . Aunty Debbie was reminding her of my degree again. So perhaps, I dunno, Ola was really angry with her. You see, Aunty Debbie used to compare us loads when we were kids. Like this one time, Ola was a few marks away from an A. She was so excited to tell her mum, but Aunty Debbie was *not* impressed. She was like, 'If you and Yinka are in the same class, then why didn't you get an A?'"

"Eesh." Nana pulls a face. "So it's always been like that with Ola? You weren't ever close at all?" Nana sucks a piece of lamb from her thumb.

"Umm . . . not really. At school, she was always closer with Rachel. They were both into makeup and hair. I was more of a nerd." I chuckle, but I feel an ache in my chest.

Nana nods slowly.

"But then sometimes she was great." I clear my throat. "You know when I told you I got teased for having dark skin? Well, Ola stuck up for me. Cussed the girls out."

Nana is quiet for a moment. "Yeah, she was like that in college too. Hey, remember that time when she got into it with the canteen guy?"

"Oh, yeah! When he tried to short-change me by 50p, right?"

Nana laughs. "Ola would *not* let it go."

We both laugh.

I sit back in my chair and sigh. "Do you know what? I was really looking forward to going to uni with Ola, you know. I thought with Rachel at Aston, and the fact that we both got into Oxford, we could, I dunno, bond a bit more. But then she met Jon, and we all know how the story ended. To be honest, I'd say things between us got worse, especially after I graduated. Aunty Debbie never stopped going on about it."

I look out of the window, which is pretty much taken up by a Jamaican flag. Hearing myself talk about this stuff out loud makes me realize how long I've buried my feelings. How have I managed to have this weirdly dysfunctional, functioning relationship with my own cousin?

"And don't forget, she's a Virgo," Nana says. "Virgos have a tendency to come across as cold sometimes, but that's only because they're trying to protect themselves. Anyway, I'll stop."

I laugh. "Let's talk about something else—your business. What's the plan? Is there anything I can do to help?"

Nana tucks in her chair so that the customer behind her can pass. I eye his plate. Curry goat with rice and peas. Yum.

"A'ight, I need to find a venue, then hold a model casting at some point. And obviously make the clothes. The designs are pretty much done. I actually sketched them a few months back. Ooh, guess what I'm calling my collection?" She doesn't give me time to answer. "Queen Mother," she says with a proud smile.

"Queen Mother? What, like the Queen of England?"

Nana laughs. "Nooo. I'm drawing inspiration from my Ghanaian heritage. In precolonial times, Queen Mothers were female leaders in the village who had massive influence. Then the White Man came along, and their power basically died. But over the years, there's been a resurgence." She raises her drink. "My collection is a tribute to them. The powerful, badass women, and the village of men and women they help raise."

I clink my can against hers. "Nana, that sounds dope. I love it. I know you'll smash it."

"But that's all the fun stuff," she carries on. "There's also the boring bits, like setting up a limited company and finding sponsorship, which, by the way, I have no idea how to do."

"Oh, my Aunty Blessing can help you with that," I say. "You know my

Aunty Blessing, the barrister, right? She's super-savvy and has loads of connections. I'll give her a call later tonight."

Nana looks relieved. "Amazing. Thanks, I owe you one."

For the next five minutes, I happily listen to Nana, feeling mega-proud and inspired. She's decided to call her fashion label Nana Badu, which I thought was fitting given that Nana's a huge fan of Neo-soul artist and fashion icon Erykah Badu and she's already set up an Instagram page.

She rests her elbows on the table and leans forward. "Now, let's talk about *your* bridesmaid's goal." She exaggerates her curiosity by batting her lashes. "Tell me. How's things going with Alex? Has he been in touch since he messaged you yesterday?"

"Not yet," I say, and my shoulders slump. I reach for my phone to double-check, and realize I have a WhatsApp notification.

After opening the app, I freeze.

"What is it?" Nana says.

"He—he messaged me." Dazed, I gaze down at my phone; I have three unread messages.

"'Hey, Yinka,'" I read aloud. "'How's your week been? Up for lunch to-morrow after church?'"

I look over at Nana again, her eyes still wide.

"He wants to see me!"

Dutty people

SUNDAY

ALEX

Hey, up for meeting before church starts?

Will save us from having to look for each other after the service

YINKA

Morning ☺

Yeah, sounds good

Meet you at the lobby, say 10.50?

ALEX

Cool ☺

Alex and I look around from our place by the buffet, gobsmacked. Every single table in All Welcome Church's favorite Chinese restaurant is occupied. Around us, a throng of aunties wearing shiny gèlès are huddling by the steaming dishes, and I can hear at least three different African languages overlapping each other.

"Wow," I exhale. "How did they get here so fast?"

"Beats me," says Alex. "Literally. They beat me to it."

I laugh. Sounds like a joke I would have made.

After the service ended, we had headed straight here. Though excited, I couldn't help but worry about my outfit. At the last moment I'd slipped on my cardigan, though I wasn't too sure if it went well with my polka dot top, so I decided I would keep my jacket on at all times. As we walked and chatted, Alex told me about his week—despite being a recent hire, he's already working late.

"But I love it," he gushed as we ambled along the pavement. "In fact, to be honest with you, I *choose* to stay late."

"Really?" Never during my time at Godfrey would I say I enjoyed working late. Ever.

"I don't think we're going to find anywhere to sit," Alex says now, as a waft of chow mein and satay sauce fills my nostrils.

"Yeah," I give in, nodding. "Maybe we should go somewhere else."

I shoot a quick glance at him. He's wearing a salmon-pink shirt (nice) under a smart navy jacket (love) and is that a muscly pec I see?

"So," he says and claps, and my eyes dart up to his face. "Any places around here that you would recommend?"

Quickly, I try to pull up a mental map and identify any restaurants or pubs in the area. But my brain is too busy being mesmerized by his pink bottom lip.

"I know," Alex says suddenly. "How about we get a takeaway, like chicken and chips?"

I think I hear the heavens open. The angels are actually singing.

"That sounds perfect," I squeak. "There's a Chicken Cottage not too far from here. By the way, do you like burger sauce?"

Alex stares at me. "Yinka!" He laughs. "I was only joking. I mean, who would want to eat *that* junk?"

I chuckle. "Well, um . . . I was joking too." I scratch my ear. "Obviously." I'm about to ask him where he wants to go, when I do a double-take.

Sauntering toward me is Vanessa, the girl I used to babysit—the one making Rachel's wedding cake—only she's not a little girl any more. She's a full-fledged woman.

"Aunty Yinka! So nice to see you!" Vanessa smothers me in a perfumey hug.

"Well, haven't you grown." And by grown, I mean genetically morphed. Vanessa looks like one of those video vixens in hip hop music videos. While I take in her growth spurt, I notice that her gaze is now directed above my head.

"Oh, sorry, Vanessa," I say, remembering. "This is Alex."

Alex smiles and stretches out a hand, and I try not to be petty and count how long they shake hands for.

"So, how do you guys know each other?" he asks as I wonder why he's now neatening the lapel of his jacket.

"Yinka used to babysit me." Vanessa giggles and swings her long blonde weave. "Obviously a long time ago."

"Sorry, how old are you?" says Alex.

"Twenty-one," she replies, and I can tell this takes him by surprise.

"Fresh out of uni," I add for emphasis. "In fact, Vanessa, didn't you just graduate last year?"

"I got a 2.1," she chimes happily. "In Spanish and English Literature."

"Nice," Alex says. "Well done you."

"*Très bon.*" I smile. *Wait. That's not Spanish.*

Vanessa turns to me. "Such great news about your cousin Rachel getting married."

I nod. "Yeah, it is."

She giggles. "Well, guess who's making her cake?"

She is so excited, I feign ignorance. "Er, I dunno. Who?"

"Me!" Vanessa actually squeals. "It will be my first wedding cake too. I'm well excited."

I notice that Alex is about to say something. "Sorry, Vanessa, but is it okay if we catch up another time? Alex and I were actually on our way out. As you can see"—I gesture to the tables—"there's hardly anywhere to sit."

"Oh, there's a couple of free seats on our table." Vanessa's words fly out like a sneeze.

"Sweet!" Alex nudges me. I grit my teeth and smile.

"How lucky, right?" Vanessa clutches her chest as she giggles. "Follow me."

Then she turns around in what seems like slow motion.

Oh, bugger. I want to cry. Her bum is pure letter D.

I glance at Alex. His eyes have flickered down. But honestly, can I blame him? It's like a solar eclipse. You can't help but look.

I *can* stop him from looking at it any further, though. I hurry in front of him and nearly trip over his foot before hugging as close to Vanessa's retreating D as I can. Well, a girl's gotta do what a girl's gotta do.

We pass the queue for the buffet. It's now about a mile long.

"Damn," says Alex, and I mutter, "Well, we wouldn't have had this at Chicken Cottage."

Vanessa swivels around. "I know!" she says. "Aunty, why don't you join the queue while Alex and I go and save our seats. Actually, give your jacket to Alex. We'll use that to save your seat."

I blink at her.

"Your jacket." She tugs at her stylish leather one. "Give it to Alex."

She might as well have said, *Yinka, give him your bra.* And with no logical reason to object, I do as I'm told.

I strip out of my jacket as Vanessa and Alex—and it feels like the whole restaurant—watch. Under the artificial lights my "go-to" cardigan looks creased and worn out. And because I bought it years ago, it's no longer long enough to cover my entire backside. Dammit. I knew I should have worn my polka dot top on its own.

I watch them set off together.

Great. Now I've got competition. And not only from Vanessa. As they weave in between tables, women are popping up like meerkats. It's like they've never seen a male of the species before.

Wrenching my eyes away, I go to join the queue then stop abruptly. Mum and Aunty Debbie are hurrying toward me. Man. I was hoping I wouldn't bump into them.

"So how far, Yinka? How is it going?" Mum smiles at me as though to say, *Has he declared that you're his wife yet?*

"Fine," I breathe out.

"Have you made your intentions clear?" she says. "That you are looking to get married soon."

"Mum, please. I just met him—"

"Your daddy and I got married within three months!"

"Okay, maybe we should give them a bit more time than a lunch date, hm, Tolu." Aunty Debbie places a hand on Mum's shoulder. "Things are done differently now. They have to get to know each other."

Mum huffs. "All this talk-talking." She kisses her teeth.

"So, Yinka," Aunty Debbie turns to me. "How's the new role treating you, hm?"

My stomach lurches.

"Um, fine," I reply nervously, then without thinking, I blurt, "I like your hat."

Aunty Debbie touches the rim. "Why, thank you," she gushes. "I actually bought it many years ago. Stella McCartney, I think."

I smile; I wouldn't know.

"Anyway, we're off now." Aunty Debbie hugs me. "Nowhere to sit. Again."

"Yinka, please," Mum hisses into my ear. "Try to make more of an effort, ehn? Try to look smart. Not always *jeans, jeans*, every day. In our church, there are many, many single women. You don't want Alex's head to be turning anyhow."

She gives my hand two ineffectual pats and casually strolls away.

W hy haven't Alex and Vanessa come back yet? I thought the plan was that they would save our seats, then come and join me in the line. I turn around again. I think the man behind me is starting to get pissed off. The restaurant somehow looks ten times busier than it did earlier, and I can't spot where they are.

I reach the buffet station, and my heart sinks as I grab a plate. Then a thought comes to me. What if I serve a plate for Alex? That way, he won't need to join the queue, and we can spend quality one-on-one time together while Vanessa goes to fetch hers? (Of course there's no way I can manage a third plate.) I smile and spoon every food onto two plates, piling Alex's especially high. Mum is always saying that the way to a man's heart is through his stomach, right?

I reach the cutlery station where I grab two pairs of forks and knives along with a few napkins. I turn around, only to bump straight into someone. Oh, Lord, it's Derek. *Why* did I agree to come to the place every single person I know has lunch on a Sunday?

"Yinka! So good to see you. Let me give you a hand with that." He reaches for both of the plates.

"No! I've got it." A bean sprout from one topples to the floor.

"Um, okay." Derek eyes the plate then me again. "So, how's it going?"

"Good, good. Actually, I need to head off. Nice seeing you—"

"Ooh, just one thing." He catches up. "What are you doing Wednesday evening?"

"Why?" Some sweetcorn topples off the other plate. Shit, it's getting heavy.

"Are you sure you don't need a hand with that?"

I back away. "No, no. I'm fine. What's happening this Wednesday?"

"All Welcome is having its first homeless outreach. Well, it's not exactly ours. We're partnering with this homeless charity, Sanctuary. They've been doing it for years."

"Sanctuary? Oh my gosh. I used to volunteer with them."

"Seriously?" Derek beams.

"Yeah." I grin. "But this was yearsss ago."

"Well, I'm glad I saw you then, as I'm actually looking for a few volunteers. The outreach will take place from seven at Peckham Arch. You know that outdoor platform just outside the library?"

"Yeah, sure."

"Oh, great. So, can you make it?"

"Sure. This is right up my street." And despite myself, I grin at Derek like a Cheshire Cat.

But then it hits me. Wednesday is the day before my job interview.

"Actually, Derek. I can't." I sigh. "I just remembered, on Thursday I have a job interview. I'm going to need the whole of Wednesday to prepare."

"Oh, sure, of course." Derek bats a hand. "No worries. Besides, the outreach will be on every Wednesday and Thursday, so whenever you're free, just swing by. Oh, and congrats on the job interview. That's really great. Who's it with? What's the role?"

My arms sagging, I squeak. "Sorry, Derek, but I really have to go. We'll catch up another time, yeah." Dammit. Why did I say that?

As I near the tables, I feel a cramp in my arms. Friggin' heck. These plates are like dumbbells. I scan the throng. Ah-hah! I see them. They're at a table at the very back, and Vanessa appears to be chewing Alex's ears off. No wonder he didn't join me in the queue.

I channel my inner superwoman and make a beeline toward him, navigating my way around tables, squeezing behind a number of untucked chairs, and stopping to greet uncles and aunties. All while carrying two plates the weight of a newborn.

Suddenly, I'm pulled back. My handbag is caught on the arm of a chair.

As I turn to rescue my bag, I hear a wail so piercing, it makes my shoulders jump. I turn back round and almost die.

Standing right below me is a crying toddler. More specifically, a crying toddler covered head-to-toe with what should have been Alex's lunch.

"God help me."

Trembling, I set down the plates and cutlery on a nearby table, grab a napkin and drop to my knees. The little boy is belting his lungs out—of course he is. He's covered in fucking chow mein!

"I'm so sorry. I'm so sorry." I'm dabbing the three-ply napkin all over his dungarees, which thanks to me and my stupid handbag will likely end up in the bin, unless there's a magical detergent that can get rid of sweet-and-sour stains.

The toddler cries even louder.

I whimper.

God, there's food everywhere. On his shoes. On his face. Behind his ears!

I look up to see everyone at the tables nearby, staring at us.

Shiiit.

Then right on cue, two hands loom and grab the boy under his armpits. I glance up. A plump woman is hoisting him to her side.

"Aunty, I'm so sorry." I'm so traumatized my words come out all jumbled. "It was an accident. L-l-let me dry for the pay cleaning. Please forgive me."

I swallow as I prepare for a series of curses to come thrashing my way, but instead, the woman yells at the boy.

"Next time you won't run off, ehn."

She kisses her teeth and without batting an eyelid at me, she struts away.

Well, that's African parenting for you. The child is always in the wrong. Even if a clumsy woman drops a whole plate of food on their head.

Shakily, I clamber to my feet. And then—*crap*—I duck down. What if Vanessa and Alex saw everything? Even worse, what if they're laughing at me?

I hover behind the table, slowing rising to take a peep.

And that's when I feel a tap.

"Jesus, Derek." I put my hand to my chest. He has his hand on my shoulder and he's looking at me as though to say, *Why are you on the floor?* To be fair, nearly everyone around us is looking at me like that.

"You need a hand?"

As loudly as I can, I hiss, "No, I can't get up."

Derek laughs. "Well, in that case." He pulls at his trousers and crouches to my level.

"Wait, what are you doing?" I ask, as though he isn't doing exactly what I've been doing for the past two minutes.

"I get it. You're embarrassed. And Yinka, that's okay. But now"—he smiles—"you don't have to be, because I'm on the floor with you."

I glance down. Derek is too nice. I wish he wasn't. It makes declining his advances twice as hard.

Above my head, an African aunty shouts, "Excuse me! You are blocking the way!"

"You didn't have to, Derek," I say, tucking my legs in further so the aunty can pass. She kisses her teeth and I think I hear her say, "*Dutty* people."

"I know what you're going to say," I add with a resigned sigh. "I should have allowed you to help me with my plates earlier."

"I've been there. Don't worry." Derek shrugs. "Remember what happened at the engagement party?"

I frown.

"I spilled a bottle of Coke down my trousers."

"Oh, yeah, I was wondering what happened." I snort, remembering his suspiciously drenched combats. Then as we laugh, I suddenly realize how this must look—classic meet-cute moment. Not that we're having a moment, of course.

"We should probably get up," I suggest, already clambering to my feet. I pretend not to see Derek offering a hand. Then he pulls a nearby chair out—ironically, the same chair that got me into all this mess—and helps me into it like I'm an elderly woman.

"Stay here," he tells me. "I'll fix you another plate." I open my mouth. "No objections. Let me help you."

I nod. Derek gives me a thumbs-up and scurries away. I lift my eyes. Every single aunty and uncle on the table is looking at me.

"Make sure you wash your hands," one says.

"He's a nice man," another says.

"Next time, face where you're going, ehn."

Then suddenly, my brain snaps like an elastic band. Alex! I whisk my head in the direction of where I saw them last.

Nothing's changed. They're still at the back table, Vanessa nattering away, Alex nodding every so often. Then they laugh, and he throws his head back. As if my heart couldn't sink any lower, Vanessa slaps him on the bicep and laughs again. I get a horrible feeling of déjà vu, as though I'm watching Femi and Latoya again.

How could you be so stupid? a voice tells me. *How could you think someone as hot as Alex could like someone as dark and skinny as you? You don't stand a chance.*

Without a second thought, I push my chair back, staggering like a drunk to my feet. Then as fast as my trembling knees can carry me, I dash out of the restaurant.

I am who I say I am

"I knew it was too good to be true. I knew it."

I throw my duvet over my head, the memory of Alex and Vanessa taunting me. After I fled the restaurant, I drove straight home and told Nana everything—Vanessa, Derek, and the epic plate disaster.

"For goodness' sake." Nana wrenches the duvet away. "Vanessa is twenty-one. Twenty-one! Don't tell me you're intimidated by a girl who was born after the Spice Girls."

"But Vanessa is so pretty," I whine. "And she's light-skinned. And curvy. Nana, you should see her now. She's practically a mini-Beyoncé. Tell me, what man in their right mind would turn down a mini-Beyoncé?"

Nana shakes her head. "So you telling me, yeah, that you're not pretty enough, huh? That being dark and skinny is not beautiful? Yinka, I'm also dark and skinny and I think I'm hot."

I twist my body to face the wall. "I'm not saying I'm ugly," I reply, and the word feels like thorns in my mouth. "It's just . . . you know how it is. Men, they have a particular type. Long hair, fair-skinned. Curvy. How often do you see women who look like *us*?"

"So that's it, then?" Nana sits beside me on my bed. "You're going to give up because you feel *insecure*?"

"You didn't see them together!" I protest, and I pull the duvet over my head again. "I bet they didn't even notice that I'd left."

Nana lets out a resigned sigh. "Girl, you need to love yourself." When she says this, a lump the size of a rock fills my throat.

"I do love myself," I mumble feebly. Well, at least, I think I do. Maybe some days less so than others. I close my eyes for a moment, until suddenly, I'm overcome by a flash of anger.

I scramble to sit up. "I blame Femi. If he hadn't shown up at Rachel's engagement, then I wouldn't have felt compelled to meet Alex. Do you know who else I blame? Ola. God, I shouldn't have allowed her to get into my head."

Nana puts a firm hand on my arm and looks me straight in the eye. Then she shuffles around so that her back is facing me, while holding up her locs.

"What does my tattoo say?" she says in her teacher-Nana voice.

Without needing to read it, I say, "I am who I say I am."

"You're what?" She pretends not to hear me.

I let out a reluctant sigh. "I am who I say I am," I repeat twice as loud.

"And don't you ever forget it," she says, dropping her fistful of locs before twisting around to give me a stern look. "I mean it, Yinka. You need to define who *you* are. Otherwise, people will happily do it for you."

"I know." I rub the back of my neck. "It's just . . . I really like Alex, and I was sure that he liked me too. You've seen our messages."

Nana takes my hand in hers. "Yinka. If it's meant to be, then it will be. And if not . . ."

I almost snatch my hand away. No. Alex and I *have* to work. I will not end up sixty and alone, the subject of pity and open prayers until people become too embarrassed at praying for the sixty-year-old singleton to pray any more. A lost cause that becomes the cautionary tale.

I sink under my duvet again. Across the room, my phone vibrates.

"The Universe has heard you," I hear Nana say after a second. "Yinka. It's Alex."

I scramble out of bed so fast that I nearly fall flat on my face. I practically rip my phone from her hand.

"Hello," I answer.

"Yinka!" Alex cries. "What happened? Where did you go? We waited ages."

For a moment, I let Alex's panicky voice wash over me. *He actually cares about me.* Then I remember that I need to answer his question.

"Sorry, uh, I had an accident."

In an even more panicky voice, Alex says, "Oh, no, are you okay?"

"Yeah, yeah, I'm fine," I say quickly before he imagines me with a missing leg. "Um, it's just that time of the month, if you know what I mean."

"Oh," says Alex, startled.

Nana shakes her head.

"Well, I hope you're okay—"

"Yes, much better. And sorry for just leaving like that."

"Don't apologize, my sister used to get them bad too. Anyway, you forgot something?"

"*I did?*" I screw up my face in thought.

"Your jacket," he replies, and I clutch my head. "Remember you gave it to me? To save you a seat."

I laugh. "No wonder I felt so chilly after I left the restaurant. So, do you have it on you?"

"Yup. I'm wearing it now. Just kidding. It's still here. Chilling on the chair I saved for you, but I'm about to head home now."

I'm so caught up in the moment that I say, "Well, can I come over and pick it up? Maybe during the week?" I amend quickly, rubbing my neck.

"Hmm. This week might be tricky. Tomorrow and Tuesday, I have this overnight work conference. Then on Wednesday, this guy that I met earlier, Derek, invited me to this homeless outreach—"

"Hold up, are you going?"

"Yeah, I thought with me being new to London, it would be a good way to meet people. Are you?"

"Of course," I say, ignoring Nana's frown. "So we'll both be there. Perfect."

"Sweet," says Alex, and I picture him grinning. "I guess I'll bring your jacket."

"I look forward to it," I say without thinking. "I mean, er, see you there."

"Cool. Well, I need to head off now. We'll catch up later, yeah. Oh, and do me a favor, please."

Anything.

"Stay away from chicken and chips. They're bad for you." He laughs.

"I don't have it all the time!"

Alex is still laughing. "See you Wednesday. Bye."

I press my phone to my chest, feeling like a teenage girl. "Nana, can you believe it?"

Nana folds her arms. "Yinka. Do you have amnesia or something?"

"What?"

"You have an interview on Thursday." She enunciates the word "interview" as though I've forgotten.

"Oh, it's just with HR." I bat my hand. "Besides, I have Monday and Tuesday to prepare."

"Hmm," she says, and she reminds me so much of Aunty Blessing. "Anyway—" She jumps to her feet. "I'm going to make a start on sketching the bridesmaids' dresses."

"Oooh, I can't wait to see them. And Nana." She turns around. "Thanks for before."

"No problem." She winks. "Remember—"

"I am who I say I am," we say at the same time.

"Pure cheese," she says.

I pull a face, and we giggle.

Operation Wedding Date is back on. Yinka Oladeji is in the running.

February

Plan 2.0

MONDAY

RACHEL

Hey chicas!

Help! I need your thoughts on décor

Found a decorator that I really like

She told me to send her pictures of what I'm after

I've whittled it down to ten

NANA

Ten! Rach, pls, tell me this was a typo

RACHEL

Actually

You're right . . .

12

OLA

Babes, send the pics through

What's the decorator's Insta?

Hope you're not going for a cheap one!

RACHEL

Hell to the no!

Okay hun. Lemme double-check

Oh, yeah, anyone know a good photographer?

I woke up this morning with a new attitude—I'm going for what I want and I'm going to get it. I read my Bible and prayed for half an hour, then I spent most of the day preparing for my upcoming interview. I did loads of research about the company before rehearsing my answers to a few common competency questions I found online.

Interview prep out of the way, I shift my focus to my next goal: Operation Wedding Date. I need to get things moving with Alex. I know I like him, and now I need to get him to really, really like me.

Using the flipchart paper and Post-it notes that I nicked from Godfrey—hey, might as well make the most of that awful legacy—I draw up my new plan.

Standing back, I tilt my head and stare at the neon-colored squares that are stuck on the paper behind my bedroom door.

OPERATION WEDDING DATE: MY PLAN TO WIN ALEX AND HAVE A DATE FOR RACHEL'S WEDDING IN JULY!!!

OBJECTIVES	TASKS	DEADLINE	KPIs
1. Be more attractive	• Buy a weave (preferably a long weave) • Wear more stylish clothes—NO cardigans permitted. Look into borrowing Nana's African print clothes • Wear more makeup—not too much. Keep it natural. • Increase my bum size by eating more pounded yam and doing 50 squats daily / bum workout on YouTube	ASAP!	• Alex compliments me • I catch Alex staring at me
2. Be more in touch with Nigerian culture	• Learn how to cook a variety of Nigerian foods _properly_ • Tell Alex (in passing) what Nigerian food I've had for dinner • Learn a few Yoruba words—YouTube? Language app? Ask Kemi for Nollywood film recommendations???	Ongoing	• Alex is curious about my cooking and wants to taste it. We spend more time together • Alex and I have better banter

Black marker still in hand, I read over the Post-its. Perhaps I'm taking my bridesmaid's goal a bit too far? What would Nana think if she saw this? Or Aunty Blessing? Or Kemi? I know what that feminist woman on Quora would say. She would accuse me of being desperate and sad for wrapping my life around a man and being a disgrace to all womankind.

I sigh. This plan does look a bit desperate. Okay, majorly desperate. But let's face it, every woman has at some point hatched a plan to win over their crush. The only difference in my case is, it's written on neon stationery, as opposed to being an accumulation of thoughts and ideas swirling around in my head.

Deciding it's okay to feel proud of my plan, I scan the task column for a good place to start. *Hmm. What about . . . pounded yam and squats?*

Twenty minutes and thirty squats later, I'm sitting in the kitchen at the breakfast table, struggling to finish my pounded yam. Ugh, why is it so soggy?

I shove the mash into my mouth—since Mum's not around, I'm using a spoon—and I'm eating it with a pool of beef stew that Nana made for dinner last night.

A moment later, I hear the slam of the front door, followed by the pattering of Nana's footsteps and the clattering of her keys.

"*What is that?*"

I follow her disgusted gaze as it lands on my plate—specifically, to the mash beside the stew. Despite my best efforts, it resembles mushy peas.

"It's supposed to be pounded yam." I sigh, and force another scoop into my mouth.

Nana laughs. And I mean, proper laughs so hard that I see her fillings.

"What happened to pizza and takeaways?" She pulls out her phone and takes a snap of my dish.

"Hey! What are you doing?"

"I'm just going to share it on my Insta Stories."

"Don't you dare!"

"Chill out, girl. I'm joking. I can't promise you that I won't use it for future bribing purposes, however." She lowers herself onto the opposite stool and I narrow my eyes at her. "Anyway, how was your day?" she says.

"Productive." I cleanse my palate with some orange juice. "Although, I still need to do more research into the company, I think. And also—"

I stop. Is "Operation Wedding Date" something I want to share with Nana?

No. I push my plate to one side. She won't get it. I could do without the lecture too.

Duh yuh waah your ier dun?

TUESDAY

Peckham Beauty Afro-Caribbean Hair & Cosmetics

26 Peckham Rye Lane

Tuesday 2 February

7.03 p.m.

x 2 Yaki 1B 16-inch Human Hair	£57.98
x 2 X-pressions Kanekalon braiding hair	£3.50
Professional Hair Extensions Thread	£0.99
Sleek True Color Lip Gloss	£4.99
Jasmine's Black Lengthening Mascara	£3.00
Luster's Pink Original Hairspray	£5.49
Total	**£75.95**

I stroll from the cashier, receipt in hand, and blink. Then I blink again.

Seventy-five quid!!!

How the heck did I just spend over seventy-five quid on hair and makeup? I kiss my teeth.

I really can't afford to spend money willy-nilly right now. Not when I don't have a job.

I swivel around, marching back to join the queue, but it now seems to have doubled in length. Ah well. It's an investment in my future. I shove the receipt into my pocket and walk down the aisle to find JoBrian. I really didn't want them to come with me to the hair shop, and specifically told them that we should meet at seven fifteen at Costa. But en route from Peckham Rye station, I saw them across the road, and although I tried to walk away and pretend I hadn't seen them, they began to call my name as though I was a celebrity. Now, here I am, hurrying down the wigs aisle because Brian has decided to try on a pixie one.

"Yinka, this place is like Ikea," he cries. "But . . . for hair!"

"Put it back," I hiss, looking over my shoulder, worried we might get chucked out. The South Asian man from behind the counter is glaring at us.

"So, what did you get then?" Joanna noses into my plastic bag.

"Just some hair extensions," I reply, not sure Joanna would get it if I said, "Some weave." She'd probably think I was going medieval and trying to make a loom.

"We good to go?" Brian has returned the wig to its rightful owner—a yellow mannequin with the tiniest nose.

I look into my bag again. "Ooh, I forgot to buy a hairnet. One sec."

I wander down the aisle filled with skincare products. I see shea butter and cocoa butter and aloe vera and—

I stop.

Lightening creams.

My eyes widen. And they're not even tucked away or hidden on the bottom shelf. They're out in the open, lots of them in every form—cream, soap, lotion, serum. Sporting words such as "bright" and "fair," and on one particular product, "white."

My jaw clenches, and I feel my fingernails dig into my palms.

"Let's go," I tell JoBrian after I return to the wigs aisle. Brian is holding up another mannequin and pretending to be a ventriloquist.

"Did you get the hairnet already?" Joanna asks.

I shake my head. "The queue was too long." I check my phone and sigh when I see the text from Nana. "Sorry, guys, my best friend locked herself out. She's the one who's living with me for the moment. She's waiting for us at Costa."

As soon as we leave the hair shop, we bump straight into a woman wearing leggings and the biggest gold earrings I've ever seen in my life.

"Duh yuh waah your ier dun?" she asks in strong patois. I shake my head.

Barely three steps later, I'm confronted with the same question.

"No, thank you, Aunty," I tell her, bending my knees a little, then rushing off.

"Wait, is that your aunty?" Joanna says after she catches up, raising her voice over the loud sounds of plucked chickens getting butchered.

"Jo, every Black woman in Peckham is my aunty," I tell her, and they both laugh.

It's the first time that I've entered the Costa in Peckham, but I might as well have entered the one in Shoreditch. Every corner, hipsters in their oversized garments and vintage attire are either sitting behind their MacBooks or glued to their phones.

Nana waves. She's perched in the corner on a red sofa flanked by two armchairs. This should be interesting. My two "worlds" have never collided before.

I wave back, then signal "one sec." We grab our drinks, and I treat myself to a hot chocolate with marshmallows.

"JoBrian, this is Nana. Nana, this is Joanna and Brian." I gesture from one to the other like I'm at a formal interview . . . "Best friend. Former co-workers."

The three of them exchange polite hellos. I take the space next to Nana, while JoBrian take the armchairs.

"What did you get?" Nana snatches my plastic bag, and despite my objection, she noses inside. "Wait, is this for you?" she says as I snatch the exposed packets of hair before shoving them into the bag. "Yinka, since when did you start wearing weave?"

"Well." I shrug. "There's a first time for everything." I avoid Nana's gaze and reach for my hot chocolate and blow over it. After the mini-lecture she gave me on self-love the other day, I don't think she'll be too impressed with my over-the-top plan to transform myself.

"Anyway," I nod to JoBrian across the low wooden table. "How are your drinks?"

They look at each other, confused. Brian answers first.

"Um, well. My one tastes like coffee."

"And my one tastes like cappuccino," Joanna says.

"And mine," Nana whispers, "peppermint."

The three of them laugh.

I pull a face. "Ha-ha. Very funny."

In unison, we all sip our drinks. I look between them. Wait, I thought I'd broken the ice?

"So Nana," Brian says finally. He puts down his coffee and crosses his legs. "What do you do?"

I can't believe this is going so well! My work friends getting on with my best friend. My life has always been so compartmentalized, so it's actually nice to see some blend.

We've all been chatting for half an hour or so when Nana mentions her plans to run a fashion show in June. Joanna and Brian immediately flood her with excited questions.

"Have you thought about inviting fashion vloggers?" asks Joanna after Nana showed them her Insta page. "YouTube influencers. Instagram models. You know, those kinds of people?"

"Ooh, that's a good point." Nana is already taking notes on her phone. "I would *love* to get someone like Patricia Bright to attend."

"You should send her some of your designs," Joanna suggests. "Ask her whether she can do a vlog on them. Her platform is *huge*."

"Oh my gosh. Why didn't I think of that?" Nana is now typing furiously.

Joanna dusts her shoulder and says, "PR queen."

"Sidenote, do you have a venue yet?" asks Brian, wiping his glasses lens against his shirt.

"I'm looking at this events hall in Old Street," replies Nana. "Got a recce this Thursday. Oh, that reminds me. Yinka, you free to tag along? Appointment is at six. I'll invite the girls too."

"Sure. Though my interview is at four. But I should be able to make it."

For the next ten minutes, Joanna offers Nana more PR tips, while Brian and I look up some other vloggers she could invite. The three exchange numbers—Joanna says she's happy to put together a press release for Nana ahead of the show. Brian just wants front row seats.

"Ooh. Before I forget." Joanna puts down her cappuccino. "Any of you fancy going to Coal Rooms this Saturday?"

"What's Coal Rooms?" I scrunch my brows. Joanna looks at me as though I've asked her what's pizza.

"It's a restaurant," she cries, and I blink at her. "In Peckham, Yinka! I thought you used to live here?"

"Yeah, well . . ." I mutter over my drink. "Before it started to change."

Joanna doesn't hear me. "They do *amazing* brunches," she carries on. "Reasonably priced too. It's been on my list of places to visit for a while."

I smirk. I always find it so funny when people recommend a place to go in Peckham. Would Joanna have suggested brunch in Peckham fifteen, twenty years ago? No, I think not. Growing up, Peckham was portrayed in the media as being so dangerous that any nonresident who risked going there would likely get shot. Now Peckham is "trendy."

"So are you guys free? Oh, and that includes you, Nana."

"I need to check with Ricky," Brian says, whipping out his phone.

"Sorry, I'm doing my hair," I reply at the same time as Nana says, "I'm working."

"Okay, how about Sunday?" Joanna suggests.

"I should be free," says Brian, looking up from his phone.

Nana shakes her head. "Sorry, no can do. I live the life of a hustler."

"Yinka?" Joanna says hopefully.

"Sorry, Jo." I take a sip of my hot chocolate. "I've got church."

"But church finishes at ten, right? Come after."

I laugh. "Jo. That's my local church. I'm going to my mum's church now. Service ends at two."

"But that's when brunch finishes." Joanna sulks. "Okay, can we meet at eleven?"

I suck in my lips. She doesn't get it.

I clear my throat. "Jo, my mum's church starts at eleven."

Joanna blinks. "*Eleven?*" She stares at me as though I'm dressed in a SpongeBob mascot. "What, so you attend church for three solid hours?"

"I go to an African Pentecostal Church," I reply sheepishly.

"Wow, I knew you were a Christian, hun. But I never knew you were *that* religious." Joanna reaches for her drink as though she needs something strong to take the edge off.

Urgh. I hate that word "religious." For some reason, whenever I hear it, I think of those radical, Bible-waving people on the streets who yell at commuters to repent now or spend eternity in hell. Oh, I hope Joanna doesn't think I'm like that.

"Or we can just go to Coal Rooms another time," Brian suggests, clearly bored of the topic. "Sooo . . . how's Tinder going, Jo?"

After Joanna provides her short update—"Brian, please. It's only been a week"—Brian shifts his attention to me: "So what's the latest with lover boy?" Full of excitement, I fill them in on Alex, keeping in all the good bits (the WhatsApp messages, the banter, the flirting, the outreach date) and leaving out all the bad bits (Vanessa, Derek, PlateGate). After twenty minutes of hijacking the conversation, I excuse myself to the toilets.

I wonder if Alex has messaged? After I've blasted my hands dry, I fish out my phone and smile. Speak of the angel.

ALEX
Hey, how's it going? How's work?
Are we still on for tomorrow?

YINKA
Hey! Indeedy we are
Thanks again for holding onto my jacket. Appreciate it
How was staff conference?

ALEX
Staff conference was decent
Not gonna lie . . . Nearly nodded off a few times lol
Enjoyed the free food doh
😝
And no worries! Shall we just meet there?

YINKA

Sounds good to me

So what you up to?

Lemme guess. You're either eating or cooking right?

ALEX

Haha! You know me well

Just had ofada rice

Was fire!

YINKA

Arrrgh, you're making me jelly!!!

Remind me again, what's ofada rice?

ALEX

Are you sure you're Nigerian?

YINKA

Covers face

I forgot! Lool

ALEX

U have it with stew with different meat and fish in it

Mad spicy

But imma Naija boy

😋

YINKA

LMAO!

ALEX

How bout you?

What did you have?

Or having for dinner?

YINKA

I'm out at the moment, so probs a takeaway lol

Got the charm and ting, innit

A brisk wind nearly causes my eyes to water. Maybe wearing mascara wasn't such a great idea. I crane my neck and glance around, Peckham library's pastel green exterior glinting in the background.

Peckham Arch has been transformed into something else. In one section, there's a group of volunteers sorting out donated items. And not too far from them is a row of volunteers behind massive chafing dishes and metallic steel pots. Hands clad in rubber gloves, they ladle food onto plates, serving two winding lines of rough sleepers. Along the outskirts are three portable toilets, a tea and coffee station and what looks like an information stand. And not too far from the dining area, made up of cushions and beanbags, are a handful of volunteers stuffing leaflets into tote bags.

My heart swells. I've missed this kind of work. Every evening I volunteered at Sanctuary's outreach, I would go home happy, even if I'd had a tough day at work. There's something about helping people that's good for the soul.

I look across the platform. It's nice to see such a large turnout, and I *love* the additions of the massive beanbags too.

"Yinka! You came!"

I turn to see Derek walking toward me. Now he's power-walking. Jogging. He hugs me.

Instead of his usual Sunday all-black uniform, Derek has on a high-vis jacket. He's holding a clipboard and there's a walkie-talkie clipped onto his belt loop.

"I thought you had an interview to prepare for?" he says as I straighten my new white blouse under my new trench coat, courtesy of ASOS's clearance section. Tonight, I'm going for a sophisticated, womanly look, as opposed to my usual casual comfort. It is a bit chilly, though. I hope I see Alex soon so that I can button up.

"Oh, I've been preparing all week. Is it okay if I still help out?"

"Sure. Of course. Let me just add your name to the registration list." Derek lifts up his clipboard. I try to scan the names upside down.

"Or I can do it," I offer. "Saves me from having to spell out my last name, eh."

Derek shrugs and hands me his clipboard and pen.

I scan the list. Ah-hah! Fifth name down: Alex Balogun. He hasn't been ticked off yet.

"Anywhere on the top is fine," pipes Derek, and I scribble my name at the top and add a tick for good measure.

"Where do you want me?" I ask. "I'm willing to help out anywhere."

Derek scratches a bald spot. "Now, let's see . . . we've got quite a number of people helping out with the mains. How about dessert?"

"Dessert sounds great," I chime, maybe a tad too enthusiastically for his question.

Derek smiles . . . smiling . . . still smiling.

"Er, shall we head there now?" I suggest, turning to walk, even though I don't know where I'm going.

"Yes, yes. Of course." Derek takes a few steps, then stops. "Oh, yeah. Where did you go last Sunday? At the restaurant."

I narrow my eyes. Then I slap my forehead.

"Oh, God. I'm so, so sorry. You were getting me another plate of food, weren't you?"

Derek nods.

I cover my mouth feeling incredibly guilty.

"Aww, don't worry about it," he says. "I get it. I'm sure you wanted to leave after what happened."

"But still! I should have told you."

"Honestly, Yinka. It's fine."

"Sorry," I mumble, and Derek smiles. Again.

"Dessert," I remind him.

"Oh, yes. Come with me."

I follow him, beaming at every person I walk past. And then I hear a familiar giggle.

Vanessa.

Dammit. Derek must have invited her last Sunday too. That man is *thorough.* And of course, she's carrying a load of cake boxes because this is what she does for a living.

Feeling a rush of panic, I jump in front of Derek so that my back is facing her.

"I've changed my mind," I squeak. "I want to do something else. Maybe something on that side."

Derek follows his gaze to where my finger is pointing at. "Leaflet-stuffing?" He sounds as though I've just turned down a free holiday.

I give a weak nod. "Well, I did say I was willing to do anything."

———

The first thing I notice when Derek escorts me to my newly assigned area is that there is no system. Well, unless you call "just make more of a mess" a system.

Lounging on a blanket are four volunteers, all wearing tracksuits. None of them look a day over eighteen. They're sitting around the pile of leaflets as though it's a badly made campfire. I watch them for a second. They wade through the pile finding one of each leaflet, then stuff a tote bag, crumpling the corners as they shove them inside, before flinging it in the general direction of a heap of tote bags that looks worse than a pile of laundry. Oh, dear.

Derek waves. "Hey, everyone. This is Yinka." He puts a hand on my shoulder, and I stiffen. "Yinka's going to be helping you guys out today."

The four volunteers look up and stare at me like neutral face emojis.

"Hi," I say cheerily, lifting my hand to wave, but also if I'm honest to shrug Derek off.

The teens murmur, "Hey," as though they'd rather be doing anything else. I wonder if their parents forced them to come.

Derek turns to me, then says, "Right. Well, I'll leave you to it." Then suddenly his eyes shoot up to a spot behind me.

I turn around to see a tall Black man wearing a hoody with a picture of Nina Simone.

"Yinka!" he says.

I frown. Who is this guy?

"It's Don. Donovan."

My eyes widen. "Ohhhh. My bad, I didn't recognize you. Long time. How's it going?"

"Good to see you, man," he says in his thick south London accent. Then to my surprise, he folds me into a hug and I get a waft of his Lynx body spray.

"Wow, you guys know each other?" Derek says, looking between us.

"Yeah . . ." My mind is still racing—is it really Donovan? He looks so different.

"We were on a gap year ting together," Donovan is now saying, much more enthusiastically than me. "That was around, what, ten years ago? I'm surprised I haven't seen you since, you know. You still live in south London?"

"Yup, Denmark Hill."

"Sorry, what's this gap year program?" Derek says.

As Donovan explains the charity work that we did in Peru, I cast a sneaky eye over him. I hate to admit it, but time has been good to him. He has bulked up considerably and he no longer wears braces. And he has hair! He had a low fade back then. My eyes graze Donovan's Pinterest-y beard, then his equally Pinterest-y hair, which consists of two cornrows in the middle, the ends tied back into a topknot. But more than that, he's being *friendly.*

"So, is today your first time, Yinka?"

"Yes, I'm here with my church."

He tuts. "'Course you are."

Just when I was going to give Donovan the benefit of the doubt, he proves he hasn't changed. Back in Peru, Donovan *loved* "debating" with me. He thought it was irrational that I believed in God, and stupid me engaged with his self-indulgent rants. That wasn't the only thing about him that pissed me off, though. Donovan was the kind of person who had an opinion on *everything.* From politics to the environment to the existence of insects. When I made breakfast, I didn't make the *tacu tacu* right. When I made dinner, the chicken slices were too large. When we went to bed in our dorm, I took too long to turn off the light. Apparently. Donovan had something to say about everything and anything. And I was so insecure back then, it really got to me. Unlike the other volunteers he took jabs at, I didn't find it funny. God, I don't know how his sweetheart girlfriend coped. I wonder if they're married now—he used to go on about her. A lot.

I try to look at Donovan's hands but they're shoved in the pockets of his Nina Simone hoody. *Woke,* I can't help but think as I stare at the iconic legend.

"So, how long have you been volunteering here?" I ask him, figuring I'll be the bigger person.

"Three years." Donovan seems proud to share this. "Man volunteers here every Wednesday and Thursday, innit."

"Oooh." *Humble bragger,* I think.

"Such a hater," he says. "Anyways." He swerves to Derek. "I thought I should let you know that Sashka and I have swapped roles, innit. So, she's gonna oversee the mains section, and I'm gonna oversee this one."

"Sounds good," says Derek. *Urgh,* I think.

I don't exactly want Donovan to be around when Alex gets here, asking me dumb questions or telling embarrassing stories about Peru. Sigh. Speaking of Alex, I pull out my phone and open WhatsApp. His status says, *last seen ten minutes ago.* I shoot him a quick message.

> Hey Alex, how's it going?
> I'm at the outreach now
> Call me when you get here 😊

"You're not here to be on your phone, you know."

I blink up at Donovan, who has his arms crossed.

"Just playing." He smiles, breaking the deadpan expression. "So you gonna give me a hand, yeah?"

The first thing I do after Derek wanders away is enforce order—thankfully, Donovan has swiftly excused himself to the toilets, leaving me in peace. I assign three of the grumpy teens a specific leaflet to find from the pile and allow them to listen to whatever music they want on Spotify using my phone data. And rather than a messy pile of tote bags, the other teen is stuffing them into large cardboard boxes, ready to be handed out at some point later on.

"Now, isn't this better?" I say, looking around at the factory-style operation. The teens are working so harmoniously.

"Someone's a natural leader," says Donovan after he returns and stands by my side.

I laugh. "Donovan, it wasn't rocket science."

"Still. You've done better than most."

I take the compliment—clearly Donovan's decided to pretend to be nice again—and shrug. "Thanks. I did this kinda thing at work. Not stuffing leaflets, obviously. But thinking up better processes and training junior staff."

"Oh, yeah?" Donovan turns to me. "So what do you do?"

"Believe it or not, I actually worked for an investment bank till recently. You heard of Godfrey & Jackson?"

"Yo, are you serious?"

Before I reply, one of the teens who's wearing a matching Adidas tracksuit approaches us, carrying a box of toiletries.

"We just found these," he mutters. "We forgot to put them in the bags."

The next five minutes are spent shoving scented soaps and toothpaste into already stuffed bags while trying to convince Donovan that although my time at Godfrey was painfully stressful, it was worth it because they paid me well. I don't think I succeeded.

"I'm telling you, Yinka," he says as we sit opposite each other on upside-down drink crates which are just about strong enough to hold up our weight. The teenagers seem to have disappeared. Cheeky buggers. "I still can't believe you went into investment banking. Sell ouuut," he says for the umpteenth time. "Sell. Ouuut."

"Why not?" I shove a toothbrush into a bag. I'd quite like to be shoving it up his backside. "And like I said, I was in the operations team. I wasn't a trader. Even if I was, what's wrong with investment banking?"

"Nothing," he says, sniffing a bar of soap before putting it into a tote bag. "I just didn't think that *you* of all people would go into that industry."

"What's that supposed to mean?" My teeth chatter. The wind is getting under my blouse, so F *it,* I do up my coat. I'll unbutton it when Alex comes. I look around. Surely he'll arrive soon.

"I'm just saying." Donovan tugs the ends of his hood-strings. "You kept banging on about how you wanted to work for a charity and whatnot, and how that was going to be the first thing you did as soon as you got back to the UK. You even cried about it, remember?"

I cover my face at the recollection of the memory. It was at one of our last dinners, when we all shared what our experience abroad had taught us.

"I believe I found my calling." Donovan mocks me, putting on a tearful voice.

"Oi! Shut it, you." I throw a bottle of hand sanitizer at him.

Donovan laughs. "I-I-I'm so grateful," he carries on, adding exaggerated sobs and sniffs and sounding very much like a tearful elderly woman. "I'm so grateful for this experience."

"Whatever, Denzel Washington." I can't help but laugh at my own joke. "Well, you can get off my back, because if you had listened carefully, you would have noticed that I used the past tense. I said I *worked* at Godfrey."

"So where you working now? Lemme guess. Another bougie bank, yeah?"

"Actually," I croak, my chest hurting a bit, "I was made redundant."

Donovan looks shocked for the first time. "Ah, man. I'm sorry to hear that, Yinks."

"Don't be." I try to sound upbeat. "I've actually got an interview tomorrow. I'll be all right."

"Oh, really?"

"And yes, it's with a bank. Don't give me that look. It's not like I have a choice. A girl's gotta pay her bills, right?"

"Well, cuz, if that's what you really wanna do . . ." Donovan trails off, then shrugs.

"And what's that supposed to mean?" I ask, despite telling myself that his opinion doesn't matter.

He pushes out his lips. "Well, when you were telling me about your work earlier, besides the money, you didn't seem to like it that much. Just saying."

"Because it's work!" I exclaim. "How many people truly love their job?"

"True, true. Not many," Donovan answers. "And do you know why? Because there's too many people out there, yeah, that are not doing what they really want to do. They stick around in a poxy job they hate for years. For what? To buy a big yard and to pay the bills? Then they wonder why they have a midlife crisis when they reach their fifties." He kisses his teeth. "Nah, bruv. Not me."

I roll my eyes. "Okay, Donovan. So what have *you* been up to these last ten years?"

"Living life, innit." Donovan spreads his hands, and I snort. "Did a bit of traveling for a while. Brazil. China. Costa Rica. Then I went into the recruitment sector, you know. For the first, what, four, five years, I was helping to recruit old white men into pharmaceutical jobs. Hated that, Yinka. *Hated it.* The money was good, though. Not gonna lie. Then after a while, I was like, nah man. This ain't for me. I'm a sick recruiter. Got the charm and ting, innit." He smiles. "But like you, I had a thing for charity work. A'ight, so, boom." He claps. "Here's what I do now. I place talented people in big charities. Save the Children. Amnesty . . . In fact, Sanctuary is one of our clients—that's how I ended up volunteering for them. Pay isn't as great but I'm much happier. Much, much happier."

"Well, I'm glad to hear you're doing something you like," I say.

"If you ever fancy a career change . . ."

"Nice try, but I'm cool. Besides, you'd be the last recruiter that I'd go to."

"Excuse you!" He looks shocked again. *Good.*

I narrow my eyes. "Don't you remember?"

"Remember what?" Donovan looks around, confused.

"How you treated me!" I exclaim. "You were a bit of a bully back then."

"A bully?" Donovan laughs, and I notice his dimples.

"Yes." I stand my ground. "You were so . . . opinionated."

"So I annoyed you?" He suggests.

"That too." I fold my arms.

Donovan finds this funny. "Elaborate."

"Well, for starters—" I reach for my mental list. "You always made a big fuss when I wasn't familiar with something."

"Like what?" He recoils.

"Like how to dice an avocado," I point out. "How was I supposed to know that there's a technique?"

"Really?" Donovan scratches his head. "Man, I can't remember." He laughs. "Well, I hope you can dice an avocado now."

I roll my eyes. "Aaand you never let things go. Remember when I told you that I hadn't heard of that hip hop group, Tribal Quest?"

Donovan is in uproar. "Oh, yeah! And they're called A Tribe Called Quest," he points out. "Terrible. Anyways, anything else?" He cocks his head and his smirk annoys me so much that I spit out my next answer.

"My faith," I say passionately. "You always challenged me about my faith. In fact, why *did* you do that? Why couldn't you just accept that I believe in God?"

Donovan makes a hissing sound followed by an expression that I do not like. "I swear, man. You Christian folks are naive."

I narrow my eyes. "We are *not* doing this again."

"I tell you now," he carries on anyway. "Believing in God is a one-way trip to poverty. Unless you're a pastor, of course."

I breathe out. "Donovan. We're adults. There's no point in us getting into an argument. Let's just accept that I'm a believer and—"

"I'm the one going to hell. Yeah, yeah. I know." He laughs sarcastically.

"No!" I tut. "I was going to suggest that we leave it like that—"

"But isn't your job as a Christian to share your faith? Yeah, Christians are very happy to preach to you, as long as you shut up and listen. But when we find holes in the Bible and ask them tough questions, all of a sudden, we're the troublemakers—"

"Donovan, I'm really not in the mood for this conversation."

"But you'd be happy to have one if I was a person of faith, right? Exactly. You proved my point. And what is so great about having faith, anyway? Give me one advantage you folks have. Because if having faith is so great, yeah, then tell me, why are there just as many sick religious people as there are nonreligious? Surely religious people would have an advantage, right? Given, you know, they believe in God and whatnot. Huh? Yinka? You don't have an answer to that, do you? Oh, please don't say, 'It's part of God's will' or whatever BS you churchy folks like to say. I swear, you Christians will say *anything*—"

"Do you know what?" I spring to my feet, and a rush of pins and needles declares war on my legs. "I'm out of here. What you want is a debate, not a conversation. Well, guess what? I'm not going to allow you to drain my energy."

I turn to walk away, but my left foot gets caught under the crate.

"Watch your step!" Donovan cries.

But it's too late.

I stagger forward, arms twisting. Thankfully, I don't fall flat on my face. But my foot pays the price.

"You all right?" Donovan says. He doesn't even try to hold back his smirk.

"I'm fine!" I retort. *Sweet Jesus, my foot!*

I swing around and hold my chin high, praying that no one else saw what happened. And with the greatest effort I can muster, I stomp away. Well, hobble.

"So immature," I mutter as I ease myself down onto the blanket where the teens were leaflet-stuffing. "He has not changed one bit. Not one bit." Surreptitiously, I take off my shoe, roll down my sock, and rub my throbbing foot.

Then I remember.

Alex!

I reach for my phone and tut. *Why hasn't he messaged me yet?* I'm about to tap on the call button when Donovan plonks himself right in front of me.

"Go away!" I tell him.

"How's your foot?" He nods to my exposed ankle.

"I came here to get away from you." I roll up my sock and put on my shoe.

"I came here to apologize," he says, showing me his dimples.

"You hardly look sorry."

Donovan amends his expression. "Okay. How about now?"

I blink at him. "You look as though you're doing a bad impression of Eeyore."

He laughs. "Okay, but really—I want to apologize—hey!"

I've jumped to my feet and answered my phone.

"Hey, Alex!" I sound super-excited, but whatever.

"Yinka, I got your message—"

"Great. Where are you?" I grin like a loon as I crane my neck.

There's a drawn-out pause.

"Actually," he eventually says, and there's a sick feeling in my stomach. "Yinka, I'm stuck at work. I'm hoping to leave in the next twenty minutes, so I might still make it. Only thing is . . . I forgot your jacket. If you like, I can go home and get it. But I don't want to keep you waiting."

I take a quick glance at my watch. We only have less than an hour to go. Alex works in central London. There's no way he'll make it in time.

"Hello? Yinka? Are you still there?"

"Yes, I'm still here." I speak quietly, afraid my voice will wobble.

"Do you mind if I just give it to you after church on Sunday?" he suggests.

"Yeah, that's fine." I try to sound unbothered.

"I'm sorry," Alex says again, and this time he really sounds it. "I only realized that I didn't have it, like, a few minutes ago."

I consider saying, "I'll forgive you, if you make it up to me," but I'm not so brave.

"You have another winter jacket to wear in the meantime, right?"

"No," I say bluntly. I laugh. "Just kidding. And don't work so hard. I know you love your job and everything, but don't forget you have a home, right?" I picture his beautiful face as he laughs.

"Right. I need to get back to work, otherwise I'll be camping here all night."

"Good luck."

"Cheers. Bye."

"You good?" says Donovan, looking at me quizzically.

I stare at my phone, disappointed.

"Yeah, I'm okay." I try to sound casual, but inside I'm throwing a hissy-fit. "It's just, my friend was supposed to come, and now he's not."

"Sounds more than just a friend to me." Donovan wags his brow.

But I am *not* in a mood to be wagged at.

"Do you know what? I'm tired of you." And to demonstrate how tired I am, I walk away.

"*Wait,* what did I do?" I hear Donovan call after me.

Yinka . . . are we cool?

THURSDAY

ALEX

Hey, U good?

Been posting some of my Nigerian dishes on my Insta

See how many you can name

Add me

@AlexKehinde_Jr.

YINKA

Listen yeah

I'm Naija thru and thru

Humble yourself child lol

And don't forget, you lived in Nigeria once. You had a head start!

I've just added you

Though it looks like your account is private

You gonna have to accept my request

I scuttle into the venue and simultaneously glance at my watch. Phew. Made it just in time. After my interview at Oscar Larson ended, I quickly bought a bagel to eat on the go, then jumped on the Tube and made my way to Old Street station. I'm buzzing—I really feel like I've nailed it.

Nana is already here, waiting by the reception desk. She looks up.

"Hey!" she says. "You made it."

We hug and she pats my face. "You're a little shiny."

I dab my forehead. "The Tube was rammed."

"The event manager will be out in a sec. Tell me. How did your interview go?"

"I smashed it." I grin. "Cara, the HR manager, was sooo impressed. The interview was pretty much conversational. All my nerves went away. Oh, and check this. Cara said she *loved* my CV. I was scared whether me being at Godfrey for eight years would work against me, but I didn't get any bad vibes from her at all."

"Oh, Yinka. I'm so proud of you." Nana bundles me into another hug. I can't stop smiling. I'm proud of myself. For the first time in days, I feel like I'm the old Yinka, who knows what she's about.

She lets go of me. "Did she mention when you're likely to hear back?"

"Latest, Monday," I reply. "Not to be cocky or anything, but I think I've got this one in the bag. Though I've still got the second round of interviews to go, and there will most likely be a third. But Cara saying that I'll hear back so soon can only be a positive sign, right?"

Nana nods. "Yeah, I've got a good feeling about this too." She looks at her phone and frowns. "Rachel's running late. And Ola's no longer coming. Couldn't find a babysitter."

I haven't spoken to Rachel or Ola since what went down at Nando's. Rachel keeps flooding our "I'm Getting Married, Biatch" WhatsApp group with photos of dresses, flowers—practically her entire Pinterest wedding board. But not once has she got in touch to find out whether I'm doing okay. Just like at school, she's pretending we're all getting on great. As for Ola, well, she's never bothered to return my calls, and yet she finds ample time to be active on Rachel's WhatsApp group. It's a bit of a slap in the face, really, given I called her to apologize. Anyway, I'm no longer going to waste my energy on her. Even just thinking about the situation is getting me annoyed.

"Nana?"

Nana and I turn to a tall, dark-haired man wearing a navy tie and white shirt. Nana extends an arm. He shakes her hand.

"Hi, there. I'm Frank, the events manager. I believe you want to have a look at the main hall?"

"I love it, I love it, I love it," Nana gushes, swirling around with her arms wide, as I take in the vastness of the rectangular hall. I gaze up at the high ceiling fitted with LED lights and steel beams, and two frosted skylights in the middle.

"We can have the catwalk here. And a DJ there." Nana is throwing her hands in different directions. "There's already a built-in bar at the back. Yinka, this place is perfect."

"It is," I agree, trying my best to visualize.

As Frank runs through the hall specs, I decide to make myself useful. I take out my phone with the intention of taking photos. But before I do that, I'll just have a quick look on Insta . . . *Hmm. Alex hasn't yet accepted my request to follow him.* I hop over to WhatsApp to see whether Alex is online. His status shows that he was last seen over two hours ago. Knowing him, he's probably still at work.

"Sorry, I have to get this," says Nana, cutting Frank off mid-sentence. "Hey, Rachel," she says after answering her phone. "You're at reception? Great!" She lowers her phone a bit. "Yinka, do you mind?"

When I arrive at the reception desk, Rachel is staring at the bulletin board wearing a long red wrap coat over her pointy leather boots and munching on a granola bar.

"They're low in calories," she says after she sees me.

"Hey," I lean forward hesitantly, but she squeezes me and says, "Good to see you, sis."

I lead the way down the corridor while Rachel vents about her terrible journey. She practically talks to herself all the way to the hall.

"Oooh, is this it?" she says as I walk in front, hearing the clank of her boots behind me. "Hey, where's Nana?"

I shrug. "Probably out back talking to the manager."

"Damn, this space is *noice*," she says, her voice echoing. "Hey, maybe I should have my wedding here."

She lets out a theatrical laugh, and I make a point of not joining her. Instead, I fish out my phone and busy myself by taking photos.

"Sooo." She turns to me. "What do *you* think of the hall?"

I snap away. Swipe through the photos. Take another one. "Like you said, it's nice." I lift my phone to take photos of the ceiling. I can sense Rachel watching me, silent confusion setting in.

"Yinka . . . are we cool?" she says, pushing each word out with caution.

Giving in, I lower my phone and turn to her.

"Rachel! I haven't heard from you. I wasn't the only one in the wrong, you know. Ola was being rude to me—"

"Oh my gosh. Is this why you're acting all funny?" She shoves her granola bar into her coat pocket, causing almonds, raisins and pumpkin seeds to scatter on the floor.

"Rachel, I'm your cousin. We're more than just friends. We're family. You could have at least messaged me."

"Nuh-uh. Don't take your anger out at me." Rachel crosses her arms. "And I couldn't *not* have gone after Ola. She was upset. What was I supposed to do?"

"Well, she upset me too." I cross my arms too, then feeling childish, I let them dangle. "I'm not just talking about when we were at Nando's. Do you know that at Kemi's baby shower she yelled at me? Called me closed-minded in front of my mum. Not just in front of my mum, but her mum too—"

"I said, I know!" Rachel says for the third time. She sighs and runs a hand over her hair. "Ola told me what happened at the baby shower. She feels terrible, you know."

I let out an incredulous laugh.

"It's true!" Then in a lower voice, she says, "She's just going through a lot right now."

I scoff and shake my head, looking up at the ceiling. "There you go justifying her behavior."

"No, I'm not!" Rachel says. "There's just . . . more to the story than you know. Anyway, shall we try and find Nana—"

"Wait a minute." I frown. "What do you mean there's more to the story?" I search Rachel's face, but she glances away. "Rachel, if there's something you're not telling me—"

"Oh, for goodness' sake, Yinka. Just let it go."

"No! Ola's my cousin too. Surely, I have the right to know if she's going through stuff. Oh, no. Is it to do with the kids?"

"No."

"Then what is it then?"

"Argh, for flip's sake!" Rachel stomps and heaves a loud breath. "If I tell you, yeah, you have to promise me you won't say anything to anyone. Not Nana. Not Kemi."

My heart rate goes up. "I swear. I promise, I won't."

Rachel looks over her shoulder, then lowers her voice, "It's to do with Jon. Ola found something out."

I blink at Rachel, stunned. Wow, I wasn't expecting that at all.

"And she's still angry at Jon? But it was ages ago! It happened in the past. And he clearly loves her. He's the father of her kids, for God's sake."

Rachel sighs. "She can't get over it, Yinka. She feels really insecure."

Everything begins to make sense—Ola's outburst at the baby shower, even her negative attitude toward Alex. And with Aunty Debbie patronizing her, I can't imagine she's feeling really good about herself right now.

"So now you know why she's being so touchy. But you can*not* tell her. She would kill me."

I place my hand on Rachel's elbow. "I promise"—I look her square in the eye—"I won't say anything."

"Sorry to keep you waiting."

Rachel and I turn around.

Nana is strolling toward us, Frank by her side.

"Frank wanted to show me the audio room," she says. "I hope you weren't waiting long."

"No, not at all," Rachel and I say at the same time. We seem to be nodding a lot.

Nana greets Rachel with a hug and thanks her for coming.

"I *love* this space," Rachel says. "Yinka and I were just saying that you should go for it."

"Yeah," I say, nodding . . . still nodding. "By the way, you're kicking our arses with your bridesmaid's goal."

"Did I tell you that I have a model casting next week?" Nana grins.

"Okay, now you're just showing off." Rachel cocks her head and I laugh. "How about *you*?" Rachel nudges my forearm. "How's things going with Alex, huh?" And playfully, she says, "Are you boyfriend and girlfriend yet?"

I chuckle. "Not yet, but wait until he sees me with my new weave hairstyle on Sunday."

Nana and Rachel's reactions are like night and day.

"You're getting a weave!" Rachel's voice is so loud. "Well, look at *you*!" She nudges me again.

"So *that's* why you bought a weave the other day?" Nana narrows her eyes.

"Oh, I was just joking." *Nearly landed myself in hot water there.* "Anyhoo, going back to your question, Rach. Alex gave me his Instagram today."

"Ooh, let's see his pics." Rachel rubs her hands.

"Sadly, we can't right now. His profile is private. I'm still waiting for him to accept my follow request, but let me check again." I fish out my phone and unlock it. "Wait, hang on."

I blink. Right at the top of my screen, I have an Instagram alert: Alex has accepted my request to follow him.

"Oh! He's online! Oh! He's just followed me back."

Nana and Rachel rush to my side and peer over my shoulder. Suddenly, I get a new notification. Then another. And another.

"Damn, girl," Rachel cries. "He's liking all your pictures."

I can't believe it. OMG. He's liked a photo of me and the girls at Zizzi's. Then one of me and Nana at Hyde Park. Hey, he's even liked the photo that Nana took of me recently at the Caribbean takeaway shop.

"Um, sorry to interrupt."

Rachel, Nana and I look up.

Frank is scratching his head. "Is there anything else I can help with or will that be all?"

Weave in

SATURDAY

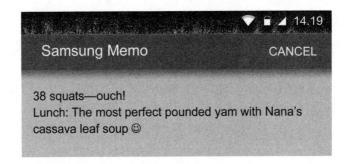

Samsung Memo CANCEL

38 squats—ouch!
Lunch: The most perfect pounded yam with Nana's
cassava leaf soup ☺

"So, how does it feel to get your first weave?" says Aunty Blessing, her hands behind me, resting on my shoulders.

We're in her living room, and she's on the sofa while I'm on the floor in between her legs. The sixteen-inch weave I bought is sprawled across my lap. I can't stop stroking it. It's so silky.

"I'm excited," I admit. "Although my bum's getting pins and needles."

"Want to take a break?"

"No, no, I'm fine."

So far, Aunty Blessing has cornrowed the Kanekalon braiding hair with my natural hair. The cornrow starts from the nape of my neck and goes round and round until it eventually stops in the middle where she has sewn down its braided ponytail. Now she's moving on to do the exciting part. With a needle and thread, she's going to sew the wefts of the weave onto the cornrow. I've only watched people have this done before, so I'm hoping she doesn't prick my scalp or sew the hair into my head.

"What made you want to get a weave?" she asks, handing me the needle and thread along with a pair of scissors. "I haven't had one since I grew out my perm and went natural twenty years ago."

"I dunno. I just . . . fancied a change, I suppose." I embark on the challenge of threading the needle. It takes me three, no four, actually, five attempts. I pull down the thread until it reaches several inches before snipping the end and handing it to her.

"Ooh, before I forget." She takes the threaded needle over my shoulder. "Your friend Nana called me this afternoon. We had a good chat."

"Nana called you?" Instinctively, I turn my head, and Aunty Blessing promptly turns me back.

"She had a few questions about setting up a business."

"Oh, yeah, I forgot I gave her your number. Were you able to help her?"

"We talked about bookkeeping and tax returns, you know, the sort of things she would need to do as a business owner. She admitted it went over her head, though—bless her—so she's going to pop by tomorrow."

"Amazing. Thank you, Aunty. I know she'll really appreciate it."

I try my best to keep my head still as Aunty Blessing sews the weave onto the back of my head. Huh, whaddaya know? It's not at all painful.

"Did she mention she needs sponsorship?"

"Indeed," Aunty Blessing says in a sing-song voice. "I'm going to reach out to a few of my contacts. Some of them like to invest in start-up businesses. I'm sure in exchange for a bit of brand promotion, they'll be quite generous; at least, I hope. I'm also going to make a contribution."

"Oh, really, Aunty?" I try to swerve my head and feel a tug as though I'm attached to a resistance band. "That's so nice of you."

"Of course I'll chip in. Bend your head down a little. Not too much. That's fine—oh, and how did the interview on Thursday go?"

"Okay, we're going to have to stop for a moment so I can show you."

Aunty Blessing stops sewing. "Uh-oh."

I fetch my phone, which has fallen in between my thighs. I open the e-mail and hand it to her.

"'Dear Yinka,'" she says. I turn around fully to see her reaction. "'Thank you for taking the time to meet with me yesterday to discuss your interest in working at Oscar Larsson. I was very impressed with your skill set,' blah-blah-blah. 'With this said'"—she's grinning now—"'we're interested in discussing your experience further'—Come on, now!— 'and we would like to invite you for a second interview on Monday fifteenth February at ten thirty a.m.' Yess!"

Holding up her hand, she says, "That's my niece."

And I feel like such a kid as I give her a high-five.

"Have you told your mum yet?" She hands me my phone back. "She'll be so relieved. And what did she say about your redundancy in the end?"

I scooch back to my original position, looking away from her. "Understandably, she was upset," I say, closing my eyes.

"Well, this news should cheer her up then—"

"Well yes, but . . . I'd rather wait. I mean, no point getting her hopes up until I get the job, right?"

I grimace, hating myself for lying to my aunty. But honestly, is me not telling Mum that much of a big deal? I guess Aunty Blessing just wants to do the right thing—given how she's a woman of the law and all. Thank God, Mum and Aunty Blessing are not the type of sisters who call each other every week.

I wait for Aunty Blessing to probe further, but to my relief, she tells me to do her another thread. I manage on the second attempt. Hey, I'm getting pretty good at this. She adjusts my head and gets back to sewing.

"Yinka, I need to talk to you about something."

My chest tightens.

"The baby shower," she says, and I feel my diaphragm relax. "Aunty Debbie's prayer was completely unnecessary. Let's just call a spade a spade—they don't want you to end up like me."

By this point, she has stopped sewing. I turn my body around. This seems like a face-to-face conversation. I've never really talked about my love life with Aunty Blessing. It's always seemed . . . taboo. Maybe because it would force me to ask her that lingering question: Aunty Blessing, how does it feel not to have found love?

Something about her reaction tells me that she has read my mind.

"You're wondering what went wrong for me, aren't you?" she says. "How come, unlike my sisters, I didn't settle down?"

"No!" I practically burst. I don't want to hurt her feelings. Then after a short pause, I add hesitantly, "But may I ask why?"

"Life," she replies matter-of-factly. "Sometimes life doesn't work out the way you plan. I had dreams of getting married. Having kids. Settling down." She smiles with her eyes. "But I also had dreams of becoming a top barrister. And as you can imagine it wasn't a walk in the park. Work became my only love. By the time I reached your age, I think the longest relationship I held down was, what, three months?"

"Wow." I chew my lip. "So . . . have you ever been in love before?"

Aunty Blessing swiftly looks past me. She shakes her head a little. "But I'm fine with that." She rubs her thighs. "Look at where I am today. I have a lovely home, my dream profession—and who told you I'm too old to find love?"

She cocks her head and I laugh. Then I remember the online dating website.

"Yes, it would have been nice to have had a husband, and a kid or two," she carries on. "But I knew deep down that I couldn't have both. Back then, female barristers were few and far between, and on top of that, I was a *Black* woman. I had to work harder. I had to prove myself. At the end of the day, I'm happy. I know I don't have it all, but what I do have I wouldn't trade for the world. Besides, I very much enjoy being an aunt."

I return her warm smile.

"You see, *I'm* responsible for my happiness." She presses a hand to her chest. "I would have lived my life disappointed if I had not known that happiness is a choice. Do you know what would be even more disappointing?"

I shake my head, not sure where she's going with this.

"Living a life that you feel pressured into." She looks me square in the eyes. "Your mum messaged me about this man that Aunty Debbie introduced you to. It seems she has high hopes that he'll be your husband in the near future." She rolls her eyes when she says this. "Now, tell me. *Do* you feel you're being steamrolled into this? Because I'm very happy to have a word with your mum. I'll tell her to ease off a little."

Her stricken expression makes me laugh. "No, no, Aunty. It's fine. Funny enough, I actually like the guy, and I think he likes me too. He's called Alex by the way. I'm meeting him after church tomorrow."

"Why am I only hearing about this now?"

"Okay, let me start from the beginning." I swing my body back around so that she can resume fixing my hair. "Let me fill you in on how we met."

As I give Aunty Blessing a quick update on Alex—the first amazing meeting, the disastrous outreach, all the Insta action since—the back of my head feels progressively heavier.

I don't tell her that as soon as I got home after Alex followed me I did a thorough audit of his account. I was pleased to see that it was nothing like his Facebook profile. No pictures of him on holiday or at nightclubs surrounded by tons of women, or any photos that would suggest that he is a low-key ladies' man. Instead, what I got were several photos of Nigerian dishes, a couple of chilled selfies, a photo of him looking ridiculously toned at the gym—my favorite—and a couple of him with his brother and late twin sister. It was only when I looked more closely that I realized his sister was the same dark-skinned girl that I saw when I was trawling through his Facebook photos at Nando's. I don't know how I didn't see it. They both have the same nose and eyes. It reminds me of that moment we shared when he first told me, and I get chills all over again.

"I *think* he likes me," I say when Aunty Blessing has finished, running my fingers through my new tresses. *Ahh, so soft.* "I just want him to come out and tell me already. What do you think I should do, Aunty? Do you think I should invite him out? After all, he is new to London."

"Sorry, you've known him for how long?" Aunty Blessings says, and I feel so sheepish when I say, "About two weeks. You're right, maybe I should just wait it out—"

"Wait it out?" Aunty Blessing kisses her teeth. "Yinka, let me tell you something. Men these days are *slow.* Send them a simple text message, you won't hear back in a week. Agree to a time to speak, they cancel or postpone. *Pfft.* I say go for it. Of course, if I were you. So what if the woman makes the first move."

I open my mouth then close it again. A smirk rolls across my lips. Well. I won't ask Aunty Blessing how she's finding online dating then.

Now you are beautiful again

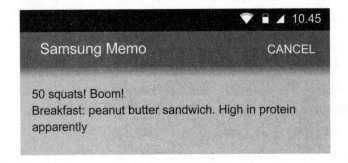

Running my fingers through my silky hair, I peer anxiously at the stream of people pouring out of the auditorium's twin doors. I'm waiting in the church lobby by the bulletin boards as Alex suggested.

I try hard to balance in my court heels, which I have not worn since graduation, and pinch the sides of my African print wraparound dress to tug it down. With Nana growing increasingly suspicious of my plan to win over Alex, I wasn't quite brave enough to ask her whether I could borrow her clothes. So I had to resort to wearing a dress that she made for my birthday. My twenty-fifth birthday. It still fits, but it is a bit tight around my hips and bum. Ooh, maybe this means my bum regime is working.

"Fine girl, Yinka!"

I immediately recognize the voice. It's Kemi, and she's walking toward me with Uche. Well, waddling. I hug them and pat her stomach.

"Check you, looking all fancy." She's eyeing me up and down. "And you've got a weave!" She touches my hair. "What's the occasion?"

I shrug. "Just fancied a change. New year, new me." I laugh.

After Aunty Blessing had finished doing my hair, I looked in her bathroom mirror and, praise be to God, I didn't get the shock of my life. Granted the weave was a little shiny, but I'm not unfamiliar with having long hair attached to my scalp; only long hair that isn't mine. I'm not going to lie, it did take some time getting used to, especially not being able to wag my eyebrows—Aunty Blessing had braided the hair underneath too tight. Thankfully, the Botox look has subsided now. Rocking a side fringe like the RnB singer, Aaliyah, I'm loving my new hairstyle. And I'm praying that Alex does too. He'd better, given how much I spent on it.

"So, how're things?" I ask, but honestly, I'm desperate for Kemi to be on her way. I don't want her around when Alex comes over. She would definitely suss out why I got my hair done.

"Urgh. Teaching this week was stressful." She pulls her face. "Seriously. I can't wait to go on mat leave. I feel like such an elephant when I stand in front of my class."

"Baby, don't say that about yourself." Uche drapes an arm over Kemi's shoulder. "You're doing great. I told you. You're beautiful." He pulls her into him and kisses the top of her head. My heart tugs a little. It's been a long time since a man called me beautiful.

Suddenly, my eye catches a glimpse of a bright blonde weave in the moving crowd.

Crap. It's Vanessa, *and* she's with Derek. I want to duck down, but my body seems to have seized up. *No, no. Please don't see me. Not now.*

"Yinka!" I hear Kemi yell. "Are you even listening to me?"

"Sorry, I'm desperate for the toilet."

"Oh. You should have said so. Well, let me not hold you up." She leans forward and we hug.

"But let's catch up soon, yeah," she says. "You hardly come round any more."

"What are you doing Wednesday evening?" I ask, remembering I need to ask her for a few Nollywood recommendations. "Mind if I come over?"

"Sure." Kemi gives me a wide smile. "I should be home by six, so any time after is fine."

"And we can show you the nursery," says Uche, giving me a hug.

"Oh, yes, the nursery," Kemi says. "We've painted it yellow."

I have a vague memory of her telling me that they were buying paint.

"Mum chose the color," she gushes. "Didn't she, Uche?" He nods.

Mum. Now I remember why I didn't tag along.

"Well, I can't wait to see it," I say, hopping from one foot to the other.

"Oh, sorry. You need to go." Kemi shoos me away with her hands.

I bustle my way toward the toilets—the opposite direction to where I'm supposed to meet Alex.

And that's when I see him.

I look quickly over my shoulder. Thankfully, Kemi is nearing the exit. Alex and I wade through the crowd and stand by the wall together.

"Someone looks nice," he says, his lips lifting a little.

A cage of butterflies opens in my stomach. Did he—did he just compliment me? Yes, yes, yes! I knew my plan was going to work. God, I'm a genius.

"Thanks." I shrug. "You look nice too." I reach out and actually touch his arm.

Alex looks down at himself as though he needs a reminder of what he's wearing today: a denim shirt, skinny jeans and sandy boots.

"I try." He gives a tiny shrug.

No, trust me, you deliver, I think to myself.

"Oh, and here you go." He proffers a large Selfridges bag at me with my jacket bundled neatly inside.

"Aww, thanks," I say.

"Apologies again," he says sheepishly.

"No, don't worry." I flap a hand. "The tenner is still in my pocket, right?"

Alex looks confused. I burst out laughing.

"Never mind. Bad joke. Soo, um, want to grab lunch? I promise not to ghost you this time, lol."

"Actually, I can't do lunch today."

The smile on my face falters.

"How come?" I ask.

"Got plans," he replies unhelpfully. "Actually . . . If you're not in a rush, I want to introduce you to someone."

Without giving me the chance to ask, "Who?" he leads me back into the auditorium and down a row of chairs.

"Mum," he says, stopping in the middle. He places a hand on the shoulder of a woman sitting in the row ahead.

Hold up. He wants to introduce me to his mum?

I lower my Selfridges bag to the chair beside me.

"Mum," he repeats, smiling. "This is Yinka."

She turns her head, then scampers to her feet like you would when you bump into an old friend.

"Ahh, Yinka!"

"Hello, Aunty." I go to bend my knees but Alex's mum hugs me over the chair between us. I feel a rush of affection as she squeezes me. Hey, I can't believe that out of all the daydreams I've had, I haven't yet thought about what Alex's mum would be like. Considering how in touch Alex is with his Nigerian roots, I would have thought she would be like my mum.

But Alex's mum seems so . . . so . . . *Western*. For starters, she's hugging me as though we're mates. And my mum would never be caught in leather trousers. *And* she has a platinum buzz haircut! Wait, is that an authentic British accent I've just heard?

Alex's mum draws back and slides her hands down my arms. I can now see her face in its entirety, and my God, she's stunning. Her complexion is a terra-cotta brown like the outside of a garden pot. And her teeth are so sparkly as though she's never eaten chocolate in her life. And her skin! It is true: Black don't crack.

"So, this is Yinka," she says, squeezing my elbows.

Wait, hold on a sec. Has Alex been talking to his mum about me?

I grin and nod.

"I love your dress!" She lifts my hands. Thank God, I shaved my armpits. "It's absolutely gorgeous," she says with a drawl.

Alex nods. "Now you look like a proper Naija girl."

I pull a face at him.

"Oh, thank you, Aunty," I say, nearly forgetting my manners.

"Where did you get it from?" she asks, lowering my hands.

"Actually, my best friend made it. She's a fashion designer."

"Shame I'm not your size." She laughs and pats her stomach. Which, by the way, is impressively toned for any woman, let alone a woman her age.

"Oh, come on, Mum." Alex nudges her a little. "I'm sure you'd look just as good."

Good! I'm practically swaying. He's attracted to me. My new makeover is working.

"Now, tell me, Yinka." Alex's mum raises a lightly penciled brow. "Has Kehinde started raiding your fridge yet?"

Who's Kehinde? I nearly say before realizing (thankfully) that Kehinde is Alex's Nigerian name. It's part of his Insta handle. Name. Whatever. "Because I tell you something," she continues, "this boy here likes to eat. And when I say eat, I mean eat." I chuckle.

"No, Aunty." I'm snuffling with laughter. "Alex hasn't raided my fridge . . . yet."

I look up at Alex, who's laughing too. Then he kisses his teeth. "Mum, please. Yinka doesn't even know how to cook Nigerian food. Do you know that this girl lives on takeaways?"

I gasp, then slap Alex across the arm. Ooh. "Aunty, don't listen to him," I say after being temporarily distracted by his muscles. "He's lying."

"Oh, there's no shame, sweetheart. But don't overdo it, okay? Otherwise, you'll pay the price when you get to my age."

"Aunty, please, don't mind him. In fact"—I feel myself stand tall—"Yesterday, for dinner, I made myself pounded yam."

Alex scoffs. "Come on. Pounded yam is easy."

I giggle nervously as I recall some of my earlier attempts.

"Can you even make proper Nigerian food?" Alex emphasizes the word by slapping the back of his hand, twice. "And by proper, I mean *proper*. You know, like moin-moin, pepper soup, ọgbọnọ."

I stall. Okay, I'm familiar with the first dish, which is a staple savory pudding made out of peeled brown beans and ground peppers and served at Nigerian parties. The second one, again, I'm familiar with, though I can't say I can take the heat. But the third one. Ogbo-what? That one's for Google.

"All right, that's enough," his mum intervenes. "I'm sure Yinka is a great cook." Then to me, she says, "I don't even know how to cook half those things," and we share a light-hearted laugh. I think I love her.

Then just as the moment is about to pass, I remember the conversation that I had with Aunty Blessing yesterday: *So what if the woman makes the first move.*

"Well, to settle this"—I fold my arms and look directly at him—"how about after church one Sunday, we have lunch at mine?"

The words vomit out of me. If he says no, I will die of embarrassment. But to my surprise, Alex says, "Okay. In that case, why don't we do next Sunday?"

"Sounds good to me," I say quickly, before he changes his mind. "Let me just put it in my calendar." I reach into my bag and look up. Alex's mum has put a hand on my forearm.

"You know you're going to have to cook a feast, right?" she says.

Undeterred, I tap open my phone calendar. "Hang on." I do a double-take. "Next Sunday is Valentine's Day." Oh, snap. I shouldn't have said this aloud.

"Oh, is it?" Alex says with a startled laugh. "Well, if you're busy, we can do lunch the following week?"

"No, no, it's fine." I may have sounded like Miss Piggy when I said this, but whatever.

Alex smirks. "You know you have six days to drop out, right?"

"I'm going to make you eat your words, mister."

"Okay, enough with the squabble." Alex's mum puts a hand on my arm again. "Sorry, Yinka, but we need to get going. I've got a train back to Bristol to catch."

Like a true gentleman, Alex helps his mum into her peacoat, then kisses the top of her head.

My throat catches. That is so sweet. They seem really close. I try to think back to the last time that Mum and I were affectionate, and my mind draws a blank.

"Nice to meet you, sweetheart."

I hug them both good-bye. Then I watch as they make their way toward the center aisle.

As soon as they reach the exit, I do a fist pump. *I've got a date,* I'm singing to myself—oh, shoot. I've got my job interview the day after. And also less than a week to learn all of the Nigerian food. *But I've got a date.* This is the most important thing. It's all thanks to my brilliant plan. And Aunty Blessing's solid advice. Who would have thought? I have to text her.

"Was that Alex's mum?"

I turn around. Mum and Aunty Debbie are making a beeline toward me.

"Were you watching me?"

"Ah, ah. Yes, now. Why not? Is it not a free country? Look at the way you greeted his mum, as if she's your age-mate, ehn? You couldn't kneel?"

"She hugged *me*!"

Then Aunty Debbie yelps, "You've changed your hair!" and they both get distracted with stroking my weave as though I'm a cute animal at a zoo.

"This is better," says Mum, visibly pleased. "This is much, much better. Now you are beautiful again."

I arrive through the front door humming Pharrell Williams's "Happy" song.

"Nana!" I yell, kicking off my heels and sprinting up the stairs. "You won't belieeeve what happened today—Hey, what are you doing?"

Nana is closing the door to my bedroom. "Missy. You've got some explaining to do." She crosses her arms.

"Hold up," I ask, "why were you in my room when I was out?" She follows me as I walk into my bedroom to put my stuff away.

"I ran out of body cream," she protests. "Come on, you know how Black skin gets after we've had a shower."

I sigh. "Okay, if we're going to live together, we need to set some boundaries."

"Fine, but not until you explain *this*." She points at my project plan. A few Post-it notes have already fallen onto the floor.

Ignoring her incredulous laugh, I crouch down and stick them back up.

"I knew you were up to something," Nana says. "I was like, Yinka getting a weave? You've never even had braids."

"Well, there's a first time for everything," I try to say breezily.

"Oh, and what's this one?" She pushes her face closer. "'Wear more stylish clothes.' 'Borrow Nana's African print clothes'!"

"I said, *look into borrowing* Nana's African print clothes. So can I?"

"No!"

"Why not?"

"I'm not getting involved in your bonkers plan. What happened to our mantra, 'I am who I say I am?' Yinka, you're essentially changing yourself for a man and I'm not having any part in it."

I roll my eyes. "I don't see it like that. We all put our best selves forward when we meet someone new. This is just that but a little more, you know, ramped up."

Nana cocks her head as though to say, *Naw, you don't say.*

"I'm putting myself out there," I continue. "Sorry, isn't this what you suggested?"

With a look of disbelief, she takes a step back.

"You and I know that is *not* what I meant. Wait. Has any of this got anything to do with Vanessa? Or the comment that Ola made? I hope you're not fixed on trying to prove her wrong."

"No!" I say. "This has nothing to do with that. Nothing at all."

"Hmm." Nana purses her lips. "If you say so."

Sister time

WEDNESDAY

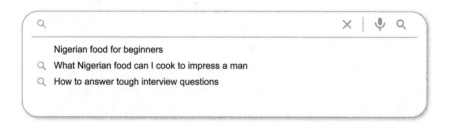

"I have to admit," I say, running my hand along a wall, "Mum did pick a great color."

I'm at Kemi's apartment, in the tiny box of a nursery room. There's a lot of yellow.

"She did, didn't she? And look, even that cot." Kemi points to it by the window. "Mum put it together, you know? She did the drilling and everything. Literally left nothing for Uche to do."

I laugh. "Well, that's Mum for you. Always willing to roll up her sleeves and do it herself. I rate her for that. It couldn't have been easy . . ."

"When Dad passed?" Kemi finishes.

I head toward the cot. "You probably wouldn't remember, as you were very young, but Daddy was a bit of a handyman. Always doing stuff to the house. Putting up shelving units, tiles, pictures . . . Although he did do a shoddy job with the kitchen floorboards."

"Urgh, those floorboards." Kemi laughs. "Like, the floor isn't supposed to move when you walk on it."

"Daddy used to do all the driving, remember?" I carry on. "Aunty Blessing told me that Mum was terrified of learning how to drive after he died. Funny, 'cause if you see the way Mum is on the road now, you would *not* believe it." I grab a furry rabbit from inside the cot and bury my chin into it. Sometimes I forget how awesome Mum is. I don't know how I would have coped if I'd suddenly became a single mother of two. I know it must have been difficult, despite how well she hid her emotions back then. I wish she would open up about her experiences now that Kemi and I are older. It might bring us closer together.

For the next couple of minutes, Kemi and I exchange childhood memories: our obsession with the park roundabout, being chased by our neighbor's pit bull and adopting a ladybird (until Mum killed it with her slipper).

"Man, I've missed this," I say. "Me. You. Hanging out. Reminiscing."

Kemi tilts her head. "I know. I've missed this too." Then after a short pause, she says, "We can still hang out, you know. Yes, I'm married and having a baby, but don't be a stranger."

I lower my gaze at the cot again. Kemi's right. I don't like how distant I've been. Maybe I should tell her about Alex. Open up more.

"Oh, gosh, I'm so sorry," she says, just as I look up. "That came out all wrong. I hope you didn't think that I was being patronizing."

"Not at all—"

"Honestly, Yinka, I didn't think—the 'I'm married and having a baby' comment."

I suppress a sigh. I wish Kemi would stop overthinking things; honestly, it would be less awkward between us.

"Don't worry," I say. "Before the baby comes, we'll spend more sister time together. I'll organize something. But hey, I need to ask you a question."

"Sure. What is it?" she says, and I notice how relieved she looks now I've changed the subject.

"It's going to sound pretty random, but . . . I want to practice my Yoruba. Yes, I know, me of all people. So my question is, are there any Yoruba Nollywood films that you'd recommend?"

Twenty minutes later, Kemi and I are sitting against the wall with our legs outstretched. I now have a YouTube playlist titled "Nollywood" on my phone.

I scroll down the list. "*Ah-bee-le-bu me,*" I try.

Kemi looks over at my phone. "*Àgbélébù mí,*" she says effortlessly. "I think it means my cross. Or my burden. I have to admit, I'm a bit rusty."

I remember when Kemi was a teen, she would sit right by Mum's feet while Mum sat on the sofa and binged on Nollywood movies. I guess it made sense given her passion for acting, but I just never saw the lure. Besides, I found Nollywood films way too long for my patience. They always ended on a cliffhanger too, and *then* there was always a part two, three and four. And most times, the film graphics were so unrealistic, they were laughable.

Kemi shrugs. "I'm not fluent, but I can get by. The ones that I used to watch with Mum were the proper villagey types. You know, the ones with witch doctors and masquerades."

I shudder. "I don't know how you weren't scared."

Kemi laughs. "The CGI was terrible—it made good comedy. How come all of a sudden you're so interested in learning Yoruba anyway?"

In a Nigerian accent, I reply, "Ah, ah! Why not now?"

Kemi giggles. "Yinka, you're something else. You'll stay for dinner?"

"Sure."

Moments like these remind me of the old days. Kemi and I would chat for aaages before realizing that we still needed to make dinner. I help her climb to her feet, rubbing her shoulders from behind as she leads the way to the kitchen. "So, what's on the menu?" I ask. *God, I hope she's not making pounded yam.*

"Jollof rice." She beams. "Or do you think Mum will mind if we have fajitas?"

"Mum? Mum's coming round for dinner?"

Kemi opens the fridge. "Sure is." She rummages out lettuce, cucumber, a pack of tomatoes and an avocado. "With the baby coming—you know, with all the boring stuff I need to get done before then—and Mum only being ten minutes away, she comes round for dinner more often."

Kemi sets down the vegetables on the counter. I grab the chopping board behind the dish rack.

Great. I really don't want to stay if Mum's going to be around. She'll only ask me about Alex, and there's *no* way I'm filling her in about our lunch date. Then she'll inquire about work and I still don't fancy telling her that I've been made redundant, regardless of Aunty Blessing's conscience.

"Jollof or fajitas?" Kemi interrupts my anxious thoughts.

"Jollof," I reply, and grab a chopping knife.

"Good choice. I made it last night."

While Kemi heats up the rice, I chop away at the vegetables. "Here. Let me help you with that." She beckons at the avocado in my hand, which I have to admit, I've been doing a bad job of dicing.

I head to the sink and wash my hands, and feel a prickle of irritation as I think back to when Donovan would take the mick out of my avocado-chopping skills.

"You didn't go to work today?" Kemi says as she cleans her hands with a kitchen towel.

My eyes pop. *Wait, does she—*

Kemi nods to my top.

I look down. Ah, yes. Wonder Woman.

"I was surprised that you got here bang at six . . ." she says. "Well, you deserve the odd day off, you work too hard. Speaking of work, we haven't celebrated your promotion yet. Hey, why don't you grab a bottle from the wine rack. Obviously, I won't be drinking, but Uche should be home from work soon—"

"I didn't get a promotion."

Kemi leans back against the counter, then blinks, confused. "What?"

I sigh. "The truth is . . . I was actually made redundant."

Kemi covers her mouth.

"Don't worry." I hold up my hands. "I'm confident that I'll get a job soon. Come on, I've got eight years' experience. And I've already had an interview. But still, I'd appreciate your prayers."

"Of course," Kemi says as though finding her breath. "When did all this happen? Does Mum know—"

"No," I say before she can even finish her sentence. "Mum still thinks I got a promotion." I wince. "Please don't say anything to her. You know what she's like."

Kemi puts a hand to her chest. "Aww, sis. You should have told me." She walks over and bundles me in a hug, leaving a slight gap to accommodate for her large bump. She buries her chin into my shoulder.

"Kemi, I'm not dying, you know." I wiggle out of her grasp, and I see her holding back the worry. Though I don't know if it's worry about me, or about what Mum would say.

"Anyway, maybe it's best not to stay for dinner if Mum's coming. I don't want her asking any questions."

"Sure, sure. I understand." She walks me to the door. "Yinka—"

"I meant what I said earlier." I quickly grab my jacket hanging over the banister. "Before the baby comes, I'll organize something for us to do to-gether. It will be like old times."

"Only I'm fatter now," she laughs, clearly deciding not to risk nagging me. "But yeah, just let me know when you're free."

"Will do." I smile. I open the door and step outside. "Oh, and ó dàbọ̀." I wave.

Kemi chuckles. "See. You'll be fluent in no time."

After a swift look both ways, I power walk down the street, praying that I do not bump into Mum.

A date and a second job interview, all in a couple of days," says Joanna on the phone. I'm approaching Peckham high street, passing another Black barber's shop. "You are on a roll. I'm so happy for you."

"Aww, thanks, Jo," I say as I step onto a pedestrian crossing. "Anyway, enough about me. How's the job search going? Ooh, better yet, any updates on Tinder?"

"Still job hunting," Joanna says, then I think I hear a smile in her voice as she says, "Buuut, I do have a date this Saturday."

"Go, you!" I shout, and a few people at a nearby bus stop turn to look at me. "What's his name? How old is he? How long have you been talking?"

"His name is Brandon." Joanna is definitely grinning now. "Thirty-seven, and for about a week. Did I mention he's a fireman?"

"A fireman? Tell me more. Have you told Brian? I bet he's well excited."

While Joanna fills me in on Brandon, how he looks (essentials first) and the chemistry they have, I spot a Chicken Cottage in the distance, and my stomach growls. I beeline toward it. As I push open the glass door, a waft of heat greets me, then the smell of fried chicken and chips. Nostalgia.

"Yes, darling, what can I get for you?" A man appears from behind the counter wearing a red polo T-shirt and a matching Fargo cap.

Joanna is still swooning over Brandon on the other end of the line.

I mouth to the man, "Sorry, one sec," and I'm about to interrupt Joanna when a familiar voice calls my name.

I turn around.

"*Wha gwan*, sis?" Donovan is slouching in a chair by a small table. He pulls off his hood then smiles. "So, what, you stalking me now, yeah?"

Laws of attraction

"Donovan!"

"No, Brandon, Yinka," I hear Joanna say through the phone. "Bran-don."

I shake my head. "Right. Sorry, Jo. Actually, do you mind if I call you back later? I'm out at the moment."

I end the call. Donovan is now on his feet. "Well, bring it in then," he says, spreading his arms wide for a hug.

I hold out a hand and stop him. "We are *not* on good terms."

"Yinks, are you kidding me? I tried to apologize, but you walked away. Anyway, perhaps this is some sort of sign."

"A sign?"

"You know, what's that thingamajig called? Oh, yeah. Laws of attraction." He shows those dimples. "Maybe that's why I'm bumping into you again. To get a second chance."

For some weird reason, my belly flutters like my insides are doing acrobatics. I really must stop with the yam.

"What can I get for you?" repeats the man from behind the counter.

I breathe out, welcoming the interruption, and glance up at the shiny menu screens above.

"Chicken and chips, please," I say without missing a beat. "Ooh, for the chicken, can I have the drumstick?"

"Drumstick?" Donovan looks at me as though I've just asked for tofu. "Fam, get the thigh. The thigh has more chicken on it."

"Err, excuse me." I hold up my finger. "The drumstick has more skin. And everyone knows that the skin is the best part."

"Fair enough." Donovan gives in. "But you'll *nyam di* drumstick quick, *enuh.*"

His patois tickles my funny bone, and despite myself, I laugh.

"Drumstick it is, then." The man smiles as he enters my order into the till.

I give the man a fiver and he hands me my change. "Two minutes," he says before disappearing off inside.

"So"—Donovan leans against the wall where all the hygiene certificates are—"you helping out at the outreach tonight?"

I look up from my purse to see the corners of his brown lips lifted to reveal white teeth.

"Um, no," I say, and his lips sag. And because I feel bad for not volunteering, I quickly add, "I have a job interview to prepare for."

"Oh, you've already got another one?"

"Well, it's with the same bank. But yeah, I've got another interview." I grin. "Girl got through to the second round."

I wait for Donovan to say, "Congratulations," or to laugh at my attempt to speak like him. Instead, he remains poker. "So you're really sticking to the banking sector, huh?"

"Donovan. Honestly. What is it to you?"

He shakes his head. "Yinka, remember what I said, yeah. Midlife crisis is a serious ting. You know what I'm saying?"

I roll my eyes.

"Your order, sir. Five wings and chips." The man sets a box down in front of Donovan, then disappears again.

"Cheers, boss," Donovan says, and he reaches for a napkin. Then after flicking the box open, he yells, "Yo, bossman. You got any burger sauce?"

"Oh my gosh. I *love* burger sauce."

Donovan lifts his head. "It's the shit, right?" he says, sprinkling two sachets of pepper all over his chips. "I mean, you can't order chicken and chips and not have it with burger sauce. It's like . . . I dunno, having a burrito without chipotle."

"Or Nando's without peri-peri."

"Yeah, yeah!" His eyes light up.

Just as Donovan stuffs a chip into his mouth, the man behind the counter returns with a squeezy bottle of burger sauce.

"Boss, you should keep this on the counter, yeah," says Donovan, and he makes a grab for the bottle before squeezing it for a good minute.

Seconds later, the man returns with my box of chicken and chips. Donovan does the honors and puts on the burger sauce.

"A bit more," I prod as I watch splats of yellow sauce burst out. "Don't be stingy now."

Donovan laughs. "You gonna eat your takeaway when you get home?" he asks as I shove a chip in my mouth. Mmm. Heaven.

"Actually, I was going to eat it at the station," I admit. "Just before getting on my train."

Donovan checks his phone. "Well, I've got twenty minutes before the outreach starts and I'm gonna eat my wings in the park, so . . ."

I laugh. "So you can chew my ear off again."

Suddenly, he places his hands on my shoulders. The intensity of his gaze makes the back of my neck warm.

"I was out of line last Wednesday. I should have respected your wishes. Hand on heart, I'm sorry."

I stare at him, stunned by his apparent sincerity. I'm waiting for him to laugh. But he doesn't.

"Okay, um, apology accepted," I say, finding my words. "Fine, I'll keep you company." I say this in a huff but my twisted lips don't quite match the attitude I'm trying to give off.

"Hey, don't act as if you're doing me a favor." Donovan nicks one of my chips.

I scowl at him. "Oi! You've got your own!"

"I'm cool with hanging out with the pigeons, you know."

"Yeah, yeah, whatever."

Donovan gives the man behind the counter a fist bump, then we leave.

It's only when we've arrived at the park and pitched up on a suspicious-looking bench that I realize I have eaten all of my chips. En route, Donovan and I reminisced about our time in Peru, and I couldn't help but notice that he laughed at *all* of my jokes. Even when I was being plain lame.

There's a slight pause while we continue to eat, which is filled by the sound of a police siren in the distance. I tap my heel on the concrete pathway that separates the stretch of unkempt grass on either side. The air has that wet dog smell, and the wind has robbed every leaf from the trees. I swear, I hate London during the winter.

"I like your hoody." I seal the takeaway box—I'll have my chicken at home. According to Nana, I chew *very* loudly when I eat fried chicken. Thanks to her I'm now self-conscious about eating it in public.

Working his way through a hot-wing, Donovan looks down at his front—at the large print of a Black man with an impressive high-top. "You like his music?" he says.

"Oh, he's a musician?"

Donovan shakes his head. "C'mon, Yinka. Big Daddy Kane. He's a hip hop legend. I swear, your hip hop knowledge is ter-ri-ble. I need to educate you, one of these days."

I shrug.

Donovan glances down and I follow his gaze to see two frowzy-looking pigeons circling our bench. He rips off a bit of skin from his wing and throws it into the grass. Like two dogs playing fetch, the birds scuttle after it.

I shudder. "Urgh. I'll never understand why God made pigeons—"

I freeze. Oh, no. I really don't want another debate.

Donovan laughs. "You can say the G-word, you know. Once upon a time, man believed in Him too."

"Who, *you*?"

Donovan nods. "Brought up in a Christian home, innit." He smiles. "You're not the only one who knows the Bible."

I watch him as he tears another piece from his hot-wing, his two new friends waiting patiently by his feet. He throws it even further and the birds make another frantic dash.

I shift slightly. I have to ask. "What happened?" Then quickly, I add, "Only if you want to talk about it, of course."

Turns out, Donovan and I can talk about theology without either one of us getting prickly. With the birds returning every so often for another scrap, he told me about his mum, who was diagnosed with lupus when he was in his late teens. About her desire to be healed and the role her church played in making her believe that she soon would be. And about the ridiculous amount of money she would give as a tithe offering every Sunday in the hope of receiving her miraculous healing. She didn't have much, yet she gave and gave and gave and received nothing back.

While Donovan explained his withdrawal from his faith, I listened, never once interrupting. It was actually quite refreshing to see this side of him and to see him lower his guard a little. For the first time, I feel like I saw him. The real him. The man behind all the swagger.

"Wow, thank you for sharing all that." I blow out my cheeks.

"So is this the bit where you gonna try and convert me, yeah?" Donovan smiles, but I see it too late.

"No, no. Of course not . . . I don't believe in conversions."

"No?" He raises a brow.

I shoot him a smile. "In my opinion, faith"—I press a hand on my chest—"is something that starts in here. You can't force the heart to believe what it doesn't want to."

Donovan nods slowly. "That's pretty deep, I give you that." He pauses. "Thank you . . . for listening. And for respecting my decision. I've never had that before." He rubs the back of his neck. "Sorry for going hard on you, all those years ago."

I flap my hand. "We were young and you were immature."

We both laugh.

"So," Donovan says suddenly, and I turn to him. "Why do *you* believe in God?"

I laugh a little, then tilt my head as I ponder.

"Reassurance, I guess," I say finally. "Reassurance that I'm not alone. That despite all the bullshit life can throw sometimes, I have someone looking out for me, fighting in my corner and giving me everything that I need to get through. Don't get me wrong, I too have moments when I wave my fist at God. But I guess, I get a sense of . . . what's the word I'm looking for . . . inner peace, knowing that I don't have to figure life out on my own, if that makes any sense at all? I dunno, I see God as a . . . friend."

Donovan rubs his chin. Dare I say, he looks slightly impressed. "Okay," he says, nodding. "I can respect that." He laughs.

"What's so funny? Was the 'God is my friend' line a tad too cheesy?"

"Cheesy?" Donovan cries. "Yinka, it was mozzarella." I laugh. He shakes his head, but I can tell that he finally sees who I really am. I feel great. Liberated even. I open my takeaway box and dig into my chicken. Screw what Nana said. I'm hungry.

"Not gonna lie, that ting looks good, you know."

I glance up. Donovan is eyeing my chicken like a predator.

"You want some, don't you?"

"Just a little." He scooches closer.

"Next time, don't feed it to the pigeons!"

I study his fingers as they rip apart my chicken. He isn't wearing a wedding band.

"Sooo, whatever happened to that sweetheart girlfriend of yours?" I ask, half-joking, before realizing I've stepped in it.

Donovan freezes. He drops the small piece of chicken and glances away.

"Sorry, you don't have to answer that," I say quickly.

He dusts his hands. "We broke up," he replies anyway.

"I'm sorry."

Donovan pulls out a crumpled napkin from his hoody pocket. "Don't be," he gruffs, wiping his hands with it. "It's coming up two years, man should be over her by now."

"But she was your high school sweetheart."

"Still," he protests. "She's moved on. I don't love her any more, I just—" He breathes out. "I hate the effect the breakup had on me. You know what I'm saying?"

"Yeah," I say. "My boyfriend and I broke up three years ago. Well, he broke up with me. Got a job in New York. Wanted a fresh start. It sucks, right?"

"Like a motherfucker." Donovan looks down and gives me a full view of his crisp cornrows. "Anyway, counseling is helping."

"Counseling?"

Donovan chuckles and he must have read into my raised brows, because he says, "Yinka, counseling isn't just for the white man, you know."

I frown. "Obviously. I just thought it was something that only married couples did."

"Nah, nah. It's for single people too. In fact, I recommend my counselor, Jacqui, to almost everyone. She's the goat."

"She's a what?"

He laughs at my confusion. "G.O.A.T. Greatest of all time. Come on, Yinka."

"Ohhh."

Donovan shakes his head. A boy passing by performs an impressive wheelie on his bike. "So," he says, "how did you cope with your breakup?"

I ponder, then realize I'm chewing as loud as *a* goat. I quickly swallow.

"Time," I say eventually. "Time and lots of ice cream."

He chuckles.

"Do you think it's worth the money? For counseling, I mean. You're essentially paying someone to listen to you, right?"

"Trust me, it's worth the investment. The more that you talk, the more you get out of it."

"Hmm."

As Donovan reaches into my takeaway box to retrieve a piece of chicken that he dropped, I feel my phone vibrate.

"Is that your friend who didn't show?" he says as I tap the screen to read a text from Nana. She's staying at her sister's tonight.

"Didn't show?" I'm baffled for a moment, and then I realize that he's talking about Alex. "Oh, no." I dust my hands, which are slimed with salt and grease.

Donovan pulls his phone out. "Oh, shit." He clambers to his feet. "Gotta go."

I think back to when I volunteered last week. Apart from Donovan annoying me, I actually had a good time. It took me back to those good days when I used to volunteer.

I stand. "Actually, I've changed my mind. I think I will volunteer tonight."

Donovan squints at me. "I thought you had a job interview to prepare for?"

I shrug. "It isn't till next Monday."

"Cool, cool. But we gotta walk fast, yeah."

I throw my takeaway box into a nearby bin.

"Admit it"—Donovan turns to walk backward, his gold chain bouncing with every step—"you're coming because you enjoy my company, innit?"

"Oh, please. Get over yourself."

He tosses his head back and laughs, and without meaning to, I notice his dimples.

If you want my honest opinion . . .

FRIDAY

RACHEL

Hey chicas

Just wondering

How's plans for my bridal shower going?

Don't forget

I want a classy afternoon tea party

Lots of champagne

Bottomless

RACHEL

Err, guys, it's been over an hour

Why hasn't anyone replied to my message?!!!

"Shouldn't you be up there?" I say, nudging Rachel. But she is busy eyeing Petros—a dark-haired, sculpted god of a man with dewy, olive skin—who is currently doing his best catwalk for Nana.

This room is hardly the Ritz. Despite stacking the chairs and pushing the tables against the walls, the walkway is still narrow. But until Nana hears back from any of Aunty Blessing's wealthy friends, a twenty quid per hour office at a local charity will have to do.

Rachel pulls one of her spiral curls. "Hun, my spot is guaranteed. Besides, I don't want to intimidate all these wannabe models."

I snort, then cover my mouth. Nana told us off earlier for being too loud.

I look around. On one side of the room are five women with different complexions and body shapes, and on the other side are five equally diverse men. Inspired by Rihanna's Savage X Fenty fashion show, Nana wants her models to represent as many people as possible. For the past ten minutes, she has called them one after the other to do the catwalk, while energetic Afrobeats plays in the background.

Checking Nana's not watching us, I lean toward Rachel. "How's wedding planning going?"

Rachel drags her eyes from Petros's bum. "Most of the important stuff is sorted, except for my dress. You're still able to come wedding dress shopping next Monday, right?"

My interview flashes to mind. Though I should be done by then. "Wouldn't miss it," I reply.

"Now, where are you guys at with planning my bridal shower? And why haven't you responded to my group message?"

"Don't worry, cuz. Ola, Nana and I are on it." That's if you can call setting up a separate WhatsApp group which we've barely used as being "on it."

"Ooh, speaking of Ola," Rachel says after she checks her phone. "She should be here any sec." She shifts a tentative glance at me. "You guys made up yet?"

I shake my head. "Not yet." Nana calls up the next model. "I was hoping to speak to her today. You know, in person." I rub my thighs. I hope I don't make a fudge of it.

"Okay, good." Rachel stops her handbag from sliding off her lap. "Because I don't want my bridesmaids bickering on my wedding day. Oh, and, what I said about Ola and Jon—"

"I won't say anything."

I return her smile, then shift my attention to the center of the room where an attractive model with voluminous red hair is strutting her stuff. A second later, the doorbell rings.

"That must be Ola." Rachel clambers to her feet.

"Let me get it." I jump out of my chair and power walk down the corridor, passing a kitchen where a cleaner is loading a dishwasher with mugs that were used earlier today.

The bell is still going. Through the glass door, I can see Ola's kids giggling. But where's Ola? I twist the lock and open the door.

"Aunty Yinka! Aunty Yinka!" The kids make a mad dash for my legs. The youngest, Daniel, is hugging one knee, while the middle child, Jacob, is squeezing the other. Ruth, the eldest of the bunch, wraps her arms around my waist, and I lower my head and peck her cornrows.

"Hey, sweeties," I say. "Where's your mum?" Jacob and Daniel completely ignore me and run into the building, Ruth tailing behind.

"Kids! No running, please!"

Ola's voice snaps my head around, and wow.

"Ola! Look at your hair."

For the first time in a long time, Ola has her natural hair out like the RnB singer Ari Lennox, only her afro puff ponytail isn't quite as long. I'm not used to seeing Ola without a weave. It's like we switched places.

"The kids aren't staying," she says, leaning in to my shoulders to give me the tiniest of hugs. "My mum couldn't babysit, and I needed a ride, so we had no choice but to bring the kids along." She slithers past me and I watch her ankle boots clack against the floorboards down the hallway.

"Yeah, sorry we're late." Jon appears by the entrance wearing a navy Barbour jacket and beige chinos.

"Oh, hey, Jon. How's it going?" I push what Rachel told me to the back of my mind. I give him a quick hug, then smooth my hand over my blouse to neaten it.

"I'm good, thanks," he says, then blinks. "Oh, wow, you changed your hair again!"

Right at the same time that he says this, I realize that the attractive model with red hair is now standing behind me, a cigarette and lighter in hand.

"Sorry, excuse me," she says. Jon and I step back so that she can pass. I look over my shoulder: Ola, kids in tow, is watching Jon like a hawk.

"Guys, say good-bye to your mum," he says.

Ola is a different person when she hugs her kids good-bye. She gives each child a loud, wet kiss and giggles.

"Come on, kids. Let's go." Jon is about to turn, then stops. "See you later, gorgeous." He kisses Ola on the cheek, and like a teenager she glances down, suppressing a tiny smile.

"Come on, kiddos. Let's get some McDonald's." Jon turns to leave as the kids break out in loud cheers. "Bye, Yinka."

"Bye, now." I close the door.

As I twist the lock, I think of my next move. It might be easier if I apologize. Keep it short and sweet.

"Ola." I turn around. "I'm—"

"Sorry," she finishes. *Wait, is she saying that she's—*

"I'm sorry," she repeats. "For overreacting, for how I behaved. I can be a right drama queen, can't I?" She looks sincere.

"No, I'm the one who should be apologizing. What I said at Nando's . . . it was insensitive and inconsiderate. But Ola, I didn't mean to be."

"It's okay." Ola shrugs and a stretch of silence follows.

Sooo, is this the part where we hug?

I test the waters by taking a step forward. Ola doesn't budge.

Fine, at least we've made a breakthrough. A small one, but still something.

"Where's Nana and Rachel?" she says.

"Follow the music." I smile.

The models have gone, and Nana has decided that since Ola and I are here, she might as well take our measurements for the bridesmaids' dresses. I'm up first and stand in the center of the room. Nana crouches in front of me, winding a measuring tape around my hips. *Thirty-eight inches. Hmm. Does this mean my bum is growing?* Ola and Rachel are sitting nearby, their feet propped up on a chair.

"How do you think the casting went?" Ola fluffs the end of her afro puff.

"Good," says Nana. "But I only liked a couple of the male models."

"Did Petros make the cut?" Rachel wails.

"Yes, Petros made the cut," Nana replies sardonically, and we laugh. "Well, I guess I can always ask my cousins," she adds, moving on to measure my height.

"Or"—Rachel quirks a brow—"you can rope in Yinka's lover boy. Hey, don't think I don't see you blushing over there."

I pull a face. "Rachel. I'm Black."

"Naw. You don't say."

"Lover boy?" Ola laughs. "So, what, you and Alex together now?"

"Not yet." I smile. "But we will be soon. Oh my gosh, Ola. I've got so much to tell you. Where should I start? Did Rachel tell you that we're following each other on Instagram?"

I whip out my phone with pride and excitement.

"*And* that's not all," I say after locating Alex's Instagram. I tell Nana to pause for one sec, then I hand my phone to Ola. "Guess who has a date?"

Rachel gasps.

"And not just on any day, but on Valentine's Day." After doing a mini-dance, I give the girls a full update of our conversation after church and meeting his mum—everything.

"Babes, this so exciting!" Rachel says. I can always rely on good ol' Rachel to be super-excited for me. "Seems like your new weave has given you confidence, huh?"

"More like your new look," Nana says under her breath, as she presses her measuring tape against Ola's leg.

I narrow my eyes at her as I sit down. "He complimented the dress you made, by the way."

I cross one leg over the other and turn to Ola, who now has a measuring tape around her waist. Like Nana, she doesn't seem that excited about my news. Instead, she keeps pursing her lips and she barely looked at Alex's Instagram before handing my phone back.

"Sooo . . ." I sway a little. "Any thoughts, Ola?"

"On what?" she says evenly.

"On what I just told you. Duh."

She pauses. "Yinka, if you want my honest opinion, something seems . . . off."

I'm so startled, I let out a laugh. "Sorry, what do you mean by *off*?"

"This . . . *crush* that you have on Alex. Not to be rude, yeah, but I think you're wasting your time."

"That was a bit harsh."

I'm surprised to hear that remark from Rachel.

"Rach, I'm only looking out for my cousin," Ola says. "I don't want her to get hurt."

I fold my arms. "You think he's too good for me, don't you?"

Ola hisses. "Now don't you go putting words in my mouth. I just think you're getting *way* ahead of yourself."

"Way ahead of myself? Ola, what are you talking about?"

She shrugs. "I think you're reading into things, no offense. Like this *date*, for example. Is it really a date?"

"It's on Valentine's Day!" I protest.

"And you're the one who has to cook?" Ola frowns. "Surely, he should be the one trying to impress you."

I sigh. Clearly, she hasn't been listening. Because if she had, she would have picked up that Alex and I banter about my cooking skills. I breathe in and out a few times. *Remember what Rachel told you. She's got her own insecurities that she's dealing with right now.*

"So how come he told his mum about me?" I say, unable to stop myself. "When I met her, she already knew my name."

Nana has finished measuring Ola, and they both drag a chair to sit opposite me and Rachel.

Ola picks at the gel flakes along her sideburns. "But you said that just before you met her, Alex met you at the lobby to give back your jacket, right?"

I nod.

"So, did it not cross your mind that your name was only brought up to his mum when he was going to return your jacket?"

I glance down. I didn't even think about that.

Ola laughs. "Oh, Yinka. See, this is what I mean. You're reading into things. I just want you to be careful. What do you think, Nana? You've been awfully quiet." She turns to her.

Nana looks at me, then back at Ola. Eventually, she says, "I think we should just wait and see how this all works out."

"Well, don't say I didn't tell you." Ola gets out her phone, probably to go on Instagram.

I'll prove you wrong, I want to say to Nana and Ola. *Especially* Ola.

"Oh, ignore these Debbie Downers." Rachel flicks her wrist and I give her a grateful smile. "As for me"—she points to her chest—"I'm down for the romance. But are you *really* going to make Nigerian food?" She lets out a raven-like cackle. "Because the last thing you want is to send him to the toilet."

I laugh nervously as I think back to the jollof rice I made yesterday. Let's just say I sent *myself* to the toilet. Despite following a recipe that I'd found online, it came out all starchy and soft, and because I forgot to remove some of the seeds from the Scotch bonnets, my tongue is still paying the price. "Actually, I was wondering . . ." I turn cautiously to Nana. She was at her sister's yesterday, and thankfully, didn't see my disastrous attempt.

Nana stares at me for a second, then blinks. "You want *me* to cook?"

"Not cook. Just, you know, help a little."

"I might be busy," she says.

"*You?* On Valentine's Day? Come on, Nana." I laugh. "You and I both know that you're free this Sunday. And Saturday. And didn't you say that you'd cook for me as part of our deal for you to move in?"

Nana narrows her eyes a fraction. "Oh, I thought you wanted me to move in for another reason."

I purse my lips. Okay. Let me not push it, in case she outs my redundancy.

Rachel looks perplexed. "You're a good cook, so . . ." She swivels her eyes as she waits for Nana to answer.

"Because—" Nana lets out a quiet growl.

"Don't forget, this is part of Yinka's bridesmaid's goal," Rachel says while Ola continues to scroll through her phone. "You want Yinka to bring a plus one to my wedding, right?"

"All right. Fine." Nana gives in with a huff. "I'll help you. But just this once."

I squeal, jump out of my seat and squeeze her from behind. "Thank you—ooh, and a tiny request," I say after remembering something extremely important. "I know you Ghanaians make your jollof out of basmati rice, but tomorrow, can we, err, stick to long grain, please?"

A romantic

SATURDAY

ALEX

Hey

We still good for lunch tmrw?

I won't judge if u decide to drop out lol

YINKA

What foolishness!

Òdè

ALEX

Ah! My girl be practicing Yoruba now!

Okay. I see you lol

And that wasn't very nice, was it 🙁

YINKA

Pèlé

Ẹ má bínù

ALEX

Lool

Apology accepted. You're forgiven

But only if your cooking is 5 stars 😩

"Err, Yinka? The last time I checked, this was *your* date, not mine. Quit faffing about," says Nana.

"I'm sorry," I say as I hover my phone over the steel pot. The smell of spice and peppers tickles the back of my throat. I take a few photos of Nana as she stirs the tomato puree and knob of butter into the frying diced onions. I'm very careful not to get her in the shot, just the wooden spatula. "It's for my Insta Story. I need photographic evidence. You know, in case Alex tries to say that I didn't make the jollof rice."

Nana scoffs. "But you're not helping me, are you?"

"Hey, that's not fair! I chopped up the tomatoes and the peppers, didn't I?"

Nana stops stirring. "You know I don't have to do this, right?"

I put my phone away. "What do you want me to do next?"

"Pour in the mixture from the blender. Then wash some rice. Please."

I grab the jug of blended tomatoes, red peppers, garlic and onions, and pour the red mixture into the sizzling pot.

"Thank you," says Nana as I fetch a bag of long grain rice from the cupboard. I pour a generous amount into a pot, fill it with cold water, then roll up my sleeves. I wash the rice, rubbing the grains between my palms until the water turns cloudy.

After too long a moment passes, I say, "Nana, can I ask you something?"

"Go for it."

"I'm not coming for you, but I really want to know why you are so against my plan. I'm finally back on the dating scene. Surely, I need to be at my best."

"But why do you need to change yourself?" she says. "Why do you think you're not good enough for Alex the way you are? If you do get together, are you going to keep up this 'new' you?"

I tip away the cloudy water and run the tap for a second rinse. "What I'm doing is no different from somebody bluffing their way to get a job—"

"And that *is* okay?" she asks as she places a number of seasoning jars on the counter.

Uh, yes. "Bad example. You know what I mean."

The rice now washed, I place the pot on the stove and fill it with some hot water from the kettle. Meanwhile, Nana unwraps a cube of Maggi stock and crumbles it into the stew with the tips of her fingers.

"I know you're thinking I'm being an uptight—*thyme,*" she says, beckoning, and I hand the dried herbs to her. "I just don't want you to think that you're not beautiful enough. Social media has got people twisted, thinking that they have to look a certain way—three bay leaves, please. Thanks. Yeah, so as I was saying, how do you know that this plan of yours isn't a slippery slope to a more drastic change?"

"A more drastic change?" I let out a loud snort. Then I quickly take a few more photos to add to my Insta Story.

"It's true!" Nana stirs in some curry powder. "That's how these things happen—gradually. I mean, no one wakes up one day and suddenly decides to bleach their skin or get bum injections. Nah, those insecurities have been festering for a while."

"Whoa, whoa, whoa. Now you're getting ahead of yourself. Skin bleaching? Bum injections? I would never."

"I'm not saying that you will. I'm saying—What I'm saying is—urgh, it doesn't matter. We're going to leave the stew to simmer for a bit. Yinka, keep an eye on that rice. We want it parboiled, remember?"

"Sure. One sec." I jab my fingers on my phone, thinking of a caption to add to my Insta Story. How about . . . **Jollof in progress.**😍 Post.

I stuff my phone in my back pocket. When I look up, Nana is glaring at me.

"I hate that you've joined Instagram."

I pull a face. "Well, I hate that your room is messy."

She rolls her eyes. "Okay, next thing. The spicy baked chicken. Can you wash the chicken, please?"

I grab the lemon juice from the fridge, and Nana hands me a tray of raw chicken. I'm pleased to see that they're all drumsticks. That's my girl.

I douse the chicken with a generous amount of lemon juice. "Did you really have plans for tomorrow? You know, for Valentine's Day?"

"Yes," she says without hesitation, and my mouth drops.

She laughs. "Don't worry. I only planned to go to the gym."

"The gym? On Valentine's Day?"

Nana leans against the radiator and shrugs. "Yinka, I told you I'm happy on my own. I'm really not fussed about getting into a relationship."

"Nana, when have you *ever* been fussed about being in a relationship? I mean, there was that one guy in college, but that lasted, what, a month? And that fling you had when you went to Barcelona for your twenty-first—"

Nana laughs and looks at her chipped black nails. "I'm aromantic."

"Oh, please. You're not a romantic."

"No, *aromantic*," she enunciates. "It's an orientation."

I blink at her.

"People like me don't really experience romantic feelings. We're not fussed about getting into relationships."

"Oh, wow. I never knew that was a thing. I mean, I've heard of asexuality. But that's lack of sexual attraction, right?"

Nana nods. "Don't worry, I only found out about the term the other day. Someone posted about it on Twitter, and I was like, wait a minute, that is so me."

"Have you told anyone yet?"

In her usual casual way, Nana says, "A few. My sister. My parents—"

"Your parents? What did they say?"

Nana shrugs. "'Well, that's the way God made you. That explains things. As long as you're happy.'"

I stop slathering the chicken. My mum would have a heart attack. Then after recovering, she'd call a prayer meeting. "Wow, I don't know what to say . . . Are you okay?"

Nana laughs. "Girl, bless you, I'm relieved. I always knew that there was something different about me. It sounds weird, but I really can't wait to start telling people."

"But what if you never experience love? Well, in a romantic sense."

Nana shrugs. "You can't long for what you don't long for, right? And that's the thing, Yinka, I don't feel like I'm missing out. If anything, I feel . . . free. I don't have to feel sad when I see my friends settling down. I don't get jealous when I see couples out and about on Valentine's Day. And it's not as though my parents are pressuring me to get married." She laughs. "They gave up on that dream a *long* time ago. So, yes, tomorrow I'm spending Valentine's Day at the gym and I couldn't be happier."

"Well, good for you," I say, putting the tray of chicken to one side. Maybe that explains why Nana is so against my plan; she can't relate to my feelings. I squirt two pumps of handwash before scrubbing my hands.

"Anyway, Rachel's bridal shower. Have you seen Ola's WhatsApp messages? She's made a to-do list."

"Oh, did she now?" I grab the napkin that is draped over the oven handle. "There's so many messages, I can't keep up."

Nana laughs. "Yeah. Don't tell Rachel. But I actually put her group on mute."

I gasp. "Nana. If she finds out, she'll kill you!"

Some men don't know a good woman even when she's right in front of them

SUNDAY

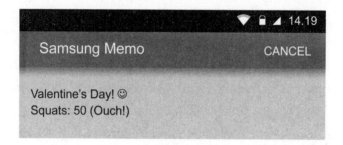

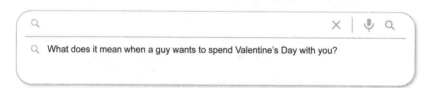

"Get long weave. Check. Look stylish. Check, check." I scan the Post-it notes on my bedroom wall, then look over at the purple ankara jumpsuit that I'll be wearing to church later on. I pinched it out of Nana's wardrobe the night she stayed at her sister's. God forgive me.

"Learn how to make Nigerian food. Hell, yeah!" With a triumphant smile, I draw a massive tick and a smiley face.

Nana and I spent close to three hours in the kitchen yesterday. We made jollof rice, gizzard with tomato stew, beef *suya* and spicy baked chicken. Although Nana did the bulk of the cooking while I passed her ingredients, I still think I'm allowed to take *some* credit. Not to mention, I chopped and fried the plantain *and* prepared the hard-boiled eggs for the Nigerian-style salad. They're all in the fridge now, covered with foil, ready to be heated up after church.

"Learn how to understand and speak Yoruba . . ." I wiggle my lips, then draw a question mark. I've been busy preparing for my interview and haven't consumed as many Nollywood films as I would have liked. Okay, okay, they were too long. Anyway, I've slipped a few Yoruba words into my WhatsApp messages to Alex, and he seems impressed.

Satisfied with the progress I've made, I move on to the next part of my plan. I scribble on a fresh pad of Post-its: "Questions to ask Alex." Now that I've won his attention, I need to find out where his head is at. Yes, he's showing signs that he likes me, but I need to hear him say so. But I can't just ask him outright. I need to be subtle. Clever. Discreet.

I write for a few minutes and stick each note onto the wall in a vertical line, then step back to review them.

1) So, Alex . . . what are your thoughts on Valentine's Day? Do you think it matters who you spend the day with?

Hmm. Maybe not . . . How about . . .

1) So, Alex . . . what are your thoughts on Valentine's Day? ~~Do you think it matters who you spend the day with?~~ Do you think the day has become over-commercialized or do you think it's still worth celebrating?

Yes. That's better.

2) You don't have a girlfriend. Oh, why is that? If you don't mind me asking.

I tap my chin. *Honestly, I see no problem with that. I'm just making conversation.*

3) So, what do you look for in a girlfriend then? You know, hypothetically speaking.

Whoa! Way too forward. That definitely needs revising. How about . . .

3) ~~So, what do you look for in a girlfriend then? You know, hypothetically speaking.~~ I hope you don't mind me asking, but when was your last relationship?

Perfect. And finally . . .

4) Do you like weddings? Because my cousin is getting married in July. It's an open invitation. Fancy coming?

I tear off the last one and scrunch it into a ball. *Too soon, Yinka. Too soon.* But the other questions will do for now. Hopefully Alex won't be too suspicious. Maybe he'll just proclaim his feelings for me without me needing to ask anything. The next stage of my plan sorted, I pick up my outfit by the hanger. Time to get ready for church.

Yinka, there is no way you made all of this food," says Alex as I place in front of him a steaming plate of jollof rice, red stew with gizzard, beef *suya* and fried plantain. "Tell the truth and shame the Devil. Your mum helped you, didn't she? She made the food and drove it here last night."

"No." I laugh as I set down the salad bowl on the kitchen table, where I have laid out my best Ikea table mats. "Trust me, Alex. She did not. She didn't even know we were having lunch today, couldn't you tell?"

We had bumped into Mum after the service. When Alex proceeded to tell her that we were having lunch at mine and that I had cooked Nigerian food, I swear Mum's eyes expanded like fried puff-puff.

Alex laughs. "Just kidding. Besides, I saw your Insta Story yesterday, when you were preparing the food."

I hide a smile. *So, you've been watching my Insta Stories, yeah?*

After I place my own plate on the table mat, I slip into the opposite chair, trying my best not to wince from the burning pain caused by all the squats. No pain no gain, right?

"Do you want to say grace?" I ask as I fold a napkin over my thighs.

Alex says a quick prayer, and we say "Amen" at the same time.

As I open my eyes it feels as though I'm in one of those really good dreams that you never want to wake up from. Hot damn, Alex is looking extra fine today. His skin has a nice sheen to it—I can tell he exfoliates—and as always, his hairline is never out of place. I inhale. He smells like what I think Idris Elba would smell like.

"Now—" Alex cuts through my wandering thoughts—"let's see if this food is as good as it looks."

Yes, yes, yes! After every mouthful of food, Alex nods and says a variation of, "Wow. This is good." He's already halfway through his plate, which is impressive given that he's done most of the talking. He's going on about how much he loves his job, which is fine, just not something I know much about. And it's not exactly Valentine's Day conversation, is it? How can I divert him from meta keywords and URLs, and get him on to my Post-it questions?

"Wow, you *really* do love your job," I say as I refill his glass of water while inwardly admiring his checked shirt. Look at me being such a multitasker.

"Sorry." Alex looks embarrassed. "I just realized I've been chewing your ear off—"

"No, it's fine." *You can nibble my ear any time.*

"So how's your job going?" Alex dabs the napkin around his lips.

My job? Wait. Didn't I tell him that I was made redundant that first time we met? Or maybe not. I'm starting to lose track of who I have and haven't told. I push my chicken to one side. Regardless of how juicy it looks, I'm not going to risk eating with my hands.

"Yinka?"

"Sorry. Um, you know. Busy." I reach for my drink, my insides twisting, not quite knowing why I don't tell him the truth. For goodness' sake, I told Donovan that I lost my job and he's a pain in the arse. There's no shame in being made redundant. It happens all the time. Okay. Deep breath. I'm going to tell him. Now.

"My mum was super-impressed when I told her that you work for Godfrey & Jackson."

"Really?" *So what else have you told your mum about me?* I want to say, but instead, I mutter, "Actually, I was made redundant."

Alex stops chewing. "Ah, man. Sorry to hear that. When did this happen? Wait, didn't you just get promoted?"

I lower my gaze. "I didn't get a promotion. It's just been one big misunderstanding. And I really don't want to get into it right now, if that's okay?"

"Of course."

"It's not the end of the world. I have a few job interviews lined up. Well . . . one." I laugh. "It's a second interview, though." I smile confidently.

"I'm sure you'll get the job." Alex raises his glass like he's going to make a toast.

"Thank you." I return his smile, relieved that he doesn't seem freaked out.

"And that aside, you've done well for yourself."

"Oh, stop it," I say, meaning, *Carry on.*

"Nah, I'm being serious. You have a nice home. A degree from Oxford. And don't think that I didn't spot the Mercedes outside."

"It's not mine," I say, then seeing his confused face, "Just kidding. It is." *Stop with the jokes, girl. You're no Tiffany Haddish.*

"Seriously, Yinka, you've got a lot going for you." He looks around my kitchen as though mightily impressed with my monochromatic countertops. "And you're *single*?" He laughs. "How is that even possible?" *Ohmigod, he likes me, he likes me, he likes me.*

"What do you mean?" I ask. In an effort to appear casual, I lean forward to cup my chin in my palm, but my elbow misses the table and jabs me in the thigh.

"It's just hard to believe, that's all." Alex stabs his fork into his plantain. "You seem like you have your entire life put together, you know? You're a nice girl. You can clearly cook. You would think someone like you would have been wifed-up by now."

I take a long sip of water to hide my growing smile.

"Well, what can I say?" I put down my glass, and because I'm feeling confident, I add, "Some men don't know a good woman even when she's right in front of them."

My eyes widen. OMG. Did I just say that aloud?

But it is as though Alex has just slept through a fire alarm. He continues to chew his food, unfazed. "Hey, now. Don't go lumping us all in the same boat. Trust me, I know a good woman when I—"

He turns his head, distracted by a knock at the door.

Dammit.

"Sorry." Nana pokes her head, then materializes with her gym bag strapped over one shoulder. She's wearing a white cropped top under a short black hoody, and leggings with the words "Ivy Park" down the side.

She's in? I immediately think, followed by, *Oh, crap, I'm wearing her clothes.*

Her eyes narrow into a squint. Bummer.

"Sorry, just need to grab some water," she says, nodding to her bottle by the sink.

"Go for it," I shrill. "Oh, by the way, Nana, this is Alex." Alex has already risen to his feet. "Alex, this is Nana. My best friend and roomie."

Alex extends a hand. "Pleasure to meet you."

"Nice to meet you too." Then she says, "Well, let me not get in the way."

As she goes to grab her water bottle, I notice her bum in the skin-tight gym leggings, and cringe on her behalf. Us J-shaped girls can't get away with clothes like that.

"Don't worry, you're not disturbing us." Alex turns to me and says, "Wait, is this your fashion designer friend? The one who made your outfit at church last Sunday?"

"Yes, that's Nana." He remembered what I was wearing. "She also made this beautiful jumpsuit."

"You know, my mum loved that dress Yinka wore," Alex says over the sound of the running water. He turns to me. "This jumpsuit is dope too. I really like the fabric, the way the diamond patterns almost look 3D. It's so stylish and feminine."

"Thanks," Nana and I say at the same time.

Nana glances at me with narrowed eyes. She's going to make me pay for nicking her jumpsuit.

"Well, it was nice to meet you," she says, heading back toward the door.

"Do you have a website or something?" Alex says to her retreating back. "My mum's birthday is coming up and I would really like to buy her one of your designs."

"I don't have a website, sorry." Nana half-turns.

I leap up and drape a hand over her shoulder. "She's actually planning to launch her fashion business this summer."

"Well, in that case, you definitely need a website," says Alex, smiling brightly. He sticks out a hand. "Say hello to your new website designer."

"Huh?" Nana stares at his hand. Okay, she might be pissed off with me but there's no reason to be rude to Alex.

"I design websites for a living." He stuffs his hand back into his pocket. "And if you're launching a business, then you'll certainly need a website.

Actually, let me give you my business card." He pulls out his wallet from his back pocket. "Have a think about it and let me know if you have any questions."

"Alex is amaaazing," I say. Okay, I haven't seen any of his work, but I am sure it's fantastic. "He's super-talented."

Nana glances at her watch. "Um, sure."

Meanwhile, Alex is still rifling through his wallet. "I swear I had a card in here," he's saying. He pulls out a handful of bank cards. I catch a flash of his work ID. *Ooh. Nice picture.*

"Do you know what?" says Nana after another glance at her watch. "You don't mind giving your business card to Yinka, do you? It's just, I've got a train to catch."

"Sure, sure."

"Nice to meet you." She hoists her bag and I go after her.

"Nana," I hiss, just as she's about to open the front door. "I'm sorry I borrowed your jumpsuit without asking."

"Borrowed?" She jerks. "Yinka, you stole it!"

"I'm sorry." I look over my shoulder. I wish she would keep her voice down. "But would you have lent it to me if I had asked you?"

Nana sighs. "I've got a train to catch. Excuse me." She opens the door and slams it behind her.

I exhale. I still don't understand why Nana is so against my plan when it's clearly working. And I just got her a website designer. If I hadn't worn her clothes and name-dropped her, Alex wouldn't have offered. And I'm sure, if I twist his arm, he'll give her a discount.

When I return to the kitchen, Alex is still on his feet, only there's a white card in between his fingers.

"Found it," he says. "Just as the door slammed."

"Don't worry. I can give it to her."

Alex presses the card into my palm, and I feel a zap of electricity as his fingers touch mine. I take a quick glance at the card. *Fancy*, I think, admiring the gold calligraphy. I stuff it into the hidden pocket that Nana wisely sewed into the side of the jumpsuit.

"Shall we?" I say, gesturing at our seats. We return to the table. I clear my throat. "Sooo, you were saying?" I bat my eyelashes like they do in the movies.

Alex ruins the moment by furrowing his brows. "Um. What was I saying?" He looks to one side then breaks out into a laugh. "God, I've got such a bad memory." He picks up his fork.

Nooo, my brain says in a whiny voice. I swear he was just about to profess his feelings for me. (Nice going, Nana.) I can't bear another week in limbo.

"Okay, same question to you," I say. I bite the bullet and lean back. "You seem to have a lot going for you too. How come *you're* not wifed-up? I mean, hubbied-up. I mean—you know what I mean." *That's basically Question 2— nice work, Yinka.*

Alex holds the base of his glass. Then after what feels like a monumental silence, he says, "I'm single because I've been grieving," and I feel like the worst person in the world.

"Oh, gosh. Your sister. Of course you are. I'm so sorry."

"Don't worry." He bats away my floundering apologies. "The truth is, I'm actually ready to start dating again."

"You are?" I say this too loudly, but whatever. "I mean, do you have your eyes on anyone in particular?" Oops, I don't think that question was on the Post-it notes. Ah, well. "I dunno. Let's see . . . Vanessa?"

"Vanessa?" Alex's eyes pop out like a champagne cork. He laughs. "Yinka, she's like seventeen. Yeah, Vanessa is pretty, but come on, she's like my baby sis."

The corner of my lip quivers a little upon hearing the word "pretty." I try to reassure myself. Vanessa *is* pretty. I can't deny that.

"So let's say Vanessa was older . . . would you be interested?"

"I dunno. I'd go out on a date with her, maybe. But nah, she's too bubbly for me."

My belly contracts a little. Okay. I'm not a bubbly person. I still stand a chance.

And just as I'm about to ask him the subtle question, "*So what was your ex-girlfriend like then?*" Alex surprises me by saying, "Actually someone has caught my eye."

"Really?" I'm praying that my bulging eyes haven't given me away, but at this point, I barely care. This is the moment I've been waiting for.

"Yeah. In fact, someone I met recently," Alex says. "And I mean *verrry* recently." He flashes me a cross between a smirk and a knowing smile.

My heart thumps. "Are you going to tell me who it is?"

"Isn't it obvious?"

Why won't he just *say*? "So I'm guessing it's someone that I know, then?"

Alex nods slowly. "Yup, very close to home," he says, and I swear I feel my blood pressure sky-rocket to the roof.

"Okay. You're just going to have to come out and say it." I dump my napkin on the table, leaning back in my chair, trying not to grin too widely. "Who is this mysterious woman?"

Alex laughs. "Wow, I really thought it was obvious. Yinka . . . It's . . . Nana."

Complete shock takes over.

"Nana? What, you mean . . . *my* Nana? You mean, the Nana you just met five minutes ago?"

"I thought the business card move was a giveaway—"

"So that was a ploy?" I wail, my voice no longer my own.

"Yes and no." Alex chuckles. "I do want to make the website for her, though. Yinka, make sure she gets my business card, yeah."

What happens next, happens too quickly for my brain to catch up.

For weeks I have literally bent over backward to get Alex to notice me. I made a fucking plan out of Post-it notes, for goodness' sake. And my hair. God, I spent so much money on this weave. Too much money, which wasn't wise given I'm jobless right now. And the squats! My thighs are ridden with pain and lactic acid. And all that friggin' *yam.* In the space between Alex telling me that he likes Nana and his instructions to pass on his business card, my shock has transitioned to anger. I'm angry that I'm being passed over yet again. I'm angry that I've wasted my time. I'm angry that I'm not considered good enough.

"Well, she's aromantic," I say.

Alex is staring at me, confused.

"*A-ro-man-tic.*" I break down each syllable. "It means she's not into dating or romantic relationships."

Still confused.

With a sigh, I pull out my phone and enter "aromantic" into Google. "See, look." I hand Alex my phone.

"Oh," he says after staring at the screen for what feels like five minutes.

"So, yeah. Sorry." I am *definitely* not sorry.

Alex lets out a rueful laugh. "Well, it wasn't meant to be." He shrugs, picks up his fork and resumes eating.

I pick up my fork too, but I no longer feel hungry. I want to throw my goddamn plate on the floor.

He's not even that fit

I shut the door, and the house resounds with an eerie silence. It follows me upstairs as I crawl into bed, under my duvet and into a fetal position.

I don't know how I sat through the rest of that lunch. I barely listened as Alex talked about the history of Nigeria. Then the politics. Then the music. All I could think was, *Alex likes Nana?* on repeat. My head started to hurt with it all, and thankfully, after I yawned a couple of times, he got the hint.

As he left, he asked me if I wanted to go to his for lunch next Sunday, and I just about managed to reply, "I'll let you know if I'm free," though really I meant, *Hell, no. Do you think I want to sit down with you after this?*

"Yinka, it's been a pleasure," he said, giving me an awkward hug. "Honestly, I love your company. It's nice to have a new friend in London. Well, you're probably my only friend."

All along he saw me as a . . . friend!

And now I'm replaying every interaction I've had with Alex in my head: from our first meeting, his smiles, to meeting his mum and our playful banter. And our WhatsApp messages! I whisk out my phone, swiping my finger up frantically.

I blink. It's as though I'm seeing our messages for the first time.

He never explicitly asked me whether I would be up for going out that first Friday. I just assumed that he did because he asked me how I was spending my evening. And even if he *was* suggesting that we do something, he is new to London after all, and it was a Friday night!

My heart is beating fast as I scroll through our later messages. I spot all the emojis. The LOLs. Our back-and-forth banter. So all along, *all along,* when he was teasing me, he meant nothing by it. Or rather, he meant friendship by it!

Now my heart is drowning. No, no. I'm sure it wasn't in my head. It can't have been. It can't! What about that time he licked his lips at me, huh? Are you telling me his lips were just *dry*? And he liked my Instagram photos! I sit up and open the app, tapping each photo that he liked.

I gasp.

Nana's in the photo. And this one! And that one! Did he only like my photos because he liked Nana? My fingers are shaking now. I'm analyzing all the signs that I thought were signs.

Alex likes Nana? My Nana. The one who wasn't even done up or wearing makeup and had on those hideous, unflattering leggings. I mean, I would have understood if Alex said he liked Vanessa, at least that could easily be explained away: another Black man goes for a light-skinned, curvaceous woman. Surprise, surprise. It would have been a hard pill to swallow, but I've swallowed it before after finding out Femi got engaged to Latoya. But Alex likes Nana. My sister, Nana. The one with the same dark skin tone and body type as mine. And it is this that baffles me. *What is wrong with me? Why am I never good enough?*

It's this thought that spurs me out of bed.

I march right over to the wall and I rip off each Post-it note.

"How could I be so stupid?" I yell, my voice hoarse and gravelly as neon-colored squares flutter to the floor.

"Stupid, stupid, stupid plan." I tear a Post-it note into tiny pieces. "I'm obviously not lovable. Not good enough."

"Hey, Yinka! What you doing?"

I'm so fired up that I didn't even hear the front door or Nana stomping up the stairs and entering my room.

"He doesn't like me, okay!" I snatch another Post-it note from the wall. "He likes you, Nana. You!"

"He likes *me*?" Nana jerks. "What, *Alex*? Yinka, are you sure?"

"Sure?" I rip another Post-it note. "Yes, I'm sure."

"What? How? We've never even hung out."

"Nana, he friggin' told me." I'm shaking. I'm actually shaking.

Nana's face is filled with shock.

"Okay, Yinka. Calm down." She puts a hand on my shoulder. "Let's sit down on the bed."

We tread over the Post-its, the paper crunching under my feet, my breath coming thick and fast.

"Breathe," Nana says as we perch on the bed. "Now, tell me what happened," she says. My head is bowed and I'm staring at my jittery thighs.

"Take your time," she says.

When I tell Nana what Alex said about her, she scoffs, "You got to be kidding me. I was literally in the kitchen for like two seconds."

"Well, you made quite an impression," I say. "*And* he's been Insta-stalking you for a while." I explain about the photos.

"Oh, no," she says. "I feel awful."

"It's not your fault," I sigh. "Urgh, he never liked me from the start. Ola was right." Then I scrunch my hair and groan, remembering. It's Rachel's bridal dress appointment tomorrow. What will I tell them?

"Eff Alex, and eff what anyone else thinks," says Nana, brushing her locs from her temples. "And do you know what, Yinka? He not even that fit."

I laugh. "Okay, let's not lie to ourselves, but I appreciate your support."

"No really, he's not. You are so much hotter than him. And kinder and funnier and smarter." Nana's warm hand on my shoulder starts to calm me down, and a seed of guilt starts to grow.

"Sorry for stealing your jumpsuit. That was out of order. And in the spur of the moment, I blurted out that you're aromantic."

Nana makes a *psh* sound. "Seriously, hun. Don't sweat it. You actually did me a favor."

I give her a weak smile. "Oh, yeah, before I forget." I reach into my pocket and pull out Alex's business card. Nana shakes her head.

"Nuh-uh. I don't want that. Yinka, he hurt you."

I force the card into her hand. "Don't be silly. You can't launch a business and not have a website."

"Well, I'll design it myself on WordPress or something."

I shoot her a look. "Nana, just because you're good at designing clothes, doesn't mean you're good at designing everything. You should take the opportunity. Take it, Nana."

"Won't that be awkward?" She glances at the card for a full five seconds.

"You *need* a website," I point out sternly.

"Fine, I'll take it, but only so you don't have to look at it. I'm not promising I'll call him." She shoves it into her pocket.

"Now, what can I do to make you feel better?" Nana is rubbing small circles on my back as though I'm a little girl who's not feeling well.

"A hand with all this," I reply feebly. Nana furrows her brows then follows my gaze to the confetti-like mess on the floor.

"Well, I can give you two," she says, jumping to her feet. Then she pulls me up and I realize I feel weak in the knees.

"So, no more crazy plans, yeah?" says Nana with a teasing smile as we stoop to pick up bits of paper.

"Yes," I say gruffly. "I'm done. From now on, I'm going to focus on myself and go with the flow—oh, crap." I slap a hand to my forehead. "My job interview. It's tomorrow."

"Have you prepared?" Nana sits up on her haunches.

"I have," I say, reaching for the bin. I hold it out for her and she puts the bits of paper inside. "It's just . . . I'm just not in the right frame of mind, that's all."

"Well, that's another thing I can help you with," she says, and squeezes my knee. "I'll run through some practice questions. You're getting that job."

After we clear the mess and help each other to our feet, Nana gives me one of those hugs you need after a shitty day.

"I'm never changing myself again," I whisper into her shoulder.

"Good," she whispers, squeezing me. "Good."

My bad

MONDAY

NANA

Hey hun

How did the interview go?

I've texted Rach already but I can't make it tonight

Few people off sick. Have to cover

See you at home x

"This train terminates here. All change, please."

We've reached Stratford station, but I can't seem to move. I'm frozen. My brain on a loop.

Was my palm too sweaty? Should I have given more examples for that question about time management? And should I really have said that perfectionism is my greatest weakness? I mean, how clichéd.

While interviewer one (Tiffany) was bright and light-hearted, interviewer two (Kevin) was stoic as a stone. He kept giving me this glare, as though I was saying something wrong; like I was a fly that he was determined to squash. And I kept stuttering! My God, since when did I have trouble saying the word "strategic"?

I lift my chin.

Please, Lord. Let me get this job.

I make my way to the exit and tap my Oyster card on the sensors, rushing through the barriers before they promptly shut again. Outside, the cold air smacks me. I walk across the bridge, zigzagging between the crowd of shoppers making their way into or leaving Westfield shopping center, its glassy paneled exterior shining like the Louvre.

I'm nervous about seeing Rachel and Ola. My big mouth just had to tell them about my stupid date. Which ended up not being a date.

I reach the bridal shop and push the door open. A feeling of déjà vu hits me, nearly as strong as the bright, artificial lights. It wasn't too long ago that I came here for Kemi's dress fitting.

The sales assistant is on the phone, so I look around at the wedding dresses on the racks and in the window display. Beads and lace and every shade from white to red. I used to have so much faith that I would wear one of these some day. But now, I'm not too sure.

"Congratulations!" says the woman, giving me a sunny smile.

"Oh . . . no. I'm here for my cousin. Rachel. Rachel Adeyemi?"

"So sorry. First day." The woman blushes and taps on the screen. "Okayyy . . . Rachel Adee . . . sorry, can you spell her last name, please?"

After the woman locates Rachel's booking on the system, and apologizes multiple times—"Sorry, the system is slow"—she leads me to the back, through a tunnel of white dresses.

Finally, we reach a wide space divided into sections where excited brides-to-be are twisting and turning in front of giant mirrors. At the very end is Ola, sitting on a velvet chair, her phone pressed to her ear. I thank the shop assistant as she leaves. Rachel must already be trying something on.

"Hey." I wave, sitting on the velvet stool opposite.

Ola doesn't acknowledge me. "Yes, I know I should have asked you first," she's saying to someone over the phone.

I wrestle out of my coat, then tug on the band of my pencil skirt.

"But come on, put yourself in my shoes." Ola's voice has risen a notch, and I take this as a signal to sit down and reach for a wedding magazine. Then in true British fashion, I turn a page, pretending that I'm not blatantly eavesdropping.

"Sorry, how was I supposed to know that she was—Look, babes. I'm sorry"—she drops her voice—"I shouldn't have jumped to—But after what I found out, can you really blame me? Anyway I'm out with the girls now. We'll talk properly when I get home. Yeah, around nine. Okay. Bye."

She ends the call and even over the gushing chatter of nearby customers, I hear her breathe out through her nose. I wait two whole seconds before looking up.

I decide not to mention the call. "Sorry, I'm a bit late," I say. "How's Rachel getting on?"

Ola makes a noncommittal sound. "Let's just say this will be the fourth dress." She fluffs her natural hair, which I'm surprised she hasn't changed yet. "She thinks they all make her look fat."

"But they do!" Rachel's voice comes from behind a curtain. Then a moment later, "Ohmigod."

"What happened?" I yell as Ola and I jump to our feet.

"*This* happened." The curtains swoosh apart.

Rachel trots in front of the giant mirror and beams, a sales assistant carrying her train behind her. She's wearing a full-on princess dress puffed out with lots of tulle and organza, and the sweetheart neckline is doing wonders for her boobs.

"Rachel, you look amazing," I squeal, while Ola cries, "Babe, this is the dress."

"I really like it," says Rachel, looking over her shoulder at us.

"Me too." I fan my face. I suddenly feel hormonal. Of course I'm happy for my cousin, but it's hard not to feel sorry for myself after yesterday. What if I really am destined to be alone? I try to squash the thought down.

"So, Yinka, how was your Valentine's Day?"

Perfect timing. How does Ola do it?

"Oh, yeah!" cries Rachel. She stops faffing with her tiara. "How did the lunch date with Alex go?"

"Go on, Yinka. Tell us about this daaate," says Ola, laughing smugly like a cheerleader. My face goes poker, but I'm sizzling inside.

If only you knew what I know about you. That would wipe the smirk off your face.

"Well, it was great." The words shoot out of me. "Alex even invited me for lunch at his this Sunday. He's going to cook. And guess what? He said I'm wifey material. Yup, I know," I add in response to Rachel's gasp. "Only thing is, his sister passed away not too long ago, so we agreed to, you know, take things slow."

It feels like an out-of-body experience, hearing myself lie. Feeling my tongue move at super-fast broadband speed.

"Yinka, this is such good news," Rachel says, clapping her hands. "Well, obviously, not his sister passing away. But the second date. And the compliments!" She fans her face and pretends to get choked up. "Oh, I feel like such a proud mum."

I deliberately avoid Ola's gaze, my senses returning to my body to pick up the debris. "Like I said, his sister passed away recently. He might not be ready for a relationship—"

"Don't jinx it!" Rachel slaps my arm. "Girl, you need to stay positive." She swerves to Ola and says, "Seeee. I told you the date would go well."

Ola and I lock eyes, and the first thing my brain thinks is, *Ha, who's laughing now!* Ola's smirk is well and truly gone.

"Well," she says eventually, "I guess the two of you proved me wrong. My bad, Yinka. Aww, Rach. I really love this dress on you." She spreads her arms wide and gives her BFF a hug.

March

Tuesday, 2 March at 11.03 a.m.

From: Howell, Cara

To: Yinka Oladeji

Subject: Vice President Operations position at Oscar Larsson

Dear Yinka,

Thank you for applying for the Vice President Operations position here at Oscar Larsson and sorry for the time it has taken us to get back to you.

While my colleagues were impressed by your CV and you clearly showed potential in the interview, we have decided to go with another candidate.

Although we will not be proceeding further with your application at this time, we welcome you to re-apply for a managerial position if you see any relevant listing in the future.

Thanks again for applying and all the best for the future.

Cara Howell

Human Resources Manager

Thursday, 11 March at 3.55 p.m.
From: Green, Sarah
To: Yinka Oladeji
Cc: Shane, Dave
Subject: Update

Hi Yinka,

Apologies for the delay in getting back to you. It's been a manic time! Yes, I managed to chase down HR at Citi. Sadly, they've decided to go with an internal candidate, I'm afraid. But they said they will keep your CV on file for the future. I know this is upsetting news and not what you want to hear, but hopefully we'll hear back from the other employers I put you forward for.

In other news, I got a new job! My last day in the office will be next Friday. But I'll be leaving you in the capable hands of Dave Shane, who I've cc'd in. He'll be your main point of contact going forward and he should be in touch in a few days to arrange a call with you. He's got your details, so no need to send.

Wishing you all the best for the future.

Best wishes,
Sarah Green
Recruitment Agent
Catasift Recruitments

Thursday, 11 March at 3.58 p.m.
From: Oladeji, Yinka
To: Dave Shane
Subject: Update

Hi Dave,

Hope you're well. And nice to virtually meet you!

Further to Sarah's e-mail below, I wondered when would be a good time to catch up? It would be great to know whether there are any openings you think that I'd be suitable for. Also, do you have any updates on my other applications?

If you want to give me a call, I'm available all day.

Best wishes,
Yinka

Thursday, 18 March at 12.44 p.m.
From: Oladeji, Yinka
To: Dave Shane
Subject: Update

Hi Dave,

Hope you're well.

I was wondering if you received my e-mail below? Before Sarah left, she said you'd be in touch to arrange a time for us to speak. Is it possible to arrange this in the next few days? As you can understand, I'm really keen to get an update on my outstanding applications, as I haven't heard from any other employers as of late.

Hope to hear from you soon.

Yinka

Thursday, 18 March at 12.44 p.m.
From: Shane, Dave
To: Yinka Oladeji
Subject: Automatic reply: Update

Thank you for your e-mail. I am on holiday for the next two weeks with no access to my inbox. I'll respond when I'm back.

Cheers,
Dave

"For flip's sake!" I thump my bed. Breathing heavily, I click "reply."

Thursday, 18 March at 12.45 p.m.
From: Oladeji, Yinka
To: Dave Shane
Subject: Automatic reply: Update

Hi Dave,

You stink at your job! Next time you want to bugger off, include
a point of contact! I hope it rains where you are!

Cheers,
Yinka

I breathe out, remembering how it used to feel at Godfrey whenever
someone sent me a rude e-mail. Then slowly, and ever so carefully, I click
"delete."

April

I'm happy for my friend

WEDNESDAY

RACHEL

Hey cuz

How are you? Are you feeling any better?

Don't worry. You didn't miss too much yesterday

Will post an update in the WhatsApp group, including when the next bridal meeting is

Rest up xx

I'm happy for my friend. I'm happy for my friend. I'm happy for my friend.

These are the words that I keep telling myself every time I glance over at Joanna and her new man Brandon, who are sitting directly opposite me and having a hard time keeping their hands to themselves.

It's the first time I've agreed to come out since the Valentine's Day fiasco and I'm already regretting it. We're at this nightclub in central London: me, Joanna and Brandon, Brian and his partner, Ricky, and Nana, and we're celebrating Joanna's new job. She's been offered a position as the PR manager at a tech company and she starts next month. With the new job, she gets unlimited holiday, free granola bars, and the company even has an office dog.

Meanwhile, the only blessing in my life these last few weeks has been the latest season of *Insecure*. And Mum's lack of contact. A few weeks ago, she broke her phone, and since Carphone Warehouse no longer sells the old Nokia model she's been using since the nineties, she had, after much persuasion, left the store with the latest iPhone. According to Kemi—who's still having frequent dinner dates with her—Mum is having a hard time adjusting to touchscreen.

They've both been *very* busy getting things ready for the baby—my God, I can't believe Kemi is due any day now—which I guess I can count as a blessing, as Mum hasn't even been in touch to ask how the date with Alex went. I've stopped attending her church, so maybe she's forgotten. I'm so glad I never told Kemi anything.

"So, Yinka," says Brandon, projecting over the cheesy pop music, which has sent many people to the dance floor. True to the photo that Joanna showed me, Brandon has spiky ginger hair, apple-green eyes and a body of a rugby player. "What do you do?"

"I'm unemployed," I say bluntly.

"Oh . . . cool." Funny enough, Brandon looks more uncomfortable than me. Then after a long pause, he adds, "What's the reason? You taking a career break?"

"No," I say matter-of-factly. And I leave it at that.

Brandon scratches the back of his neck. He smiles awkwardly. "What's that you're drinking there?"

I lift my glass. "Oh, this? Tap water."

Brandon throws back his head and laughs.

"It's the only thing I can afford," I say with a deadpan expression.

"Oh, sorry. Let me get you a drink."

"It's fine. I'm only teasing. It's lemonade. But I am unemployed, though. Didn't make that bit up."

"Oh, my God, I love this one! Who fancies dancing?" says Joanna, the girl who never dances. Drink still in hand, she pulls Brandon from his seat, her skater dress twirling as she cha-chas away. Brandon looks frankly relieved to be taken away from me. Brian is next up. He doesn't drag Ricky with him because he hates dancing.

"Girls?" Brian looks over his shoulder.

Nana turns to me with an "I'd rather watch paint dry" expression.

"We're going to wait until they start playing RnB and hip hop," I say.

Ricky shakes his head as Brian pushes his way through the crowd.

"What is he like?" Ricky says as he scratches his stubble. "Anyway, you girls fancy another drink?"

"I'm good, thank you," I say after Nana politely declines. Ricky heads to the bar.

I'm glad that Nana and I are alone, there's so much that I want to talk to her about. She's been so busy working—sometimes I hear the drill of her sewing machine well after midnight—that we haven't been able to catch up as much these days.

Fine, if I'm honest it's more than that. She's been off with me ever since I told her that I'd lied to Ola and Rachel about Alex.

"Yinka! This is getting absolutely ridiculous," was what she actually said when I admitted it. "All this lying! I thought you were a Christian."

"I'm human!" I snapped back. "Ola was being really snarky. And technically, I didn't lie. I just . . . exaggerated the truth a little."

But it was when I asked her to back up my story that she really blew up.

"You want me to tell the girls *what*? That you lied about how the date really went? Or about the fact that you didn't actually get the promotion? Or maybe even about your extreme transformational plan?"

"Hey, that's not fair," I cut in, wounded. "I didn't ask to lose my job. And you were there when I abandoned my plan! And it's not exactly easy saying, oh, by the way, the person I really liked, likes my best friend."

The silence that followed was astronomical.

Finally Nana sighed. "I just thought, I dunno, you would have told the girls that Alex likes somebody else or something like that. We're all supposed to be friends. We're supposed to be honest with each other."

"I will tell Rachel and Ola in my own time."

"Please do, Yinka. For your own sake."

But I still haven't. And since I heard that I didn't get the Oscar Larsson job, Nana seems to be giving me a break. But she's also clearly not forgiven me.

I sidle closer to her. The music is so deafening that I'm going to have to speak right in her ear.

"How's the website going?"

She turns from the throng. There are a lot of comically drunk people on the dance floor who suddenly think they can bust a move.

"Great," she says brightly. "Alex is good at what he does. I'm not going to give too much away, though. You'll see the website when it's done."

I nod in time with the music, which is again another pop song. Sigh.

"And how's the working relationship?" I ask after a tentative pause. I mean it genuinely—I don't care about Alex any more. He's in the past.

Nana shrugs. "It's not awkward, if that's what you're hinting at. It's all strictly profesh. Althooough, he does ask about you from time to time."

I roll my eyes.

True to his word, Alex invited me to his place for lunch, the Sunday after Valentine's Day. Amicably, I declined his offer. I told him that I was now attending a local church, shorter commute and all that. Still, he continued to WhatsApp me. And because I didn't want him to get suspicious, I continued to reply. But when he asked me out for a drink the next Friday, I knew I had to break contact. So I sent him a voice note explaining that I was too busy and stressed with job hunting to do anything at the moment, and that I'll let him know when I'm free again.

"We missed you yesterday," says Nana, grabbing the wheel of our conversation. In response to my frown, she clarifies. "Rachel's bridal meeting. How come you couldn't make it? Anything to do with your little white lie?"

"No! I had a headache."

Nana doesn't even try to hide rolling her eyes. "Rachel kept asking me about the latest with you and Alex—"

"What did you say?" My voice is so loud that it actually causes a passing man to look over his shoulder.

"I told them that we've both been so busy, that we haven't had a chance to catch up—"

"And what did Ola say?"

Nana folds her arms. "She didn't say anything. So you can stop looking at me like a fox caught in broad daylight. Honestly, Yinka, you can't avoid the girls forever. Rachel's bridal shower is this Saturday!"

To my relief, Rihanna's "Umbrella" starts playing—well, a weird remix version.

"Ooh, this is our cue." I pull Nana's arm. And despite her objections, I prod her along to the sweaty dance floor.

Weave out

FRIDAY

History	Ctrl+H

Recently closed
Good excuses for not going to a bridal shower—Reddit

"How're things going between you and Alex?" says Aunty Blessing as she hacks a blade at a piece of thread. It's déjà vu: once again, I'm sitting on the floor between my Aunty's legs in her living room, only this time, she's taking out my weave. "The last I heard, you said my advice worked and he was coming round to yours for lunch. I don't want to pry, but you never got back to me when I texted you about it."

"Yeah, well, things didn't work out," I reply. "Is it okay if we don't talk about it?"

"O-kaaay." Silence fills the room, save for the blade that she's sawing against the thread. "Talking of other things, a few of my contacts have come through. They've agreed to sponsor Nana's fashion show. Isn't that brilliant?"

"Yeah, Nana told me yesterday. Thanks again, Aunty."

More silence.

Aunty Blessing clears her throat. "Any update on the job front?"

"Nope." I emphasize the p. "No update since the wave of rejections I told you about. The recruitment agencies have gone quiet on me too."

"Have you chased them up?"

"One has gone on holiday. But yes, I've chased the others. Sometimes even twice a week."

"Hmm." Aunty Blessing tilts my head. "This is so strange. I thought with Godfrey on your CV, you would have got a job by now. Have you asked the interviewers for feedback?"

I let out a laugh. "Oh, yes, *I've asked*. Apparently there just happens to always be someone with more experience than me. I'm always *thiiis* close but never get it."

Aunty Blessing drops a weft of tattered weave onto my lap. It's lost its sheen. I dispose of it into a plastic bag, trying hard not to remember how much I spent on it.

"Well, you know what they say," she says, hacking at another thread.

"What, Black people have to work twice as hard?"

"No, well yes, but that's not what I was going to say." There's a pause. "What I was trying to hint at is . . . maybe these rejections are happening for a reason. Are you sure you want to stick with the investment banking sector?"

"Aunty, I'm not interested in working for a charity."

"I didn't say it had to be a charity. Just, maybe, a different sector." I feel the breath she puffs out on the back of my neck. "Now what does your mum think of all this?"

"What do you mean?" I'm praying that my wobbly voice doesn't give me away.

"You not having a job yet," she clarifies. "I imagine she's quite worried."

"Um . . . yeah," I say, grimacing. That's not exactly a lie—she's always worried about me.

I run a finger along my hair, touching the cornrows free from the weave. It's going to be so strange seeing my face with my short, kinky hair again.

"Yinka?"

Oh, no. Here it comes.

"I didn't want to offer if you'd decided to change sector, but I recently met a man who works for a boutique investment bank. Maybe I can ask him to pull a few strings?"

"Oh, would you?" I'm so excited I whip my head around.

"Of course," she says with a gentle smile. "I can't remember what his role is or the name of the bank for that matter, but I do know he's very senior. His name is Terry Matthews. I can't promise anything, but I'll have a word. In fact"—she rises to her feet—"I'll text him now."

I watch her bare feet patter over to the coffee table where her phone has been charging. She picks it up and types quickly. There's a strange smile on her face—one usually reserved for when you text a friend a witty comment or a funny meme.

Then something hits me. It's after nine. Quite late, in my opinion, to be texting someone you have a business relationship with. Unless you *don't* have a business relationship with them.

"Aunty"—I scratch my itchy scalp, doing my best to quell a growing smile—"sorry, how did you say you know Terry?" and knowing that she hasn't.

"Oh, at a networking event," she says coolly. "We exchanged business cards and kept in touch." She sets her phone back on the table, then without looking at me, returns to the sofa where she adjusts my head between her legs until she's comfortable.

Mmhmm. I smile broadly as she resumes. Who is she trying to fool?

After Aunty Blessing finishes taking my weave out, I stand in front of her bamboo mirror, tugging at my wispy dead ends, which are entangled with dandruff and old hair grease.

"I think my hairline has receded," I whimper. "Look." I press down my unruly hair and shove my forehead under her nose.

"You're just being paranoid." She laughs and flaps me away.

My protest is curtailed by my vibrating phone. In unison, we look down at the sofa.

It's Mum.

"I'll call her back later," I say at the same time that Aunty Blessing picks it up.

"Aunty—"

My mouth falls open as she answers it.

"Hello, Tolu. It's Blessing—Oh, wow! Yinka! Kemi's having the baby!"

This is your mess, not mine

By the time Aunty Blessing and I arrive at King's College Hospital, Mum has already christened the baby seven times: at one point, he was Olúwaṣẹ́gun, then later, Olàlàbí, then intermittently, Chinedu, an Igbo name that Uche and Kemi picked. The area surrounding Kemi's bed is packed, crammed with adoring visiting aunties sitting on chairs, which I'm still not sure are technically allowed to be removed from the waiting area. Aunty Debbie is standing at the foot of the bed, taking photos on behalf of Big Mama, who is happily chomping through her second packet of plantain crisps, content with admiring the baby from afar. I'm pretty sure we are causing a major fire hazard.

Sitting on the edge of the bed, Uche perched on the opposite side, I cradle an arm around my sister as she looks adoringly at their creation. The baby is so fair-skinned and tufts of silky, black hair sprout from his crown. I can't believe Kemi's a mum. My baby sister, a mum. The same girl that I used to pick up from school and help with her homework. Now she has an entire family. And as her older sister, I feel helpless that I can't offer her any advice. Just like when she was getting married, I'm useless. I didn't even get round to organizing our catch-up.

"You birthed a human being," I say, trying not to wallow in self-pity.

"I know!" Kemi says. "Sis, you should have seen me. I was screaming as if I was possessed or something."

"Please. *Abeg.* You're not possessed." Mum comes back in and swoons for the hundredth time. In an attempt to find better phone reception, she stepped out into the hallway to call family back home in Lagos and tell them the good news. Despite that, all we have heard for the last ten minutes is, "Hello? Hello? Can you hear me now?" and "Speak louder. I can't hear you."

"Uche was amazing." Kemi presses her clammy head against her husband's, and at this, Mum pats Uche's shoulders. "My son here was as calm as a swam."

"*Swan*, Mum," I correct her. Kemi laughs and Uche thanks his mother-in-law. It's a shame that neither of his parents got their visas in time. A new thought comes to me. "Mum, how was Daddy when you went into labor?"

Mum doesn't even bother to think about it. "I can't remember. *Oya*, everybody." She addresses the room. "Everybody, let us pray. We have to give thanks to God."

After Mum finishes an epic prayer—*No weapon formed against the baby shall prosper*—the midwife kindly asks that all visitors step outside so that she can show Kemi how to breastfeed the baby.

"I'll give you a hand," says Uche.

Big Mama cries, "Ah, what hand can you give her? Are you not a man?"

Everyone laughs, and leaves the ward as loud as they came in. Aunty Blessing and I are left to do the heavy lifting, and return all the chairs to the waiting area. There's a handful of other visitors in the room, and now we're all seated in our own small huddle while we wait for Kemi to finish feeding. Uche stayed in with her, despite Big Mama's jokes.

"Thank God for His mercies." Big Mama raises her palms skyward.

I shift my gaze from her scraggly toenails to see Mum frowning at me.

My stomach tightens. Uh-oh. I hope she's not going to bring up my job or ask me about Alex.

"Why did you go out with your hair like this, ehn?" she says, as though seeing me for the first time.

My insides relax.

"Tolu," Aunty Debbie says, pronouncing Mum's name like an English person and repeatedly tapping her on the knee. "You did it again. Earlier, you forgot to pray for Yinka."

Insides *clench*.

"It's okay," I say. "We're in public."

This doesn't deter Mum. "Ah! Yes! Funke, you're right. Yinka, I'll pray for you now."

"Make it brief." Aunty Blessing stashes her phone away.

I look around wearily. Fab. We've got an audience.

"Okay, quick prayer." Mum slaps her thighs and gets up. "Dear God," she says hastily, holding her hand in the air, and I'm so frustrated, I don't close my eyes. Instead, I fold my arms like a stubborn child, avoiding the stares of those nearby who are now more intrigued by our soap opera than the one on the TV screen. "Also bless my daughter, Yinka Beatrice Oladeji. Thank you for the blessings you have bestowed upon her in the last few months. From her job promotion to her new boyfriend, who we pray that by this time next year will be her *huzband*. In Jesus' name. Amen."

Mum's prayer is so quick that it takes me a second to react, and then another second to realize that Aunty Blessing is throwing daggers at me.

"That wasn't too long," Mum says, sitting down gracefully, clearly oblivious to her gawking audience.

"Yinka has a boyfriend!" cries Big Mama, shimmying her shoulders. "Ehhh! I didn't know. We thank God!"

"And a job promotion," says Aunty Blessing, cocking her head to one side. "Funny, because Yinka was at my place earlier and she didn't mention it."

"Um . . ." I fluff my hair, forgetting how dirty it is. I stare back at her. I'm trying to communicate with my eyes that I'm sorry and didn't mean to deliberately lie, and please don't throw me under the bus.

To my relief, Aunty Blessing doesn't say anything more. Instead, she turns her head as though to say, *This is your mess, not mine.*

"It's because Yinka is so modest," says Aunty Debbie, darting me a knowing smile. "She never likes to boast about her achievements. But with the baby not around to distract us, Yinka, now's your chance. So, how's the new job going, hm? Oh, and Alex?" She wiggles her brows. "The last I heard, your mum said you had lunch together—"

"Oh, yes!" Mum shuffles around in her seat. "I've been so busy with Kemi, I forgot. So what did you cook him, ehn? And why haven't I seen you at church?"

I look from Mum to Aunty Debbie, eager expressions on their faces. Big Mama stuffs a handful of plantain crisps into her mouth. I glance at Aunty Blessing again, but she looks just as keen to hear what I'm about to say. So does the elderly woman sitting nearby who has stopped reading and is openly staring.

Lying got me into this mess and lying won't get me out of it. Doesn't it say somewhere in the Bible that the truth will set you free? Or is that quote from *Liar Liar*? Either way, it's true.

"Ah, ah! Speak now!" Big Mama says impatiently.

I look down, take a deep breath, then glance up again. Here goes.

"Mum. Aunty Debbie." I look from one to the other. "I'm sorry, but I've got some bad news."

"Ah!" Mum shoots forward to the edge of the chair, her hands on her head wrap. "Bad news? Oh, God. What happened?"

"Alex doesn't like me," I say, ripping off the Band-Aid quickly, and Mum shrieks, "*Yeh!*"

"What do you mean?" cries Aunty Debbie, while Big Mama scoffs and then chokes.

"He likes someone else," I explain, my pits sweltering. "He told me. Over lunch. To my face."

"Oh, God!" Mum presses her palm to her forehead and shakes her head. "This cannot be happening. This cannot be happening."

Aunty Debbie narrows her eyes. "Who is she? Give me a name."

"I don't know, what does it matter." I bite my lips. "And that's not the only bad news."

"There's more?" Mum and Aunty Debbie cry at the same time.

I glance over at a very subdued Aunty Blessing, and she nods slowly. "Go ahead, Yinka."

"Wait, let me drink my water first," says Big Mama, pulling out an Evian bottle in an attempt to stop the choking.

I wait for her to take a big gulp before I speak. "Um . . . I didn't get a promotion," I confess, and there's a pantomimic gasp.

"You didn't?" says Aunty Debbie, clutching her invisible pearls.

I shake my head. "No. I actually lost my job. I was made redundant."

Aunty Debbie pinches her nose like she's about to cry. Mum gapes at me as though she's having a mini-stroke. Big Mama says, "Ohh, you lost your job. I'm sorry to hear that. Don't worry, God will provide," and tucks back into her plantain crisps.

"Ah, but this doesn't make sense now." Mum looks confused. "Back in January, you told me you got promoted. When did this all happen?"

I scratch my head. "Um, in January . . . a few days after Kemi's baby shower."

Mum catches her breath. "So you lied?"

"Not on purpose," I say, my voice a trembling mess.

"She was nervous to tell you," says Aunty Blessing, and she reaches over and places a hand on my knee.

"This is why things didn't work out with Alex," cries Mum, stabbing a finger at me. "You lied and God doesn't like liars."

"Mum!" I'm not even shocked by her over-religious response. "This is why I didn't want to tell you. I knew you would be disappointed, and I didn't want you to worry about me being unemployed. And technically, I didn't lie," I add before Mum can launch into her counter-attack. "When I told you I got the promotion, I actually thought I had got it. And maybe I should have told you straight after I got the news that I was being let go, but you went ahead and told Alex and you were so excited—"

"So this is your mother's fault, hm?" Aunty Debbie bites back like a chihuahua. Mum's reaction is more like a pit bull's.

"What have you been doing all this while you have been at home, ehn?"

"Er, applying for jobs." Shouldn't it be obvious?

"Everyone needs to calm down." Aunty Blessing races to my defense. "Don't worry, I'm making use of my contacts," she says. "I know someone who works in investment banking, and he's pretty senior too. Everything will be okay. Yinka will get a job. The earth will carry on spinning."

"And what about Alex?" Mum cries, still attached to her dream son-in-law.

"There's no Alex!" Aunty Blessing's voice rises. "For goodness' sake, Tolu. Alex isn't the only bachelor in London."

"But we're running out of time!" Mum's outrage fills the entire waiting area. Meanwhile, Aunty Debbie sits with her arms crossed as though no longer invested in the situation.

"It's okay. We will continue to pray now," Big Mama keeps saying in an effort to appease Mum.

"Yinka is thirty-one. Thirty-one!" Mum cries. "How long must I wait until she marries, ehn? Three? Four? Five years? *Oya*, where's my bag?" She swivels around and snatches it from the floor. "I'm going to call Aunty Chioma."

I have a flashback of Aunty Chioma at All Welcome Church, trying to set me up with her playboy son, Emmanuel.

My heart thumps. "Mum. Please don't call her."

But Mum is too busy rummaging for her phone.

That's it. I don't have to take this. Yes, I've lied, but I don't have to listen while Mum pimps me out.

I grab my coat and walk away. Thankfully, no one calls me back, but as I reach the door, I bump straight into Uche.

"Oh, I was just on my way to come and get you all."

Fighting back tears, I wrestle into my coat. "Sorry, Uche. I'm heading off now."

"Already? Oh, okay. I suppose it is late."

I glance down as I zip up my coat.

To my relief, all he says is, "Do you want to go and say good-bye to Kemi, then? I'll see you later."

He heads toward the waiting area, leaving me standing by the vending machine where above my head are two arrow signs—one for the maternity ward, the other for the exit.

I imagine that guilty look Kemi will give me if I tell her what just happened. And how I'll feel if I ruin her special day.

I keep my head down as I scurry toward the exit, texting.

YINKA

Sorry, sis. Desperately need to wash my hair lol

Sorry I didn't say bye. Congrats again x

Plan 3.0

OPERATION WEDDING DATE: MY PLAN TO HAVE A DATE FOR RACHEL'S WEDDING IN JULY!!!

OBJECTIVES	TASKS	DEADLINE	KPIs
1. Meet a guy virtually	• Sign up for online dating Hinge? Tinder? Christian Mingle?	ASAP!	• I meet a decent guy who is not a perv or a misogynist and is capable of holding a conversation • I do not get catfished
2. If all else fails, meet Emmanuel	• Ask Mum for Emmanuel's number and call him	Last resort	• We hit it off • He reassures me that he is not a player and that he's looking for a long-term relationship

Now look at what you've done

Hello. Hello, Yinka. I've been trying to call you. Why won't you pick up your phone, ehn? Anyway, I've texted you Emmanuel's number. Make sure you call him o! I don't want to hear any stupid nonsense, that he's not your type. You're getting old now. Beggars can't be choosers. And what are you planning to do now that you don't have a job, ehn? I can't believe you lied to me. Kai! May God forgive you. Do you have enough money? Please. Let me know o. Don't be suffering in silence if you're struggling to pay the bills. Anyway, give me a call when you get this. Ó dàbọ̀.

Today is Rachel's bridal shower, and all afternoon my mind spins anxiously. Have Ola and Rachel's mums already told them what happened? How will they react when I tell them the truth? Dammit. I knew I should have trusted my gut and told them before the shower. And will Mum ever let me forget that I lied to her? What if I exhaust every possible option and have no choice but to attend Rachel's wedding alone? What if I spend the rest of my life alone?

I shake my head to dislodge the thoughts. *Come on, Yinka. Be optimistic.* At least I know where I went wrong. I put all my eggs in one basket. I did it with Alex and that job at Oscar Larrson. Well, now I'm going to broaden my horizons. As discreetly as I can, I reach for my phone and open the Hinge App, which I downloaded last night. See, I've already got four notifications.

> Wassup baby. You look fine
>
> Do you taste like chocolate? Wink, wink
>
> You are my Eve and I am your Adam
>
> Sexy eyes

I blow out my cheeks and stuff my phone away. It's okay. It's hardly been twenty-four hours.

Sitting forward, I tune in to the chatter on my side of the table. Jasmine, the extrovert with Kate Middleton–esque brown hair sitting to my left, is talking.

"My husband proposed to me in the Lake District," she's saying. "Up in a hot air balloon."

I quickly tune out again.

I gaze around. Kudos to Ola for finding this place. It's one of those posh hotels with chandeliers and marble floors. You know, the ones with Baylis & Harding handwash in lavender-scented toilets. We have a private room booked for a few hours of afternoon tea and games. We've already done the games—"Guess Who Knows Rachel Best" and "Make a Wedding Dress Out of Toilet Roll"—and the speeches, to which Rachel and a couple of others shed a few tears, and now we're all just chatting around the table, eating leftover cake until we get chucked out. Only a few more minutes and I'll be able to escape.

I glance over at Rachel, sitting at the head of the table, which Nana and I decorated with confetti and mini pom-poms. She adjusts her bride-to-be sash and steals a tart from the cake stand.

"Cheat day," she says, holding the tart like it's a champagne glass. She mimics toasting to herself and scarfs it.

I smile. I'm not quite sure how much weight she has lost since setting her goal, but she looks great. And happy.

I look around the long table. Everyone is wearing either floral or pastel-colors. I must look gothic in my dark cocktail dress.

"You all right?"

Directly opposite me, Ola shoots me a look of concern. Today her natural hair is gelled back and held down with lots of pins.

"Yeah, I'm fine. Why?"

"You've been quiet, that's all."

"I think I'm coming on my period," I whisper.

"We're all girls here," she laughs. "Now eat up. Paid forty-five quid for this."

I force a laugh and pick up my brownie, my intestines knotting, as though I'm really having menstrual cramps. I don't *think* Aunty Debbie has told Ola about my nonexistent promotion. Or that things didn't work out with Alex. I chew miserably.

Right. As soon as the rest go home, I'm just going to tell Ola and Rachel the truth.

"So, who's next?" says Jasmine. She has been prying into everyone's love life for the last hour. And now she's started this stupid conversation about when everyone first met their other half.

Jasmine surveys the table. "How about you?" she says, nodding to Ola. "I see a ring on your finger. How did *you* and your husband meet?" She obviously only thinks hetero relationships count.

Ola picks up her teacup and blows over the rising steam. "At uni," she says.

"Oh, how sweet," says another girl called Gemma after Ola fails to elaborate.

"Very," Jasmine agrees. "So, how did he propose?" She bats her long lashes.

Ola has her hands clasped around her cup, still blowing over her tea.

I wonder what she's going to say. It's not like her and Jon got married after years of being uni sweethearts. They got married because their parents believed it was the right thing for them to do. So there was no proposal. No engagement. No big wedding—well, at least not by Nigerian standards.

"Well, it wasn't as fancy as yours," she says eventually.

I take a sip of my lukewarm tea.

"But it was perfect. Jon took me out for a picnic and hid the ring in a cake."

"Ohmigod, that is so sweet," cries Jasmine over a chorus of "aww's." "Sorry, excuse the pun." She cackles.

I squint at Ola, who seems quietly pleased with the table's reaction.

"I didn't know this," says Nana. She is sitting to my right and can clearly read my mind.

Ola shrugs. "Well, now you do. Okay, that's me done. Gemma?"

While Gemma recites how she met her husband, I take fleeting glances at Ola. *Did she—did she just make that up?* It's common knowledge that Ola and Jon didn't have a traditional engagement.

"And how about you?" says Jasmine, tilting her head toward me.

I blink as though I've been caught sleeping while on the job. "How about meee . . . ?"

"Are *you* in a relationship?" she clarifies, her eyes sparkling with curiosity.

"Not yet," I say abruptly, followed by Nana, who quickly says, "Neither am I."

"What about Alex?"

I stare back at Ola. She knows. Dammit. Aunty Debbie has only gone and told her.

"Are you guys still taking things slow?" she says, raising her pinkie as she brings her tea to her lips. From the corner of my eye, I can see Nana watching me.

"Ooh. Who's Alex?" Jasmine gushes.

I sigh. "Things didn't work out." And as casually as I can, I shove a large piece of the brownie into my mouth before dusting my fingers.

"No!" Ola looks genuinely shocked.

Okaaay. Maybe she didn't know.

"He likes someone else," I say to Ola, ignoring Jasmine's whiny cries to be looped in. "So you can go ahead and say, 'I told you so.'"

"I wouldn't do that," says Ola with an empathetic expression, and I search her face for an inkling of a smirk. "I had my suspicions about you and Alex, yes—" She breaks off, as though knowing this line of thought wouldn't be helpful right now. "But at the end of the day, there's no shame. We've all been there before."

I hear Rachel cackling in the background as she takes multiple selfies with her friends. Ola gives me a tiny smile. It sends a warm feeling through me. Of course Ola would be understanding. She went through something similar. Granted, what Rachel told me about her and Jon happened years ago. But still, she can relate.

"When did you find out?" she asks. I'm so touched by Ola's kindness that I think, *Sod it*. I might as well tell her everything.

"I actually found out on Valentine's Day," I admit.

"He broke your heart on Valentine's Day?!" An overdramatic Jasmine blinks at me, aghast.

"But I thought—" Ola's brows knead together in confusion.

"So did he say who he liked?" Funny that this question comes from Jasmine. The girl who knows nothing about anyone in this scenario.

I turn to Nana, who seems pretty preoccupied in straightening her utensils right now.

"Yinka, you don't have to say who it is," she says. But it's too late.

"Nana?" Ola's compassion morphs into shock. She's wearing the same expression that I probably had when I sat across from Alex all those weeks ago. "You mean Nana? *Our* Nana?"

"Yes, me." Nana breathes out, and Jasmine says, "What the fuck?"

"How? When?" Ola can't even get her words out. She tries again. "Okay, start from the beginning. When did Alex and Nana meet?"

"Like I said, it was on Valentine's Day." I turn to Nana, and she glances down like she's embarrassed. "Nana popped into the kitchen briefly while Alex and I were having lunch—"

"Hold up. This doesn't make any sense." Ola pushes her chair back. She places both hands on her temples. "What about what you told me and Rachel? You know, that evening we were at the bridal shop."

"Eh? I heard my name." Rachel stops taking selfies and sits up. "What about me? What happened at the bridal shop?"

"Don't you remember?" says Ola while the fifteen women in the room stare at me, my insides tangling like headphone wire. "You said that Alex saw you as wifey material, that he couldn't believe you were single but because his sister had recently passed, you guys were going to take things slow. Was that all a lie?"

"No!" I say louder than I intend to. "Why would I lie about his sister passing? But the other bits . . ." I breathe out, irritated with myself. "I might have exaggerated. Well, no, I lied. The truth is . . . he sees me as nothing more than a friend. After he met Nana, he actually asked me to set him up with her—"

"But I'm not interested so that's the end of that," Nana jumps in before I can finish and further embarrass myself.

Ola's mouth falls and to dramatize her shock, she looks side to side. "Wow," she says, as though she's out of breath. "I didn't see *that* coming. So do you mean to tell me, yeah"—she covers her mouth, and to my surprise, her shoulders begin to bop—"that Alex fell for Nana?" In hysterics, she reaches for a napkin, her eyes welling.

"Okay, let's just drop the entire conversation," says Nana.

But Ola is rocking back and forth like a neighing horse. Meanwhile Rachel, clearly having a delayed reaction, says, "Wait. So Alex likes Nana?"

"I'm sorry." Ola dabs the pointy end of her napkin against her lower lash line. She bites her lip, only for a bubble of laughter to burst out of her again. "Come on, you have to admit," she says between splutters. "This is friggin' hilarious. And you made all that food!" Tears are leaking now. "Sorry, Yinka. But I can't. I can't."

I watch Ola laugh away, and my body heats up like an iron. I'm aware that Nana's calling for Ola to stop, but all around me goes black, my blinkers on Ola.

I can't believe she's laughing *at* me. At my heartbreak. At my pain. Just because Alex and I were never together, doesn't mean my feelings don't count. I thought that of all people, Ola would understand. I thought she would understand because she had been cut in the same way.

"Fuck you, Ola."

Like bullets, my words fly out.

"Excuse me?"

"She didn't mean that." Nana puts a hand on my shoulder.

"How dare you?" I spit, and there's a scraping sound as Rachel pushes back her chair and rushes over. "How dare you sit there and laugh at me?"

Ola, still finding the situation funny, pulls one of those faces that commuters exchange on the Tube when someone gets a bit prickly. "Okay, calm down. No need to make a scene. And don't speak to me like that. Who do you think you're talking to?"

"You're such a bitter person."

"Sorry, how am I a bitter person?" yells Ola over Rachel, who cries, "Girls. Please."

"For months"—I carry on anyway—"I've kept my mouth shut to keep the peace between us. And what do I get in return? A slap in the face."

"Yinka! That's enough," says Rachel.

"What?" Ola jerks, and then she kisses her teeth. "*Abeg.* I'm not even going to entertain this conversation. It's not my fault that you lied."

"And it's not my fault that Jon wanted to be with me!"

"I said that's enough!" Rachel cries, but my volcano has already erupted.

"Yes, Ola. I know that the same night Jon broke up with you, he told you he had developed feelings for *me*. But then you told him you were pregnant, so he *had* to marry you. And what did I do after finding out this information? I didn't laugh in your face as you're laughing at me now. I kept my mouth shut. And for what?" I fling out an arm. "To be repaid like this? Oh, and that picnic proposal that she told you about earlier?" I nod profusely at Jasmine, who looks stunned. "Yeah, that was BS. You know what, I should have laughed in your face then."

By the time I've stopped shouting, a tense silence hangs in the air.

"Now look at what you've done," says Rachel, as Ola's chair crashes backward and she storms out of the room.

"Oh, yes, because it's always my fault!" I yell this at Rachel. Then, as she dashes after Ola, "Yes, you go after her like you always do."

"Rach, wait!" Nana is next to go, running after the bride-to-be, who cries, "My day is ruined!" as she rips off her sash and throws it on the floor.

The doors swing closed. Slowly, I face everyone. They're all staring at me as though I'm a monster.

"Well, enjoy the rest of the bridal shower." I snatch my jacket and bag from my chair.

It is only as I go to open the doors that I notice no one makes a sound. No one runs or calls after me.

Do you think I have time for this?

Hey, this is Rachel. Leave a message. (Beep!)

Hey, Rach. It's Yinka . . . again. I know you're really angry at me, and you have every right to be, but I'm so, so, so, so sorry. I'm know there's no excuse but . . . can we talk? Call me back, please. Bye.

"Rachel! Thank God, you picked up." I run a hand over my hair. I've tried calling her at least eight times already. Now it's close to eleven and I'm nearly in bed.

"What do you want?" she says, her voice like ice.

I sit up. "Rachel, I'm so, so sorry."

"You promised, Yinka. You promised me you wouldn't tell Ola."

"I had to!" I protest. "She left me with no choice."

"No, you didn't." I've never heard Rachel this angry before. "Ola is really upset—"

"Oh, yes, because we don't want to upset Princess Ola."

"Excuse me?"

"You heard me. You *always* take her side—"

"And *you* always put me in the middle."

"In the middle?" I let out an incredulous laugh. "You hardly back me. Even when Ola's in the wrong, you *still* take her side. Ever since we were kids. *Always* having an excuse ready to justify Ola's behavior."

"Oh, Yinka, you sound so childish." Rachel actually laughs. "You know what, I'm not going to engage in this conversation." I try to interrupt, but she speaks over me. "I'm getting married in less than three months. Three months! Do you think I have time for this? This issue, beef, whatever it is that you have with Ola, sort it out between yourselves and quick. Because I'm *not* having my wedding day ruined like my shower was."

"Well, in that case, tell Ola that I'll be waiting for my apology."

"You see! This is exactly what I mean. Do you know what, don't speak to me until you've made up!"

To my shock, Rachel ends the call.

Twenty minutes later, when Nana gets home, I'm swiping madly on Hinge. Honestly, why did I think going on here would take my mind off things? What sane person asks a stranger, *"Can I see your tits?"*

"Come in!" I yell after Nana knocks.

She walks in and perches on my bed. "I brought you some cake," she says, and hands me a piece wrapped in a table napkin.

"Thanks." I put it on my bedside table. "Sooo, it looks like I ruined Rachel's bridal shower."

Nana doesn't respond straight away. "Not exactly." She shifts slightly. "We ended up going to karaoke. I wanted to call you, but Jasmine said it was best for you and Ola not to be in the same room. You know, to give you some space."

"It's okay. I'm not offended." I return to mindlessly swiping through profiles. I can feel Nana watching me.

"Are we really not going to discuss what happened then?" she says finally.

I let out a deep breath and place my phone facedown on my lap. "Surely, Rachel and Ola filled you in."

"Yes, but I want to hear your side of things."

I run a hand over my hair. Where do I even start?

"Rachel told me something—it was when we were venue scouting with you. Something that Ola had found out and didn't want me to know about. She told me so that I knew why Ola was acting weirdly."

"Right—you mean this stuff about Jon fancying you back at uni?"

I nod. "Just before Ola told Jon that she was pregnant, Jon told her he had developed feelings for someone else. Well, he told her it was this random girl on campus. But all along, it was me. She only just found out."

"That's mad. And how did she find out?"

"Apparently they were talking about the past, and I'm guessing, maybe, that Ola probed Jon about this random girl he had developed feelings for, I dunno. I don't know what in the world provoked Jon to tell her the truth—maybe he thought since it's been over ten years and they have three kids, she wouldn't see it as that much of a big deal. But, yeah, Jon told Ola that this random girl he'd developed feelings for was actually me. So essentially, I was the other woman. Well, almost."

"Yikes."

"When Rachel told me, I was like, now that explains why Ola has been so catty to me over the last few months. And why she randomly yelled at me at Kemi's baby shower—"

"Sorry, rewind." Nana cuts in. "Did you suspect that Jon had developed feelings for you at the time?"

"Hell no." I scrunch my face. "I mean, he was always commenting on my hair, but that was about it. He never flirted with me. We didn't even hang out. Trust me, Nana, I was just as shocked as you when Rachel told me. I was like, Jon liked *me*?"

"Damn."

"So now can you understand why I'm so angry at Ola? I didn't laugh in her face when I found out that Jon liked me, so she shouldn't have laughed when I told her that Alex liked you."

"Fair enough," Nana says. "But Yinka, you're better than this. You don't have to stoop to her level. And causing a scene at Rachel's bridal shower." She shakes her head.

"Please, Nana, I feel guilty as it is. I'm going to make it up to Rachel. But I don't regret standing up for myself. Let's face it, Ola and I have never really been friends. We were only friends by default because we're cousins. Now we can stop pretending and go our separate ways." I pick up my phone and resume scrolling.

Nana is quiet for a moment. Then in a low voice, she says, "You've changed."

"Excuse me?"

"I said, you've changed, Yinka. And not in a good way."

I scoff. "Sorry, why am I the only one receiving all the blame? I hope you're giving Ola the same energy."

"I've already had a word with Ola. She shouldn't have laughed at you. But I'm not talking about Ola right now, I'm talking about you."

"Oh, please. Enlighten me, guru."

"You made a plan out of Post-it notes!" she says. "A plan to change yourself. For a man. And you've been lying. And stealing—"

"Erm, I've apologized for taking your jumpsuit."

"Look, one thing I know for certain is that the Yinka I've seen over the last few months isn't the Yinka that I know and love."

As Nana launches into a monologue about the various different ways that I've changed, I start swiping through my phone again.

Ooh. He looks cute. Scratch that. I can't date a smoker.

"Can you see where I'm coming from?" Nana says at the same time that my heart stops.

I squint.

Wait. Is that—is that Donovan?

"Oi!"

Nana snatches my phone and holds it out of reach.

"Give it back!" I yell.

"You weren't even listening to me, were you?" She ignores my cries and looks down at the screen. "Seriously?" she says, glancing back at me.

"What?" I make a swing for my phone again. "Didn't you say I should put myself out there?"

"Not like this," she says.

"Okay, gimme my phone." I let out a short laugh. "I've taken out my weave, which you were so vehemently against. And you took away the one guy I actually liked. Honestly, what more do you want from me?"

Nana looks at me, her lips quivering in shock.

"Thank you," I enunciate as she slaps my phone into my palm. I glance down and unlock it, going straight back on Hinge to make my point.

"Fine," she mutters. She stomps out of the room, and I don't bother to look up. Instead, I relocate the profile.

I wasn't seeing things. There he is, with his beard and cornrows and those annoying dimples. Donovan. I read his one-sentence statement: **You should message me if you can hold a conversation.** *Typical.*

"I'm only doing this because I care about you."

Nana has burst back into my room. She's brandishing a white business card. "His name is Francis Kirkland. He's a professional counselor. My co-worker recommended him—"

"Nana, you're overreacting. I don't need to see a counselor."

Still, she forces the card into my hand as though I'm refusing money. "Call him first thing on Monday."

"Or what?" I fold my arms.

Nana folds hers too. "Or . . . I'll move out."

May

Sod it

MONDAY

Monday, 3 May at 12.09 a.m.
From: Shane, Dave
To: Yinka Oladeji
Subject: Update

Hi Yinka,

Hope you're well.

I just realized I never got back to you. Apologies. It's been manic ever since I returned from my holiday.

Sadly, no updates from any of the employers Sarah put you forward for.

Will be in touch if I hear anything.

Cheers,
Dave
Catasift Recruitments

I pause the finale of *How to Get Away with Murder* and put my laptop down. I stroll to the bathroom while simultaneously opening the Tinder app, plonking my bottom on the toilet seat. After stumbling across Donovan's online dating profile, I've had no choice but to delete my Hinge account. I just pray that he didn't see my profile. That would be extremely awkward.

I can't believe I'm on Tinder. (Sigh.) The one dating app I didn't think I'd sign up for, but here I am. It's hella addictive. Joanna and Brian were of course in favor when I told them about it last Friday.

"About time," Brian said as we sat in the All Bar One that I had avoided going to for months.

"Thank you," I said loudly, sipping my expensive lemonade. I pulled a face. "Nana thinks I shouldn't be dating right now."

"What?" Joanna screwed up her brows.

"I know, right! Anyway, how's the new job?"

From the light in her eyes, I knew she was going to say . . .

"I love it. I love the people. I love the culture." Joanna listed each thing she loved with her fingers. Then after Brian and I had asked enough questions, we moved on to talk about her boyfriend, Brandon. It seems like they're very happy.

"And how about you, Brian?" I asked, trying to shake off the weird feeling in my chest. *I'm not jealous. I'm not jealous. I'm happy for her.*

Brian was still hating his job. And I hated myself for feeling relieved.

"So how are things with you?" he asked, slowly stirring his drink with a straw.

I looked at my phone. "Still job hunting."

True to her word, Aunty Blessing put me in touch with Terry Matthews, and despite e-mailing him my CV about a week ago, I have not heard back. Aunty Blessing did say that he is a very busy man, but still, I was hoping for something sooner.

Joanna diverted the conversation. "Ooh, how's Nana? How are plans for her fashion show going?"

I scratched the top of my ear. Since Nana gave me that business card, I've been trying my best to avoid her. She thinks that I've booked a counseling session when really I chucked the card the night she gave it to me. I just think she's being overly dramatic. Let's hope she doesn't find out that I'm fobbing her off. I'd hate to see her move out. I really can't afford the entire place alone.

"She's great," I said eventually. "Very busy. Understandably."

I excused myself to the bar and checked my WhatsApp messages. Rachel's "I'm Getting Married, Biatch" group has been quiet for a while. Not like I'm expecting to hear from either her or Ola. And since then, my main companionship has been my new friend, Tinder.

Ten minutes have gone by, and I'm still on the toilet seat, swiping left.

No. No—hang on. I recognize this guy.

Marcus. Where have I seen him before?

I'm racking my brain, trying to remember why I recognize those blue eyes, when I'm interrupted by an incoming call from Kemi. I feel a pang of guilt.

Since Kemi gave birth, I've only been round once. It's not like I'm not happy for her. God, my heart swells when I see the way she looks at Chinedu. Even now, a little part of my chest aches because I may never have that. Years ago, when I was with Femi, I could dream of having a family and it didn't seem far-fetched. But now, any time the thought comes to mind, it's punishing. And this is what has kept me away. This and Mum always being at Kemi's place. I'm not exactly in her good books right now, and the atmosphere is unbearable. I make a mental note to try to visit at a time when Mum's not there.

"Hey, sis," I say, feeling bad that I didn't contact her first.

The sound of Chinedu wailing in the background is what I hear first, followed by Kemi. "Yinka, I'm stressed out. I feel like my brain is going to explode. Why won't he stop crying?"

"Isn't Mum with you?" I ask. I have absolutely no idea how to help her.

Kemi sighs. "Mum had to pop out." Over Chinedu's screams, I hear Uche say, "Here, give him to me." Then I hear a whimper, but it's not from the baby. Kemi sounds worn out.

"I knew it would be hard," she's now saying, her voice breaking. "But I never knew it would be *this* hard."

As she pours her frustrations out—something about painful nipples?— I find myself contemplating whether or not to swipe right on the twenty-eight-year-old, animal-loving marketer, saying "hmm" and "bless you" hopefully in all the right places.

There's something about Marcus's easygoing smile that's making me hover. Where have I seen him before?

Then it hits me.

Marcus is the guy who Brian showed me when Joanna set up her Tinder account. At the time, I thought he was cute, but Joanna wasn't feeling him.

I ponder which way to swipe. Marcus is white. What would he make of my kinky hair and dark lips and chocolate skin?

"Sod it," I say under my breath, and swipe right.

"What did you say?"

"Nothing. Carry on."

As Kemi continues her rant, the screen changes within seconds. I can't believe it. We're a match!

I start to stand up, then freeze. Oh no. He's just messaged me.

Feeling jittery, I sit back on the toilet seat again, my hand holding the towel rack for support.

Hey, Yinka. How's it going?

My belly flips. I reply:

Hey, Marcus. I'm good. How are you?

There's the unbearable wait of the three dots. Get a grip, girl, he's a bloody stranger!

"Yinka!"

The abruptness of Kemi's voice makes me jump.

"Sorry, I missed that. What was it that you were saying?"

She huffs. "Have you even been listening?"

"What? 'Course, I have." I take Kemi off speakerphone. Marcus will just have to wait. "You were ranting about your tender nipples, weren't you?"

The frostiness of the silence confirms that I'm way off.

"You know what?" My little sister sounds proper huffy. "You're obviously too busy, so let me not take any more of your time—"

"Kemi, wait . . . I was on the toilet."

"Oh," she says. "You should have said."

I reach for the unraveled toilet roll and tear a piece. "Look, why don't we do something this Saturday? I still haven't forgotten the one-on-one time I promised before you gave birth. I know it's a bit late, but I still really want to."

"Well, it's going to be me, you, plus Chinedu," she reminds me.

"Even better. Hey, maybe I can bring some oils and foot scrubs. Give you a foot massage while you're breastfeeding."

Kemi laughs, and I sense that she hasn't laughed properly in a good while. "I would love that," she says softly.

"Perfect. I'll be round yours, say . . . three?"

"Sounds good. Oh, and how's the job search going? I've been meaning to ask you. Mum's really worried. I'm sorry that she found out about the redundancy."

I sigh. "It's going okay. And don't apologize; I only have myself to blame. Anyway, see you Saturday."

I end the call and race back to Tinder. Marcus has replied.

I'm not one for small talk, so excuse my bluntness. We like the look of each other, if we were in a bar we'd exchange numbers, wouldn't we?

He gives me his mobile number.

Add me on WhatsApp. PS—I'm legit lol

There's a fluttering in my stomach. All of a sudden, I feel hot. Excited. And equally nervous. Why is Marcus so keen to talk? Oh no. I hope he doesn't have a fetish.

I stare at the screen, unsure of what to do. But the longer I leave it, the more likely Marcus will think I've got cold feet. I'm just going to be open-minded and message him.

Well, as soon as I've washed my hands.

Jheeze, man. I was only asking

WEDNESDAY

Wednesday, 5 May at 6.34 p.m.
From: Matthews, Terry
To: Yinka Oladeji
Subject: Interested in working at Comperial

Dear Yinka,

Please accept my apologies in getting back to you so late.

Comperial is currently undergoing an internal restructure, so there will be quite a few job openings at various levels. It would be good to arrange a time to meet. I'm afraid I wasn't able to see your CV attached. Can you resend?

Terry
Director of Management & Strategy

I stare at my receipt. Twenty quid. Not bad. Twenty quid hardly breaks the bank.

"Jo!" I pick up her call as I power walk out of the hair shop. I've just purchased a sixteen-inch, straight wig made out of synthetic hair (hence the price). Yes, I'm unemployed, and yes, I shouldn't be spending money right now, but it was an emergency. Marcus wants to meet up this Saturday, and in my Tinder profile I have long hair. God knows how he'll react if I show up rocking my short fro.

Speaking of Marcus, we talked on the phone for ages. I love him! Not *love*, love him . . . you know what I mean. Marcus is charming. Straight-talking. He doesn't hold back on the compliments—which I *love*—and as well as being a nonsmoker and a Bryson Tiller fan, he's also a Christian. (Bonus.)

I'm not going to lie: I wish Rachel and I were on good terms right now, as I know she would be super-excited for me. I did think about telling Nana, but considering her dislike of my plan, I doubt she wants to hear about my love life. Besides, she's busy preparing for her fashion show. I don't want disrupt her "creative energy."

"It's going to be a short date," I tell Joanna, pressing my phone to my ear. I'm heading in the opposite direction to Peckham Rye station because I'm desperate for some plantain chips.

"How come?" Joanna asks.

"I promised my sister that I'll pop over. Remember I mentioned she had the baby recently?"

"Then why not just meet up with Marcus in the evening?"

"And risk getting kidnapped? Hell no!"

Joanna laughs, then I hear a beeping sound. I look at my phone. It's Nana.

"Jo, do you mind if I call you back later?" I end my call with Joanna and answer Nana's.

"Hey, how's it going?" I say, wondering why she's calling. "Don't tell me you forgot your key at home."

Nana laughs. "It was *one* time. Actually, I'm calling to find out how your counseling session went? I believe it was today, right?"

I stop dead in my tracks. A man nearly bumps into me from behind and curses. A few weeks back, Nana asked me when my counseling session was, and to get her off my back, I told her a random date. Dammit. How did I forget? I'm usually good at remembering things.

"It was canceled," I say, trying not to splutter. "Yeah, at the last minute. Francis was unwell."

"Oh," says Nana, as I resume walking. I can't tell whether or not she believes me.

"Looks like I'm going to have to reschedule." I approach the pedestrian crossing and spot lots of beanbags and people in the distance. *Oh yeah, the outreach is on today.* I haven't volunteered since that time I fell out with Donovan.

"Sorry, Nana, is it okay if we catch up later?" I say, getting in before her. "I'm actually volunteering right now." I end the call and cross the road.

When I reach the platform, I look around. No sign of Donovan. Though I do see Derek and Vanessa helping out in the dessert section. Vanessa waves. Derek puts down his cake box and jogs over.

"Hey! Long time," he says as we hug. "Up for giving us a hand with the dessert?"

I'm still looking around searching for Donovan.

"Yinka?"

"Huh? Sorry, Derek. Actually, I think I might just mingle, if that's okay?"

"Sure. Go for it."

Derek heads the other way as I weave between huddles of people sitting on beanbags. Today, spaghetti bolognese is on the menu, and it seems to be going down a storm. I spot an unoccupied beanbag opposite a hollow-cheeked woman with dark circles around her eyes. She's talking to a Middle Eastern man sitting beside her, a sleeping bag draped over his shoulders.

"Is this seat taken?"

The woman gives me a toothy smile. "Nah, love. Come join us," she says, and I plonk myself on the beanbag and almost get swallowed whole.

"Wow, these beanbags are comfy," I remark, trying to find my balance. "Sorry, I hope I didn't interrupt your conversation?"

"Nah, not at all." The woman bats a hand. "I'm Kelly, by the way, and this is my mate here, Farsheed."

Farsheed presses his palms together. "Sorry, my English no good."

"Nice to meet you." I shake their hands. "I'm Yinka. So," I smile, "how's the bolognese?"

For the next few minutes, I carry on chatting to them. Well, Kelly does most of the talking while Farsheed nods and hmm's. We talk about everything from how we like to drink our tea to our appreciation of Peckham and its strong community. This is why I love volunteering—meeting all sorts of people from all walks of life. Giving something back and getting priceless moments like these in return.

"I thought I recognized your big head," comes a voice out of nowhere. I look up. Donovan is standing over me wearing a Nike vest and shorts.

"Oh, great. You." I clamber to my feet and we hug. I stagger back. "Jheeze, man. You're dripping wet."

"Sorry, just came from the gym, innit." I notice his biceps—*Why am I noticing his biceps?*—then immediately scowl at him.

"So that's why you're late," I snap.

"Oh, you were looking for me, yeah?" Donovan laughs. He lifts up his vest to wipe his flushed face, and now I can see his very defined abs.

I turn hastily. "Kelly. Farsheed. This is Donovan."

They exchange hellos. Afterward, Donovan tells me he needs a hand with the tea and coffee.

"As long as you bring her back, yeah," says Kelly. "We were having a lovely chat, weren't we, Yinka?"

I grin.

"No disrespect to the other volunteers, but they're always asking me questions like, how did I end up on the streets? Blah, blah, blah. But this one"—Kelly gives me a wink—"she's a real one, she is. Ain't that right, Farsheed?"

And whether or not Farsheed has understood, he nods.

I flop back into one of the chairs tucked behind the trestle table. For the past five minutes, I've been helping Donovan serve tea and coffee. Although, the words "help" and "serve" are a bit of an overstatement, when all I've really done is add a splash of milk and a teaspoon of sugar into plastic cups. And I didn't manage to get that right half the time.

Donovan slips into the chair beside me. "Anyway, it's been a minute. So what's happening with you? Where you working now?"

"I'm still job hunting."

"What about that interview you told me about?"

I shake my head.

"Aww, man. Sorry, Yinks."

"It's okay." I try to sound breezy. "My Aunty put me in touch with this managing director at a boutique investment bank. Apparently, there's a lot of job openings coming up. Anyway, he asked me to send him my CV, because stupid me forgot to attach it to my original e-mail."

Donovan leans back in his chair. "That's a shame 'cause I have the perfect role for you."

I laugh. "Go on, then."

Donovan leans forward, elbows on his knees. "Sanctuary is looking for someone to oversee their Woolwich outreach. I think you'd be great at the job, still."

"What, because of that *one* time you saw me help those teens stuff leaflets?"

"No," he says slowly. "Because you're good with people. Even Kelly said so. You've got transferable skills, and experience working with the homeless. Yinks, you're more qualified than you think."

"Thanks," I say, flushing, then immediately blame it on the heat. Okay, it's only sixteen degrees, but that's hot for the UK.

"I'm leading the recruitment, and I want to put you up for the role. The salary is decent for charity work, not gonna lie. Anyway, the deadline is May seventeenth. Let me at least send you a job spec."

"All right." I give in.

Donovan blinks. "Cool. Um, let me get your e-mail address then." He hands me his phone.

"Might as well add your number, innit," he says. "Just in case, you know, for any questions."

I type in my number, sucking in my lips to quell a smile. *Wait, what am I smiling for?*

"This MD," he says after I hand him his phone, "you sent him your CV yet?"

"Not yet," I say, stroking my hair. "I was going to make a few tweaks first."

"Well, I can look it over, if you like? Offer you my expertise."

"Oh, would you?" My eyes light up. "Thanks, Donovan. That would be amazing."

"No problem. Let me give you my e-mail address."

I dig out my phone, and I notice Donovan's fresh cornrows as he taps on the screen.

"Here," he says, handing it back. Just above his e-mail address, he's saved his number.

"Anyway, enough about work," I say in what I hope is a breezy tone. "How's things with you? Ooh, how's counseling?"

Donovan rolls up his sleeves. He sighs. "Jacqui has given me homework."

"Okaaay?"

He reaches for a plastic cup. "She wants me to think about why I'm so resistant to dating."

I hear the word "dating," and Donovan's Hinge profile flashes to mind. "Err, isn't that the whole point of seeing her?"

"I know, but she's making me think about *things*, like, 'What's the worst that can happen if you put yourself out there?'" He says this in a voice that I'm pretty confident doesn't sound like his therapist. "And she's making me do things. Like, can you believe that man has set up an online dating account. You heard of Hinge?"

"Yeah."

"I joined that not too long ago. Haven't really used it."

"When is this homework due for?"

Donovan wrinkles his nose. "To be honest with you, Yinks, it's been an ongoing homework for a few months now."

"A few months!" I nearly scare away an approaching man. "Sorry. Tea? Coffee?" Donovan and I rush to our feet. He brews a teabag in a plastic cup while I wait to add a drop of milk and some sugar.

"Donovan, that's insane," I say after we've served the man and flopped back in our chairs again. "Why are you so scared to start dating again?"

"I dunno. Fear of rejection, maybe."

I give him a smile. "Want to know what I think?"

"Go on."

"I think your counselor is a crutch."

"A crutch?"

"You heard me." I roll my neck to add a bit of sass.

Donovan laughs.

"Nah, I think it's great that you're doing therapy, so you don't bring old baggage into any future relationship. But you're never going to get into one, unless you put yourself out there." For a quick moment, I consider telling

Donovan that this is what I've been doing lately but something holds me back. So instead, I say the next thing on my mind. "You know what else I think?"

He leans back. "Go ahead, Oprah."

I lower my voice to a whisper. "I think you need a bit of faith."

"A bit of what?"

"I said, a bit of faith!" A pigeon nearby flaps away. "I'm not talking about religion," I say quickly. "I mean, faith in yourself." I tap his knee, before hastily removing my finger. "Donovan, you need to have faith that you're worthy of love and that you'll find it. That's not to say you won't get hurt, but faith is about believing that there are better days ahead, even when you can't see the full picture."

I let my words hang in the air. I can tell that he is mulling over them.

His dimples reappear. "They teach you that at church, yeah?"

I nudge him. "You see. Church isn't so bad."

After a moment, Donovan folds his arms behind his head. "So, what's *gwarning* with you? What's the deal between you and this *friend*?"

The sight of his muscles makes my heart thump, and feeling flustered and irritated, I say, "We're good, thank you very much. Now leave me be."

Donovan lowers his arms. "Jheeze, man. I was only asking." He stands up and begins to stack a few of the plastic cups. I wait for him to bust a joke, to pry into this "friend," to ask questions. But nothing.

I open my mouth to speak, but Donovan gets there before me.

"I just need to check on something, yeah." And without looking back, he walks away.

Please call Yinka a cab

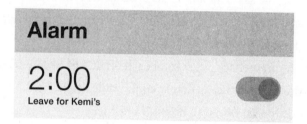

Alarm

2:00
Leave for Kemi's

"I can't believe I'm doing this," I say to myself as I look at the blue dot on my phone's GPS.

I was excited, a bit nervous, optimistic even, this morning when I squeezed into my skinny-skinny jeans and off-pink blouse. But now that I'm here, I'm absolutely bricking it.

I glance up at the pub, its ramshackle bricks with giant murals. Welcome to Shoreditch. I rake my fingers through my wig, the strands like silk as they glide between them. Okay. It's going to be a quick date to confirm that Marcus is who he says he is, then when my phone alarm goes off at two, I'll make my way to Kemi's.

I send the pub's address to Joanna and Brian for safety precautions.

Good luck Brian immediately messages back, followed with a wink emoji.

Propelled by two smokers standing nearby, I push open the pub door and I'm hit with a waft of heat. Inside is considerably nicer. It has a cool vintage feel with its dark paneled walls and flooring. And in true Shoreditch style, the bartenders are all wearing beanies.

It's just gone one o'clock, so the pub is busy. Nevertheless, I spot Marcus by the window, on his phone, sitting behind a small rustic table. I'm grateful that he's looking down as it gives me another chance to shift my wig a bit.

I take a breath, then navigate my way between bodies and chairs and tables, loud laughter and chatter overlapping the background guitar music. Marcus glances up and stands, smiling.

"You came," he says, spreading his arms while I hold out a hand.

"Of course," I reply, or rather croak. I allow him to hug me. He smells of fresh aftershave with a twinge of coffee.

As Marcus draws back, we stare at each other. Just like his photo, he has magical blue eyes and there's that friendly smile again. He may not be five eleven—five nine, I'd say—but he's still a hottie.

Marcus gestures at the stool opposite. I take a seat, wondering if he felt my thudding heart. And what he thinks of me. He didn't compliment me. Why hasn't he complimented me?

He laughs. "You can take off your jacket, you know."

I look down at myself. I'm wearing a puffer jacket. Zipped up.

After I've peeled off my coat, I realize I have nowhere to put it so I drape it over my lap like a British Airways blanket. Just as well, my thighs are jittery. Gosh, I am bloody nervous.

Marcus is wearing a green and blue checked shirt. "Am I what you expected?" he says. "Or were you keeping your jacket on for a reason?"

I laugh, and I can tell from the crinkles that have appeared around his eyes, that he's glad he's broken the ice.

"You're all right," I tease, feeling warmed by his gaze. "And me?" My voice goes up a bit when I say this.

Marcus smiles. "You're drop-dead gorgeous."

"Thanks." I give him a coy smile.

He smiles back.

"How about I get us a drink," he says, standing. "You know, to ease the nerves."

"Yeah, that would be great, thanks. I'll have a lemonade, please."

Marcus laughs. "Okay, now I *know* you don't want to stay long. Get a proper drink. Don't be shy. It's on me. I know, how about I get us a bottle of red. Or white?"

I bite my lip and immediately regret doing so. (I'll have to reapply my lippie.) I drink alcohol, yes, but not in the friggin' afternoon, and not for a first date.

But Rachel's wedding is not too far away, and remember, Yinka, you're *not* closed-minded, so . . . "Red would be fine," and I tell myself that I'll have *one* glass.

Three glasses later . . .

"I can't believe you're scared of cats." Marcus is looking at me with goggling eyes as though I've just told him that I've got a phobia of chocolate or something.

"They look evil," I protest.

Marcus gasps. "Take that back! I have four cats, you know."

"Four!" I nearly topple out of my stool.

"Three live with my mum."

"Well, remind me to never to go round your mum's then."

Marcus shoots me a coquettish smile. "But you'll come round to mine?"

"I'm not makinnng any . . . p-p-romises."

He smiles at me and rests his arms on the table. God, he looks hot. And

I'm having fun. Lots of fun. Tipsy, sloshy head, slurred words kinda fun. Marcus was right. The wine has eased my nerves.

"Should I get us another bottle?" He shakes the empty red and quirks a blondish brow.

"And get me drunk? Hell, no!" I flail my arms for some reason when I say this.

Marcus chuckles. "I think you already are," he says, clearly amused.

"Shit! I'm not supposed to get drunk." *Sorry, God.*

"Why?" Marcus is still bemused. "Are you babysitting this afternoon or something?"

My heart stops. Baby. Chinedu. Kemi. I rummage for my phone.

"Shit!" I say again after I realize the time. "It's just gone three!" How come my alarm didn't go off? Oh, crap. I'm such a twit, I set it for 2:00 a.m. not 2:00 p.m. I stagger to my feet, shoving my coat on. "Sorry to leave you like this, but I'm supposed to be at my sister's like . . . right now."

Marcus rushes to his feet and says, "Hold up. Wait, wait, wait." But I'm elbowing my way to the door.

Outside, the spring air hits me and so does my lack of orientation. I can't remember which street I came from, or how to stand up straight, for goodness' sake.

"I've got you," Marcus says as I stumble into his arms. He steadies me, gripping my shoulders.

His eyes flicker down to my lips. "Let me call you a cab," he says after a moment.

And after I resist the urge to kiss him, I manage a shaky nod.

'm so, so sorry." I burst into Kemi's apartment like an addict—hands twitchy, pores oozing with sweat. I'm struggling to keep my eyes open.

Despite Marcus getting me a cab, it took ages to get there. The traffic was horrific. Even worse when I reached south London to the point I almost wished I'd taken the train. That's if I could walk properly. See, Yinka, there's a reason why God sets limits.

"The traffic was really bad," I say to Uche at the front door. His head rolls back as though I've just sprayed body mist in his face.

"Where are they?" I'm startled by the eerie silence.

Uche rubs his nose. "In the nursery. But Yinka, just to give you a heads-up, she's not in the best of moods."

After somehow making it down the corridor, I knock on the nursery door and enter, rolling apologies.

"Shhhh," Kemi hisses, physically shoving me out of the door while holding her white robe together. "I literally just put him to sleep."

"Kemi. I'm sorry," I say as she closes the door behind her.

She scoffs and shakes her head. "You don't even want to be here."

"*What?* Oh, Kemi. You're just tired and stressed out—"

"I'm tired of constantly making an effort with you." The sternness in Kemi's voice startles me. "*Begging* you to be my sister. To listen to me. If you don't want to spend time with me or talk to me over the phone, fine. I know it must be awkward for you now that I'm married and have a baby. But just stop making empty promises, okay?"

The weight of what Kemi's saying knocks me to the ground and it takes me a moment to recuperate. I could come back fighting. Tell her that she doesn't understand. That there is a lot I haven't felt able to tell her these last few months. Then there's Mum. Mum who constantly compares us. Mum who now appears to be her best buddy, always spending time together.

"Kemi, lessss jussst sit down." I say this clearly, or maybe not. Kemi narrows her brows, and her angry expression morphs into shock.

"Um, why are you slurring?" She eyes me suspiciously. "Ohmigod." She sniffs. "Yinka, you're drunk, aren't you?"

I try to protest but this only makes matters worse, as she uses the opportunity to sniff my breath.

"Yes, you are!" she cries. "You reek of alcohol! I can smell it! And you wanted to be around my child?" She clutches her white robe as though I'm someone dangerous. "Uche!" She raises her voice. "Please call Yinka a cab."

And for the second time this Saturday, I clamber drunkenly into the backseat of a car.

"I'm sorry," I tell Kemi.

But she tightens her robe and turns away.

Call me Virgin Mary

SUNDAY

Sunday, 9 May at 1.22 p.m.

From: Daley, Donovan

To: Yinka Oladeji

Subject: Your CV and Sanctuary's Outreach Manager job spec

Hey Yinka, you good?

Attached is the job spec for the Sanctuary job I was telling you about. I also had a look at your CV . . .

With my sister now part of the ever growing "I'm angry at Yinka" club, I decided I needed to take my mind off things, so I accepted Marcus's invitation to come over after church. Really, I shouldn't have; I barely know the man. But with Rachel's wedding around the corner, I can't afford to waste time. And he seemed pretty non–serial killer to me.

Clean, modern and monochromatic, Marcus's apartment in Greenwich is just what I expected. Further evidence that he's not a psychopath. I think. We've just had lunch—shepherd's pie, he got the recipe from the BBC website—and now I'm waiting for him on the sofa while he stacks the dishwasher. Lunch was amazing. He earned extra points for being a good cook. We definitely have chemistry.

"You've got an impressive book collection," I call out as I stare at the colorful spines on his shelf. *We Should All Be Feminists. Things Fall Apart.* Okay, this man is cultured.

"Thanks," he calls from the kitchen. He insisted that I shouldn't help him clear up, and also told me that he has a surprise for me.

"Close your eyes," I hear him say, followed by light footsteps.

"Oh, I hate this part." I obey anyway.

"Are your eyes closed?" he says.

"Firmly." I'm relishing the excitement.

The sofa sinks as he perches beside me. "Okay. You can open them."

"Arrrghhh!" I stumble back.

Bundled in Marcus's arms is a furry gray cat.

"This is Chloe." He strokes the cat behind its ears, laughs, then kisses Chloe on the head. And I swear that animal cut her eyes at me.

To my relief, she fidgets, and Marcus lets her go. She scampers out the door without looking back.

"Was that my surprise?" I say, retreating from the edge of the sofa.

Marcus laughs then stops when I don't. "Okay, bad joke. Let me make it up to you."

He walks out of the room again, and when he returns, he's holding a bottle of wine and two glasses.

"Oh . . . okay . . ." I say as he sits on the sofa beside me.

Marcus pours a generous amount of wine into a glass.

"Just a little," I say quickly as he starts to fill the second one. *Be open,* I tell myself. *Relax.*

He sets the bottle on the floor, then hands me a glass with a smile. *God, he's sexy.*

We clink our glasses and check each other out as we sip.

He stares at me with those gorgeous eyes of his before stretching out an arm and resting it casually on the top of the sofa. Then slowly, he reaches for my hair, and with soft, delicate fingers, he fiddles with the ends, his eyes trained solely on my lips.

Oh shit. I remember my wig, then imagine his reaction if it suddenly fell off.

Marcus is still touching my hair, his gaze intense now.

"You're gorgeous, you know that?" he says, and I flush all over.

Before I can tell him to kindly refrain from touching my hair—he obviously hasn't been with a Black woman before, otherwise he would know this is rule number one—he puts his glass on the floor and does the same with mine without asking.

Suddenly, he's closer. He's sitting right up next to me. My heart seems louder than usual, my breath is coming up short and slow. For a while, he just looks at me, his eyes flickering over my face. Then at the same time, we latch onto each other, our tongues lashing as though we're fencing. I feel butterflies. Fireworks. A tingling between my thighs. God, it's been so long.

As Marcus cradles me, my mind swoops to my wig. He's pushing me backward, all with the force of his mouth, so now my spine is squished against the armrest, but I don't care.

"Your lips are so soft," he says, this time in a low whisper. He kisses my neck and I giggle. Then his mouth indulges mine, his tongue sweet and warm.

Okay, we should probably take it slow. But I haven't kissed a man since Femi. It's not like we're going to have sex or anything. I just want to be in the moment.

And for a good while, I am in the moment. Until Marcus gropes my breast.

"Hey, slow down, tiger," I hear myself say with a sputtering laugh.

But Marcus only gropes harder.

"You like that, don't you?" he says gruffly as he massages the little flesh beneath my bra. Sigh. It's a pain having small tits.

Marcus's fingers have now wormed their way to the zipper of my jeans. He's poking at my knickers—which are old and fading and from Primark—and he's breathing, "You're so wet, aren't you? Tell me you want it," as he kisses my neck.

My senses jolt and instantly, I wake up. "Okay, that's enough," I snap as he presses harder and lets out a groan. "I said, that's enough!" And this time, I shove him. Marcus draws back and clambers off me.

I push myself up against the armrest, and do my zip up quickly.

Marcus looks ruffled, though thankfully, not annoyed. "Got carried away there." He gives me a rueful smile.

There's a pause for close to a minute as he adjusts his shirt while I pat down my wig, praying the center parting is still in the middle. I bite my lip. I have to ask.

"You didn't expect me to have . . . sex with you, did you?" I say, cringing slightly.

Marcus's eyes widen into two shiny marbles. "No, of course not. I just got lost in the moment, that's all." He runs a hand over his blondish hair, which is now disheveled from me stroking it earlier. "It's only date number two so . . ."

He looks at me as though I should fill in the rest.

"So it's still early days, right?"

He grins at me as though I've given him the right answer. After pecking my lips, he reaches down and grabs both our drinks. He hands me my glass. I swallow.

"So, if it was, saaay, our eighth date, would you still call it early days?"

Marcus makes an incredulous *pfft* sound. "Yeah, as if we'll manage for that long."

I gulp. Shit. This is bad.

"Well, the thing is . . ." I stop to clear my throat. "Um, well, I'm not in a rush to have sex any time soon. And by any time soon, I mean, by the eighth date . . . and any dates after that."

Marcus frowns as though he has misheard me. "What do you mean?" he asks, shifting slightly.

"I mean—" I let out a sharp exhale. "I mean, I'm saving myself for marriage."

His mouth expands to the size of a golf ball. "Are you serious?"

"Yes," I manage to say, and he practically winces. "I thought you would have guessed."

"Sorry, Yinka, but how would I have *guessed?*"

I flounder. "Well, for starters, um, we're both Christians. Sorry, I assumed when we had that conversation about our faith that we were on the same page."

The conversation I'm referring to is one we had on the phone before we met for the first time. I asked Marcus about his faith and he was pretty candid about it. He attends a Methodist church and grew up in a Christian home. For some reason when he told me this, I thought, *Phew. That will make the conversation on celibacy easy.* But as I'm sitting here, my thighs rubbing as they jiggle, it's fair to say I was greatly mistaken. Gosh. I'm so stupid. Not every Christian is the same.

"So what, you're a . . . *virgin?*" Marcus might as well have said a tomato. Or a lobster.

I sigh. This is *exactly* why I don't open up to people about my sex life. Or lack of.

"But you're in your thirties," he cries.

"Yup. I'm a thirty-one-year-old virgin woman. Call me Virgin Mary."

Marcus doesn't laugh at my attempt to lighten the mood. Instead, he blinks at me, his expression still one of immense shock.

"Wow," he says, "that's impressive but *very* rare. Wait—are you telling me that you and your ex didn't do any funny business?"

I glance away. "We made out, yeah. But sex . . . no."

"Bloody hell," he exhales, taking a gulp of his wine. He stares ahead at the black TV screen, clearly in shock.

I bite my lip. "Will this be a problem?" In the wait that follows, my heart is thundering.

To my relief, Marcus eventually faces me. The corner of his lip has lifted a little. "No," he says softly, and my stomach contracts.

Consumed with a wave of affection, I shuffle closer, resting my palms on his cheeks. "Thank you." I gaze into his eyes. "Thank you for being understanding." I press my lips against his again, and he jolts.

"Whoa!" Marcus says, shifting back. "I, uh, really don't think that would be a good idea, do you?"

"You're right," I reply, embarrassed. I retreat to my side of the sofa.

We need to talk

"Your call has been forwarded to the T-Mobile voicemail service of 07916—"

"Argh!" I end the call, heaving in frustration. I haven't heard from Marcus since Sunday. After we'd cleared the air, he relaxed a bit—thanks to the red wine—and we watched a movie, his arm around me for two solid hours.

So now I'm standing outside the Costa in Peckham before meeting Jo-Brian, agitated to have reached Marcus's voicemail, yet again. How have we gone from *that* to *this?*

"Spare change, please."

I look up from my phone to see a man with tired, hooded eyes wearing a long coat.

"Sorry, I've got no change."

The homeless man shuffles away, and my heart drops. I dig into my bag.

"But I've got this." I go after him, holding out a Yorkie bar.

The man's smile is like the keys on a piano. "Thank you," he says, taking the chocolate.

"What's your name?" I ask, just as he turns away.

He looks at me as though he has never been asked that question before. "Thomas," he says, and his eyes crinkle as he smiles.

"Thomas. You know, I've always been fond of that name. Hey, do you know about the homeless outreach happening tonight?"

"Outreach?" Thomas looks confused. "Sorry, I'm not from around here."

"Yeah, it's on every Wednesday and Thursday from seven at the outside platform near Peckham library." I look at my phone. "You're in luck, they've just started. I think you should go. There'll be food and drink and lots of friendly people."

Thomas doesn't need any further persuasion and clasps my hand. "God bless you," he says, and I put my hand over his. Just seeing how grateful he is makes my throat catch.

"Do you know how to get there?" I ask.

Thomas makes a startled expression. "Come on, darling. I may not be from Peckham, but everyone knows where the library is."

Inside, Costa is bustling. But I spot Joanna and Brian in the corner, sitting on the leather sofa side by side. I go toward them. Squint. Wait, is that . . . Nana?

"What are you doing here?" I ask her. I do the rounds of hugs before slumping in the chair beside Nana.

When she doesn't respond, I sense that something is off.

"We need to talk," she says finally.

"We?" I look around. Joanna gazes down. Brian lays a hand on the table.

"Yinka, we care for you," he says.

I laugh. "Okay, what's going on, guys? And Nana, why are you here?"

"I'm here because you've changed," she says. "Not for the better."

I flutter my eyes. "Oh great, this conversation again?"

"She told us." Joanna finds her voice. "She told us about your plan and your out of character behavior—"

"Out of character behavior?" I shake my head. "Nana, I can't believe you called my friends behind my back. And Joanna, Brian, you were the ones congratulating me for joining Tinder!"

"But we didn't know," says Brian. "We didn't know you were vulnerable and in a bad state. But since Nana lives with you, she saw everything. She told us everything."

I slump back in my chair. "Is this some kind of intervention?" I steal a quick glance at my phone again. *Damn you, Marcus. Damn you!*

Joanna itches the side of her face. "Yinka, you lied to Nana about going to counseling—"

My head swings toward Nana. I struggle to find an excuse.

"We're worried about you."

For some reason, Brian's remark makes me laugh.

Nana nods to my phone. "You need to delete Tinder. Hand me your phone." She goes to grab it; I snatch it away. "Hand it over, Yinka."

"Guys! Guys!"

We continue to struggle as Brian bangs the table.

"Let go of it," I grunt.

Suddenly, my phone buzzes and Nana backs away. I glance at the screen. Oh goodie, it's Marcus.

"Marcus! Hey!" I swivel around so my back is facing Nana. I'm hoping I sound casual and not like I've just been wrestling with my best friend. "What happened to you? I've been trying to reach you. I called you like five times—"

"Fifteen times," he corrects. "Fifteen."

"Well, pick up your phone then," I say, annoyed, and behind me I hear Nana ask JoBrian, "Who's that?"

"I was worried about you." I pout and run my fingers through my wig. "Are you okay? Did you lose your phone?"

Marcus inhales as though he's breathing through gritted teeth. "Stop calling me," he says angrily, and I blink in surprise.

"Okaaay, I know I called you fifteen times—"

"Fifteen times?" Nana cries.

"—but I was genuinely worried. I haven't heard from you—"

"Well, you don't need to be," Marcus cuts in. "Stop calling me. In fact, don't ever call me again."

"Excuse me?" I feel like I've just been punched in the ribs and left to die. "Why?"

"We won't work." Marcus sounds short-tempered, not like the man I know. Or thought I knew.

"Marcus." I can hear every tremble in my voice. "Are you—are you *dumping* me? Wait, is this because of what I told you?"

Marcus sighs as though I've been keeping him on the phone for hours. "We're not together, Yinka. And look, you can't expect a man to wait *that* long. It's old-fashioned, and quite frankly I'm pissed off you weren't honest with me sooner."

"Honest with you?" I lose it. "Well, sod off and have a nice life, because I'm not compromising my virginity for anybody. I'll find a man who's happy to wait till marriage and I'm glad it won't be *you*."

I end the call, seething.

"What a jerk," I say, swiveling around again. Shit, the whole of Costa must've heard that.

Brian and Joanna are visibly shell-shocked.

"Are you a virgin?" Joanna says, lowering her voice.

Under the table, Nana puts a hand on my knee.

"Yes," I mutter eventually. Man, this is awkward.

Or is it?

Why shouldn't I be proud that I'm a virgin? For years, I've compartmentalized my faith, worrying about what others might think about it. Well, I'm tired.

"I'm saving myself for marriage because in the Bible, sex is something sacred. And while I respect that everyone makes their own choices, I wish that society didn't make me feel alien for mine. So, yup. There you have it. I'm a virgin."

The silence that follows barely lasts a second.

"Yinka, you should have told us," says Joanna, and Brian says, "Yeah, especially when we shared all those sex stories."

"I don't want you to stop being yourselves," I say, looking between them. "And I don't want you to treat me differently."

"Then be yourself," says Nana, giving me a long look. "You need to embrace who *you* are."

"I think you being a virgin is commendable," says Joanna with a light shrug.

"You do?"

Brian pushes up his glasses. "Totally," he says. "You should be proud, Yinka. Not many people stick to what they believe in. Hey, you should get a T-shirt that says, 'Virgin and Proud.'"

"Okay, don't get me that for Christmas," I laugh, and my spirits lift. "Or my birthday. Or ever, actually."

"And that Marcus guy sounds like an arsehole." Joanna wrinkles her nose. "I would be grateful if I were you. You dodged a bullet."

"Maybe . . ." I rub my cheek. "Don't get me wrong, Marcus has every right to not want to be with me. But don't, you know, ghost me. That's just rude."

Nana clears her throat. "Now going back to why we're here." She removes her hand from my knee, her face the bearer of bad news.

I fold my arms. "I don't need counseling."

She shakes her head. "Sorry, hun, but I think you do."

I look over to Joanna and Brian. They're no help, nodding somberly and explaining why they're so worried about me.

But I'm hardly listening, my mind racing ahead, planning my next move. I can't possibly go back to Tinder and risk meeting another Marcus. And because of Donovan, Hinge is a no-go. I guess there's always Christian Mingle, but do I really want to pay? Oh, God. Why can't I just meet someone normally? What am I doing wrong?

But I won't get an answer. Not here anyway.

"Sorry, guys. Gotta go." I lurch to my feet.

Joanna says, "Hey, where you going?" followed by Nana's, "Er, we're not done yet."

"I just remembered." I tuck in my chair. "I'm supposed to be volunteering tonight."

When I reach the homeless outreach, I spot Thomas slumped back on a beanbag eating a burrito. He seems to have made two friends—one of whom is Kelly, can you believe it. I wave at them and they wave back, grinning.

I look around the platform. The weather is pleasantly warm. Donovan is with a group of volunteers on cushions sorting out the donated items. I pat the sides of my wig and stride toward him.

"Hey!" I say enthusiastically.

Donovan clambers to his feet, dusts his hands and hugs me. "You good?" he says, drawing back.

Grinning at him, I wait. This is usually his cue. Any second now, he'll mention something about the Laws of attraction. But he doesn't say anything, and so for five whole seconds I'm smiling at him like a loon. He frowns.

"Er, I like your jumper," I say quickly. "Let me guess. Run-DMC?"

Donovan looks down at himself where there is a print of three Black men wearing thick gold chains, matching hats and Adidas tracksuits.

He smiles. "Brushing up on your hip hop, yeah?"

I smile, grateful to have restored our banter.

"How comes you didn't get back to me?" he says.

I frown, unsure of what he means.

"Your CV," he reminds me. "I e-mailed it to you. I added some Track Changes. Overall, it was really good."

I slap my forehead. "Damn, I'm so sorry. I saw your e-mail but I got distracted. Thank you for doing that. I'll send it to Terry tonight."

"What about the job spec I sent you? Did you have a look at that? The deadline is next week. You gonna go for it?"

I chew the inside of my mouth. "I haven't looked at it. And . . ." I sigh. "Honestly, I'm not too sure if I want to go for it. It just feels like too much of a risk."

Donovan looks at me as though I've just told him I never want to eat chicken again. "That's a shame," he says. "You would have been good at the role, still."

"But thanks for thinking of me," I say, and he glances away.

"I'm just going to say hello to my friend, yeah." He nods to a disheveled-looking woman, idling in the distance.

I watch him walk away. Suddenly, he turns around.

"Your mum's church," he says. "Remind me of the name again?"

"All Welcome. It's on Old Kent Road. Um, why?"

"No worries."

For the next ten minutes, I carry on from where Donovan left off, sorting the donated men's clothes from the women's. Then I spot Derek stepping out of the portable toilets and for a moment I just watch him. I tilt my head. Hmm. Derek isn't *that* bad. He's no Alex or Femi or Donovan. No, not Donovan, what am I saying?

And without giving myself a second to change my mind, I clamber to my feet and go after him.

"Derek!" I tap his shoulder.

"Oh, hi, Yinka. Great to have you back. You did such a great job last time." I clear my throat. "Um, do you have a moment?"

We settle for the patch of grass near the library. There's a bench and I don't know whether to sit or stand, so in the end I kind of fall.

"Are you okay?" he asks as he lowers himself down on the grass next to me.

"Yeah," I reply. I'm absolutely bricking it. "Derek, I just wanted to say . . . this might sound crazy, but . . . sorry, I'm trying to gather my thoughts."

"Don't apologize. Take your time."

I breathe. "Okay, what I'm trying to say is—"

"Aunty Yinka!"

I turn.

Vanessa.

After Derek and I have clambered to our feet, she hugs me and tells me how pretty my hair is, before turning to Derek.

"I'm off now," she says, gripping the strap of her handbag. "I have over thirty cupcakes to make tomorrow."

"Well, I know you'll ace them," says Derek. Then quicker than a blink, he kisses Vanessa. On the mouth.

What?

"Bye, babe," she says to Derek, giving him a feline stare.

"Bye, sweetheart," he says back, squeezing her arm adoringly.

"See you, Aunty." Vanessa hugs my now frozen body, then strolls away.

"Sorry, you were saying?" Derek turns to me. I'm guppying like a fish.

What the hell? Not even Derek wants me.

"Um, I just wanted to let you know that—that sadly, today will be my last day." I swallow. "I won't be able to volunteer again."

I feel like I'm losing myself

THURSDAY

Rachel ▸ shared a post
1h

Not long until my wedding! Eeeeek! So excited. Can you tell? 😄 😄 😄

👍 8

👍 Like   💬 Comment   ➦ Share

After I returned home yesterday, I deleted the Tinder app. Nana saw it as progress, and I didn't really have the energy to tell her it was more like giving up.

"Are you sure you'll be okay?" she says now, sitting at the foot of my bed, her jacket on, key in hand. "It's a shame that I've got to bartend this evening."

I nurse the mug of hot chocolate that she's made me.

"If you're still awake, we can talk more when I'm back," she offers. "I'm happy to just listen, you know."

"Okay," I say, as this is what she wants to hear. "Oh, and I'm sorry for snapping at you in Costa. I know you were only trying to help. And that time when I said you took Alex away from me, I was just angry. I didn't mean it."

Nana puts a hand on my leg. "Don't sweat it." Then she goes, leaving me alone with my thoughts.

Lying there, all my brain can do is think, *Why? Why is my love life such a struggle? Why does no one want me? Why am I not good enough?*

After a while I sit up in bed. I feel the need to do *something*. Rachel's wedding is in two months. I'm running out of time. I have to do something. Now.

I reach for my phone. No. I'm done with online dating. Another thought comes to mind. I chase it away.

No, Yinka. You're not in a position to be closed-minded.

So I rush out of bed and fetch my wig lying on the dresser. I attach it to my head and shift it a few times so that it aligns with my hairline. Finally, I give it a quick brush, and tap on a bit of cherry lippie.

Back in bed, I whizz through my WhatsApp contact list. I stop at the name Emmanuel, take two deep breaths, and click on the video icon. It rings. Again. And again.

After the fifth ring, it dawns on me that I haven't seen Emmanuel since I was twelve. I try to refresh my memory of him: left ear pierced, caramel skin, chipped eyebrows—yes, because that was the "cool look" at the time, thanks to the likes of So Solid Crew.

By now, I've counted the tenth ring. With a sigh, I go to tap on "end call," when suddenly, the call connects and we're staring face-to-face.

Okaaay. Player rumors aside, Emmanuel is *fit*. He has a nice stubble and shape-up, and he has ditched the chipped eyebrow look.

"Yo, who's this?" he says, his brows twisting like The Rock.

"Hi, Emmanuel," I say. "It's Yinka."

"Yinka?" He looks confused. Not even a flicker of recognition runs across his face.

Oh, God. There's a sick feeling in my stomach. I'm sure Mum said Emmanuel was waiting to hear from me.

"Yinka," I say again. "We knew each other when we were kids?" And because Emmanuel's expression doesn't change, I add, "You know, the one who you went to Sunday school with? Lived in Peckham."

"Oh," he says to my relief. "Oh, so *you're* Yinka." His eyebrows rise. "Okay. My mum did say you might call."

I smile. "Yes, I am she." I raise my phone higher to catch a better angle. "This is awkward," I say after an extended pause. God, I wish I had planned a few questions. "So, how's it going?"

Emmanuel's eyes remind me of a chameleon's. They flicker everywhere but at me.

"Good," he says flatly. "Life is good. Can't complain." I wait for him to ask me the same question, but he doesn't.

"Great," I say to avoid another lull. "Life is good too. Can't complain."

"Cool," Emmanuel says.

More silence.

"Sooo . . . what do you do for work?" I say this calmly, but inside I'm panicking. Maybe I caught him at the wrong time.

"I'm a plumber," he answers in the same mechanical tone.

"That's handy." I chuckle. "Excuse the pun."

Emmanuel doesn't laugh. He doesn't even chuckle or—*throw me a bone*—smirk. Instead, his pupils are still busy chasing the elephant in the room.

"Okay. I know this is awkward, me video calling you out of the blue. Would you like me to call you normally? Or maybe another time? Or you can call me in your own time?" I add quickly. "Whenever you're free."

Emmanuel sucks in his lips as though he's in pain and he needs to scream. God, I know this is painful but give me *something*, man.

"The thing is"—he rubs his neck, laughs a little—"when my mum told me about you, I actually had a *different* person in mind."

"Oh," I say, startled, not prepared for that answer. "Who did you think I was?"

Emmanuel smiles, an awkward smile. He's still rubbing his neck. "Do you remember that light-skinned girl?" he says finally, and I stiffen. Jemimah was the light-skinned girl that all the boys liked in Sunday school. "Yeah, for some reason, I had in mind you were her."

"I see . . ."

"It's nothing personal against you," he rushes to say, and I have no desire to hear what he's about to say next. Tears are burning the backs of my eyes and I'm desperate to get off the phone. "It's just my preference," he finishes. "But you're pretty for a dark-skinned girl, though—"

I hit "end call" before the tears come. I've heard enough. Suddenly, I'm hyperventilating. Crying like a child who has just broken her toy. I snatch off my wig and toss my phone to one side, not even caring when it bounces off the bed with a thump. I feel so stupid. Humiliated. I'm taken back to the younger me on the playground. I feel . . . *ugly.*

I thrust myself out of bed, stomping toward my mirror where I'm confronted with my dark complexion. I cry louder. Gasping for air.

I am the problem. I will never find love, because *I'm* the problem. All along I was wrong. It's not what I need to *do,* but *who* I need to be.

After wiping my face furiously, I pick up my phone then snatch up my car keys. I don't bother with my wig. I grab my coat and leave.

It takes me longer than usual to reach Peckham. God, the traffic is intense. Thankfully, the hair shops are still open and I rush into the same one I went into a few months back. I head for the skincare aisle, knowing exactly where to stop.

I grab a handful of all types: creams, soaps, gels, lotions—all promising lighter skin. Fair and beautiful.

I head toward the cashier, my arms full, not giving a damn who sees me. There's a short queue. I stand behind a plump woman, her acrylic nails clutching two packets of weave.

Aware that my eyes are puffy and red, I stare at the floor, relieved to take a step forward every so often. I'm third in the line now. Nearly there.

Then, just as I'm about to step forward, I hear a little girl say, "Excuse me, please."

When I look at her, my heart swells. She has rich chocolate skin with short kinky hair tied back in pigtails, and as I stare at her, I see . . . I see . . . me.

"Yinka, you're beautiful." I'm hearing Daddy's voice. *"Don't let anyone tell you otherwise. Remember, the midnight sky is just as beautiful as the sunrise."*

I look down at my chest, the array of lightening products pressed against my arm. I feel physically sick.

"I said excuse me, please," the girl says again. I step back and watch her skip past, the hem of her dress swishing above her white socks until she grabs the hand of a man wearing a durag.

What am I doing? I come back to my senses, and a single tear falls.

I scurry out of the queue, apologizing to the South Asian man who yells, "Next, please!" and hurry up the aisle. I stuff all the products back, not caring that I've placed them all wrong on the shelves.

Outside, my emotions are overwhelming and for the first time in Peckham, I feel disoriented. I can't drive. Not in this state. I need somewhere private.

Blindly I make my way to the park where Donovan and I ate chicken and chips all those weeks ago, collapsing on the same bench. I wipe my eyes. Tears fall. Wipe them again. More tears fall. Giving up, I allow myself to cry, making ugly blubbering sounds.

"Yinka?"

I look up. Donovan is nearing me, holding a takeaway box. I immediately wipe my face. For flip's sake, can't I go anywhere without seeing this man?

"Hey, what's wrong?" He rushes over to the bench, casting the takeaway box to one side before wrapping his arm around me.

"Everything!" I clap my knees in exasperation. "Why am I never good enough?"

"Is this about your job situation?" He draws his face closer to mine.

"No. It's not that. It's—it's . . ."

"Family?"

"No, not family. God, I feel so embarrassed."

Donovan rubs my shoulder, and I feel his strong gaze on me. I keep my eyes fixed on my thighs, which have stopped shaking.

"It's about that guy, isn't it?" he says after a moment.

I look up, and a wave of emotions hits me, a rush of blood to the head.

"I just want to be accepted, okay! Accepted for who I am. How I look. What I believe in. I shouldn't have to compromise myself. Including my bloody virginity. You accept me for who I am. Take it or leave it. I'm tired of changing myself."

Donovan stares at me. My chest is heaving.

"Sorry." I glance away. "I—I don't know what came over me."

"Don't apologize," he says. "Don't be sorry for who you are. Or what you believe in. No woman should ever feel like they have to compromise themselves, and especially not you. Now, I don't know what went down with you and this friend of yours, but the person you're meant to be with will treat you like a queen."

For some reason, this makes another tear fall. And then another.

"Aww, come on. Yinks." He pulls me into him. I cry into his shoulders.

"I feel like I'm losing myself, Don."

He tightens his grip, burying his chin in my hair.

"I feel like I'm losing myself, and I don't know how to get myself back."

What brings Yinka here today?

MONDAY

DONOVAN

Hope today goes well x

JOANNA

We're so proud of you. x

Jacqui isn't what I expected. Neither is the room we're sitting in, with its warm lighting, turquoise sofa and yucca plant in the corner. On the table beside me is a glass of water and a Brita jug. Jacqui is sitting opposite me, her hair in braids, shoulders wrapped in a shawl. She's wearing trainers— Retro New Balance with orange shoelaces.

"Now," she says, adjusting her notepad lying on her lap. We've just run through the terms and conditions—things I have to commit to, like doing my "homework," which frankly sounds a bit terrifying. "What brings Yinka here today?" She smiles.

I blow out my cheeks and touch my hair, digging my fingers through the coils. "Gosh, where do I even start?"

"Anywhere that is comfortable for you," she replies, and I glance down at her feet. Unlike mine, they're perfectly still.

It seemed like a good idea at the time, taking down the number of Donovan's counselor. But now that I'm here, I'm not too sure. I can't tell Jacqui about my Post-it note plan. The squats, the pounded yam diet—I'm cringing even just thinking about it. And as a fellow dark-skinned woman, I *cannot* tell Jacqui that I nearly bought a range of lightening products.

So instead, I say, "Is it so wrong to want love?"

Jacqui gives me a nod, which I'm guessing means, *"Tell me more."*

"I want my happily ever after," I say, and I surprise myself with my defensive tone. "Sorry, I . . ." I breathe out. "I just have this fear. This fear that I'll never—" I break off, not wanting to say it aloud. "I want to find love and get married one day. Yeah, I know, it's the twenty-first century, so this makes me a bad feminist, right?"

I reach for my glass of water, needing to hold on to something. I already know what Jacqui is going to say. She'll tell me all the reasons why marriage doesn't equate to happiness, as though I don't already know this.

So when Jacqui shakes her head, no, my brows shoot up in surprise.

"I don't think it does," she says sagely. "It just shows that you're human. And as humans, we have an intrinsic need to find and maintain relationships. So no, Yinka, there's nothing wrong in wanting these things. But you mentioned the word 'fear.' Tell me, is that a fear of yours? That you'll never find love or get married?"

My mouth parts. I feel as though I've walked into a trap that I didn't even know I had a role in making. I sense that Jacqui realizes this too, as she relaxes back in her chair.

"Maybe we should start with this?" she says. "The catalyst that perpetuated this fear. For many people it's more than one thing, but let's start with the first thing that comes to your mind."

Without needing to think, I say, "Femi. My ex-boyfriend."

I've never been a loquacious person, but once I start talking it's hard to stop. It's as though someone has reached into a bathtub and pulled out the plug, and now all the murky, dirty water is whirling beyond my control. I tell Jacqui that ever since I was young, I've been an overachiever. That this served me well in my education and career, and so, naturally, I had faith that I'd find love and marry one day too. So when I got with Femi—sweet, ambitious, handsome Femi—he didn't just solidify my plans, he boosted my confidence. My life was all going as I'd hoped it would. Then all of a sudden, he didn't want to be with me.

"I met his beautiful new fiancée recently and I was like, ah-hah!" I raise a finger. "So that's why you left. You wanted someone better. Someone lighter—" I break off, then continue hastily. "And now I'm convinced there must be something wrong with me. Is there something wrong with me? Sorry, you're the one supposed to be asking the questions."

Jacqui finishes the note she's scribbling. "Don't apologize," she says, and there's a twinkle in her eye. "Remember, there's no right or wrong way of expressing yourself." She tilts her head. "It sounds as though you went through some heartbreak, huh?"

I nod several times.

"From what I'm hearing, you're feeling hopeless. Your ex-boyfriend has managed to meet someone and you haven't. That's what brought about this fear, isn't it? But Yinka, tell me. What if you never find love or get married? How would you ultimately be?"

The very thought is excruciating. "I would like to say I would be happy because finding love doesn't define who I am." Aunty Blessing flashes to mind. "But honestly, Jacqui, I would be disappointed. Then there's dealing with my family and friends. I don't want to be the one everyone feels sorry for."

Jacqui does another of her "go on" nods, but my throat is tingling. I don't want to elaborate. Then after an immense silence, she says, "You know, it may be that it's not so much fearing being alone, as fearing you're not good enough," and I feel as though she is holding up a mirror.

"A person who doesn't believe in themselves may think that they are not worthy of love," she carries on, and I knock back my water to stop my gathering tears from leaking out. "Yinka, I want to help you confront your underlying fears head-on. The goal here is for you to be happy as a single woman *now* while retaining your faith that you'll find love because you deserve it. In other words, to embrace the present and not fear the future. Does that make sense?"

Unable to speak, I give a weak nod. And when she glances down, I wipe the corner of my eye.

"Now, if you don't mind," she says, looking up again, "I want to touch on something you said earlier. When you mentioned Femi's new fiancée, I was intrigued by the words you used."

I take a long glug of my water as Jacqui refers to her notes again, hoping she's not going to ask what I think she's going to ask . . .

"You said, and I'm going to quote you here, 'I met his beautiful new fiancée recently and I was like, ah-hah! So that's why you left. You wanted someone better. Someone lighter.'" She looks up.

"Oh, did I?" I give a nervous chuckle. Then I peer at the clock behind me. How has only twenty minutes gone by?

"Okay, let's leave that for another day," Jacqui says finally. *Thank God.* "Now, going back to Femi, walk me through how you coped with the breakup. What thoughts were running through your head?"

"I guess I buried myself in work," I admit, reflecting on my days at Godfrey. "I worked at an investment bank as an operations manager. Didn't particularly like it."

"What about your attitude toward love? What was it like then?"

I push out my lips. "Strangely, optimistic." I tug the end of my sleeve. "I always told myself that I would find love in my own time. It was the mantra I used when people brought up my singleness. Like I said, I was convinced that my life was all going to plan."

"Would you say it was your crutch?" Jacqui asks, and I let slip a quiet gasp. This was the same question I posed to Donovan when we talked about his reluctance to start dating.

"Yes," I say eventually. "That's right."

Jacqui and I discuss practical ways that I can overcome my fear of being alone and boost my self-confidence. From meditation to words of affirmation. *Hmm. Maybe I can write a few of these on my Post-it notes?* We also discussed the importance of embracing singleness and taking time out to be at one with yourself—a task she set me for this week's homework.

"So, Yinka"—Jacqui unwinds her shawl—"can you imagine that you're lovable even if you're single?"

I think of Aunty Blessing again. "Yes . . ." I clear my throat. "I think—I think I can."

Pregnancy doesn't stop ears
from working

Monday, 17 May at 3.08 p.m.

From: Matthews, Terry

To: Yinka Oladeji

Subject: Interested in working at Comperial

Hi Yinka,

Thanks for sending your CV. It's very impressive. I actually
think you'd be great as a strategy project manager (see role
description attached). Are you available to come to our offices
next Tuesday at eleven?

Terry

I make a mental note to reply later. Therapy has got me in the talking mood,
and there's only one person I want to talk to right now.

"Hey." Kemi answers the door in a flat tone and gives me the briefest
hug. "How's it going?" she says as she slumps back on the sofa.

"Just came from counseling."

"Counseling?"

I gaze over at Chinedu, sleeping peacefully in his crib. I join Kemi on the sofa. "I need to talk to you about some stuff."

I tell her about everything—well, not Marcus but everything else—including how my singleness has taken a toll on me over the last few months.

"Yinka! Why didn't you tell me?" she cries.

"Because I'm supposed to be your older sister, the one that's supposed to have her *ish* together. *And* you were pregnant," I add.

She frowns. "Pregnancy doesn't stop ears from working."

"Yeah, I know. It's just…" I sigh. "Kemi, I'm sorry. I'm sorry that I showed up here tipsy the other day. And for all the times I haven't been there for you. You're always making an effort to spend time with me. But I kept avoiding you … well, Mum."

"Mum?" Kemi looks startled. Chinedu gurgles, and we freeze for a moment, then he settles. "So you weren't avoiding me?"

"'Course not," I say as Chinedu quietly babbles to himself. "But these days you love to spend time with Mum. The only thing is, when I'm here, too, Mum always harps on about me being single. Then you apologize, thinking it's your fault. That's why I left the hospital without saying goodbye. My love life was put under the spotlight. *Again.*"

"Oh, Yinka. I'm so sorry—"

"But that's the thing, Kemi. I don't want you to be sorry. You're happily married with a beautiful baby. There's nothing for *you* to be sorry about. The truth is, you feeling sorry makes me feel even worse about myself."

Kemi opens her mouth—like she's about to apologize—then closes it again.

"My issue is with Mum," I carry on. "*I'm* sorry I allowed that to affect our relationship." I'm not sure who reaches for whose hand first.

"You know"—Kemi licks her lips—"when we were younger, I envied the attention Mum gave you."

I squeeze her hand and she places the other on top.

"You were the bright, clever one," she goes on. "You *earned* Mum's respect. She admired you. You got the grades, or rather, you got the grades in the subjects that mattered. So for years I fought for her attention. Why do you think I understand Yoruba and can make Nigerian food better than you?"

It's my turn to stare at her, shocked.

She exhales. "Then when I got engaged, things changed. She was finally proud of me. Yinka, I spend time with Mum because, because . . . I've longed for her."

"Oh, Kemi." I pull her to me and rock her slightly. She clings to my shoulders. All this time I've thought I have no role as an older sister. And all this time she's needed me.

"So it's Mum's fault," I say. We laugh as we draw apart. "Now, how about that pampering session I promised you? I still have those foot scrubs." I reach for my bag. "But please tell me you've clipped your toenails!"

Can we be normal again?

> I am worthy of love
> I am who I say I am

"Drumroll, please."

At Nana's request, Aunty Blessing and I drum our hands against our knees. Nana leans over Aunty Blessing's desk as she signs a few papers.

"That's it. It's done," she says, straightening up, and Aunty Blessing and I break into applause. "I'm officially the company director of Nana Badu Limited."

"So how do you feel?" says Aunty Blessing as I stare awestruck at her hair. For the first time in ages, she's wearing it down and it's way past her shoulders.

"Nervous but excited." Nana lets out a relieved sigh. "Oh, and thank you, Aunty, for taking the time to run through it with me." She bundles her paperwork into a folder then perches on the arm of my chair.

"So, not long to Rachel's wedding." Aunty Blessing sags back in her seat, and in my peripheral vision, I notice Nana glance down.

I know, I want to say. I also can't believe it's been weeks since I last spoke to Rachel and Ola. I do miss them.

"Yeah, not long now." I feign excitement. Maybe I should call them? Talk it out, like I did with Kemi. Nana had reminded me that I could talk to Jacqui.

"Ooh, Terry," Aunty Blessing says to my relief. "Has he got back to you?"

I nod. "On Monday. There's this project management role he thinks I'll be good for."

"That's fantastic," she says, while Nana squeezes my shoulders.

"But truthfully . . ." I wring my hands. "I'm not interested."

Aunty Blessing actually laughs. "You've got to be kidding me."

I laugh too. "Please, hear me out. I don't want the role because . . . I'm going to pursue a career in the charity sector."

Aunty Blessing and Nana turn to look at each other.

"Wow." Aunty Blessing exhales. "What brought this on?"

I think back to my counseling session with Jacqui. "I need to get in touch with who I really am," I say. "Not try to be the person the world wants me to be."

Aunty Blessing smiles. "Love it."

"Have you seen any charity roles that you're interested in?" Nana asks.

I nod. "My dream job. An outreach manager at Sanctuary."

Aunty Blessing blinks. "Wait, isn't that the homeless charity that you used to volunteer for?"

"It sure is," I say in a sing-song voice. "A friend—I mean, I know someone who is recruiting for the role, so I've got a way in. Speaking of which"—I glance at my watch—"I was hoping to catch him at the outreach tonight. I'd better get going." I rise to my feet and Nana stands too.

"Oh, I'm so happy for you." Aunty Blessing envelops me in a hug. "You see, my dear, in life, you will face many, many pressures. But it's important that you only do what *you* want to do, in your own time and at your own pace. If you can remember this, you'll live a very happy life. Anyway, I'm glad you're off. Because your Aunty's going *out*." And with that, she flicks her hair. "See you at Chinedu's christening."

"I guess I'll meet you at home," I tell Nana as she grabs her rucksack from the floor.

"Actually, do you mind if I tag along? I left my key at home."

"Oh, I can just give you mine." I swing my bag from my shoulder.

"No, it's okay." She links my arm. "Besides, we're due a catch-up. Now, tell me about this friend with the job contacts."

"Well, I wouldn't call him my friend," I say with a small laugh. "He's okay but a bit of a know-it-all."

I stroll down the corridor, Nana in tow. Aunty Blessing is singing Whitney Houston's "I'm Every Woman" in the bathroom.

"Someone's in a good mood," says Nana, and we both laugh. For some reason, her laugh stirs something in me. It reminds me of our shared good times. Nana has been with me through thick and thin.

"Nana. Thank you," I say when we reach the bottom of the stairs.

"For what?" she asks.

"For being such a true friend, pushing me to see a counselor. You were right." I sigh. "I was such an idiot."

Nana offers me a warm smile. Her eyes tell me that she recognizes me again. "You know I got you, hun."

———

When we arrive at Peckham, the sun is still bright. That's one thing I love about late spring—it doesn't get dark till around nine.

Derek spots me. "Hey! What you doing here? I thought you said you were taking some time out to focus on your career?"

I rack my brains. *Crap. What can I say?*

Then it hits me. What if the question that I should be asking myself isn't "*What can I say?*" but rather "*What should I say?*" I realize I have a lot to say to Derek about how I treated him these last few months. He's a good person and I've been avoiding him like the plague. And just because I don't like him romantically, doesn't mean we can't still be friends.

"Derek, I've come here to tell you that I'm sorry."

"Sorry?" he says. "For what?"

"Sorry, Nana. Can you give us a sec?"

Nana nods and takes a step to the side.

"For how I've treated you," I carry on, thinking back to how I felt when Marcus avoided me. "I don't know if you've noticed, but I have been kinda avoiding you these last few months."

Derek laughs and bats his hand. Then after I fail to join him, he says, "Okay, I have noticed. But honestly, Yinka, it's fine." He shoves his hands in his pockets. "And I'm sorry if I came across as, you know . . . overbearing. Yes, overbearing," he repeats after I frown. "But I only made the extra effort because I wanted things between us to be normal . . . I know I freaked you out a little when I told you I liked you."

"Well, clearly that's not the case now." I smile and nod to Vanessa a few meters away. "She's a sweetheart, she is. How long have you guys been together?"

Derek grins. "Yeah, she's great, isn't she? Oh, and two months this Sunday."

I smile. "You know what, Derek? I miss hanging out. Can we be normal again?"

He proffers a hand. "Deal."

After I've made up with Derek, it doesn't take me long to find Donovan. He's with the tracksuited teens, leaflet stuffing, using the same system that I showed them all those months ago.

I pull Nana along with me. Donovan is rapping along to Drake's "God's Plan," and I smirk at the irony.

"I can't keep you away, can I?" Donovan greets me with a hug. I haven't seen him since I ruined his hoody with my snot and tears last Thursday.

"Oh, this is my friend, Nana."

Nana sticks out her hand. "I'm guessing you're Donovan, then."

Donovan frowns. "Come on, sis. Bring it in." They hug.

"Yes, yes, my brother. I love that album." Nana nods to the print on Donovan's T-shirt.

Donovan looks down at himself. "Wait, you know about Black Star?"

"Err, who doesn't?"

And as I expect, Donovan throws a side-glance my way. He laughs. "Just kidding." My heart races as he leans over and squeezes my shoulders.

"Ooh, sorry. I have to get this." Nana points at her buzzing phone and strolls away.

"So"—Donovan turns to me—"how did your first session go?"

I notice his toned arms and I feel my cheeks warm. I'm getting that same feeling I have whenever I see Michael B. Jordan on TV.

"Huh? Um, I mean, yeah, not bad." *Were his eyelashes always this long?* "You were right. Jacqui is a goat."

Donovan chuckles heartily. "You mean *the* goat. *Now* do you think therapy is a worthy investment?"

I push out my lips. "It's still early days."

"Just remember, yeah, you only get out of it what you put in. Anyway, any word from that MD? I'm not gonna lie, Yinks, I'm sad you missed the deadline for that Sanctuary job."

"I missed the deadline?" I say this right at the exact same moment Nana returns.

"Sorry about that," she says. "Yinka, that was your neighbor—"

"My neighbor?"

"Yeah. Turns out your car is blocking hers, so we need to head home. Like, now."

"Why does my neighbor have your number?" I frown, genuinely perplexed.

But Nana is too busy hugging Donovan good-bye. "You know what?" she says, standing back. She looks at Donovan from head to toe. "You have a good height, you know. How do you fancy walking in a fashion show?"

The first thought I have as we draw closer to my house is, How can my car be blocking my neighbor's car when hers is not even there?

I turn to look at my friend. "Nana, what's going on? And I was really looking forward to volunteering tonight."

"Oh, please," she says. "You just wanted to spend time with Donovan."

"What?" I push open my front door, ready to list the one hundred and two reasons why I can't stand that man, when I hear a hum of chatter.

"Oh, God. Someone's in the house." I grip onto Nana, my heart thumping.

But when the door to the kitchen swings open, I'm surprised to see Rachel.

"Finally. What took you so long?"

My shoulders go slack. God, I've missed her.

"Now before you say anything—" Rachel holds up her hand, then stands aside. Ola is sitting at the breakfast table. "I'm not here to play mediator but my wedding is in two months. And according to Nana, neither one of you has called the other. Since I'm not going to take sides, the best I can do is get you in the same room."

Slowly, I walk into the kitchen and stand across from Ola.

"Nana and I are going to step outside, and the two of you *will* talk." Rachel places Nana's key on the counter.

I watch Nana lead the way out of the kitchen, and just before Rachel goes, she squeezes my shoulder.

I turn to Ola. She looks . . . *sad.*

I feel an urge to apologize and be done with it. But then I think, no. We need to have a proper conversation.

So I sit on the opposite chair, and I pretend that I'm in Jacqui's room again with its turquoise sofa and warm lighting and the yucca plant in the corner, and feel something stir within me. Then I start to talk. I tell Ola that I'm sorry that I outed her secret and for all the mean things I said. I tell her how I feel like I've been paying the price for her mother's behavior toward her and how it feels to walk on eggshells and be blamed for every one of our fallings-out. I tell her how much I miss her. The cousin who would stick up for me, even over something as trivial as being short-changed by 50p.

By this point, Ola is holding back tears. I place my hand over hers and stroke her knuckles.

"We haven't been open with each other for years, have we?" I whisper.

And for the next several minutes, Ola pours out her heart and I listen, never once interrupting or letting her hand go. She tells me about her marriage and how she feels like a wife only by default—because if she hadn't got pregnant then she and Jon wouldn't be together. She tells me about how hard it is for her to trust anyone—she's constantly watching Jon's every move—and how this has strained their marriage. She tells me that Jon is always reassuring her that he loves her, and yes, the picnic proposal did happen, but she didn't tell anyone about it because she doubted his love.

"Despite all Jon's reassurances," she sniffs, "I couldn't help but think that he loved me as the mother of his children, not the love of his life. And then, when he told me recently that it was *you* he'd liked way back when, I felt so insecure. Why do you think I ditched my weave?" She pulls her tightly coiled ponytail. "I know it sounds silly, but I've never had much confidence. Even when I was a kid. I think I have my mum to blame for that."

"I know the feeling," I admit, and my voice wobbles. "Though it's more about whether or not I'm in a relationship. You know, my mum compares me with you too."

My lips are trembling now. My heart aches. *Sod it.* I get up and throw my arms around her.

"I'm sorry," we keep saying. We wipe each other's eyes and cheeks, only for tears to fall again. I've wanted this for so long.

"Look at us, blubbering like two grown babies," Ola says, and I laugh. "Oh, yeah." She sniffs. "I heard about your redundancy. Are you okay?"

I take a deep breath before explaining why I lied.

"Don't worry," she says. "I would have done the exact same thing. No *way* I'd risk a lecture from my mum!"

We laugh again, then her smile vanishes.

"I'm such a mess," she whispers, staring blankly straight ahead. "Jon, he deserves better."

During the silence, I stroke her hair, not in a rush to speak. Eventually I say, "Ola, don't take this the wrong way but . . . have you considered counseling?"

In your own time

> Psalm 139:14—I praise you because
> I'm fearfully and wonderfully made
>
> Phenomenal woman, that's me

Today, Jacqui's wearing Adidas Superstars—white shell toe trainers with three blue stripes on the outer side. I've just been telling her about my great week and how I've repurposed my dozens of Post-it notes to write words of affirmation to myself, including my favorite poem "Phenomenal Woman" by Maya Angelou. They're all stuck up on my bedroom wall shaped in a heart. I also tell her about my decision to change careers. Yes, I missed the Sanctuary job deadline, and I'm still gutted about that, but I'm not going to give up. I want to work for a charity.

"I have to say," says Jacqui, adjusting her pashmina, "you do seem chirpier this week."

"Thanks!" I flash my teeth.

"Now, if it's okay"—she looks down at her notes—"there's something you mentioned last week that I would like us to discuss today." She pauses briefly.

I shift. "I know what you're going to say." I sigh. "You're talking about that comment I made, right? How I thought that Femi wanted someone better . . . someone lighter."

Jacqui snuggles in her chair. "Are you happy for us to start there?"

I run a finger over my thigh, feeling Jacqui's gaze on me. There's no easy way to tell her that I considered lightening my skin. But like Donovan said, you only get out of therapy what you put in.

"I have this belief . . ." The tears are already collecting in my throat. "This belief that the reason why I'm still single is because . . . I'm not beautiful enough. You see, for years"—I allow a tear to fall—"I've searched for someone who looks like me, with my complexion, my figure, my hair, to be the chosen one. But when I look at all the famous Black men, their wives, their girlfriends, they don't look like me." I reach for a tissue, pulling the pointy end while what feels like anger rumbles in my chest. "Let's face it, Jacqui. The women who grace magazine covers are usually light-skinned, Latina or white. In music videos, they are the desired ones. Light-skinned women are seen as more beautiful. Full stop. In fact, only a few weeks back, this guy told me straight to my face that I'm not his preference. And do you know what his consolation prize was? Well, at least I'm pretty for a dark-skinned girl. It broke me, Jacqui. It broke me. And that's why . . . and that's why . . . and that's why I considered lightening my skin."

My confession roars out of me. I put my hands to my face. I'm shuddering. Crying loudly.

"I'm sorry. I'm so sorry." I dab my cheeks with my scrunched-up tissue, but it's so badly crumpled and wet, it's useless. A hand falls on my shoulder.

"It's okay to *feel.*" Jacqui is on the sofa beside me, and she lowers her head close to mine. "Don't suppress it. Let it out."

So I do. I feel. I feel from the tingles in my toes right to the hairs behind my neck. I feel when I shut my eyes, where I'm that little girl again, hating herself even more than she hated the bullies.

"Tell me," Jacqui says after I quieten. She offers another tissue and I blow my nose. "Was there ever a time when you felt beautiful?"

I train my eyes on her rug, squeezing the tissue, praying for my tears to go away.

"You know, my daddy used to call me beautiful, but now he's dead, so . . . so, I don't know."

For what feels like the first time in forever, I talk about the loss of my dad, the bullying, and how when Daddy was alive he reaffirmed my beauty, and how since he died I've always been looking to men to make me feel better about myself.

"You see, this belief you have, that you're not beautiful enough. It's not a fact, it's a by-product of your life experience. And Black history. You've heard of colorism?" Jacqui raises her brow. "It's been dividing our people for generations. And do you know what the sad thing is? It has made our people believe this lie—that the closer one is to being white, the better one is. Sounds silly when I say it aloud, doesn't it? But a lie can appear true when it has been told for centuries."

While we were talking, I couldn't help but think of Mum and her obsession with long hair. Colorism. Texturism. They're part of the same thing.

"And what about your mum?" asks Jacqui as though she's read my mind. She's still sitting on the sofa beside me. "You've said a lot about your dad, but where does your mum fit in to all of this?"

I surprise myself with a laugh. "Sorry, it's just . . . she's part of the reason I'm here. She's always pressuring me to get married. But I don't see what talking about her will achieve. She's set in her ways. She's Nigerian, so—" I bring my tongue to a halt. I realize that I don't know Jacqui's heritage. "That's not to say all older Nigerian folks are set in their ways," I backtrack. "It's just the way my mum is."

Jacqui's smile is reassuring. "Don't worry, I get what you're trying to say about the generations. I grew up in a Caribbean household so there are many similarities. Now back to your mum—I know you said you don't want to talk about her, but you already have."

Jacqui is like a human bat. She picks up everything.

"I guess it's just something I have to live with."

"But how does it feel, this constant pressure to get married?"

"Annoying! Sorry, I didn't mean to raise my voice. And it's not just my mum. My Aunty Debbie puts pressure on me too. Well, maybe pressure isn't the right word to use. Basically, she goes out of her way to help me with my love life but only ends up embarrassing me. But I don't see her all the time, so I can cope with that . . . to a point."

Jacqui does another one of her iconic slow nods and after a while of me not saying anything, she asks, "Do you think your mum is aware of how you feel?"

I open my mouth to reply then close it again. Surely, Mum *knows* how I feel. She must. Or does she? Maybe all this time that I've been refusing her potential suitors for me, she just thinks I'm being . . . stubborn.

"Do you know what, Jacqui?" I say. "I really don't know the answer."

"But would you want your mum to know how you feel, if you had it your way?"

"I guess so." I shrug. "But we don't have that kind of relationship where we can be open with each other over a cup of tea. Oh no. Don't tell me that's my homework for next week?"

Jacqui smiles. "Don't worry, it's not. For next week, I want you to write a letter to your younger self, preferably handwritten. It's a way to get things off your chest. But for now"—she places her notebook on the floor—"I want you to engage in a therapeutic exercise called chairwork. Yes, chairwork," she repeats after I look at her as though she's speaking a foreign language. "Basically, this exercise is when you have an imagined conversation—in this case, it will be with your mum. I understand that you've accepted the relationship you have with her, but it's clear that the pressure she puts on you is causing some pain. So this is a chance for you to speak your inner mind, even if you never get the chance to do it in person. Now"—she nods to the empty chair opposite—"in your own time."

Later that day . . .

Dear Yinka,

You are now a full-grown woman! Can you believe it?
I remember the days when you used to say you couldn't
wait to move out so that Mum would stop nagging
you about your homework. Well, congrats, you. You've got
your own place now. Do you know that you've also got a degree
from Oxford? Anyway, I'm not writing to you to tell you
about your achievements—and trust me, baby girl, there
are many—but I would be lying if I told you that the bullies
who called you dog poo are the only challenges that
you'll face.

You'll grow older and face many more challenges as you
navigate this world as a dark-skinned woman. There will be days
when you'll take pictures and feel like crap when you look at the

photo and can hardly see yourself. And there will be days when you'll look at Kemi and wish you had her skin tone. The thought, "If only I was lighter" will cross your mind, and you will think this each time a guy shows no interest in you, and when the love of your life breaks your heart.

Dear younger self, I am telling you this so that you can save yourself from many years of pain and insecurity. My message for you is . . . be ready. Be ready for the world you're about to enter. Because the world of today doesn't fairly uphold women who look like you. As a dark-skinned woman, sadly, you do not look like today's standard of beauty. So be ready, baby girl. Be ready and stand ready. Be ready to walk into any room with your chin held high and your shoulders rolled back because, yes, your rich chocolate skin does deserve a seat at the table. Define your own definition of beauty. Don't wait for society or any poxy magazine to do it for you. Don't wait for social media (oh, you'll find out what that is). And most definitely, do not wait for any man to affirm the beauty that you are. Tell yourself that you're beautiful each and every single day. Remember, Yinka, you are God's handiwork. Remember what Daddy said about the midnight sky being just as beautiful as the sunrise. All shades of brown are beautiful, including yours.

You are enough, Yinka. You. Are. Enough.

Proud of you, baby girl. So, so proud.

I love you . . . I love myself.

Yinka x

In Jesus' name we pray, Amen

SATURDAY

> *I am beautiful. I am beautiful.*
> *I am beautiful.*

It's like Kemi and Uche's wedding all over again, only in a less fancy venue—a community center in New Cross. Today is the day of Chinedu's christening celebration and the hall is buzzing.

Sitting cabaret style are at least three hundred guests—Mum went crazy with the invitations—and we're all now eating and drinking our way through a mountain of jollof rice, yam pottage and red gizzard stew. Pastor Adekeye is the MC, while the best of Shina Peters plays in the background. Wearing matching white traditional lace, Kemi and Uche are at the high table on the stage, taking turns carrying a restless Chinedu. At my table are Mum, Aunty Blessing, Aunty Debbie and her husband, then there's Ola, Jon and their three kids. I'm glad to see there's no awkward vibes between me and Ola. In fact, she gave me a proper hug earlier and whispered in my ear that she starts her counseling next week. At this rate, Jacqui will have to start paying Donovan commission.

So far I've been able to avoid having a direct conversation with Mum, but not for much longer . . .

"Yinka," she leans over. Reluctantly I bring my gaze back. "Things didn't work out with Emmanuel, ehn?"

Oh, for goodness' sake. Are we really going to have this conversation now?

"No," I say simply. I take a sip of my Supermalt.

"What happened *this* time, hm?" says Aunty Debbie, rolling her eyes.

"Is now the right time and place to be having this conversation?" Aunty Blessing comes to my rescue as always.

I dart my eyes across the dozens of round tables with guests from both sides of the family. I wish I was sitting at Rachel and Gavesh's table with Nana.

"And how's the job search going?"

Aunty Debbie does not know when to stop.

"Fine," I exhale, remembering to breathe. I try to recall something that Jacqui told me—that I can control how I respond to others. But just as I'm doing so, Aunty Blessing says, "Don't worry, Debbie. She's applying for her dream job. Isn't that right, Yinka?"

I purse my lips. Bummer. I haven't had the chance to tell Aunty Blessing that I've missed the deadline for the Sanctuary job I told her about.

"Well, that's good," Aunty Debbie continues. "I'm sure having a degree from Oxford on your CV will help." She's saying this to me, but she's really directing it at Ola.

I shoot a quick glance at Ola. The shift in her face is minute, but I've been on the receiving end of harsh words enough times to recognize what hurt looks like. And rather than the usual feeling of guilt I often have when Aunty Debbie puts us in a situation like this, I feel infuriated.

Thankfully, the tension is released by the arrival of Pastor Adekeye, whose mustard yellow suit immediately lifts my mood.

"Tolu," he says, bending over to speak to Mum. "We are due for another prayer." He points at item five on the program in his hand.

"Oh, yes," Mum cries. "Thank you for reminding me."

She pushes back her chair and scrambles to her feet, when I hear myself say, "Actually, Pastor, can I pray?"

Everyone turns to me, visibly stunned. Except for Pastor Adekeye, who says, "Yes, that would be lovely. Come with me."

As I arrive on stage, Kemi gives me one of those double-take looks as though I've stepped out of the changing room naked.

Pastor Adekeye signals to the DJ to stop the music. "Okay, we have a very special guest," he says, bringing the mic too close to his mouth. "As you all know, this is Yinka, Kemi's older sister," he says, addressing the audience. "Yinka has kindly offered to lead us all in another prayer. So take it away." He pats my back, then hands me the microphone before stepping to one side.

"Thank you," I say, not quite into the mic. I survey the hall. The guests are still chatting among themselves, and my tonsils are wobbling in the back of my throat. I'm absolutely bricking it.

I close my eyes. "May we all bow our heads, please." Thankfully, it doesn't take long for the chatter to settle. In fact, the hall becomes so quiet that I can hear the thudding of my heart in my ears.

I take a breath and moisten my lips. "Dear God," I begin. I wince at the sound of my own voice. It sounds jittery and shaky, as though I'm on the verge of tears. "We thank you for this occasion and for bringing us all here today."

I'm suddenly aware of how tight my gèlè feels around my head.

"We thank you for my sister, Kemi—who I love so, so much. And for her amazing husband, Uche, who's absolutely perfect for her. We thank you for Chinedu, the latest addition to our family. God, bless them richly and give them good health."

I get my first chorus of Amens and a hushed, "Yes, Lord," from Pastor Adekeye. *Thank God, I haven't passed out yet.*

"I thank you for my mum," I continue, "who is the backbone of our family. I love her dearly. God, please bless her."

Another murmur of Amens. Mum's is the loudest.

"And I thank you for my uncles and aunties. In particular, my parents' sisters—Aunty Blessing, Aunty Debbie, Big Mama, and the many others who are in Nigeria and abroad. They have not only looked out for my mum, but also for me and Kemi. God, bless them."

A third round of Amens. Oh, and a "Hallelujah!" from Big Mama.

"I also want to pray for myself." If the hall can get any quieter, it has, and tiny goosebumps prickle along the sides of my arms. "Firstly, Lord, thank you. Thank you that I'm alive to witness this day. But I also want to say . . ." I swallow. My heart is now in my throat. I'm like an Olympic diver on the edge of a springboard. "Th-th-thank you for this season," I finish. *No, Yinka, be more specific.*

"Thank you for this season of singleness," I amend.

There are three or four Amens—two of which come from Kemi and Uche. Other than that, the hall is stiflingly quiet. The same silence that you get when a comedian makes an offensive joke and the audience is unsure whether or not to laugh. The back of my ankara *bùbá* feels sticky, but I power on.

"For many people," I continue, and there's a new tone to my voice—confidence—"singleness is something to be ashamed of. It's something negative, to be prayed away. But I thank you, Lord, for this blessing." (Cue in the mutters and murmurings.) "Because without it, Lord, I wouldn't know how

to be a better person. How to better love my family. My friends. Myself."
(Kerfuffle and murmurings increase a few decibels.) I hear Pastor Adekeye
whisper into my ear, "Yinka, *oya*, round up."

Then I hear Mum. She's near the stage, somewhere to my right. She's
hissing, "Yinka, stop this bloody nonsense. Stop it right now!"

But I'm not done yet.

"Lord—"

"Yinka, get down!"

"If there is one thing I ask of you, it is that I find love *only* when I'm ready.
And when I do find love—which I ultimately know I will—let me be in the
position to give and receive it as a more confident, whole person who
knows her self-worth."

There. I've done it. I've bloody done it. *Oops. Sorry, God.*

Kemi yelps a mighty "Amen!" and so do a few other people in the
crowd too.

"Yinka." Pastor Adekeye calls my name like a warning.

But I've said what I had to say, and I feel incredibly proud of myself. Now
all that's left to say is . . .

"In Jesus' name we pray, Amen."

The muttering just about drowns out my closing, with the exception of
my dear sister, who's shouting, "Amen, preach it, sis!"

I open my eyes. It's just what I expected. Many conferring, shaking
heads. A few kissing their teeth. But what I do not see is one person with
pity in their eyes. And that makes me feel empowered.

And then I see Ola. She's on her feet, clapping. Then Aunty Blessing
stands up. Jon joins in too. Now Kemi isn't the only one to cry, "Amen!"—
they're all shouting it. Oh, and now Rachel has joined. Gavesh. And oh
my gosh, there's Nana. Before I know it, every millennial-looking person is
on their feet. They're whooping. They're clapping. My heart is bursting
with joy.

And then Pastor Adekeye wakes up from his daze and grabs the mic from me. "Okay. Thank you, Yinka, for that, ehhh . . . very untraditional prayer." Then quickly, he adds, "But we still pray you find a *huzband*, Amen."

The majority of the hall say, "Amen," and that's okay. They're not wishing bad on me. But it feels absolutely friggin' amazing to have spoken for myself for once.

The music, as requested by Pastor Adekeye, resumes playing, and when I turn around, Kemi is right there to give me the biggest hug.

"I'm so proud of you, sis," she whispers.

Tears prick my eyes. But I swallow them away, knowing who I have to face next.

Mum is at the foot of the stage, her arms crossed, chest heaving. I can hear her muttering in Yoruba, then—

"What is wrong with you? Have you lost your mind? Have you bloody lost your mind?"

Aunty Debbie scurries over, and not far behind is Aunty Blessing.

"How embarrassing," Aunty Debbie keeps saying. "Yinka, you know you embarrassed the family up there, don't you?"

"Okay, let's not *actually* embarrass ourselves by making a scene." Aunty Blessing's no-nonsense voice carries weight. Aunty Debbie looks over her shoulder and hisses something under her breath.

All the while, Mum just glares at me.

"Come with me," she says.

In the private room where we left our belongings earlier, Mum is pacing up and down, repeating, "Why now?"

I stand there waiting. I feel ready for it.

At last, Mum stops. "Yinka. What did I do to you for you to be treating me like this, ehn? Why would you embarrass me in front of all my friends?"

I take a breath. "Mum, what did I say that was so embarrassing? Was it calling singleness a blessing? Because if so, in what way is that embarrassing?"

Mum's expression twists into disbelief. Usually, I wouldn't have said this aloud. Usually, this is something I would have said in my head. But how long must I carry on like this? Playing it safe? Replying with silence? If there is one thing the chairwork has revealed to me it is, boy oh boy, do I have a lot to say. If I can stand up for myself in front of three hundred people, I can do the same in front of one.

"Yinka, all we have done is pray for you. Why don't you want to settle down, ehn? Why won't I pressure you? You're no longer a young woman. *Shebi*, you want to end up like your Aunty Blessing?"

"So is this what you're scared of, hm?" I'm not yelling but there is a power to my voice. "Me ending up like Aunty Blessing, or is it me ending up like you?"

"What?" Mum looks incredulous. It's as though I've just renounced my faith or told her I'm going to be a stripper. My heart quickens at the sight of her expression, but I press on.

"Daddy." My lips are trembling now. "Why don't you talk about him?"

"What are you talking about? Yinka, please. Don't insult me."

"No, you don't, Mum," I cry. "Whenever I ask you about him, you tell me I ask too many questions or shrug me off."

Mum scoffs and laughs. "You want to insult me today."

"See. You can't even deny it, can you?" Tears are gathering now as I remember what I said during the chairwork exercise. My heart is beating so fast.

"Mum," I say, my voice quivering. "Mum, look at me, please."

She just about turns her head.

"You've never mentioned how it felt to lose him," I say. "To be a single mum. To no longer be a wife. You've never mentioned what it was like to have your future changed."

Mum folds her arms, but there's a shimmer in her eyes, as though she's holding back tears too.

"Mum," I say again, "do you fear I'll be alone just as you are now?" My voice is weak, but the message is clear.

All at once, Mum breaks down, yelping loud sobs, tears gushing in thick streams. She yells Daddy's name. "Kunle! Kunle!"

"Oh, Mum." I go to her. Hot tears fall as I wrap her into me. We cry loudly. Neither of us in a position to comfort the other. *Although this is comforting,* I realize. It hurts seeing Mum break down, but we're actually hugging. I can't remember the last time I've hugged Mum like this, if at all.

"I just want you to be happy," she says into my shoulder through a snuffle of sobs. "I had to be strong for you and Kemi. I had to be strong."

For a while we just cling to each other, neither of us knowing what to say, swaying slightly. During the exercise with Jacqui, I spent twenty minutes speaking to an invisible Mum, and yet this moment of silence feels much more uplifting. As another tear rolls down my cheek, slipping through the corner of my lips, I realize how freeing it is to say what I think. To stand up for myself. I realize how much less of an effort it is to be my authentic self, as opposed to trying to be someone else. I love this feeling. I love this Yinka. I can get used to her.

June

Own it

FRIDAY

RACHEL

Exactly one month to go before my wedding!!!!!!!!!
💍👰🏾

Original Destiny's Child reunited!

YINKA

Can't wait!!!!!!! Woop! Woop!
Think we need a new name though
Girls, any suggestions?

OLA

Ooh, what about Bride's Beaches

Get it?

YINKA

Haha
Or . . .
The Support Bras?
Lool

NANA

Orrrr

We can just use an acronym

How about . . .

NORY?

OLA

YORN? Lool

RONY?

YINKA

I know! I know!

How about . . .

ORNY

😆

OLA

LMAOOOOOO

I'm dead

💀

NANA

I actually choked on my drink

RACHEL

😳

I swear Yinka

You're the queen of lame jokes

If someone had told me at the beginning of the year that I would be sitting next to Mum at Nana's fashion show taking selfies, I would have laughed in their face. Seriously. And yet, that's what we're doing. Smiling, cheeks squished up together and trying to stay in the frame.

After Mum and I had a good cry in the private room at Chinedu's christening party, we agreed that it was best to talk tomorrow at her place after church. The following day, we flicked through her wedding album and Mum talked about Daddy and how romantic he was. I can see now why she is so keen for me to have that too. We also talked about Aunty Debbie—Mum agreed to have a word with her—and how it feels to be compared to Kemi.

"Okay, I'm sorry," Mum said, a hand on my knee. "From now on, I will be more mindful of what I say."

And finally, my big announcement: that I'll be following my heart and pursuing a career in a charity organization. Mum's views on charity jobs has not changed, but she warmed to the idea when I told her about the better work-life balance.

"Does this mean you will have time to find a *huzband*?" she said.

"*Mum.*"

"I know, I know. I'm just joking."

I haven't found a job yet. But I'm not going to give up until I do.

Aside from job hunting and spending more time with Mum and Kemi, counseling has been going well, and the insight I get about myself only continues to grow.

After Mum and I have inspected the selfie—it's a bit blurry, but it will do—I turn to my right to look at Ola. Not just Ola, in fact, but Ola and Aunty Debbie. I can only assume that with Ola attending counseling now, the two of them are making progress too.

"What do you think?" says Ola, looking at her mum before darting a glance at me.

Nana's fashion show has yet to start, but still, I'm expecting nothing short of "excellent" from Aunty Debbie. For starters, the hall looks a-mazing. Straight ahead is a T-shaped catwalk illuminated with LED lights, and behind that is a massive screen displaying dream-like visuals that move in sync with the pumping dance music. In the front row are VIPs—vloggers, bloggers, *O.M.G. Is that Patricia Bright?*—and photographers are crouching near the stage, cameras ready.

"Well?" Aunty Blessing says, tilting her head.

We all stare at Aunty Debbie, waiting for her to answer.

"It's . . . wonderful," she says at last.

Ola and I clap.

"So do you still think that Nana made a mistake then?" Clearly counseling has given me no filter. "A few months ago, Aunty, you said Nana should have gone to uni—"

"Me?" Aunty Debbie looks flabbergasted. "No, I think you misunderstood. I said it would have *helped* if she had gone to university."

Ola and I smirk.

"But I have to say"—Aunty Debbie adjusts her cuffs—"she clearly is an ambitious girl. I'll give her that."

"Sooo," Ola says tentatively. "Would you say it's not essential to have a degree? That it's more about having ambition, working hard, not giving up?"

"A degree is still important," Aunty Debbie quips. Then she softens. "But yes, I suppose, those qualities are just as valuable."

"And passion." I turn to Mum, who is distracted by the massive overhead banners with "Nana Badu" printed in fancy gold writing and the logos of her sponsors beneath. Alex helped Nana create the logo when he designed her equally impressive website. Hmm. That's a thought. I wonder whether he'll be here today. I haven't seen him since the lunch of shame.

"What was that?" Mum shifts her attention back to me.

Smiling, I say, "It's important to do what you love. What makes you happy."

"Yes." Mum smiles. "Happiness is the utmost importance."

"And on that note . . ." Ola scratches her hair. She has returned to wearing a long weave again. "I've got an announcement to make."

"You're expecting another baby!" Mum says.

Ola snorts. "No. What I wanted to say is"—she takes a breath—"I'm going to become a freelance makeup artist."

"Wow, congrats, Ola." I squeeze her shoulders, and Aunty Blessing says, "Well, good for you."

"I'm good at makeup so I thought, hey, why not. Plus, I can fit it around the kids."

Mum says, "Good. I'll be calling you from now on. Any time Kemi does my makeup, I look like a clown."

We all laugh, except for Aunty Debbie.

"Mum?" Ola places a hand on her mum's knee.

Aunty Debbie remains poker, and we all hold our breath.

Suddenly, she breaks out in a smile. "So does this mean I get a discount then?"

Ola and I exhale with laughter.

"Hold on," Mum says. "I want a discount too."

A slightly out of breath Rachel appears from behind us wearing a white robe, her hair half-straightened. She does the quickest genuflect, then turns to me and Ola. "Nana needs you."

Backstage the atmosphere is buzzing: people everywhere, some half-dressed and others wearing brightly patterned garments. There are photographers, vanity mirrors, ooh, body art. A strong smell of hairspray punctures the air. Among the hubbub, I spot Nana, on her knees, her face vexed, hemming a model's lace mermaid skirt.

"Argh!" She drops the pins. "Why the fuck is everything going wrong today?"

Whoa. Nana must be stressed out. She never curses.

"Okay, I need to get ready," says Rachel. She makes a swift dash to the right. Ola and I ask Nana whether she's okay.

"No!" She clambers to her feet. "One of the models just canceled. I don't need this right now. Not on the most important day of my life."

"Okay, breathe." Ola demonstrates by breathing in. "Can't you just get one of your other models to step in?"

"It's not as simple as that." Nana sighs. "I want all the models to show-case my collection together at the very end. Great. Now my vision is all messed up." She blows out her cheeks.

"I'll step in."

Nana blinks at me.

"I'll be the model. Hopefully, the clothes will fit?"

"Yeah, she's about your size and height. But Yinka, are you *sure*?" Now Nana doesn't look as desperate. "Let me at least show you the outfit first before you commit to anything." She pulls out a garment cover from a nearby rack.

"Oh," I say after she zips it open. "It's a . . . swimsuit."

"A monokini," she corrects, and she twirls it by the hanger. I eye the tribal prints, the cut-out slits. Ooh, and it's backless.

"Yinka, are you *sure*?" Ola is saying while Nana says, "You don't have to do this, you know."

"No. Hand me that—whatever it's called. Me and my J-behind are going to rock that catwalk."

Nana hugs me. "You're a lifesaver."

I squeeze her. "No, it's time for me to be there for you."

"Hey, make space for me." Ola throws her arm around us.

"What are we all hugging for?" Rachel says, rushing over.

"Yinka's our new model," says Nana as we draw apart. "Quick. Get changed. Then go to hair and makeup."

"I'll do her makeup!" Ola volunteers.

As quick as I can, I strip out of my clothes before sliding into the monokini and a pair of heels. "Um, Nana. I'm also going to need a razor stick."

After I've sorted out my bikini line, I hurry to hair and makeup, and en route, I spot Donovan chatting to the other male models. *Oh yeah, I forgot Nana talked him into it.* The tallest of the bunch, he's wearing these cool dip-dyed shorts and a red dashiki vest. We lock eyes and he smiles.

At last, and with only one minute to go, I'm standing behind the stage with the other female models. In our bold colors and Nana's edgy designs, we look both confident and powerful, like African royalty. We embody the strength of Queen Mothers.

Hugging my exposed waist, I crane my neck. Nana is studiously watching a screen that shows everything that's happening on stage.

"Okay, thirty seconds!" she yells, and everything goes dead quiet. "And remember, guys. Own it." She gives me a wink.

The music goes on again. The deafening, loud, pumping kind. And after a deep breath, I let go of my waist.

Three minutes. That's how long the standing ovation went on for, after Nana delivered *the* fashion show of the year. Three words: she smashed it. Photographers, bloggers and fans are ambushing her as though she's Beyoncé.

"Congratulations!"

As soon as Nana breaks away, Ola, Rachel and I join her family by half-throttling her with a hug, before loading her with a bouquet of flowers, kisses and compliments.

"Girls, thank you so much for your help earlier," Nana says. "And Rachel, Yinka, you killed the runway."

Everything happened so quickly—one minute I was being ushered on to the stage, the next I was physically on it. Suddenly, this confidence came out of nowhere and I was strutting, hands on hips. I didn't care that the majority of my body was exposed, including my J-shaped bum, which I've now decided to stop referring to it as. I wasn't in my head, worried about the bright lights, or if I would fall off at the end and break my neck. Instead, I was in the moment, reciting the letter to my younger self: *Yes, your rich chocolate skin does deserve a seat at the table.*

"So out of the three of us, you smashed your bridesmaid's goal," says Rachel, patting Nana on her back.

"Nuh-uh," says Nana. "Rach, surely you've reached your weight goal by now?"

Rachel smiles. "I haven't, but I'm flattered you think I have. Truthfully, I ditched my diet months ago. When I thought about it, I was like, hey. I want to look like myself on my wedding day. And I love my curves!" She puts her hands on her hips.

"While we're on the topic of goals," says Ola. "I've got some news to share."

As Nana and Rachel gush over Ola's news to become a makeup artist, I scan the crowd and the rows of chairs. I don't spot who I'm looking for, but I do spot a familiar face.

"Alex!" I say after slipping into the crowd.

He looks up from his phone. "Hey! Long time." He leans over and hugs me.

"So, how's things?" we say at the same time.

Alex chuckles. "Ladies first."

Over the background noise, I tell him about my decision to have a career change. He tells me about his work with the same animated expression as always. And while we are chatting, I keep thinking, *Alex isn't a bad guy. There's no reason we can't be friends.*

"Alex," I say after he stops talking. "I've got a confession to make. You know that time when I made you Nigerian food? Well . . . I had a helping hand. And if you're willing," I quickly add as he laughs, "I would love for you to show me how to make proper Naija food one day."

I return to the girls with a cooking session with Alex in my calendar. Joanna and Brian have joined them, Brandon and Ricky in tow.

"Ooh, we've got something for you," says Brian after we've gushed over the best bits of Nana's fashion show. Joanna hands me a gift bag.

"Aww, guys. You shouldn't have." I squirrel into the bag as though it's Christmas Day. I gasp.

"We thought you could use it to jot down your thoughts after counseling," says Joanna as I awe over the beautiful notebook, its sleeve made out of wax fabric.

"And what's this?" I push the tissue paper to one side and pull out a damask pink hair bonnet.

"You weren't able to get a hairnet that time," says Joanna as I rub the cap against my cheek. *It's silk!*

"Aww, thank you, guys." I embrace them together. Jeez. Shame on me for thinking that they were out of touch with Black culture. As I draw back, I catch Donovan staring at me. I excuse myself.

"Well, look at you, Miss Naomi Campbell." We hug. Thankfully, he's back in his own clothes again.

"Well, look at you, Mr. Michael B. Jordan."

Donovan smiles.

I clear my throat. "I got some news to share with you—"

"Oh, yeah? I've got some too. But go ahead, you first."

I roll back my shoulders. "I'm . . . going to pursue a career in charity."

I stare at Donovan, waiting for him to yell, "*I told you so!*" Instead, he says, "Well, this makes my news ten times easier. Remember that Sanctuary job I was telling you about? Guess who got shortlisted for an interview?"

I frown. Donovan nods to me, a smile growing on his face.

"How—when? I didn't even apply."

Donovan laughs. "*I* put you forward for the role. Remember that time you sent me your CV?"

My mouth drops. "Are you being serious? Did I really get shortlisted?"

"Yup. So, I was right all along, yeah?"

My lips twist into a smile. And overcome with happiness, I'm unable to help myself; I throw my arms around him. "Thank you, Donovan," I whisper.

After I've let him go, my friends magically appear.

"We were wondering where you got to," says Nana, giving me a wink.

Rachel wastes no time introducing herself, even checking Donovan out while she's at it.

Brian whispers to me. "Cor, he's a stunner."

Ola throws me a *"You go, gurl"* look before extending a hand.

Joanna behaves like a normal human being. "Nice to meet you, Donovan."

While Donovan gets to know everyone, I stand back and watch, grinning. So, this is what it looks like when my worlds blend.

July

Where's your plus one?

SATURDAY

Friday, 9 July at 4.17 p.m.
From: Huang, Martin
To: Yinka Oladeji
Subject: Next steps

Dear Yinka,

It was great speaking to you on the phone just now.

Congratulations again on your appointment as Outreach
Manager. We can't wait for you to join the team.

As I said over the phone, you truly impressed us during the
interview with your passion and enthusiasm. We think you'll fit
right in!

I'll be in touch next week with your contract, but any questions
in the meantime, please get in touch.

We look forward to welcoming you to Sanctuary.

Best wishes,
Martin Huang
Head of HR

I look one last time at the e-mail I received yesterday and allow myself to feel another surge of excitement before focusing on the scene around me. This wedding is what I'd call glam galore: think a copper and rose-gold palette, with lots of white silk flowers, chandeliers and fancy Chiavari chairs. And at the center of it are Rachel and Gavesh. From the back of the candlelit hall, I stare at them dancing, their eyes firmly locked. Rachel is stunning in her princess dress and her gold multilayered headpiece, and Gavesh looks so gorgeous in his sequined jacket with its puffy sleeves and matching crown-like hat.

How they managed to plan their special day within six months is beyond me. Though they both come from different cultures where weddings are an equally big deal, somehow they fused their traditions beautifully without killing each other.

With a glass of bubbly in hand, I watch as the saree-and-*àṣọ̀ ẹbí*-wearing guests on the dance floor spray Big Mama and Gavesh's mum with American dollars while they drop it like it's hot. Kemi's dancing too. She has slipped into her flats and is showing everyone how low she can go now that she no longer has a bump to contend with.

"Hey, you." Nana drapes her arm around me and gives me a peck on the cheek. We look like twins today in our pink saree-inspired bridesmaids' dresses. Nana has done an amazing job.

"I'm so happy for Rachel and Gavesh. I mean, look at this." I spread my arms.

"Yeah, they should be proud of themselves." Nana looks around for a moment, then nudges me. "You too."

"Me?" I laugh a little. "Let's be real. I didn't contribute that much."

"No, I'm not talking about the wedding. I'm talking about how far you've come. I'm so proud of you, sis."

"Aww." I give her a side hug and we sway a little.

"Sooo, where's your plus one?" In an exaggerated manner, she swivels her head.

"Plus one?" I frown. "Girl, you know I abandoned my bridesmaid's goal a long time ago. The goal is to love myself and that's still a work in progress."

"You didn't invite Donovan?"

"Nana, we're just friends." I take a sip of my bubbly, pretending not to see her cock her head, like *yeah, right.*

"Anyway, this is my jam." She hoists up her dress, pecks me on the cheek, then rushes to the dance floor to shake a leg to yet another Afrobeats song.

"Yinka."

It's Aunty Blessing. And she's got someone with her.

"I would like to introduce you to someone." With a grin, she gestures at the silverfox of a man who kind of looks like Sean Connery (obviously after his Bond days). "This is Terry Matthews."

I blink, then remember my manners.

"Sorry, nice to meet you." I shake his proffered hand.

"Blessing tells me you've got a new job?"

I glance at my Aunty, who is still manically smiling. "Yes. I recently got a job as an outreach manager at a homeless charity. I know. Worlds apart from what I was doing before. Oh, and I'm sorry I didn't meet you that time."

Terry bats a hand. "Don't worry. And congratulations. It's important to do what makes you happy."

I glance at Aunty Blessing again. She looks the definition of happy.

"Okay, let me introduce you to my other niece." Aunty Blessing slips her arm through Terry's. "Ooh, I see her. Yinka"—she hugs me—"we'll catch up later, my dear."

I watch them meander their way around the hall, each round table adorned with white linen, gold candelabras and silk flowers.

My first thought is, *I wonder if she met him on that dating website?* Then my second thought is, *I'm so, so happy for her.* Just goes to show that you can find love at any age.

Beaming, I make my way to the buffet station. Those—I think they're called watalappans?—are absolutely to die for. En route I see Ola with her arms around Jon's neck, dancing. Our eyes meet and she waves. Jon turns his head and waves too. It's nice to see the two of them being affectionate.

Just as I'm about to reach for a dessert plate, I feel a light tap on my shoulder and turn around. It's Femi.

"Yinka, so good to see you." I'm greeted with a hug . . . and now a squeeze . . . wow, and a wide smile. I forgot that he was going to be at the wedding. And now that I'm seeing him in the flesh . . . I wait for the familiar sensation of nerves and anxiety to kick in. Nope, it doesn't come. So, I guess I don't care any more.

"Hey, Femi. Good to see you too. Where's Latoya?" I glance over his shoulder.

Femi's jovial expression vanishes. He seems preoccupied with the floor.

"We broke up," he says at last, his face glum.

"Oh my gosh. I'm so sorry." I now feel terrible for asking. Okay, I feel a tiny bit glad, but mostly awful.

"We kind of rushed into things, whatever." He shrugs, but I can tell he's hurt. "She was still in love with her ex, so . . ." He manages to lift his gaze an inch.

"Femi. I'm . . . I'm truly sorry."

"Don't be." He runs a hand over his head, and I congratulate myself for not gawking at his biceps. "In fact, I should be apologizing to you." He exhales. "Yinka, I'm sorry that we didn't work out. Sometimes I wonder if breaking up with you was a big mistake."

I stare at him, dazed. Everything around me vanishes. And as I gaze at him, I realize that I'm actually waiting. I'm waiting for a feeling. Vindication. Longing. *Something*. But nothing comes except for the realization that I'm well and truly over him.

Femi realizes this too. He shifts uncomfortably in his shiny shoes. Then he clears his throat and says, "You look beautiful, by the way."

"Thanks." I scratch my elbow. Hey, what do you know? That word did nothing for me either. A few months ago, my heart would have swelled from the compliment.

"So is your mister here?" Femi swivels around, and just as I'm about to say no, Donovan appears.

Wait, *Donovan*?

"Look at you, looking all fancy," he says, bundling me into a hug while my mind is trying to process why he's here.

"Sorry, my bad. I'm Donovan." He stretches a hand toward Femi, and the look on Femi's face is priceless.

"Well, it was good seeing you." Femi nods to me, then he does this weird half-wave at Donovan and scurries away as though he needs to pee really badly.

"Lemme guess. The ex?" Donovan cocks his head. I'm so used to seeing him in his woke hoodies, I'm taken aback by how attractive he looks in a suit.

"Yes," I answer after admiring his neat beard. "What are *you* doing here?"

"What am *I* doing here?" Donovan staggers back as though my words are bullets. "Nana said you wanted to invite me, but was too chicken to ask."

"That girl!" I spin my head, and not to my surprise, Nana's watching. She gives me two thumbs up. Sneaky.

Then as though tonight is the night of guest appearances, Mum and Aunty Debbie magically appear by our side. Aunty Debbie is in my good books right now, because she managed to compose herself after I failed to catch Rachel's bouquet.

"Hello, Aunties," Donovan says just as I'm about to introduce him. From the looks of things, however, both Mum and Aunty Debbie already know his name. *Huh?*

"Donovan came to All Welcome last Sunday." Aunty Debbie has clearly read my baffled expression.

Mum says, "We recognized him from the fashion show, so we thought, you know, we'd introduce ourselves."

"Oh, did you now?" I notice their familiar mischievous expressions. And wait—why the heck was Donovan at All Welcome Church?

"Anyway, we just thought we'd say hello," says Mum, already adjusting her wrapper to leave.

I blink. This is a miracle. I'm standing side by side with an (objectively speaking) handsome man and she's not even sizing him up as a potential *huzband?*

I'm still in a state of shock as I watch them go.

"Okay, since when did you start attending All Welcome?" I ask, gathering myself.

Donovan chuckles, then rolls his eyes. "First of all, it was *one* Sunday. And it's not my cup of tea."

"But why?" I laugh a little. "Not why wasn't it your cup of tea. Why were you there in the first place?"

Donovan's response doesn't come straight away. "I guess talking to you about faith made me want to, you know, revisit what I had in the past. I'm not saying I'm a Christian now, but I'm definitely . . . intrigued. In fact, you heard of the Alpha course? Yeah, man starts that in two weeks."

"Well . . . I'm speechless."

Donovan grins and my belly flutters.

"Oh, and we should celebrate. I knew you'd get the job. You free next Saturday?"

My lips curl into a smile.

"What?" he says, and my smile broadens. "I'm not taking you anywhere fancy, you know. Probably Chicken Cottage or something."

"Chicken Cottage?" I laugh.

"Okay, fine. Nando's?"

I notice his dimples as he laughs. "Donovan! You know what you're suggesting is called a date, right? I mean, I thought you were terrified to ask women out?"

Donovan scratches his head. "Yeah . . . but not you." Then as though he can't bear being serious for a moment longer, he adds, "So are you free next Saturday or what?"

"Yes." I'm smiling so hard, I can feel the muscles in my cheeks. Then pretending to be blasé, I add, "If I must."

The iconic intro of Cameo's "Candy" blares from the speakers: *Bom, bom, bom, bom, bom-bom, bom-bom, bom.*

On cue, flocks of people dash to the dance floor to join the dancers who have already arranged themselves into rows and are now trying to agree on what leg they should start with once the bass drops.

"Yooo!" Donovan whips his fingers. "Made it just on time." He grabs my hand and stops when I tug him back.

I wiggle my lip. "I don't know how to do the electric slide."

His mouth drops. "But you're Black."

"Well, then I must be the only Black person in the world who doesn't know how to do the Candy dance."

Donovan laughs. "Don't worry, I'll teach you." He takes my hand again.

We reach the dance floor and stand side by side facing the same direction as everyone else.

"Look. It's easy." He takes two steps to the left. Two steps to the right. Two steps backward. Two steps forward. Kicks foot out—*hello!*—ninety-degree turn, then does the same move all over again.

Donovan is right. The electric slide is easy. (Gosh, I missed out at Kemi's wedding.) After one wrong start and two wobbly turns, I've found my rhythm.

"There you go," says Donovan encouragingly. "See. You're getting the hang of it."

I take two steps to the left, another two to the right, and I spot the faces of loved ones among the crowd.

Rachel, Gavesh, Nana and Ola.

Two steps backward.

Aunty Blessing, Aunty Debbie, Big Mama and Mum.

Two steps forward.

Kemi, Uche, Chinedu and Ola's kids.

Swerve, kick, turn—

"Oops, sorry, Donovan."

Hmm. God, you clearly have a sense of humor.

Acknowledgments

First, I want to thank God for entrusting me with this story and for blessing me with the gift of writing. I'm grateful every day. To my husband, Martin, if only I had more pages! Thank you for encouraging me over the years and for making sure I didn't give up. I really appreciate all those times you listened to my ideas, gave me feedback and provided a shoulder to cry on whenever I was overwhelmed. Oh, and thank you for taking off my glasses anytime I passed out after a long day.

To my wonderful parents: I love you so much. Thank you for all your support and wisdom. Thank you, Dad, for nurturing the writer in me when I was young by buying me all those Jacqueline Wilson books. Thank you, Mum, for all those motivating WhatsApp messages you've sent me and for your countless prayers. (Shout-out to your church group!) To my equally wonderful in-laws: thank you for your genuine interest in my writing and well-being. Your positivity really helped. To my siblings and cousins: thank you for being successful in your own endeavors. You were my role models without even knowing it. As for my many aunties and uncles here in the UK, Nigeria and the U.S., thank you for always showering me with love. Grandma and Sister Donna, thank you for keeping me in your prayers too.

To my godsent agent, Nelle Andrew: In Donovan's words, "You're the G.O.A.T!" Thank you for believing in me from day one (even when my writing still needed a bit of work!). I truly appreciate your passion and expertise. And massive thanks to the rest of the squad at Rachel Mills Agency—Charlotte, Alex and Rachel. Thank you for championing Yinka abroad.

To my UK editor, Katy Loftus: You're everything I've wanted in an editor and more. Thank you for being such a talented person to learn from. For your passion, energy, and bags of enthusiasm. You really helped take Yinka to the next level. To my U.S. editor, Pam Dorman: Honestly, I feel so blessed. Thank you for your valuable advice on storytelling, for pushing me to become a better writer and for that much-needed pep talk. Jeramie and Marie, thank you for all the hard work you've done behind the scenes and for being such great in-house cheerleaders. Vikki, Julia Jason and the design team, thank you for absolutely smashing it with the look and feel of Yinka. You really brought it to life! Thanks also to Jaya Miceli for the amazing cover! And to everyone at Viking UK and Pamela Dorman Books, thank you for believing in Yinka and investing in me.

Huge thanks to my copyeditor, Mary Chamberlain. Thank you for being so meticulous and for getting the story timeline watertight! Massive thanks to Deborah Balogun for your brilliant line-edit and to Maria Adebisi for your valuable beta-read report. Thank you both for ensuring that all the cultural references were spot-on and for making my story even more authentic. And thank you Nicole Wayland and Megha Jain for your superb proofread.

To Aki, Joe and Nelima at The Literary Consultancy: Thank you for shortlisting my story for the Pen Factor Writing Competition 2019. Since I won, you haven't stopped shouting about Yinka. (Please don't stop!) As always, I'm truly grateful. And thanks to Thalia Suzuma (my TLC reader) for your invaluable manuscript assessment report. Everyone at Spread the Word: Thank you for hosting such fantastic writers' events—they were worthy investments! Special shout-out to Aliya Gulamani for her ongoing support. And thank you to Davinia Andrew-Lynch, one of my early readers. I will never forget that time you had coffee with me and shared your thoughts.

To all my sensitivity readers: Alex and the team at AUREA, thank you for your great and reassuring feedback on my portrayal of aromanticism. Conor

Duckworth at Glass Door Homeless Charity, thank you for your helpful insight on my portrayal of homelessness. Beryl Tomlins, thank you so much for running a "mock" counseling session with me. I couldn't have written Jacqui's character and the therapy chapters without you! Seyi Afolabi, thank you for looking over the fashion-related scenes. Alex Lee, Lola Adelaja and Louis Blackburn, thank you for allowing me to pick your brains on the world of investment banking.

To my amaaazing friends, I wish I could name you all! Thank you for your love, support and prayers over the years, and for not growing tired of my same ol' writing updates. And thanks to my girls on the Creative Ladies WhatsApp group for spurring me on. To my lovely former co-workers at Carers UK: Thank you for all your much-needed encouragement and for not yawning when I told you that I spent my weekend writing. Again.

I have to give a shout-out to my girl, Issa Rae. If you ever read this book, I'm a HUGE fan! Thank you for creating your TV show, *Insecure*. I drew a lot of inspiration from it, especially as there are very few shows centered on Black female friendships. And thank you, Mara Brock Akil. *Girlfriends* and *Being Mary Jane* provided massive sources of inspiration. Thank you for being a trailblazer and for telling Black stories. Also, big-up to *The Wrap Party* and *Chuckie Online*. Honestly, listening to your podcasts helped me hone Donovan's voice. You guys cracked me up when I needed a boost.

Last, but not least, thank you, Jackie Ley, for giving me the idea to turn Yinka's blog post into a novel. Our encounter was definitely divine. I'm forever grateful.